DOUBLE EAGLE

AWARD-WINNING SCIENCE fiction author Dan
Abnett adds to his existing pantheon of memo-
rable characters with a tale of airborne war and
bravery in the face of ultimate defeat. The Sabbat
Worlds Crusade spans whole planetary systems,
untold billions of men and women selling their
lives dearly. The Imperial world of Enothis stands
dangerously on the brink of destruction as the
mutated hordes of Chaos evoke worldwide carnage in the name of their daemonic gods.

The elite pilots of the Phantine XX fighter corps
know it is probably a suicide mission. The entire
Enothis squadron has been decimated. They are
the only hope for victory and for the countless terrified refugees fleeing in panic before the Chaos
advance. Can they hold up the Chaos advance,
buying precious seconds until reinforcements
arrive? In the lightning-fast white-knuckle terror of
aerial combat, can they hope to win against an
enemy possessed by daemons?

More Dan Abnett from the Black Library

· **RAVENOR** ·
RAVENOR
RAVENOR RETURNED

· **EISENHORN** ·
In the nightmare world of the 41st millennium,
Inquisitor Eisenhorn hunts down mankind's most
dangerous enemies.

Includes the novels
XENOS, MALLEUS,
and HERETICUS

· **GAUNT'S GHOSTS** ·
Colonel-Commissar Gaunt and his regiment, the
Tanith First-and-Only, struggle for survival on the
battlefields of the far future.

The Founding
FIRST AND ONLY
GHOSTMAKER
NECROPOLIS

The Saint
HONOUR GUARD
THE GUNS OF TANITH
STRAIGHT SILVER
SABBAT MARTYR

The Lost
TRAITOR GENERAL

A WARHAMMER 40,000 NOVEL

DOUBLE EAGLE

Dan Abnett

For my father
with love and plastic cement.

A special note of thanks to Tony Cottrell
for his advice, suggestions and patience.

A BLACK LIBRARY PUBLICATION

First published in Great Britain in 2004.
Paperback edition published in 2005 by BL Publishing,
Games Workshop Ltd.,
Willow Road, Nottingham,
NG7 2WS, UK.

10 9 8 7 6 5 4 3 2 1

Cover courtesy of Forge World.
Map by Nuala Kennedy.
Double Eagle icon designed by Andrew Walsh.

A CIP record for this book is available from the British Library.

ISBN 13: 978 1 84416 090 7
ISBN 10: 1 84416 090 4

Distributed in the US by Simon & Schuster
1230 Avenue of the Americas, New York, NY 10020, US.

Printed and bound in Great Britain by
Bookmarque, Surrey, UK.

See the Black Library on the Internet at
www.blacklibrary.com

Find out more about Games Workshop
and the world of Warhammer 40,000 at
www.games-workshop.com

It is the 41st millennium. For more than a hundred centuries the Emperor has sat immobile on the Golden Throne of Earth. He is the master of mankind by the will of the gods, and master of a million worlds by the might of his inexhaustible armies. He is a rotting carcass writhing invisibly with power from the Dark Age of Technology. He is the Carrion Lord of the Imperium for whom a thousand souls are sacrificed every day, so that he may never truly die.

Yet even in his deathless state, the Emperor continues his eternal vigilance. Mighty battlefleets cross the daemon-infested miasma of the warp, the only route between distant stars, their way lit by the Astronomican, the psychic manifestation of the Emperor's will. Vast armies give battle in his name on uncounted worlds. Greatest amongst his soldiers are the Adeptus Astartes, the Space Marines, bio-engineered super-warriors. Their comrades in arms are legion: the Imperial Guard and countless planetary defence forces, the ever-vigilant Inquisition and the tech-priests of the Adeptus Mechanicus to name only a few. But for all their multitudes, they are barely enough to hold off the ever-present threat from aliens, heretics, mutants – and worse.

To be a man in such times is to be one amongst untold billions. It is to live in the cruellest and most bloody regime imaginable. These are the tales of those times. Forget the power of technology and science, for so much has been forgotten, never to be re-learned. Forget the promise of progress and understanding, for in the grim dark future there is only war. There is no peace amongst the stars, only an eternity of carnage and slaughter, and the laughter of thirsting gods.

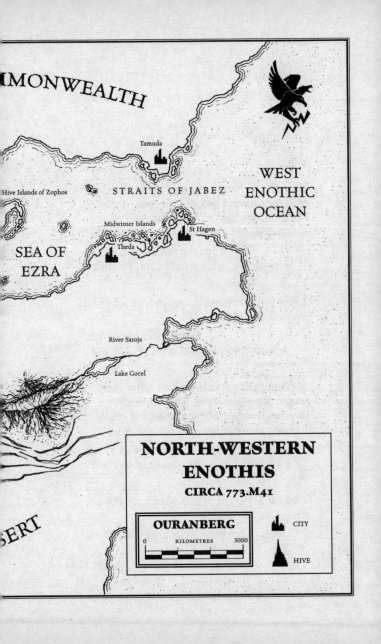

MONWEALTH

Tamuda

STRAITS OF JABEZ

WEST
ENOTHIC
OCEAN

Hive Islands of Zophos

Midwinter Islands

St Hagen

SEA OF
EZRA

Theda

River Saroja

Lake Gocel

NORTH-WESTERN
ENOTHIS

CIRCA 773.M41

OURANBERG

0   KILOMETRES   3000

CITY

HIVE

DESERT

'Strong men have conquered the land,
Bold men have conquered the void,
Between land and void lies the sky,
And only the bravest men ever conquer that.'

– from the dedication to the
Hessenville Aviator Scholam, Phantine

'I give you command of the air. It is up to
you how you take it.'

– Warmaster Macaroth,
despatch to Admiral Ornoff, 773.M41

'We had planes. We flew them. They had
planes. They flew them. There was some
shooting involved. All that mattered, really,
was who was still flying at the end of it.'

– Major August Kaminsky (73 kills),
six weeks before his death in 812.M41

'I intend to get out of this alive if it's the last
thing I do.'

– Commander Bree Jagdea, at Ouranberg

TARGET FOUND

THEDA

Imperial year 773.M41, day 252 – day 260

DAY 252

Over the Makanites, 06.32

IN THE SIDE RUSH of dawn, the peaks glowed pink, like some travesty of a fondant celebration cake. Hard shadows infilled the cavities like ink. Streamers of white cloud strung out in the freezing air three thousand metres below.

Hunt Leader was just a cruciform speck in the bright air ahead. He started to turn, ten degrees to the north-west. Darrow tilted the stick, following, rolling. The horizon swung up and the world moved around. Slowly, slowly. He heard the knocking sound and ignored it.

At least the inclinometer was still working. As he came around and levelled the column, Darrow reached forward and flicked the brass dial of the fuel gauge again. It still read full, which couldn't be right. They'd been up for forty-eight minutes.

He took off a gauntlet and flicked the gauge once more with his bare fingers. He felt sure the lined mitten had been dulling his blows.

The dial remained at full.

He saw how pinched and blue his hand had become, and pulled the gauntlet back on quickly. It felt balmy in his insulated flightsuit, but the cabin temp-stat read minus eight.

There was no sound, except for the background rush of the jet stream. Darrow looked up and around, remembering to maintain his visual scanning. Just sky. Sundogs flaring in his visor. Hunt Three just abeam of him, a silhouette, trailing vapour.

The altimeter read six thousand metres.

The vox gurgled. 'Hunt Leader to Hunt Flight. One pass west and we turn for home. Keep formation tight.'

They made another lazy roll. The landscape rose up in his port vision. Darrow saw brittle flashes of light far below. Artillery fire in the mountain passes.

He heard the knocking again. It sounded as if someone was crouching behind the frame of his armoured seat, tapping the internal spars with a hammer. Pulsejets always made a burbling, flatulent noise, but this didn't seem right to him.

He keyed his vox. 'Hunt Leader, this is Hunt Four. I've–'

There was a sudden, loud bang. The vox channel squealed like a stabbed pig.

The world turned upside down.

'Oh God-Emperor! Oh crap! God-Emperor!' a voice was shouting. Darrow realised it was his own. G-force pummelled him. His Commonwealth K4T Wolfcub was tumbling hard.

Light and dark, sky and land, up and over, up and over. Darrow choked back nausea and throttled down desperately. The vox was incoherent with frantic chatter.

'Hunt Four! Hunt Four!'

Darrow regained control somehow and levelled. He had lost at least a thousand metres. He got the horizon true and looked around in the vain hope of seeing someone friendly. Then he cried out involuntarily as something fell past his nose cone.

It was a Wolfcub, one wing shorn off in a cascade of torn struts and body plate. Flames were sucking back out of its pulsejet. It arced down and away like a comet, trailing smoke as it went spinning towards the ground. It became a speck. A smaller speck. A little blink of light.

Darrow felt his guts tighten and acid frothed inside him. Fear, like a stink, permeated the little cockpit.

Something else flashed past him.

Just a glimpse, moving so fast. There and gone. A memory of recurve wings.

'Hunt Four! Break! Break and turn! There's one right on you!'

Darrow leaned on the stick and kicked the rudder. The world rolled again.

He put his nose up and throttled hard. The Wolfcub bucked angrily and the knocking came again.

Throne of Earth. He'd thought his bird had malfunctioned, but it wasn't that at all. They'd been stung.

Darrow leant forward against the harness and peered out of his cockpit dome. The aluminoid skin of his right wing was holed and torn. Hell's-teeth, he'd been shot.

He pushed the stick forward to grab some thrust, then turned out left in a hard climb.

The dawn sky was full of smoke: long strings of grey vapour and little black blooms that looked like dirty cotton. Hunt Flight's formation had broken apart and they were scattering across the heavens. Darrow couldn't even see the bats.

No, that wasn't true. He made one, bending in to chase Hunt Five, tracer fire licking from its gunpods.

He rolled towards it, flipping the scope of his reflector sight into position before resting his thumb on the stick-top stud that activated the quad cannons in the nose.

The bat danced wildly across the glass reticule of the gunsight. It refused to sit.

Darrow cursed and began to utter a prayer to the God-Emperor of Mankind to lift his wings and make his aim true. He waggled the stick, pitching, rolling, trying to correct, but the more he tried, the more the bat slipped wildly off the gunsight to one side or the other.

There was a little smoky flash ahead, and suddenly Darrow's Wolfcub was riding through a horizontal pelt of black rain.

Not rain. Oil. Then debris. Pieces of glittering metal, buckled machine parts, shreds of aluminoid. Darrow cried out in surprise as the oil washed out his forward view. He heard the pattering impact of the debris striking off his nose plate and wing faces. The bat had chalked Hunt Five and Darrow was running in through the debris stream. Any large piece of wreckage would hole him and kill him as surely as cannon-fire. And if so much as a demi-mil cog went down the intake of his pulsejet...

Darrow wrenched on the stick and came nose-up. Light returned as he came out of the smoke belt, and slipstream flowed the oil away off his canopy. It ran in quivering lines, slow and sticky, like blood.

Almost immediately, he had to roll hard to port to avoid hitting another Cub head on. He heard a strangled cry over the vox. The little dark-green interceptor filled his field of view for a second and then was gone back over his shoulder.

His violent roll had been too brutal. He inverted for a moment and struggled to right himself as the mountains spread out overhead. That knocking again. That damn knocking. He was bleeding speed now, and the old pulse-engines of the K4T's had a nasty habit of flaming out if the airflow dropped too sharply. He began to nurse it up and round, gunning the engine as hard as he

dared. Two planes rushed by, so fast he didn't have time
to determine their type, then another three went per-
pendicular across his bow. They were all Wolfcubs. One
was venting blue smoke in a long, chuffing plume.

'Hunt Leader! Hunt Leader!' Darrow called. Two of
the Cubs were already climbing away out of visual. The
sun blinded him. The third, the wounded bird, was diving slowly, scribing the sky with its smoke.

He saw the bat clearly then. At his two, five hundred
metres, dropping in on the Cub it had most likely
already mauled. For the first time in his four weeks of
operational flying, Darrow got a good look at the elusive foe. It resembled a long, sharp, elongated axe-head,
the cockpit set far back above the drive at the point
where the bow of the blade-wings met. A Hell Razor-
class Interceptor, the cream of the Archenemy's air force.
In the dispersal room briefs, they'd talked about these
killers being blood red or matt black, but this was pearl-
white, like ice, like alabaster. The canopy was tinted
black, like a dark eye-socket in a polished skull.

Darrow had expected to feel fear, but he got a thrill of
adrenaline instead. He leaned forward, hunched down
in the Wolfcub's armoured cockpit, and opened the
throttle, sweeping in on the bat's five. It didn't appear to
have seen him. It was lining up, leisurely, on the
wounded Cub.

He flipped the toggle switch. Guns live.

Closing at three hundred metres. Darrow rapidly cal-
culated his angle of deflection, estimated he'd have to
lead his shot by about five degrees. God-Emperor, he
had it...

He thumbed the firing stud. The Wolfcub shuddered
slightly as the cannons lit up. He saw flash-flames licking up from under the curve of the nose cone. He heard
and felt the thump of the breechblocks.

The bat had gone.

He came clear, pulling a wide turn at about two hundred and seventy kilometres an hour. The engagement had been over in an instant. Had he killed it? He sat up into the clear blister of the canopy like an animal looking out of its burrow, craning around. If he'd hit it, surely there would be smoke?

The only smoke he could see was about a thousand metres above in the pale blue sky where the main portion of the dogfight was still rolling.

He turned. First rule of air combat: take a shot and pull off. Never stick with a target, never go back. That made *you* a target.

But still he had to know. He *had* to.

He dipped his starboard wing, searching the peaks below for a trace of fire.

Nothing.

Darrow levelled off.

And there it was. Right alongside him.

He cried out in astonishment. The bat was less than a wing's breadth away, riding along in parallel with him. There was not a mark on its burnished white fuselage.

It was playing with him.

Panic rose inside pilot cadet Enric Darrow. He knew his valiant little Cub could neither outrun nor outclimb the Hell Razor. He throttled back hard, and threw on his speed brakes, hoping the sudden manoeuvre would cause the big machine to overshoot him.

For a moment, it vanished. Then it was back, on his other side, copying his brake-dive. Darrow swore. The Hell Razor-class were vector-thrust planes. He was so close to it that he could see the reactive jet nozzles on the belly under the blade-wings. It could out-dance any conventional jet, viffing, braking, even pulling to a near-hover.

Darrow refused to accept he was out-classed, refused to admit he was about to die. He twisted the stick, kicked the rudder right over and went into the deepest dive he dared execute. Any deeper, and the Wolfcub's wings would shear off its airframe.

The world rushed up, filling his vision. He heard the pulsejet screaming. He saw the glory of the mountains ascending to meet him. His mountains. His world. The world he had joined up to save.

Behind him, the pearl-white enemy machine tucked in effortlessly and followed him down.

Theda MAB North, 07.02

SOMETIMES – TIMES LIKE this perfect dawn, for instance – it amused August Kaminsky to play a private game. The game was called 'pretend there isn't a war'.

It was relatively easy in some respects. It was quiet, and the night chill was giving way to a still cool as the sunrise came up over the city. From where he sat, he could see the wide bay, hazy in the morning mist, and the sea beyond it, blue-grey, glittering. The city of Theda itself – a mix of pale rockcrete towers, low-rise hab-stacks and pylon steeples – was peaceful and quiet, huddled on the wide headland in a quaint, antiquated manner, as it had done for twenty-nine centuries. Sea birds wheeled overhead, which spoiled it slightly, because he envied them their wings and their freedom, but still, at these times, it was easy to play the game.

Theda was not Kaminsky's birth-town (he'd been delivered, a silent, uncomplaining infant. forty-two years earlier and three thousand kilometres north in the Great Hive of Enothopolis on the far side of the Zophonian Sea), but he had, unilaterally, adopted it. It was smaller than the Great Hive, prettier, a littoral town that understood the mechanisms of the sea and, with its universitariat and its many scholams, was famous as a seat of learning. It was older than the Great Hive too. The Old Town quarter had been standing for three hundred years when the first technocrats began sinking their adamantine pilings into the Ursbond Peninsula to raise Enothopolis. Theda, dear old Theda, was one of the first cities of Enothis.

Kaminsky had adopted Theda partly because of its distinguished past, mostly because he'd been stationed there for six years. He'd come to know it well: its eating houses, its coastal pavilions and piers, its libraries and museums. It was the place he'd always longed to return to every time he snapped the canopy shut and waved the fitters away. And it was the place he always had come back to.

Even the last time.

'You there! Driver!'

The voice broke through his thoughts. He sat up in the worn leather seat of the cargo transport and looked out. Senior Pincheon, the Munitorum despatcher, was coming over the hard pan towards him, three aides wobbling along in his wake like novice wingmen. Pincheon's long robes fluttered out behind him and his boots were raising dust from the dry earth. His voice was pitched high, like the seabirds' calls.

Kaminsky didn't like Pincheon much. His game was ruined now. The senior's call had made him drop his eyeline to take in the ground and the airfield. And no one could pretend there wasn't a war when they saw that.

Kaminsky opened his cab door and climbed down to meet the senior. He'd been up since five waiting for despatch, sipping caffeine from a flask and munching on a coil of whisp-bread.

'Senior,' he said, saluting. He didn't have to. The unctuous man had no military rank, but old habits, like Kaminsky himself, died hard. Pincheon had a data-slate in his hands. He looked up and down Kaminsky, and the grubby transport behind him.

'Driver Kaminsky, A? Vehicle 167?'

'As you well know, senior,' said Kaminsky.

Pincheon made a check in one of the boxes on his slate. 'Fuelled and roadworthy?'

Kaminsky nodded. 'As of 05.00. I was issued coupons for sixty litres of two-grade, and I filled up at the depot before I came on duty.'

Pincheon checked another box. 'Do you have the chit?'

Kaminsky produced the paper slip from his coat pocket, smoothed it flat, and handed it to the senior.

Pincheon studied it. 'Sixty point zero-zero-three litres, driver?'

Kaminsky shrugged. 'The nozzle guns aren't really accurate, senior. I stopped it when it wound over sixty, but the last few drops–'

'You should take care to be more accurate,' Pincheon said flatly. One of his aides nodded.

'Have you ever fuelled a vehicle from the depot tanks, senior?' Kaminsky said lightly.

'Of course not!'

'Well, if you had, you might know how tricky it is to get the wind exact.'

'Don't you blame me for your inaccuracies, driver!' Pincheon sputtered. 'Essential resources such as fuel must be managed and rationed to the millilitre! That is the task of the Holy Munitorum! There's a war on, don't you realise?'

'I had heard…'

Senior Pincheon ignored him and looked at the nodding aide. 'What's zero-zero-three of a litre two-grade at base cost?'

The aide made a quick calculation on his pocket slate. 'Rounding down, ten and a half credits, senior.'

'Round up. And deduct it from the next wage slip of driver Kaminsky, A.'

'So recorded, senior.'

Pincheon turned back to Kaminsky. 'Transportation run. Personnel. Pick up within thirty minutes from the Hotel Imperial in–'

'I know where it is.'

'Good. Convey them to the dispersal point at MAB South. Do you understand? Fine. Then sign here.'

As he signed his name, his stiffened fingers struggling with the stylus, Kaminsky asked: 'Are they fliers? Navy fliers at last?'

Pincheon huffed. 'Not for me to say. There's a war on.'

'You think I don't know that, senior?' Kaminsky asked.

As he took back the slate and the stylus, Pincheon looked up at Kaminsky's face and made eye contact for the first time. What he saw made him shudder.

'Carry on, driver,' he said, and hurried away.

Kaminsky climbed up into his battered transport and turned the engine over. Blue smoke coughed and spurted from the vertical exhausts. Lifting the brake, he rolled the ten-wheeler down the gentle slope of the hardpan and drove off along the field circuit trackway, following the chain link fence.

The game was certainly ruined now. No pretending any more. Here were fuel bowsers, smeared with treacly black promethium waste, armoured hangars, repair sheds reverberating with the noise of power tools, lines of primer coils on their trolleys, electric munitions trains parked and empty on verges of swishing sap-grass.

And airstrips. Cracked rockcrete looking like psoriatic skin in the early light, with eight-engine bombers sulking on their hardstands, props like sabre-blades raised in threat, hook-winged Shrike dive-bombers under tarps, fitters and armourers working around them.

Beyond the strips, facing the sea, lay the long launch ramps of the Wolfcubs, stretched out like exposed spinal chords, glinting and skeletal in the rising sun.

Five Wolfcubs sat on taxi-racks at the head of the ramps. Bottle green with grey undersides, they were tiny, one-man planes with stubby wings and tails, their rocket engines raised above their backs, their nose guns muzzled. They looked squat, leaden.

But Kaminsky knew how they felt to fly. He knew how they rose off those catapult ramps, throttles right back, pulse-engines farting and popping as the airflow fired them to launch velocity. The belly-dropping jink as they cleared the ramp end and lifted up into the blue, raw and throbbing. The cold smell of the cockpit. The reek of rubber and steel, promethium, nitrous, fyceline. The feel of being aloft, alive...

God-Emperor, how he missed it.

At the gate, beside the staked revets and the heavy blast-fences, he pulled over to let a munitions convoy roll in. He glanced up into the driving mirror and, for a moment, saw himself.

More than anything, more than even the airfield full of prepping warplanes, the sight of himself reminded August Kaminsky that his cherished game was only pretend.

There was, inescapably, a war on.

Theda Old Town, 07.09

HE COULDN'T SLEEP. It was anticipation mostly, the prospect of a new war to survive, but his body clock was still running on shipboard time, and to him it was late afternoon.

Just before six by the chronograph on his night stand, he gave up on his bed and got up. It was cold and not yet light. In the adjacent rooms, the other men of *G for Greta* were sleeping. He could hear snoring, particularly the volcanic rumble of Bombardier Judd. The Munitorum had issued them billets in a once-handsome pension on Kazergat Canal, and they'd piled in late the previous afternoon, leaving their packs in a heap in the hallway, eagerly laying claim to rooms. The younger men had broken open liquor and got down to the business of getting drunk so they could better sleep off voyage-lag. He'd had a glass or two, but the cheap escape held little attraction.

He and the other flight officers had swung the best rooms. He'd had to order a disappointed Orsone out to make way for him. 'Find somewhere else,' he'd told the young tail-gunner. But the room wasn't much of a trophy. The carpet had long gone and the plaster was crumbling. Pitch-washed sheets were nailed over the windows in place of curtains. Damp patches blotched the ceiling like sores. There was a smell of fatigue and faded grandeur. That's what years of warfare did to a place. They certainly did the same to a man, after all.

The old woman who ran the pension had told him that there would be no hot water until after eight, and he hadn't come that many parsecs to start a tour by standing under a piss-cold shower. He'd got dressed in the half-light – boots, breeches, fleece-vest – and started to pull on his flight coat. But his fingers had then encountered the insignia sewn into the thick quilts of the garment, the captain's bars, the squadron badge, the name-strip that read 'Viltry, Oskar'. He had put it aside and opted instead for a more anonymous tan leather coat.

The landing was dark. On the floor above, the crewmen of *Hello Hellstorm* were slumbering, with the crews of *Throne of Terror* and *Widowmaker* on the floor above that. The retinues of *K for Killshot* and *Get Them All Back* were billeted on the ground floor. The other six crews of XXI Wing 'Halo Flight', Imperial (Phantine) Air Force were tucked up in another pension down the street.

Viltry activated a glow-globe. The light was dim, but enough to light his way down the creaking staircase. In the hall, there were ancient books stacked on the mantel of the ornate but flaking fireplace, but those that he touched in the hope of finding an hour or two's distraction fell into dust.

He let himself out onto the street. It was chilly and quiet, except for the gurgle of the canal. A van rumbled by on the far side of the canal, its headlights cowled as per blackout procedures. He walked a few paces, noticing the stumps, regularly spaced, where iron lamp stands had been removed from the boulevard for the war effort. He tried to imagine the place in peacetime. Elegant, glass-hooded lamps, purring electric cruisers on the grand canal, prosperous Imperial citizens going about their business, stopping to greet and talk, dining at terrace taverns now long boarded-up. There would have been students too. The briefing documents said that Theda was a scholam town.

In truth, he realised, he knew precious little about Enothis. Precious little apart from three things: it was an old, proud Imperial world; it was strategically vital to this zone of the Sabbat Worlds; and he, and thousands of other aviators like him, had been drafted here from off-world at short notice to save it from extinction.

He noticed passers-by suddenly – other pedestrians out in the early light, dressed in dark clothes, all hurrying in the same direction. He heard the chime of a chapel bell ringing out seven of the clock, calling them to worship. Viltry followed them, crossing a bridge over the canal, hanging back.

By the time he reached the Ministorum chapel on the far bank side, the dawn service had already begun. He stood for a moment outside, listening to the plainsong chants. Above him, in the cold, grey light, the bas-relief facade showed the figure of the God-Emperor gazing down on all mankind.

Viltry felt ashamed. He bowed his head. When, eight years earlier, he had sworn to give his life as a warrior in the service of the God-Emperor, he hadn't realised how damn hard it would be. He'd always wanted to be an aviator, of course. Phantine's unusual topography bred that instinct into all its sons and daughters. But the cost had been great. Two years before, during the final onslaught to liberate his home world from the toxic clutches of the Archenemy, fighting alongside the Imperial Crusade forces of Warmaster Macaroth, he had almost died twice. Once as wind waste over the Scald, then as a prisoner of the vile warlord Sagittar Slaith at Ouranberg.

In the two years since then, Viltry had been unable to shrug off the idea that he should be dead already. He was living on borrowed time. His tutor at the scholam had drummed into him the concept of Fate's wheel. He'd said that it spun at the Emperor's right hand. It spun for balance, for symmetry. What was given would be taken, what was loaned would be paid back. A life saved was only a life spared.

His had been saved twice over. There was a reckoning to be had. And here he was, on another world, charged with the duty of fighting to save it. The reckoning would be here, he was sure of it. Fate's wheel would turn. He had been spared twice so he could live long enough to see his home world saved. Now he was fighting to save another man's home world. This, surely, would be where the accounts got squared.

The crew of *G for Greta* had seen this fatality in his every action, he was sure of that. They knew they were flying on a doomed bird. Doomed by him, cursed by him. He'd lost one crew over the Scald, and he should have gone with them. Now Fate's wheel would bring another crew down with him in its efforts to even the tally.

He'd asked for a transfer, been refused, asked for a non-operational posting, had that turned over as well. 'You're a bloody fine flight officer, Viltry,' Ornoff had told him. 'Get rid of this fatalistic nonsense. We need every man-bastard with airtime and combat experience we can get. Enothis will be tough as nails. Our ground forces are in hard retreat from Sek's legions. It'll come down to a bloody air war, mark my words. Request denied. Your Navy transport leaves orbit tomorrow at 06.00.'

Viltry looked up at the graven image of the God-Emperor, hard-shadowed in the sluggishly rising sun. It looked disapproving, scowling at his timid soul, fully aware of the cowardice in his heart.

'I'm sorry,' he said, out loud.

A woman in a long black coat, coming late to the service, looked round at him. He shrugged, bashful, and held the chapel door open for her.

Light, and a chorus of triumph dedicated to the Golden Throne of Earth, washed out on them both. She hurried in.

He followed her, and closed the heavy door behind him.

Over the Makanites, 07.11

THIS ONE WAS GOOD. Daring. Young, most likely, desperate to live. Weren't they all?

The dive was magnificent, foolhardy. Flight Warrior Khrel Kas Obarkon, chieftain of the fifth echelon, which was of the Anarch, and so sworn to he that is Sek, decided he would like more of this boy's kind in his echelon come the showdown. The boy flew, as they say, by the claws. Such a scream dive. Obarkon didn't know the runty little enemy pulsejets could achieve that.

It seemed almost a waste to slay him.

Wound tight in his grav-armour, auto-pumps and cardio-centrifuges compensating his circulation, Obarkon committed his Hell Razor steeper still, adjusting the trim, slicing down through the air like a knife at point eight of mach. His cockpit was dark save for the winking lights of his instruments, which reflected off the black, patent-leather gauntlets encasing his hands. The stooping Wolfcub was a bright orange pip on his auspex display.

How was it surviving? Pilot skill or luck? The young had little of the former and, sometimes, barrels of the latter. The dive was testing the enemy plane right to the limits of its airframe. A single degree deeper and the descent would strip the wings away at the cabane or blow out the inductive motor.

Behind the matt-black glass visor of his full-head helmet, Obarkon smiled. His face, so seldom seen, was a grizzled tissue of fibre and poly-weave reinforcements. His eyes were augmetics, linked directly to the warplane's gunsights by spinal plugs.

At three hundred metres, the Wolfcub pulled out, dragging a long, aching turn up and away to avoid the ragged peaks, its jet engine spitting and foundering.

Another surprise. Another admirable display of skill. Or luck.

Obarkon tilted his stick and nudged the reactive thrusters, pulling out of the dive non-ballistically, mocking the laboured struggles of the smaller plane. It had been locked in his gunsight for two minutes now. The target finder was chiming over and over again.

Attention…
Target found.
Target found.
Target found.
Why hadn't he killed it?
I want to see what you've got, Obarkon thought.

The Wolfcub veered around a peak-top, letting the cross of its shadow flicker across the sunlit snow, then tipped its wings hard to steer around another crag. Obarkon kept his Hell Razor almost level to execute a following path, ripping through the air like a heat-hungry missile. The Wolfcub was still in his crosshairs.

Suddenly, around the next peak, it disappeared. Obarkon frowned and swung about, assuming the boy had finally misadventured and flown into a cliff wall. For the first time in nearly three minutes, the target finder bleeped *lock lost… lock lost… lock lost…*

No, not dead. There he was. The little wretch. He'd somehow flick-rolled the Wolfcub around the promontory and swung back the way he'd come, gunning low on full thrust.

Obarkon lifted his shiny black-clad hands off the stick and clapped. Very fine indeed.

A warning note sounded and Obarkon snapped it off with a curse. He was down to reserve now, almost at the critical fuel threshold. That meant he had no more than two minutes left before he had to turn for home. More than that, and he wouldn't make it to Natrab echelon aerie.

'Game's done now,' he hissed through chapped lips. He surged the Hell Razor forward and it went fluidly, responding perfectly, sure as a shark. 'Reacquire,' he told the auto sight. He'd made five kills already, another ace day, but this boy would make a nice round six. He'd dallied too long, playing games.

The target pipper chased and bleeped. The Wolfcub was pulling wide rolls and staying low, keeping the twisting furrows of the peak line between itself and the hunter.

Target denied…
Target denied…
Target denied…

Obarkon cursed in the name of his most foul god. The little bastard was slipping away. By the skin of his teeth. By the claws. He had allowed too much grace. Now the enemy was mocking him.

He got a partial target, then lost it again as the fugitive Wolfcub banked perilously around a crag. They both passed so close that snow blizzarded up off the crag in their combined wash.

Another partial. Obarkon fired. Dazzling tracers laddered away from his machine and cut the cold, mountaintop air. Miss.

Another turn, another partial, another futile burst. Obarkon throttled up and soared around, using reactive thrust to viff his machine out wide on the Wolfcub's eight.

It was running for all it was worth, burning at full thrust. Obarkon got a true tone at last.

Target lock.

Target lock.

Target lock.

'Goodnight,' he muttered, bored of the game now. Hardwired thumbs dug at the trigger paddle.

Cannon fire lanced down through the air ahead of him. Obarkon felt a tiny vibration and a sudden display told him he'd been holed in one wing-sweep. Out of the sun, a second Wolfcub was diving on his tail, its nose lit up with muzzle flash. Just a glance told the expert chieftain that this second Cub was piloted by an idiot, a man far less capable than the spirited boy he had been chasing. It was coming over too shallow, wobbling badly, desperately. It had no real target lock.

But still, it was behind him and gunning madly.

The warning sounded again, impatient. He'd reached critical fuel threshold.

He was done here. Enough. Obarkon traversed the reactor ducts and powered off almost vertical, pulling out of the chase. The second Wolfcub went by under him as he climbed, bemused by the sudden exit.

Obarkon climbed into the sunlight, gaining altitude and speed. He turned his beloved Hell Razor south.

This broiling air war was just getting started. There would be another day.

And another kill.

Hotel Imperial, Theda, 07.23

KAMINSKY MADE A good run across the northern sectors and arrived outside the Hotel Imperial well inside the time Senior Pincheon had allocated for the job. The only slight delay had been a queue of market stallers lining up to get onto Congress Plaza for the midweek moot. These days, it seemed to Kaminsky, the Old Town kept to its bed until after eight, as if afraid of what horrors might roam in the dark hours of night.

He rolled in under the wrought iron frame of the hotel's awning, quietly wondering how long it would be before even that was taken for war metal, and glanced around. There was no one about except for an ancient old porter dozing on a folding chair amongst a half-dozen deactivated cargo servitors, and a gaggle of housekeepers smoking lho-sticks together by the service door down the side of the building.

Kaminsky was about to get down out of the cab when the glass and varnished wood of the hotel's front doors flashed in the early sunlight, and a mob of dark figures strode out purposefully towards him.

They were fliers, he knew that at once by the swagger of them, but not locals. Nor were they wearing the black and grey coats and flight armour of Navy aviators. There was at least a dozen, dressed in quilted taupe flightsuits and brown leather coats, carrying equipment packs loosely over their shoulders. They were unusually tall and well-proportioned individuals, slender and uniformly black-haired where the average Enothian was robust and fair.

And they weren't all male. At least three of them – including, it seemed, the figure leading them towards the transport – were women.

Kaminsky got out and walked round to the back of the transport to drop the tailgate. He nodded a greeting to the first of the newcomers, trying to get a decent look at the insignia on the coat sleeve, but the young man spared him not a second glance and simply hoisted in his kit bag and climbed up after it.

Only the woman paused. She had cold, searching eyes and a slim jaw that seemed to be set permanently in a gritted clench. Her black hair was cut unflatteringly short.

'Transport to Theda MAB South?' she asked Kaminsky. She spoke with an offworld accent that sounded rather odd and nasal to him.

'Yes, mamzel. To the dispersal station.'

'That's "commander",' she corrected, hauling her lithe figure up into the transport. 'Carry on.'

Kaminsky waited for the last of them to climb aboard, then shut the gate. He limped back round to the cab and started the engine.

Phantine. That's what it had said on the woman's silver shoulder badge. Phantine XX, embossed on a scroll backed by a double-headed eagle that clutched lightning bolts in its talons.

Kaminsky had been a student of aviation history since childhood and, though he'd heard of a world called Phantine, he had no idea why a flight wing should bear the name.

He drove them through Vilberg borough and turned south towards the base. On Scholastae Street, a pair of Commonwealth Cyclones went over at about five hundred metres, turning north and west. Kaminsky looked up to watch them pass.

In the driving mirror, he saw the fliers in the back do the same.

Theda Old Town, 07.35

THE SERVICE HAD finished, and the faithful were filing out, most stopping to light candles at the votary shrine. Candles for the lost, or those who might soon be.

As usual, as she did every morning, Beqa Meyer lit three: one for Gart, one for her brother, Eido, and one for whoever might need it.

She was tired. Night shift at the manufactory had really taken it out of her. It had been a struggle not to sleep through the hierarch's reading. If she'd been any warmer, she surely would have dozed off. But her coat was too thin: a second-hand summer coat, not even lined. Perhaps next month, with her next wages and what she had put aside, she'd be able to pick up a thermal jacket or better from the Munitorum almshouse.

As she turned from the candle-stand, she knocked against someone waiting their turn to light an offering. It was the man she'd seen by the church door on her way in for the service. Tall, dark-haired, an offworlder. He had a sad face. He was dressed like a soldier, and had that scent of machine oil and fyceline about him.

'My pardon, mamzel,' he said at once. She nodded 'no harm', but kept a distance as she went by. He'd been talking to himself when she'd first seen him. A stranger, maybe with battle-psychosis. That was the sort of trouble she didn't need.

In fact, the only thing she needed was her rest. She could be home by a quarter to the hour, and that would give her three hours' sleep before she'd have to rise and dress for her day job at the pier. When that was over, at evening bell, she'd have an hour to nap before the night shift at the manufactory began.

She hurried out through the templum doors into a cold street where full daylight now shone, and made her weary way back towards her hab.

Over the Thedan Peninsula, 07.37

'HUNT TWO, YOU'RE making oily smoke.'

The flight leader's anxious voice cut over the vox. There was no immediate response from Hunt Two. Darrow sat up in his seat and scanned around in the morning light. The scrub plains and grass breaks of the Peninsula swept by, two thousand metres under him, a wide expanse of greys, dull whites and speckled greens.

Down at his four were Hunt Eight and Hunt Eleven, with Hunt Leader running to starboard on the same deck as Darrow himself. Hunt Two and Hunt Sixteen were off and low at Darrow's port.

Six planes. Six planes were all that was left from the engagement. They'd left all the others as flaming pyres littering the snowcaps of the Makanite Mountains.

And it might only have been five. Darrow knew he surely would have been chalked by that white killer had not Hunt Leader, sweeping back in a desperate effort to rally his few remaining machines, run in at the last moment, cannons blazing, and driven it off.

Major Heckel – Hunt Leader – kept asking Darrow if he was okay as they pulled what remained of the formation back together. Heckel sounded extraordinarily worried, as if he felt Darrow might have simply scared himself to death in the frantic chase. But it was probably shock and the ache of responsibility. So many cadets dead. One of the squadron's black days.

And there had been so many in the last few months. Darrow wondered how officers like the major coped.

But then Heckel was only three years Darrow's senior, and had gained his rank through the accelerated promotion caused by severe losses.

'Hunt Two. Respond.' Even over the distorting vox, that tone in Heckel's voice was clear as day.

'Hunt Leader, I'm all right.'

He wasn't. Darrow had a good angle down at Hunt Two. Not only was he cooking out a steady stream of grubby smoke, he was losing altitude and speed.

What was it? Coolant? Smouldering electrics? Some other lethal eventuality Darrow hadn't even thought of?

How long had they got? By his own map and bearing they were forty-six minutes out from Theda MAB North, longer if Hunt Two maintained its rate of deceleration. Darrow's fuel gauge still showed full, but by Heckel's calculation, none of them were likely to have more than about fifty minutes in them. Especially not Darrow, given his excessive aerobatics.

'Hunt Flight…' Heckel's voice came over the comm. He paused, as if frantically trying to make up his mind. 'Hunt Flight, we're going to divert to Theda South. That should shave fifteen, maybe twenty minutes off the flying time. Confirm and line up on me.'

Darrow confirmed and heard the others do so too. It was a good decision. Flight command would rather get six Wolfcubs back at the wrong MAB than none back at all.

Darrow switched channels and heard Heckel banter back and forth with Operations as the reroute was authorised.

Then he heard the knocking again.

He was about to call it in when Hunt Eight began screeching over the vox.

'Hunt Two! Look at Hunt Two!'

Darrow craned his neck around. The wounded Cub was gently arcing down away from the formation. Its smoke trail was thicker and darker now. It looked heavy and sluggish, as if much more gravity was weighing down on it than on the other planes.

'Hunt Two! Respond!' Darrow heard Hunt Leader call. 'Hunt Two! Respond!'

A faint crackle. '–think I can hold the–'

'Hunt Two! Bail, for Throne's sake, Edry! Cadet Edry… Clear your plane now before you lose too much height!'

Nothing. The Wolfcub was just a dot at the end of a line of smoke far behind and below them now.

'Edry! Cadet Edry!'

Come on, Edry. Get out of there. Darrow strained to see. With their fuel loads so low, none of them could risk turning back. *Come on, Edry. Come on! Let us see a 'chute! Let us see a 'chute, Edry, before–*

A small flash, far away in the grey-green quilt of the landscape. A small flash of fire and no 'chute at all.

Theda MAB South, 07.40

BY THE TIME the transport turned off the highway onto the field approach way, it had been joined in convoy by three others. They waited in turn to be checked off by weary-looking PDF sentries at the west gate and then rumbled on down a steep cutting onto the field basin.

Commander Bree Jagdea raised herself up on the hard bench of the jolting transport and looked around. Theda Military Air-Base South covered over twenty square kilometres of low land south-west of the city itself. She could smell the coast a few kilometres north, and the sea air had layered a light morning haze across the field that the sun was just beginning to cook off.

Vast defences ringed the field. Ditches and dykes, blast fences and stake lines, armoured nests for Hydra batteries, pillbox emplacements for raised missile cylinders. There was a patched perimeter track, busy at this hour with military trucks and weapons carriers moving both ways, and a leaner inner ring of anti-air batteries. To the south end of the field stood the great housing hangars and rockcrete armouries, to the north Operations control and the stark derricks and pylons of the vox, auspex and modar systems.

A hash-shape of crossed airstrips covered the main inner area, the primary runways large enough to manage the big reciprocating-engined bombers the locals flew. Jagdea saw a few of them parked on a hardstand in the distance. Magogs, big and old and ugly. They'd used them back home on Phantine during the final offensive, desperate to get aloft anything that could fly and fight. Here they were a standard bombing mainstay. No wonder Enothis had been punished so hard.

But most of the local machines had been shipped out to clear the field for the newcomers.

Jagdea and her flight had arrived in darkness the night before. This was their first proper look at the base. It would serve; it would have to.

Work gangs from the Munitorum were already busy making field conversions. Labourers were proofing up more hard-wall silos for the arriving machines, and in one place were beginning to dozer up one of the old runways to make additional parking bunkers. The newcomers' aircraft, over seventy of them already, were dark shapes under netting in the clusters of anti-blast revetments to the east. There was a muddle of activity – chugging generators, clunking excavators, bare-chested rock-drill operators, growing heaps of spoil – all across the inner landscape of the field.

Jagdea glanced at the chronograph strapped around the thick cuff of her flightsuit. They were right on time. Their transport had left the perimeter track and was bumping towards the nearest of the huge drome hangars.

'Up and ready, Umbra Flight,' she ordered. The eleven aviators under her command gathered up their kits as the transport rolled to a stop.

Jagdea jumped down and took a deep breath. 'Here we go,' she muttered to Milan Blansher, her number two. Blansher was a grizzled veteran in his forties, his career tally of twenty-two kills the finest in Umbra Flight. He said little, but she trusted him with her life. He had unusually pale, distant eyes for a Phantine and sported a thick grey moustache, partly to lend himself an air of avuncular seniority, mostly to help conceal the ridge of white scar tissue where a piece of shell casing had split his face from his right nostril, down across both lips, to the point of his chin.

'Here we go indeed,' he murmured, and hoisted his kit onto his shoulder. The others clambered down. Van Tull, Espere, Larice Asche with her hair up in a non-regulation bun, Del Ruth, Clovin, the boy Marquall, Waldon, forever whistling a melody-less tune, Zemmic, jangling with his cluster of lucky charms, Cordiale, Ranfre. Almost all of them made the superstitious bob down to touch the ground.

Vander Marquall didn't. He was gazing across the field, watching three machines of the Enothian Commonwealth Air Force crank up for launch. They were powerful, twin-engine delta-form planes, an Interceptor pattern known as Cyclones. Started from trolley-mounted primer coils, their massive piston engines sucked and thundered into life, kicking out plumes of blue smoke from the exhaust vents as the heavy props began to turn to a flickering blur. They rocked impatiently at their blocks as the ground crews rolled the carts aside. Marquall could see the two-man crews in the glass nose cockpits making final checks. Though most Commonwealth wings had been withdrawn to make way for the offworlders, a flight of these Cyclones had been left on station to fly top-cover tours while the Imperials bedded in.

'Coming, Marquall?' Jagdea asked. He turned and nodded.

'Yes, commander.' Marquall was the youngest aviator in Umbra by four years, and the only one with no operational combat experience. Everyone else had seen at least some action during the Phantine liberation. Marquall had still been in the accelerated program at Hessenville when hostilities ended. He was eager and, Jagdea believed, reasonably gifted, but only time would really tell his worth. He had the classic saturnine good looks of a Phantine male, and a white, toothy grin that people either found winningly charming or unpleasantly cocky.

Umbra Flight strode off across the apron towards the hangar, followed by another flight of aviators spilling down from a second transport. Jagdea took a glance back at their own ride. In the cab, the Munitorum driver nodded briefly to her. She could clearly see how one half of his face was lost in burn scarring, as if soft, pink rose petals had been plastered across his skin.

They walked into the vast drome hangar. The air inside smelled cold and damp, with a tang of promethium. The interior space had been cleared, except for a lone Shrike under tarps in a corner, and a stage of flakboards supported by empty munition crates had been raised along the west wall. A chart stand and a hololithic displayer had been set up on the staging.

A group of more than twenty aviators was already waiting inside. They stood near the stage, their kit bags at their feet. Like the men who had come off the second truck, they were Navy pilots, wearing grey flight armour and black coats. Some of them sported augmetic eyes. They greeted their colleagues from the second truck, but both groups looked dubiously at the Phantine as they came in, and stayed apart from them in segregated groups. Jagdea regarded them casually as Umbra Flight dropped their bags and made a huddle. The Navy fliers kept glancing their way. Jagdea knew the Phantine Corps was unusual, and that set them apart from the regular Imperial aviators. It undoubtedly would mean rivalry and a pecking order, she accepted.

They were tough-looking brutes, sturdy and thickset, with pale skins and cropped hair. Most of their flight-suits were reinforced with plating sections or coats of chainmail, and their heavy leather coats were often fur-trimmed. Many had ugly facial scars. Several displayed medal ribbons and other honour sashes.

'Sixty-Third Imperial Fighter Wing,' Blansher whispered discreetly in her ear. 'The Sundogs, as they like to be styled. I believe that one there, the big fellow with the flight commander pins, is Leksander Godel. Forty kills last count.'

'Yeah, I've heard of him,' she answered lightly.

'The other bunch are the 409 Raptors, I believe,' Blansher went on, 'which would make that unassuming fellow there Wing Leader Ortho Blaguer.'

'The same?'

'The very same. One hundred and ten kills. See, he's looking at us.'

'Then let's look somewhere else,' Jagdea said and turned away.

'Orbis at your six!' Pilot Officer Zemmic suddenly cried out loudly, his voice echoing round the drome. Dismounting from another transport just now drawn up outside, a dozen more Phantine fliers were marching into the hangar. Jagdea felt instant relief at the sight of familiar faces. Orbis Flight, comrades and friends. At the head of them strolled their commander, Wilhem Hayyes.

The two wings clustered together and greeted each other.

'Nice of you to join us,' Jagdea grinned as she shook Hayyes by the hand.

'Nice of you to wait for us,' Hayyes replied. 'I trust there are still some bats flying for us to hunt.'

A hush suddenly fell. A final group of aviators, all Navy men, had just entered the hangar, making a late entrance that seemed to Jagdea calculatedly theatrical. There were only eight of them. Their armoured flight-suits were matt black and their suede jackets cloud-white. They wore no insignia or rank markings whatsoever, except silver Imperial aquilae at their collars.

'Holy crap!' Jagdea heard Del Ruth whisper. 'The Apostles!'

The Apostles, indeed. The celebrated wing of aces, the very elite. Jagdea wondered which one was Quint, ace of aces, which one Gettering. The tall one, was that Seekan or Harlsson? Which one was Suhr?

There was no time to ask Blansher. Escorted by a dozen aides and tactical officers, an imposing figure in the uniform of a fleet admiral came in and took the stage. It was Ornoff himself.

All eyes turned to him.

'Aviators,' he began, his voice soft but carrying. 'At 18.00 yesterday evening, I met with Lord Militant Humel in the War Ministry at Enothopolis. The lord militant, as you must be aware, has been prosecuting the war here on Enothis for the last nine months, in the name of Warmaster Macaroth and the God-Emperor of us all.'

'The Emperor protects!' one of the Apostles said smartly, and everyone eagerly echoed the words.

Ornoff nodded appreciatively. 'I hope he does, Captain Gettering. In the meantime, we will have to do. I presented the formal orders sent to me by the Warmaster to Lord Militant Humel, and at 18.30 hours precisely, the Lord Militant formally handed command of the Enothis theatre to me.'

Spontaneous applause broke out across the hangar floor.

'For now, the land war on Enothis is done. Now the air war begins.'

Theda MAB South, 07.46

MAJOR FRANS SCALTER glanced at the co-pilot alongside him in the cramped bubble canopy of the thundering Cyclone, got a thumbs-up, then turned to wave the ground crew off.

He adjusted his mask. 'Operations, Operations. This is Seeker One. Seeker Flight is ready for departure. Awaiting permission.'

Scalter had his hand on the wheel-brake lever.

'Seeker One, Operations. Roll them out. Main is open. Fly true and may the Emperor protect you.'

'Thank you, Operations. Seeker Flight, on my lead.'

Scalter released the brake, and opened the throttle gently. Bucking, the twin-engined plane began to creep out off the hardstand towards the main runway. Its wingmen followed. The combined roar of the six engines resounded across the field.

Scalter rolled to the start position, and made a final adjustment to the trim. At his side, Artone opened the radiators and made the fuel mix a little richer for a lusty take-off.

'Seeker Flight–' Scalter began.

Artone suddenly held up a hand.

'What?'

'Red flag!' said Artone urgently, pointing down the field.

'Throne! What now?' snarled Scalter. 'Operations, this is Seeker One. We've got a red flag. Please confirm our clearance.'

There was a pause. Then the vox fizzled. 'Negative clearance, negative clearance, Seeker Flight. Abort now and clear main. Roll off to revetments fifteen through seventeen and stand down. Repeat – Negative clearance, abort and clear main.'

'What the hell's going on?' Scalter demanded.

'Wounded birds,' the vox replied. 'Wounded birds inbound.'

Twenty kilometres short of Theda MAB South, 07.46
THEY COULD SEE the spread of the field, slightly hazy in the morning light. Guide paths were popping off. The knocking from behind Darrow was now constant.

Major Heckel called in the fuel load from each Cub in turn. All were miserably low. Darrow could only answer full as he had no other reading. Hunt Sixteen had begun to dribble smoke in the last ten minutes, and its pilot reported rapidly dropping hydraulic pressure. Hunt Sixteen had taken at least two hits to the belly during the brawl over the mountains.

'Hunt Flight, this is Hunt Leader. Sixteen and Four have landing priority. Let them go in first and we'll follow as soon as they're down. Confirm.'

Darrow stretched his shoulders against the harness. Heckel wanted Sixteen down before it died, and he wanted Darrow down as quickly because he was most likely flying on empty.

'After you, Hunt Sixteen,' Darrow voxed, allowing the Wolfcub to come around ahead of him. The Cub's streamer of smoke pulsed clear then white, clear then white, like a ticker tape.

The knocking grew yet more insistent. Darrow began his approach.

* * *

Theda MAB South, 07.47

'YOUR FIGHTER WINGS,' Ornoff told them, 'are five of the first to arrive on station here along the southern coast. In the next seventy-two hours, a total of fifty-eight wings of the Imperial Navy… and its affiliates…' he added, with a nod to the Phantine, 'will be deployed at airfields along the entire littoral. Forty-two fighter wings, sixteen bomber flights. To say that you will be supporting the local Commonwealth squadrons here is a mis-statement. You will form the front line in the air. The stalwart Commonwealth forces who have, let me remind you, been fighting this theatre for months now, will take a supportive role. God-Emperor willing, this may allow them precious time to repair, refit, recrew and rest.'

He turned to the chart behind him. 'I don't need to tell you to familiarise yourself with the topography, channel use, and the location of friendly fields. Encryption codes will be changed on a daily basis. The Archenemy is listening.'

Ornoff paused and slid his open hand down the chart pensively. 'The situation here is grave. Lord Militant Humel's land forces, ably supported by the Commonwealth armies, almost succeeded in driving the Archenemy off this world. However, in the last two months, fortunes have reversed disastrously. The Archenemy, whose remaining surface stronghold is around the Southern Trinity Hives – here – has resupplied in great force as part of the counter-offensive launched last year through the Khan Group as a whole. The Lord Militant's land forces are now in harried retreat northwards through the Interior Desert… this region, here. Some have already reached the Makanite Range, and are struggling through the passes there. Our task – your task – is to help as many of them reach the safety of the Zophonian Coast as possible. We are to supply comprehensive air cover to the retreating columns of armour and infantry. That means denying the enemy airspace, and prosecuting their land forces with aerial strikes. Enothis will only be saved if sufficient portions of allied land forces can be brought back to the coast intact. There, with resupply, they can make a stand, a counter-attack to meet the Archenemy invasion.'

Ornoff looked back at them all. 'Expect to be flying sorties round the clock. A thorough strategic plan will be executed as soon as all the wings are on station, at which point your wings may be reassigned to other fields. In the meantime, you will be flying ad hoc missions at the discretion of Operations to supply cover until we are at full strength.'

Ornoff raised a hand and beckoned one of the staffers who had entered the hangar with him onto the stage, an older man in the flight kit of a Commonweath pilot officer. 'I've invited Commander Parrwood here to brief you on climate and terrain peculiarities. Before he does, any questions?'

Godel, the Sundogs' flight commander, raised a gloved hand. 'What are we to expect here, admiral?'

'Superior air power,' Ornoff replied crisply. 'Hell Razor and Locust-class fighters, Tormentor and Hell Talon-class fighter-bombers. The Archenemy is flying a large number of locally-made machines. There are also reports of heavy bombers, of a type yet undetermined. Many of their planes exhibit extended range, which may indicate mass carriers in the desert.'

'When do we get in their reach?' one of the Apostles asked.

'Unless you deny them, Major Suhr, at their present rate of progress, the Archenemy wings will have range enough to begin attacking these coastal bases within the month. That is an eventuality I don't want to see.'

'And you won't, admiral,' said Suhr, 'because we *will* deny them.' There was a general murmur of approval.

'Now, if Commander Parrwood would be so kind we–'

Ornoff's words were cut off as a hooter began to drone outside. In a moment, it was chorused by others. A deep, ominous moaning wailed out across the field.

The aviators exchanged glances. Ornoff looked at his aides and hurried off the stage, heading for the hangar doors. Everyone followed.

Outside, in the bright sunlight, they clustered on the rockcrete apron, scanning the glassy sky. Path lights had been lit along the main runway track, and recovery vehicles were growling out of sheds along the north perimeter.

'Someone's in trouble,' Blansher muttered.

'There!' one of the Navy pilots called, pointing.

Low in the southern sky, tiny dots. Jagdea heard the distant, burping putter of pulsejets.

'That's low,' said Asche. Several of the dots were hanging back, but two were hoving in. They could see sunlight flare off canopies. The lead plane, a little dark-green monojet, was dragging a string of vapour behind it.

'Not good,' said Jagdea, staring.

Beside her, Marquall said, 'What?'

'If he's going to land, let's hope he gets his cart down.'

Over Theda MAB South, 07.51

THE SMOKE COMING out of Hunt Sixteen was getting thicker, and had started to plume out fat and heavy as their airspeed dropped. Darrow had to adjust height to stop himself flying in blind through the vapour. Hunt Sixteen was pitching low, and it forced Darrow to sit up high, higher than he would have preferred for an approach.

There was a slight crosswind. He felt his tail skidding, and he trimmed to compensate. According to the airspeed indicator, he was getting dangerously near critical stall.

'Come on, Hunt Sixteen!' he cursed. 'Come on, Phryse! Get that bird down!'

'Hold your water…' the vox chattered. 'I think… think my bloody cart's hung.'

'Clear it, Phryse!' Darrow heard Hunt Leader urge over the channel.

'Trying… damn thing's stuck… lever's jammed. Bent. I think…'

A bleeper sounded in Darrow's cockpit. Fuel out… even though the damn gauge still read full.

'I've got to sit *now*!' he called.

'Okay, okay! S'all right, Enric. I've got it now. Lever's pulled. Cart down.'

Theda MAB South, 07.51

EVEN AS THE Cyclone's engines whistled down to a dying chop, Scalter wrenched open the window slider of the canopy and stuck his head out, searching the sky.

'Operations!' he yelled, but then realised that pushing his head out of the window had pulled his mic-cord to full extent and yanked the plug out of the vox panel.

'Damn it!' he yelled, struggling back inside and banging his head. 'Damn it!' He fumbled for the end of the cord.

'Got it!' cried Artone, ramming the plug back into its socket.

'Operations! Get a flag up! Signal! That Cub's coming in with its undercart up!'

'Clear the channel, Seeker.'

Scalter clunked off his harness, threw open the side hatch and fell out onto the ground. Artone was fast on his heels. The crews of the Cyclones in the revetment bunkers next to them had dismounted too.

Scalter ran up the embankment towards the main strip, waving his arms. Red flares had gone up over the field. Bleeding smoke, one wing hanging heavy, the Wolfcub was really low. The noise of its pulsejet was a drawn-out, plosive blurt.

Its undercart was locked up in its belly.

'Up! Up!' Scalter yelled. He fell on his face as Artone tackled him and brought him down short of the rock-crete track.

The Wolfcub came in, over and past them both. Just shy of stall speed, it began to drop its tail, about to settle onto gear that wasn't there.

The underside of the tail hit first. There was an abrasive shriek. Metal shards and grit flew up in a hot grind of friction. Immediately, the tail came back up, bouncing, pitching the Wolfcub down straight on its nose. The Interceptor came apart, shredding aluminoid off its frame. The port wing crumpled and flew off. The pulsejet, coughing flames, sheared off its mounts, crushed the already buckled cockpit, and detonated as it lifted clear. Liquid flame boiled out across the runway.

High on its six, Darrow stared in disbelief. He'd just lowered his own undercart, and the added drag had dwindled his speed even more. There was no runway any more, just a lake of fire and a mass of tangled wreckage.

'Abort, Hunt Four!'

Darrow slammed on full emergency thrust and trimmed for maximum lift. His Cub shook and fought, tired of flying now. He hauled on the stick.

Jet screaming, Hunt Four cleared the debris by scant metres and zoomed through the leaping fireball of the crash. Darrow's canopy blackened with soot. There was smoke everywhere. As he came clear, he saw loose flame dancing along his wings.

'Request secondary runway!' he yelled.

'Runway is clear—' the vox sang. He came around, rising and turning as tightly as he dared. He wouldn't stall. Not now. Not now. The stick was like lead. He came about onto the track, dropping fast but true. He had it now.

Red lights fluttered across his instruments. He felt a lurch. The engine had flamed out. Zero fuel or nothing like enough airspeed, he couldn't tell which. Didn't have time. Didn't care.

The Wolfcub fell out of the air onto the ragged runway. The undercart survived the first hard bounce, but not the second. It disintegrated in a scatter of chrome struts and torn rubber. The machine made a third bounce on its belly, cascading sparks into the air. Body plating ripped away. The slide went wide, turning the dented nosecone right, folding a wing like paper. Darrow screamed, his arms over his face, shaken like a bead in a tin.

They came running from all directions, from the silos, from the fitter barns, from the main hangar. Recovery trucks, their hooters blaring, kicked up dust and stones as they raced over the verge sides.

Jagdea and Blansher were amongst the first of the aviators to reach the wreck.

'Back! Get back!' a tender driver screamed at them.

'Get him out then!' Jagdea yelled back, slamming past the barrier of the man's outstretched arms.

The canopy hood of the downed Cub wrenched backwards, and the pilot dragged himself out. His plane was almost on its side, pinning a broken wing under it, surrounded by debris. He staggered towards them, shaking his head dizzily as the crash-crews ran in towards the wreck with retardant sprays.

The young man's face was black with soot and oil. When he pulled off the breather mask, his lower face was pink and clean. He blinked at Jagdea and Blansher.

'Shit,' he said.

'Good landing,' Blansher said, offering an arm to support him. The pilot sagged heavily, shaking.

'Good… landing…?' he coughed.

Blansher smiled. 'You walked away from it, didn't you?'

DAY 253

Interior Desert, 10.10

THE FURY OF PARDUA was dead. Its power plant had been running sore and hoarse for the last hundred kilometres, and the coolant needles had been buried in red for the last twenty. The driver had managed to get it just about off the main track before the engine uttered its death-rattle, and now the venerable Conqueror-type battle tank was slumped as if in repose.

The fine, dry sand was slowly dimpling under its sixty-two tonnes and it was beginning to keel, submerged up to the axles on the port side.

LeGuin walked around it once, feeling the heat radiating off its metal hull on his face. There was a clatter of tools and one of the regimental aux techs appeared out of the rear hatch, his face red and shiny from exertion.

'Well?' asked LeGuin.

'Coolant's dry and the main cylinder block has just fused. Running too hard, too long. And there's sand in everything.'

49

LeGuin nodded. 'Strip out anything portable or consumable. Munitions, batteries, vox, pintle weapons, any water or fuel in the reserves. Strip it out and transfer it to transports. Make it fast, trooper.'

'Yes, captain.'

LeGuin glanced round at Lieutenant Klodas, the *Fury's* commander. His driver, loader and gunners stood nearby in a shabby, respectful group, caps in their hands, like mourners at a funeral. LeGuin saw that Klodas was trying not to cry.

'No wasting surplus water, please, Klodas,' he said. 'We've got a bloody long way to go yet.'

Klodas sniffed and nodded. LeGuin felt bad for being so hard on the junior officer. Losing a steed, as LeGuin well knew, was like losing a best friend, sibling, parent and faithful hound all in one go. The average tanker lived in his machine, fought with it, killed from it and had been saved by it. He owed it, he trusted it and knew its foibles. To leave it for dead at the side of a desert track seemed… criminal.

Besides, simply as a piece of military technology, these tanks were priceless. Precious few of the original units remained in active service. The great forge worlds were manufacturing modern pattern copies as fast as they were able, but the craft was getting lost, many of the tech secrets were being forgotten, or had never been recorded. LeGuin himself knew, as a bitter certainty, virtually no forge worlds were now capable of hand-crafting the specialist L/D cannon for a tank hunter.

Fury of Pardua was one of the 8th's oldest Leman Russ examples, painstakingly maintained and repaired for twenty-three centuries. Even in its current pitiful state – seized up, burnt-out and fried dry – it deserved to be recovered and hauled away for full salvage or refit.

But that wasn't going to happen. There was no time, no resources and – if they all stood there much longer – no one left alive.

LeGuin looked back down the trail. In the glare of the blow-torch sun, a column of men and machines wound towards him across the sandpaper terrain, blurred by heat and dust. Every ten seconds, another tank or carrier grumbled past, kicking up grit. LeGuin's eyes were at a permanent squint. The retreat column stretched back as far as he could see, and it was only one of a hundred or more threading their way desperately across the scorched earth and billowing dunes of the north-western sief. Such was the fate of Lord Militant Humel's great 'land armada', which had almost reached the gateways of the Trinity Hives to purge Enothis, before being turned back by the unbelievable ferocity of replenished Archenemy forces.

The abject wreck of the *Fury of Pardua* seemed to Captain LeGuin an appropriate symbol for this disastrous retreat: a great, proud beast from another age, beaten to extinction by the foe and the climate, left to rot into the consuming sands where only future archaeologists might ever expose its dry bones again.

LeGuin looked north, watching the dust trail of the vehicles that had passed ahead. Men trudged beside crawling machines, as thirsty for water as the vehicles were for oil. Some rode on fenders or straddled body plating. Every few kilometres something needed to be repaired, dug free or pulled out of soft sand by the Atlas teams. The *Fury* was not the first piece of armour to be abandoned at the roadside. The miserable route back to the Trinity Hives was marked with the corpses of machines that had died along the way.

Died or been killed. The Archenemy was not letting them run unmolested.

Klodas had flagged down a half-track weapons carrier, and his crew was formed into a human chain to ship what was salvageable from the Conqueror.

'Don't take too long,' LeGuin told him.

LeGuin walked back to his own steed, wiping his brow with a hand that came away black with perspiration and grit. As he walked, he looked up into the relentless sky. Where would the next attack come from? Up there? Or, as the vox-reports from back down the column suggested, were the enemy land forces now beginning to nip at their heels too?

The *Line of Death* sat waiting for its commander. As he climbed up, he patted its flank, even though the sun-roasted metal scorched his hand. The *Line* was an Exterminator-type assault tank, its chassis the same basic pattern as the heavier Conqueror. Its turret-mounted twin autocannons could produce an astonishingly savage field of rapid firepower. The tank was painted dust-red, though that wash was scuffed down to the chrome base metal in many places. Its name was painted on the turret's mantlet, and its regiment – 8th Pardus Armoured – was embossed above the sponsons beside an Imperial double eagle crest.

LeGuin clambered over the drums of spare munitions webbed to the rear cowling and hopped up into the turret. Matredes, his gunner, was waiting for him in the top hatchway.

'We going?'

'Yeah.'

Matredes shouted down to Emdeen, the driver, and the V12 engine revved. They lurched onwards, treads clattering, and rejoined the file.

The *Line* had not been LeGuin's for long and, though he tried to bond with the steed, they were not tight. For most of his career, LeGuin had been a Destroyer man, commander of the tank killer *Grey Venger*. Thirty-four kills they'd shared, until *Venger* had fallen to enemy fire on the shrine world Hagia three years before. LeGuin might have happily burned with his steed, but his life had been saved by the selfless action of an infantry scout called Mkoll, a man LeGuin respected enough not to be angry with.

On his return to regimental headquarters, they'd assigned LeGuin this can. He'd wanted another Destroyer, naturally, for that's where his skills and training lay, but there were just none available. On the rare occasions one of that ancient marque came up for transfer or reassignment, it was usually a reconditioned hulk with lousy bearings, a rebored engine and some useless firework in place of the precious, specialist L/D cannon.

So, disguising his disappointment, LeGuin had become an assault tanker, riding his new steed in with Humel's doomed Enothian campaign.

The *Line* spurred forward. Under the present circumstances, the memory of his disappointment seemed ridiculously insignificant and made LeGuin smile. So, he hadn't been assigned the steed he wanted. Shame. If only that was the worst thing he had to deal with now.

All that mattered at this moment was what was going to get them first: the desert or the enemy.

Even with the internal compartments filter-sealed, it was like an oven in the Exterminator. LeGuin dared not use the air exchanger for fear of depleting fuel even further. Matredes was studying the charts by the light of a red bulb overhead, and he said something. LeGuin had put on his ear-baffles already, and now he switched on the internal intercom.

'Say again?'

'Another forty kilometres, and we should be reaching rougher terrain... open karst. That'll mark the beginnings of the rift.'

LeGuin nodded. The rift, and the mountains beyond it, represented the second and third of the great barriers the columns would have to overcome in order to reach safe territory. The desert was just the beginning. But it gave him some sense of hope. These were palpable markers that he could tick off.

LeGuin popped the hatch and sat up, taking the electroscope Matredes passed to him. The *Line of Death* was travelling in the forward quarter of the retreating column. According to unconfirmed rumours, some of the Imperial elements had already reached the Makanite passes, on the doorstep of safety. According to other rumours, enemy rapid assault units had reached there too, gunning to deny them.

He scanned ahead through the scope, trying to brace against the lurch of the machine. Every view was filtered by heat haze and whirling dust. But there did now seem to be something far ahead. A slender blue-white line. Mountains, or a daylight dream?

The vox chattered something he didn't quite catch. A moment later, he didn't need it repeated. Flickering shadows shot north overhead, and he heard the rush of afterburners above the roar of the tank's engine.

Two dark red shapes in the bright sky, moving as fast as arrows, curled in low above the column ahead. He saw flashes, sprays of sand, then heard the rolling *crump* of detonating munitions. A kilometre away, something caught fire and began to smudge the sky with a thick spout of oily, black smoke.

'Alarm! Alarm!' he shouted into the vox. The *Line's* turret weapons were already cranked to maximum elevation, but there was no point wasting ammo at this range. In the distance, he saw the choppy flashes of tracers from Hydra carriers in the front file.

Two more bats went over, using the convoy's long dust wake as a marker to line up on their targets. Matredes was rotating the turret, but LeGuin shook his head. A troop truck three vehicles forward of them leapt into the air in a brilliant eruption of flame, and showered burning debris in all directions.

They hadn't even seen that one coming.

The vehicles ahead of them swerved. The hit truck was a stricken mass of blazing, twisted metal. Burnt bodies, some stripped naked by the blast, littered the sand.

Another troop truck, turning to avoid the ruin, hit soft sand and dug in. It rocked violently, wheels spinning and digging deeper, engine over-revving. The infantrymen in the back leapt down with spades and chains.

'Full stop! Get the cable!' LeGuin yelled to Matredes, who clambered out at once with Mergson, one of the sponson gunners.

'Tie it up! Tie it up!' LeGuin shouted at the men on the ground as Matredes and the gunner fetched the hawser coil from the starboard panniers. They had to be quick. The enemy warplanes habitually dumped their payloads on the head of the column to slow it down. Then they delighted in coming about down the stationary line, strafing as they went home.

'Come on!'

Surface-to-air from the column ahead. Tracer, some wild cannon fire, small-arms. Some idiot tried a shoulder rocket. It went up, useless as a white flare in daylight. Where were they? Where the bloody hell w–

Booom! One went right over at zero altitude, rocking the tank on its torsion bars with the shockwave. By the time it had gone by them, it was already pulling off. The track five hundred metres ahead was swathed in fyceline smoke from the deluge of cannon fire it had stitched down the line. New fires had started. Something big – a tank's magazine, most likely – blew up with a dry roar.

'Come on, Matredes!' LeGuin bawled. Most of the troopers had thrown themselves flat when the bat went over, but LeGuin's men had got the cable lashed around the truck's bull-bars.

'Ease off! Get him to ease off!' LeGuin shouted to Matredes, indicating the truck driver, a Munitorum drone who was still thrashing the daylights out of the vehicle's drive shaft in an effort to self-right.

'Emdeen?' LeGuin voxed to his driver. 'Nice and easy back step, no jerks, or you'll amputate its rear end.'

'Understood, captain,' Emdeen voxed back. 'Fifteen segs, mind.'

Fifteen segs. LeGuin laughed despite the situation. A Pardus tanker was permitted to sew a little stylised track segment to the edge of his uniform collar for every year served active. Emdeen was reminding his captain that he was a fifteen year vet and didn't need to be told how to tow a cargo-10 successfully.

LeGuin had thirteen segs of his own.

His laughter stopped as he saw the next bat. Low, head on, red as an open wound. Weapon ports flashed as it came on. Tormentor-class, LeGuin presumed. Maybe a Hell Talon. He didn't care. He knew tanks. Planes looked all the same to him. It might as well have been a frigging flying pixie, it was still intent on murder.

The bat's cannon fire chewed along the track, kicking dirt up in man-high bursts with the rapid precision of an industrial belt press. A STeG armoured car wearing the dusty livery of the Enothian PDF ruptured like an eggshell and rolled on its side. The raking blasts atomised the front end of the water tanker.

Then the shots stitched right across them. Half a dozen of the troopers from the stranded truck were mown down, their bodies flung aside, or into the air, or into pieces. The air filled with up-flung dust and dirt. LeGuin lost sight of Matredes, but saw Mergson clearly as he was hit. Everything below Mergson's waist vaporised in a blitz of flame and fibres.

'No!' LeGuin screamed as he dropped back into the turret for cover, three shells spanking off the *Line's* top armour.

The bat had already hammered past, but as he'd dropped, LeGuin had seen a second one right behind it.

Raging, he seized the yokes of the main turret's twin mount, threw the autoloader lever and began to fire.

The turret rocked. He couldn't see a thing through the prismatic sight, certainly not a target.

A waste of munitions? Let me miss first, LeGuin reasoned, *then* tell me that.

Over the Makanites, 12.01

FLIGHT TIME WAS coming up on one hour. Twenty thousand metres of clear air down to the frosted mountains below them, three-tenths cloud. Visibility clear to forty-plus.

Strapped in his flight armour and breathing air-mix through his mask, Viltry looked up out of his Marauder's shadowed cockpit into the bright realm of the sky. Ahead, and slightly high, *Hello Hellfire* was cruising smoothly, leaving long, straight, pure-white condensation trails behind her. The sunlight glinted off her polished-alloy silver.

It was almost serenely quiet apart from the background thrum of *G for Greta's* four ramjets. According to the auspex, there was nothing in the air except their six plane formation for a hundred kilometres.

Viltry clicked his intercom. '*Gee Force*, check in.'

That was *G for Greta's* other nickname. *Gee Force Greta*. Orsone had coined it, and it had stuck.

'Bombardier, aye.'

'Nose, aye.'

'Tail, check.'

'Turret, aye.'

Lacombe, Viltry's navigator, looked round from his position and made a finger-'o' with his gloved hand.

'How far?' Viltry asked the navigator.

'Coming up on the waypoint, sir. We want to make a turn bearing east ten in the next five.'

'What's it called again?'

'Irax Passage. I believe, named after a local species of alpine herbivore that–'

'Thanks, Lacombe. War first, history later.'

'Sir.'

Viltry switched channels. 'Halo Flight, this is Halo Leader. Prepare to come about bearing east ten on my mark… three, two, one… mark.'

The angle of the sun tilted. The tactical bombers turned. *G for Greta, Hello Hellfire, Throne of Terror, Mamzel Mayhem, Get Them All Back* and *Consider Yourself Dead.* Except for heavy operations, Halo seldom lofted all of its dozen birds for one sortie. Six was standard, and these six had been picked by straw poll. *Widowmaker* had been drawn, but then switched out because of a vector duct problem. *Mamzel Mayhem* had taken her place. The *Mamzel* was Halo Two, Kyrklan's bird. As Viltry's second-in-command, Wassimir Kyrklan usually led sorties with the other half of the flight while Viltry's half was in turn-around. It was unusual for them to be flying together.

'Make your descent by five thousand,' Lacombe said.

'Copy all flight, descent by five thousand.'

There was a change in engine tone as they began to drop. The ice-capped peaks began to seem terribly close.

'Lacombe?'

The navigator's sharp eyes switched between the terrain-scanning auspex and the cockpit view. 'Looking for a point turn. Yacob's Peak. Plot brief says it stands at the mouth of the pass.'

Another slow minute. 'Come on, Lacombe.'

'There it is. Twelve kilometres and closing. We need to lose another two thousand now. Brief advises wind shear once we enter the pass.'

Viltry nodded, easing the stick. 'Halo Flight, Halo Flight. Point marker twelve kilometres and closing. Stoop by three, and watch for crosswind.'

'Halo Two, understood.'

'Following your lead, Halo Leader.'

A photo-scout Lightning from the 1267th Navy (recon) had run this pathway at dawn, identifying a cluster of Imperial armour and artillery units halfway up the pass, with Archenemy heavies tight on its tail. Apparently, a local squadron had spotted the area the day before, shortly before getting stung by enemy air cover.

'Halo Flight, watch the air,' Viltry voxed. He switched to intercom. 'Gunners? Locks off. Eyeball scans now, like your lives depend on it. For they surely do. Judd?'

A crackle. 'Captain, sir?'

'Kiss the children for me, bombardier.'

Crackle. 'I'll tell them you said night-night.'

In the bomb bay below Viltry, Judd gently armed the payload, and then snuggled up to the foresight reticule on his belly.

The ragged pinnacle of Yacob's Peak rose up ahead of them, a snow-caked jab of rock. Viltry could see the mouth of the pass now. His heart began to beat faster. It was going to be tight.

'Halo Flight, Halo Flight. On it now.' He tried to keep his voice calm. 'Come about the point marker and drop hard by number sequence. The Emperor protects.'

All of the planes repeated that catechism.

Three... two... one...

The six Marauders, now formed in line astern, banked hard around the rock spire and followed *Gee Force* down the chute, swinging low and chasing hard. The promised wind shear rattled them brutally. Then, for a few moments, the canyon walls were so close on either side that the pilots expected to see friction sparks at their wingtips. But the chasm began to widen out. The pass descended. Snow cover, a ridgeway, a well of black rock with curling ice-sheets. It widened to five hundred metres-plus. Viltry kicked in some throttle, dropping *Gee Force* down to a sense-whizzing low fifty. At the stick of *Mamzel Mayhem*, right behind *Gee Force*, Kyrklan grinned. Low fifty, in a Marauder doing 400 kph, boxed in by a granite canyon. Only Oskar Viltry had the balls to lead off like that.

Kyrklan had been flying Marauders for just a year less than Viltry, and for the last six had been Viltry's second in Halo. He loved the man, and would follow him anywhere. In Wassimir Kyrklan's opinion, no one quite knew how to play a four-ram bird the way Viltry did. It was a gut thing, a nerve thing. Like he was born to it. When Viltry had gone missing, presumed lost, over the Scald in 771, Kyrklan had mourned not just for his friend but for the generations of Phantine pilots to come. They would never see Viltry fly, never learn, never understand. The fact that Kyrklan had gained flight command was no consolation. He'd had to lead the wing in on the Ouranberg raid. Viltry would have done that job better. Now the captain was back and everything would be four-A.

Kyrklan pushed his dangling mask up to his face. 'Slow down, eh, Osk?' he laughed into the vox.

'Say again, Halo Two?'

'Nothing, Halo Leader. Let's go get.'

In the juddering cockpit of Halo Lead, Viltry shivered. Inside his armoured gauntlets, his knuckles were white. *This is it. This is the one. Fortune's frigging wheel. This is the payback. Death. Death now. Death now—*

'Target sighted!' Judd sang out.

They had just whipped over a straggled formation of Imperial armour, over two hundred vehicles hemmed in on a shelf of the steep pass. Up ahead, mobile batteries and heavy cannon began to punch the air with shot.

Viltry's hands were quivering on the stick. 'I can't...' he began.

'Captain?' Lacombe asked, looking round at him.

Holy Throne! Just do it. Just do it! Viltry shook himself, and screamed into his mic. 'Forward guns fire now! Now! Judd! Fry them!'

Naxol, in the bow turret, began firing, kicking out backwashing flame around the plane's nose as he raked the ground positions.

'Load away!' Judd reported. *Gee Force* lifted suddenly as the belly and wing weight let go.

A ripple of flame below. Then *Mamzel Mayhem* added to it, then *Hello Hellfire*. It whipped up into a firestorm. The others, in swift succession, followed.

By then, *G for Greta* was banking up out of the pass, the crystal mountainscape under her. Sucked back into their harness rigs by the extreme G, her crew was still cheering.

Levelling out at five kilometres over the peaks, Viltry sagged over the controls for a moment, breathing hard.

'We cooked them! We cooked the bastards and–'

The voice was shrilling from Gaize, the turret gunner.

'Shut up. Shut up!' Viltry yelled. 'Shut up for Throne's sake! Pick up your visual scanning right now or we won't get home! Do you hear me? We won't frigging well get home!'

Theda MAB South, 12.12

THE SKY WAS empty, but Pilot Officer Vander Marquall wasn't looking at it. He was looking at his bird.

The I-XXI Thunderbolt sat on its skids in an anti-blast revetment on the east side of the Theda South field. It was a hefty beast, fourteen tonnes dead weight without fuel, with a blunt group of cannons for a nose and a body that swelled out into forward swept wings around the thrust tunnels of the double turbofan engines. The canopy was set amidships, giving the Bolt a reclined, louche look.

It was painted matt grey, with the marks of the Phantine XX on its tail and nose. Its exposed engine ducts glinted copper.

Racklae, Marquall's chief fitter, looked up from under one of the gun housings. 'Be good as new, I promise,' he said.

Marquall grinned. Racklae's subs were just finishing up the nose art paint job on the bird. The Phantine stylised eagle, clasping the jagged lightning bolt, with the name 'Double Eagle' beneath it in inverted commas.

Marquall became aware of someone coming up behind him. He turned, and stiffened in surprise.

It was Captain Guis Gettering of the Apostles, his white suede flight coat almost glowing in the midday sunlight.

'Sir, I–' Marquall began.

Gettering calmly removed one of his chainmail gauntlets and slapped Marquall across the face with it so hard that the young man was knocked down onto one knee.

Dazed, stunned, his face grazed by the chain, Marquall looked up.

Guis Gettering was striding back to his hardstand.

'What…' gasped Marquall, rising with the assistance of his fitters. 'What the bloody hell was that about?'

Theda MAB North, 12.26

WHEN DARROW FINALLY got back to his station, it seemed like the place had been abandoned. He stood for a few minutes on the sunlit assembly yard and looked out across the main field. A kilometre away, along the western side of the area, he could see rows of big machines under nets. Imperial birds, Marauders. Darrow could just make out fitter crews at work on the heavy fighter-bombers. To his north, Munitorum crews were dismantling six of the twelve launching ramps used by the Wolfcubs. Activity, but all of it remote.

The complex of operations and barrack buildings behind him felt deserted and empty. He wandered up the main steps and into the cool gloom of the main hall. Darrow was wearing a borrowed pair of old overalls. His clothing had been ruined in the crash. He'd managed to keep hold of his aviator boots, and his heavy leather flying coat, though one sleeve of it had been badly torn. He'd refused to let the medics toss it away.

They'd insisted on keeping him in Theda South's infirmary overnight for observation, even though it was clear to anybody that he was fine apart from a few scratches and bruises. In the morning, he'd been forced to wait, twitchy with impatience, to fill out forms and incident statements. Only then had he been written up cleared and allowed to snag the first available transport back to North.

He just wanted to get back, get into the routine again and put the previous day, that terrible day, behind him.

No one seemed to want to let him do that. The forms, the medical checks, the incident statements. Even the transport driver who'd brought him back from Theda South seemed like a sick jibe. The man's face had been a mess of pink scar tissue.

The entry hall was empty. Nobody hurried past along the polished wood-tile floor. He walked past the gilt-lettered rolls of honour on the panelled walls, one for each Commonwealth squadron, including his own, the 34th General Intercept, and under the brooding hololith of the late Air Commander Tenthis Belks. It was a time-honoured custom for all pilots to salute the old man's portrait as they went past. Darrow didn't feel like such frippery today.

There was no one in the day office, or behind the desk at company and area. Darrow went down to the dispersal room, but there was nobody there either. The air smelled of over-brewed caffeine and stale smoke. A circular regicide board, its game unfinished, sat on one of the small tables.

Darrow went back out into the hall, and walked down to the station chapel. On the wall beside the double doors hung a blackboard where the names of the dead and missing were written up prior to the morning service. He stood for a moment and stared at the list written there now. The dead cadets of Hunt Flight. Such a damnably long list. But for five names, it was a roll call for the entire wing.

He opened the doors and looked into the chapel. It was quiet and very dark, save for the daylight falling in multi-coloured rays through the lancet windows at the far end. There was an odour of wood-wax and floor polish, and also fading flowers. Someone was sitting down at the front, at the end of the first pew. Darrow couldn't make out who it was, and felt reluctant to disturb them.

Retreating back into the hall, Darrow noticed for the first time the printed posts tacked up on the wallboards outside the day office.

He started to read them.

Major Heckel came out of the chapel and walked over to him.

'Darrow?'

'What… what is this?' Darrow murmured.

Heckel could hear the tinge of anger in the pilot cadet's voice. 'You just got back then?' he asked. 'You're checked out? You're all right?'

'What does this mean?' Darrow snapped, pointing at the posts.

Heckel's face was pinched and pale, and he seemed to shrink back timidly from Darrow's bitterness.

'It's just the way things have worked out, Darrow.'

'Did Eads sign off on this?'

'It was his decision, he–'

'Is he here?'

'Yes. Yes, he is.'

'I want to see him.'

Heckel bit his lower lip and then nodded. 'Come on.'

The major led the way up the front stairs to the main operations chambers. Their boots rang on the hard wood. Heckel seemed to have a need for small talk.

'Everyone's been given day leave,' he said, almost cheerfully. 'As of this morning. Everyone... Well, news like that, yesterday. Sort of knocked everybody back. And as we were about to go into turnaround and move out to make way for the Imperials, well, it seemed like the best thing, so Commander Eads issued passes and...'

Darrow wasn't really listening. The door to the main operations room was open, and he saw unfamiliar personnel in Imperial Navy uniforms stare out at him as he went by.

They reached the commander's outer office and Heckel ushered Darrow in. Darrow noticed how badly the major's gesturing hand was shaking. Really shaking.

The outer office was empty. The desks there had been cleared, and transit cartons labelled with the aquila badge were stacked up in the middle of the well-worn floor. Heckel knocked gently at the inner door. He was answered by a grunt.

They went in. It was pitch-black inside.

'Sir...' Heckel began.

'What? Oh, my apologies.' There was a click, and the steel blast shutters over the windows retracted to let the daylight in.

'I forget, sometimes,' Eads said.

The entering daylight revealed Air Commander Gelwyn Eads behind his brass desk in the bay under the main window. The walls of the office were covered with

hololiths – formal squadron group shots, individual
pilot portraits, pictures of Wolfcubs and Cyclones,
cheerful scenes from base formals and dinners, a picture
of Eads with old man Belks. A tattered Commonwealth
flag was suspended in pride of place over the fireplace.

Eads was sorting data-slates and charts into filing
boxes around his desk. He was a short, wiry man in his
sixties, his grey hair shaved so short it looked like metal
filings coating his scalp. Little, round dark glasses covered his eyes.

'Make yourselves known,' he said. 'It's you, Heckel,
am I right?'

Eads had been blind for nineteen years. He had
refused augmetic optics. There was a dermal socket
behind his left ear which allowed him to plug into operation systems and 'see' tactical displays during sorties,
but that was the only compensation he made for his
disability. The plug was in now, permitting him to identify and sort the data-slates using the code-reader sitting
on the desk.

'It is, sir,' said Heckel. 'And Pilot Cadet Darrow.'

Both men saluted with special formality. Long ago,
Eads had decided that men probably weren't bothering
to salute him properly because he couldn't see, and had
taken to saying 'Call that a salute?' to anyone who vis-
ited him. As a consequence, everyone saluted him with
more care and correctness than they did sighted officers.

'Call that a salute?' Eads said, and smiled. 'Make yourselves easy. Hello, Darrow. Are you recovered?'

'Yes, commander.'

'Good to hear it. They want me to pack up and leave.
The Navy. I suppose I should be thankful for their coming, but it sits uneasily.'

Eads rose, unplugging himself from the code-reader,
and walked around the desk. He used a sensor cane,
topped with the Enothian crest in worn silver, which

trembled in his hand if he came too near to obstacles. He hardly needed it in his own office, he knew the layout perfectly. Eads walked over to the fireplace and touched the edge of the old flag. Then he pointed at some of the framed hololiths.

'Company dinner, wintertide 751. Wesner looks particularly pissed in that shot, doesn't he? His cravat is terribly skewed. That's… that's Jahun Nockwist, standing next to his Magog, with his fitters. Old Greasy Barwel and his team, Emperor bless them. There, that's *Humming Bird*, my first Cub. Bad old lady. Dropped me in the Sea of Ezra after a flame-out in '42. I imagine she's still down there, crusted into some reef.'

He turned to face them. 'Am I correct?'

'Yes, commander,' said Heckel. 'Every one.'

Eads nodded. 'I only know because I remember where I hung them.' He took one of the pictures off the wall, weighed it in his hand, and then carried it over to the desk. It went into one of the boxes. 'I don't suppose I'll hang them in my new office, wherever that ends up being. Barely any point. I won't be able to see them. I mean, remember how they looked. Might as well nail empty frames up. Still, I should take them.'

Eads was still for a moment, deep in thought. Then he swung his dark lenses round at them again.

'I imagine this is about the re-assignment, Darrow.'

'Yes, sir. I'm disappointed to say the least–'

'I'm sure you are, cadet. I damn well would be. But I'm not going to change my mind. With the losses yesterday, we've scarcely got enough serviceable K4Ts to keep even twenty of the 34th flying, and that's with pilots sharing Cubs between sorties. We're scaling the wing down, we have to. Once we've shipped out to another field, we need to trim the numbers. Some pilots will remain active… pretty much Vector Flight and Quarry Flight. Others will be stood down for the time being. Experienced pilots get priority, Darrow. I'm sorry. Hunt Flight was a cadet section. And – forgive me for putting it so bluntly, Heckel – there are precious few of Hunt left. Darrow, you'll be reassigned to ground duties, and probably moved back to Zophos Field or Enothopolis in reserve. It's just the way it has to work.'

'Yes, sir.' Darrow's teeth were gritted.

'Reserve isn't so bad, Darrow,' Eads added. 'You'll be kept plenty busy, rewarding work. And if things come good, you could be flying again before the end of the year.'

Darrow nodded.

'Darrow?'

Yes, sir. I… Yes. I nodded, sir.'

'Nodding doesn't work for me, airman.'

'Sorry, sir.'

Eads walked back around his desk and resumed his seat. 'Tell you what,' he said. 'Just get it off your chest, Darrow.'

'Sir?'

'Speak your mind. Let's get it done with.'

Darrow glanced at Heckel. The major's face seemed even paler than before, and his hands were both clearly shaking. But he shrugged an okay to Darrow.

Darrow cleared his throat. 'I know I've only been operational four weeks. I'm a cadet. All of that. And yesterday was a… a …'

He looked at Heckel. Heckel frowned and shook his head.

'Anyway, I believe I can fly, commander. I mean, I can fly well. I've hardly had the chance, and I hate to trumpet myself. But yesterday, I really felt I… There was this bat and…'

'Yes, Darrow?'

Darrow felt stupid even trying to say it. 'It doesn't matter, sir.'

Eads sat forward and lifted a data-slate out of the pile to his left. He put it down in front of him. 'Your modesty does you credit, cadet. I have Heckel's report right here. It's… How should I put it? Glowing, isn't it, major?'

'It's just an account, sir,' said Heckel.

'You took on that bat and flew your boots off. Instinctive, brilliant. The major praises you in no uncertain terms. Hell, If I'd seen you fly the way he said you did, I'd be calling for a commendation.'

'You said that?' Darrow murmured.

Heckel stared at the floor. 'Just reporting what I saw, cadet.'

'So, well done,' Eads said.

Darrow blinked. 'Sir… If I've earned such praise… If I've shown what I can do… why am I being sent to reserve?'

'My choice, Darrow. Don't you go blaming Heckel for this. His recommendation was to get you a transfer to Quarry Flight. But there's this little matter…'

'Sir?'

'It was your first combat. Your first fly-fight. You did well, but that's the way first fly-fights go. Novices usually die in those situations. The ones that survive seem to punch above their weight. And almost always, that's down to luck. You did gloriously in one sortie, Darrow, but that doesn't make a career. I decided to send you to reserve for that reason.'

'Commander?'

'Luck, cadet. I think, yesterday, you used up an entire lifetime of luck. You used it all in one dogfight. If I keep you active, you'll be dead the next time you go out.'

Darrow didn't know what to say. He blinked. His mouth was dry.

'So, are we done?' asked Eads.

'Sir,' they both said, and left the office.

Heckel caught up with Darrow on the stairs.

'I'm sorry!' he said.

Darrow looked back up at him. 'God-Emperor, don't be sorry, sir,' he said. 'You didn't have to make a report like that.'

'I only wrote what I saw, Darrow. That piece of airmanship was fantas–'

'You saved my life, sir. Gunning in like that. He had me. You saved my life.'

Heckel hesitated, caught in the sunlight of the stairwell. 'I did what I could,' he said.

'You saved my life. He had me,' Darrow repeated.

'But–'

'Thank you,' Darrow said.

Darrow continued on down the stairs and strode along the hall past the chapel. Only then did he notice the smudge.

On the blackboard, the service of honour. The names of Hunt Flight. At the bottom of the list was a name that had been written up in chalk and then smudged off.

It was his own.

Theda MAB South, 13.01

THE CHAINMAIL AVIATOR's glove thumped onto the desktop like a lead weight.

'I borrowed that from stores,' Bree Jagdea said. 'So, do you want to explain or should I smash you round the face with it?'

Wing Leader Etz Seekan looked down at the glove for a moment. His manicured fingers drummed deftly on the edge of the desk.

'Let me see…' he said softly. He was a beautiful man, perfectly built, with twinkling blue eyes and a captivating grin. His dark hair was superbly groomed and oiled, and his manner was annoyingly relaxed and charming.

He looked up at Jagdea. 'Part of me wants you to – what was it? – smash me round the face. Just to see Ornoff when it comes to filing charges. But I don't think that will get us anywhere. Why don't you sit down?'

He gestured to the armchair in front of his desk.

'I prefer to stand,' Jagdea snapped.

Seekan shrugged. 'Around this time, I like to take a small glass of joiliq. Can I interest you in one?'

'I prefer to – no, you bloody can't!'

Seekan shrugged and rose. He walked over to the cabinet and poured a very small measure of liquor into a tumbler. 'I've heard about you,' he said.

Jagdea stiffened. What the hell did that mean? Part of her wanted to gush: I've heard about you too, all of you... all the Apostles. The finest fliers in the western Navy. Quint, ace of aces, Gettering, Suhr... and always Seekan. Wing Leader Seekan, master of the Apostles. Never a famously high score, but renowned for his leadership and tactics. Loved by his men. Seekan, the Imperial hero.

She chewed her lip instead.

'About me?' she said.

'Not you particularly,' Seekan said. He thought about that for a second and then frowned. 'Throne, I didn't mean to offend you. I meant the Phantine. The only founded Imperial Guard regiment who are fliers. Because of the nature of your home world, isn't that right?'

'Yes.'

Seekan nodded. He raised his glass and rolled the spirit around inside it. 'All other air wings come under the command of the Imperial Navy, except yours. That makes us allies rather than kin.'

'I suppose.'

Seekan smiled. 'And you value female pilots as much as men. Females are few in the Navy. This is a rare...'

'Pleasure?' asked Jagdea.

'"Thing". I was going to say, "thing".'

'There is no viable land on Phantine,' Jagdea said. 'Everyone learns to fly, men and women. Our ability is said to be intuitive and exceptional.'

'The same has been said of the Apostles.'

'You have no reason to celebrate your own virtues. The Apostles' reputation is clear enough.'

'Thank you.'

'So... would you like to explain why your man struck my pilot with a glove like that?'

'Because he was angry.'

'Angry? *Angry?*'

'Are you sure you wouldn't like to sit down, commander?'

'Answer the damn question!'

'Captain Guis Gettering... Sixty-two kills. His bird is called the *Double Eagle*. He was offended that your man would copy that name for his own plane.'

'That's it?'

'What else can I say?' Seekan shrugged.

'My pilot will rename his plane. No offence was intended. In return, I suggest your Captain Gettering makes a written and formal apology to Pilot Officer Marquall. Then the matter may be concluded without higher attention.'

'My pleasure,' said Seekan. Jagdea turned and strode to the door.

'Commander?' Seekan called. She paused in the doorway and looked back.

'Good flying,' he said.

Over the Lida Valley, 15.16

IT WASN'T AN auspicious start to their first official sortie. A bright, promising day had turned sour in the time it had taken to get their machines aloft. At ten thousand metres, with a lousy eight-tenths cloud, and an even more lousy side wind, they were running up the wide valley of the River Lida towards the mountains.

Jagdea's normally sweet-running Thunderbolt, serial Zero-Two, was flying rough and heavy. Too long in the belly-hold of a Navy carrier, Jagdea supposed. The devoted maintenance crews had done their best to keep systems at optimum, but there was no substitute for regular flying time. Apart from the delivery run to Theda MAB South, all the Thunderbolts in Umbra Flight had been out of use for three and a half months.

Then again, she wondered, maybe it was her. Serial Zero-Two wasn't the only thing not to have flown in three and a half months. Jagdea felt clumsy and inept. She'd even made a sloppy job of take-off. They'd had simulators on the carrier of course, regular sessions to keep them sharp, but it wasn't the same, just like turning a bird's turbofans over on the flight deck every morning wasn't the same.

Good flying. Seekan's presumably honestly meant remark now seemed like a jinx.

They were flying in unit teams of four machines. With her were Van Tull, Espere and Marquall. Blansher had the second unit four about forty kilometres behind them, and Asche the third, running a wide patrol over the Littoral. Essentially, Umbra Flight had split into three independent Interceptor units. That was optimum size for routine hunting or opportunist intercept work. If more than three or four Thunderbolts tried to share the same slice of sky, things tended to get a little crowded.

Anyway, this wasn't a hunt. It was a shakedown. A little wind-in-the-hair run to get pilots and machines into the swing of things. Umbra Flight had traditionally been a Lightning wing, but after the liberation of Phantine, they'd switched to the heavier Thunderbolts, and come to love them during the air war on Urdesh Minor. Sometimes Jagdea missed the sprightly performance of the III-IX Lightning, the exhilarating rates of its climb and dive, the darting grace of its turns. The Thunderbolt was almost half as heavy again and, at lower speeds, particularly climbing, it felt as if it barely had the power to lift its massively armoured body. But it was heavy and robust, and could soak up the sort of punishment that would send a Lightning fluttering to its doom like a moth. It had longer legs too, and a snout-full of killware. Where the Lightning was a playful ambush-cat, the Thunderbolt was a full-grown carnodon. Blansher had once said that a pilot flew the Lightning for the joy of flying, and the Thunderbolt for the joy of killing. That seemed about right to Jagdea. She adored her Bolt. It was muscular, indomitable, responsive.

Except on days like today. The port fan was simply not running clean. There was nothing on the display, but she could feel it, something in the rhythm of the engine tone.

She checked the fuel. Roughly a third gone, and they hadn't opted for reserve tanks. She keyed the vox.

'Umbra Four-One Leader to Four-One Flight. Let me hear you.'

'Umbra Three, Four-A.' Of course he was. Van Tull was always Four-A.

'Umbra Five, I'll be fine once I've remembered what the controls do.'

'Roger that, Five. I know the feeling,' Jagdea returned.

'Umbra Eight. Okay here.'

Marquall sounded unhappy still. The stupid business with Gettering had knocked him back, the last thing a novice wanted on his first day out. He'd tried to make light of it, remarking that his Bolt was now called *The Smear*, because Racklae hadn't had time to do any more than paint out his nose art with a wash of undercoat. But Jagdea knew he'd been hurt.

'Let's refresh the pattern, flight,' she said. 'Eight, you slip into point, Five and Three change over. I'll take the hanger.'

They all responded, 'Okay'. A nice little manoeuvre test to get them flexing their brains Jagdea reckoned, and getting Marquall up in what was technically lead position might do his confidence some good.

'On the mark… three, two, one… execute.'

Unit fours flew in a line formation, with one machine forward and another two flanking to rear on either side. The fourth, or 'hanger', flanked one or other of the wingmen to rear, forming an asymmetrical V. It was an excellent pack formation, each pilot covered by his comrades, the hanger able to switch from side to side as needed. Currently, Jagdea was in point, with Van Tull to her port and Espere to her starboard, Marquall at Espere's five as the hanger.

On her mark, they shuffled the deck. Jagdea throttled down and slid back out of the point of the V. Van Tull rolled three-sixty high and Espere did the same, but in reverse and low, until the two wingmen had swapped places. Marquall peeled out low, then gunned forward under the V and pulled ahead before dropping to cruise speed and coming up gently. The two wingmen then matched speeds and flanked him sweetly to his five and seven. Jagdea throttled back again, just a touch, and came around onto Espere's five.

Textbook. The first thing that had gone right all day.

'Nice work, flight. Very slick. Let's stay put for another five.'

The undercast was thinning. They had about six-tenths cloud now, and dark patches of the Lida's arable valley appeared below them, distant patchworks of field-systems, irrigation webs and hydroponic rafts.

'Flight Leader?' It was Van Tull.

'Go, Three.'

'Check your auspex. I'm tagging eight or nine contacts below us at twelve kilometres, south, inbound.'

Sure enough. Jagdea's scope showed seven pippers, moving north-east at under three thousand metres. Not eight or nine, but that could just be the conditions masking returns.

'Umbra Four-One Leader to Operations. Come in, Operations.'

'Receiving, Umbra Four-One Leader.'

Jagdea reached forward with her heavily-gloved left hand and transmitted the auspex fix.

'Four-One Lead. Should there be anything up?'

'Plenty, Four-One Leader, but not there.'

'Understood, Operations. We'll check it out.' Jagdea shifted in her seat, and tweaked the air-mix a little richer. 'Lead to flight. I'll take a look.' That was the hanger's job, to peel off for sweeps. 'Hold it here and come around three points south.' There was no time to shuffle the deck again, which meant she was leaving Marquall at point. A good idea? No time even to worry about it. 'Umbra Eight, you have point. Stand by to stoop if I need you.'

'Read that, Leader. I've got it.'

At last. A touch of excitement in the boy's voice. Good. He could do with this. Besides, Van Tull was right there, solid and dependable. And Espere was a consummate wingman.

Jagdea kicked the afterburners a touch and rolled out, feeling the delicious punch of G as she inverted and began to dive away, wide, to the left of the trio V. The long dive loaded power into her wings, and she was touching two thousand kph as she closed on the targets. Enough load to pull off beautifully if they were friendly. Enough punch to turn it into an intercept if they weren't.

Five kilometres and closing.

Four.

The sky was suddenly very clear, less than four-tenths cloud. The vast green rift of the Lida Valley stretched out beneath her, and for the first time she could see the hazy line of the Makanites.

Three kilometres. There they were. Below her still, but closing at an alarming rate because they were travelling towards her, and adding her speed to their own. Nine machines. Clustered rather than in formation.

At two kilometres, she identified their pattern. Cyclones. A flight of Cyclones, Enothian PDF. The delta-winged double props were painted in a grey and white dazzle, and running north hard, possibly at the top of their performance.

What the hell were they doing here? Were they... running?

Instinct made Jagdea flip off the red safety covers of her main guns.

'Cyclone intruders, Cyclone intruders, this is Umbra Four-One Leader–' she started to say into her vox-mask.

But she stopped. One of the tail-end Cyclones wobbled and exploded. The brief fireball was fuel-rich and sent streamers of white smoke twirling away into the clear air. The flaming debris dropped towards the field-system below.

Something crimson and hooked ran in past it so fast it was climbing out of range again before Jagdea had realised what it was.

'Bats! Bats! Bats!' she yelled into her vox.

Theda seafront, 15.20

THEY'D WANTED TO celebrate. Of course they had. First run in a new theatre, and a fine one at that. But Viltry hadn't felt like celebrating. It had taken a lot to just get them home. The final half-hour, fuel low, belly-light, weapons all but empty. So exposed, so vulnerable. Operations insisted nothing in the enemy's air force could reach the Littoral and the home-stretch, but Viltry had been sweating so much on the last section, he'd been able to pour moisture out of his flying gloves when he took them off.

The field had come up, Theda North. Even closing in on the beacon lights, he'd still had the distinct feeling that something was going to come down out of nowhere and kill them hard.

The field. The outer circuit. Blue flags all round. Power down to minimal, just kissing the edge of stall speed for *Greta's* massive airframe.

Then in over the cross, balancing the Marauder as he brought the vector nozzles around, switching from forward flight to vertical. A squeeze or two of viff, a hunkering, and then down. Intact, alive.

The rest of Halo came back around them.

Judd and the boys had already earmarked a tavern near the billets. They got out, loud and full of themselves, scattering flight kit onto the hardpan as they whooped and slapped hands.

'I'll join you later,' Viltry told them. 'Paperwork.'

He'd taken the longest shower in the history of the Imperium of Man, standing silent and naked under tepid water in the stinking rockcrete stalls behind dispersal, then changed into a spare uniform suit he'd had the presence of mind to bring in his kitsack. He put on his tan leather coat. His hands were still shaking.

The crew was already gone. Viltry found a transport that was doing a run down into the centre of town to pick up a Navy crew, and hitched a ride. It dropped him off on a corner where the old temple road met the fish-market.

There was no one around. Viltry walked north, away from the dark and boarded streets of the town towards the coast. He could smell the sea.

He had no real idea where his billet was. Someone would know, when he was ready.

The piers came as a real surprise. He turned a dank street corner and suddenly found himself on a bright and windswept esplanade. Ahead of him, beyond an iron railing, a reinforced seawall and a narrow curb of grey foreshore, was the sea itself. There was no one in sight, except a truck that groaned past. He crossed the wide roadway and came up to the railing. The sea fascinated him. There were no seas on Phantine, not liquid ones anyway. The sun was slipping down, into the lazy, low part of the afternoon, and the sky was yellow. The endless water seemed indolent and slow, hissing in a languid rhythm against the crusty beach. The water was making frothy breakers at the shore, but beyond that, it formed into a sinuous expanse of rolling gunmetal, stretching away to the vague horizon. It reminded him of the Scald.

Three long piers, their ornate ironwork painted white, marched out from the esplanade over the water. Though faded and rundown, Viltry realised they had once been pleasure palaces. There were shuttered arcades, dance halls, flaking posters advertising weekly match-dances and cordial functions. He was utterly taken with the idea of stepping out on an iron-and-wood bridge that crossed to nowhere, the sea sucking beneath him.

He walked down the strand a little way until he came to the entrance arch of the nearest pier. A chalkboard had been propped up against the ironwork gate. 'Palace Refreshments. Table service, sea views,' it read.

He liked that. That would do.

Warily, he walked in under the iron arch and out along the pier. The sound of the sea was much louder now. He could see the surge of it between the boards beneath his feet. It made him dizzy and excited, and those things helped to mask the kernel of fear he was carrying in his heart.

The cafe was at the end of the pier. Everything else was shut up and derelict. As he approached, he was able to smell caffeine and spun sugar. Viltry had never been this far out from dry land. He'd never walked over an ocean.

The cafe was huge, a testament, perhaps, to former glory days, when pleasure seekers had packed Theda's seafront and come in search of sea views and refreshments. Tables formed rings inside the great circuit of lattice windows. Some of them were occupied: old men and women in mumbling groups, a couple of Commonwealth troopers looking tired and wan. Music was playing from the kitchen area. A handsome Thracian waltz.

Viltry took a seat at a window table, and watched the sea some more.

'What will you have?'

He looked up. The girl in the blue-striped dress and apron had appeared from nowhere. He picked up the table-card hastily. 'A… a pot of caffeine.'

'Anything to eat?'

He was still studying the card. Very few things made sense.

'A smoked ham sa–'

'No ham,' the girl said. 'Sorry. No poultry, either.'

'I *am* hungry,' Viltry realised.

'The lorix is good. With bread.'

'Then that's what I'll have.'

She disappeared. He looked back at the sea. Grey, mobile, immense. He'd seen skies like that. The weather was turning.

The girl returned with a tray. She unloaded the caffeine pot, cup, sugar-bowl, and a plate with bread slices and a dish of something. He poured the caffeine as she departed, then examined the food. It smelled savoury, quite nice, but he wasn't sure what it was. Or how to eat it. He tried some, but found it was salty and far too

meaty for his liking. He swallowed anyway, but left the
rest. The bread was all right. He ate that instead.

'THERE'S A FUNNY bloke over at sixteen,' announced Letrice. 'Offworlder, I'd say.'

Beqa looked and stopped wiping the counter. 'I'll deal
with him. You're off now anyway, aren't you?'

'I got a date,' Letrice grinned. 'Fancy flyboy from the
PDF. His name's Edry. He's nicely handsome.'

'Have fun. Don't do anything I wouldn't do.'

'No thanks. That wouldn't leave me much,' Letrice gig-
gled, and began taking off her apron.

Beqa cleared a few tables and then walked over to the
window table.

It was him. The sad-faced offworlder she'd seen at the
templum the day before. The one who'd been talking to
himself.

She hoped he was stable now. Her shift was coming
to an end, and that gave her just over an hour to nap
before the night-shift.

'Everything all right, sir?' she asked.

'Yes, yes. Fine.' He didn't look up. Throne, but his
expression was so miserable.

'The lorix? Not to your liking?' she asked, lifting the
uneaten dish onto her tray.

He looked up, then said, 'Um? No, I'm sure it was
fine. It was fish, wasn't it?'

'Shellfish.'

He nodded. 'I'm afraid I… I've never eaten fish
before. Or shellfish, whatever that is. It's a bit… funny
tasting.'

'You've never eaten fish?'

'I… I mean, my world… No seas, you see…'

'Oh. So, you must be hungry?'

'No, I ate the bread. I'm fine.'

'Well, okay,' she said and cleared his table.

He still sat looking out at the sea when her shift ended and Pollya came on for the night. The sun had set. The sea was as dark as oil.

He'd ordered another cup, and was sipping it while he stared at the rolling waters as they crashed against the shore.

Over the Lida Valley, 15.29

GUNS LIVE, JAGDEA turned and rolled in on them, her Thunderbolt trembling with power. Six Locust-pattern bats, the lightest and most nimble of the Archenemy's vector-planes, all painted crimson or mauve, were harrying the heels of the Cyclone pack.

They were all over them. To her left, she saw another Cyclone explode, and another pitch left, trailing tarry smoke as it foundered down in a wide sweep towards the ground.

Two Locusts slipped under her, but she had the third, braking back to trim over on another Cyclone. In the hairs, pipper blinking.

Jagdea thumbed the gun-stud.

Serial Zero-Two lurched as the twin-linked lascannons in the nose spat off.

Brilliant daggers of light flew out of her machine, zagging down through the sky towards the bat. Struck, it rolled over and staggered sideways, then started to make white smoke as it curved away, falling, falling.

'Bag one,' Jagdea snarled into her mask. 'Four-One Leader to flight, I have engaged. I repeat, I have engaged.'

She half-heard a response from Marquall, but the meaning of it was lost as she inverted again, viffing hard to increase her turn rate, her ears popping with hard-G as she sidestepped an incoming Locust. A glimpse. The blinking flashes of the gunports, the blur of mauve wings.

As she came nose up, throttle out as far as it could go, she saw two Cyclones blunder past, followed by a banking Locust. All three were in view for less than a second.

None of Umbra Flight were carrying rack weapons on this sortie, certainly nothing guided or air-to-air. Jagdea would have to rely entirely on boresight shooting.

She pushed the nose over and kicked right rudder, heaving the heavy machine around. The horizon swung madly. A Cyclone went by under her, emitting sporadic brown smoke. The banking Locust had already pulled out of sight, but there was another, scarlet like blood, turning in towards the wounded Enothian machine.

She made another deep dive, fans shrieking, G pressing the mask into her face and making her see spots. She had the Locust for a moment. Then it viffed sideways on its reactor jets, a non-ballistic wobble to the side, but instinct set her ready to do the same and compensate. It was purely a gut thing that she got it right: the Locust had gone the way she would have done.

Jagdea punched las-shots at it and hit something, because the slipstream suddenly filled with black smoke and shreds of wing casing. The Locust vanished, then she made it out again as she rolled. It was heading away east. Was it going down or running? There was no way to confirm. The old, foremost rule: don't stay on a target.

She came around again and made a shallow climb that slid her between two of the racing Cyclones. Her auspex began bleating. Something had a lock on her. She rolled, craning her head back over her left shoulder, then her right. Where the hell was it? Las-shots scorched past her port side and her machine bucked hard. There were suddenly raking scorch marks on her port wing. She rolled and turned again. Still the lock held. More shots, stitching past on her right now. She dipped her wing and banked out, catching her speed and opening the reactor nozzles so she almost turned end on end.

The Locust went right by her, overshooting. She saw the bone-white kill marks under its canopy sill.

THREE THOUSAND METRES above her, Marquall began his turn, standing on his port wing, gazing down at the spiralling machines through the cloud cover below. Van Tull and Espere matched his turn.

'Stoop and sting,' Marquall instructed. God-Emperor, but he'd waited his whole life to say that for real.

'On your lead, Eight,' Van Tull responded calmly.

'Just say when,' added Espere.

'My mark… three, two… mark!'

The three Bolts curved away, speed climbing as they dropped. Intercept dive. Marquall could see Jagdea, and two of the bats. The other machines were local prop-drives. He was coming down on them so very fast…

Guns! Throne of Earth, he'd almost forgotten to switch live in his excitement. He wrenched back the switch cover. There was a bat, snaking left under his wing. Surely, they'd seen the three Bolts coming down on them? Who cared?

He had a lock, and he squeezed. His machine rocked as it unloaded. Marquall swore aloud. He'd meant to select autocannon, but the toggle was across on las. He'd sprayed off almost half his battery load in one go and not even hit anything.

Except… Over there, a Cyclone. Falling, coming apart, weeping flame. Marquall blinked hard, sweat drooling inside his mask. *Shit, no!* Please say he hadn't done that! Please!

'Eight! Have you got a malfunction? Marquall?' Van Tull's voice exploded out of the speakers.

Marquall snapped awake. He'd only been staring at the Cyclone for a second or two, but that was more than enough. His dive had punched him down through the fight layer. A miserable overshoot.

'I'm okay, I'm okay!' he yelled, and instinctively pulled on the stick. It was a rookie mistake. He was coming up far too hard, bleeding off all the power he'd gained from the dive as his machine struggled to climb again. His airspeed dropped to a crawl.

'You stupid fool!' he cried aloud.

'Eight? Say again?'

'I'm all right!' he snapped, swinging into a wide, curving turn to nurse some speed back into his wings. Almost at once, a Locust went past in front of him. With a jolt, he fired wildly, missed.

Pearly las-shot dwindled away in front of him. A tone sounded. Weapons batteries out. He'd just done it again. He hadn't deselected, and now his primary weapons were spent and dry. All thirty shots wasted in two futile bursts.

JAGDEA HAD LOOKED up as her three wingmen came stooping into the fight. Van Tull's machine went over across her two, and expertly splashed a banking Locust. The bat fire-balled, and Van Tull's Thunderbolt rolled as it swept through the flame wash, its slipstream sucking fire and debris out behind it in a curious string. Espere made a fine pass, but his chosen target viffed at the last moment and went wide. Espere flattened neatly, dummied, and then rolled out left chasing another bat.

Jagdea wasn't quite sure what was going on with Marquall. The kid had come in like his arse was on fire, and unloaded a ridiculous quantity of las-power. Virgin nerves? Maybe. Maybe that explained why he'd also dropped long and then mushed off all his power in the worst dive recovery she'd seen outside of flight school.

She wanted to break off and go to cover him, but the Locust was back on her, getting intermittent locks as she jinked and twisted.

'Four-One Leader to Umbra Five.'

'Go, Lead!'

'Espere. Cover the boy, for Throne's sake!'

'On it!'

Espere turned his Bolt over and burned towards Umbra Eight. It was wallowing now, making tentative jinks.

'Eight, this is Five. You okay?'

'Yeah, I'm… yeah.'

'Eight, do you have a weapons malfunction?'

'Negative, Eight.'

'You just nailed the sky with what looked like full batteries.'

'Negative, negative. I'm fine.'

Espere shook his head. He was tense himself. Very tense, and it wasn't just the fly-fight. Alone amongst the pilots of Umbra Flight, Pers Espere had not settled well with the Thunderbolts. He missed his old Lightning more than he could explain. In dispersal, the others would sit around, lauding their Bolts, and talking about them like they were lovers, wives, husbands. Espere just didn't feel that way. His machine, serial Nine-Nine, did not suit him. It was an old machine, a veteran bird, lovingly maintained by the fitter teams. Espere didn't know if it was Thunderbolts in general that disagreed with him, or Nine-Nine in particular. He was fighting with it all the time, wrestling to get it to do what he wanted. He had come to loathe the prospect of each sortie.

In an Imperium where diligently-maintained war machines were often ten, twelve, fifteen times older than their pilots or drivers, there were plenty of tales of particular planes or tanks carrying a jinx. Cursed machines, plaguing the lives of their users until they were themselves destroyed. Serial Nine-Nine had a long and patchy record. Six pilots dead or maimed at the controls, two bad landings, three major refits. Espere had once asked Hemmen, his chief fitter, if Nine-Nine

was jinxed. Hemmen had laughed, not altogether reas-
suringly, and said not. The following morning, there'd
been a refuelling mishap. A junior fitter had been
torched so badly he'd left the skin of his hands fused to
Nine-Nine's fuselage.

He tried not to think about it, even though he'd made
four kills in his old Lightning, and none in this
machine. It was constantly coming home with shot-
holes to patch.

Espere settled in beside Marquall's machine. Espere
was an expert wingman. He knew how to fly cover and
watch a fellow pilot's back. That's why Jagdea had called
him to do this, and that's what he'd do. But he was
tense. Marquall was alarming him with his antics. There
was a gauge light on for a drop in lube-pressure. What
was that about? Had he taken a hit he didn't know
about?

Mind on the game, Pers. Mind on the game. The boy
needed all his help.

'Come about, Eight. Let's see if we can't do some good
here.'

He looked over at the machine alongside him, and
saw Marquall's red-helmeted head nod eagerly, his
thumb coming up. Sunlight glinted off the canopy.

Sunlight glinted off something else.

'Break! Break! *Break!*' Espere yelled. The two Bolts
scissored up and away violently as the mauve shape
snapped by. Espere's damage recorder started beeping.

'Eight? Where are you?' Espere rasped, struggling with
the stick as he tried to right the plane.

'I can't see it! I can't see it!'

Espere could see him well enough. Marquall was
above and to his right, turning really badly into a terrible climb. Espere hit the juice and started to rise.

'Pull in, Eight! You're going to stall if you turn that
tight!'

Silence. The horrendous weight of high G was preventing the kid from answering.

Don't black out… don't black out… Espere willed. Shit! There was the bat again, stooping in from the east, cannons blazing. Marquall's Bolt shuddered as it was hit, but the impact seemed to settle him out. Or snap him awake.

Espere hit reheat and came around hard in a port turn-and-roll, viffing gently to set himself up on the Locust as it crossed. He'd be damned if he'd let the kid get killed on his virgin run.

Espere opened up. Autocannons. A neat burst with good deflection. The Locust trembled, side hit, and then broke left.

Then, out of nowhere, there was another bat, coming in straight. Espere kicked the rudder and came in tight, shielding Marquall's bird with his own machine as he tipped his nose towards the attacker.

Marquall saw what was happening about a second too late. Espere's plane rocked wildly. Pieces of plating sheared off, part of the rudder, part of an engine duct. The canopy shattered but stayed on. The Locust went by under them both like a comet, doing well over 500 kph.

'Umbra Five! Umbra Five! Are you all right?'

Umbra Five wobbled and began exuding a trickle of grey smoke.

'Umbra Five?'

'I'm okay,' Espere's voice answered. 'I'm okay.'

ESPERE HAD BEEN hit, Jagdea was pretty certain of that. As she threw her bird to and fro, the bat on her neck, she glimpsed Espere take a slice-by.

Where was he now? No way of telling. She was banking and the world was coming round. The bat was right on her.

She pulled into a crisp turn. The auspex collision monitor suddenly squealed.

A Commonwealth Cyclone was flying right across her path.

Jagdea slammed the stick forward to avoid it, and went under the delta-wing, her turbofans shrilling as the Thunderbolt started to power dive. The ground was rushing up at her, the curlicue line of the Lida, the squared-off field beds and hydroponic assemblies. Getting out of this dive was going to be hard.

Target lock wailed. Okay then, harder still. The bat was on her, following her down.

Coming out of this, she'd have to pull three or four Gs. That was possible, provided the pilot was ready for it. She tensed her torso and legs, the recommended 'grip' manoeuvre, and yanked the stick.

Here it came. Wham! Already she weighed about a thousand kilos, feeling her heart and lungs pressing on her diaphragm. Spots in front of her eyes. The start of tunnel vision. 'Grip' position helped hold the blood in her head so she wouldn't black out.

She levelled off at around fifty metres, so low over the agricultural waterways her plane raised a bow-wave of spray off the field ponds. She glimpsed water aurochs scattering across a field. Bank to the right, to avoid a pump station's tower, then left again. Her slipstream ripped the plastek sheeting off a field of waterbeet. The bat was right on her six. Target lock. *Ping! Ping! Ping!*

She hit the speed brakes, her harness snapped her back into her seat. The bat went right over her, starting to turn and climb desperately.

She viffed into its reactive turn and hammered it with three salvoes from her lascannons. It turned to port, apparently unharmed, then suddenly screwed over into a nosedive and planted itself so hard into the middle of a hydroponics raft, the impact sent a tidal wave ripple flushing out beyond the field boundaries.

Jagdea turned south, rising, as a column of smoke boiled up from the farmland behind her.

'Lead, you with us?' Van Tull voxed.

'Four-A,' she replied. 'Umbra Five, you okay?'

'Fine,' Espere responded.

The remaining Locusts had fled. Jagdea had Four-One turn in to escort the rest of the Cyclones home. She'd made two kills, with one probable, raising her career tally to nineteen. Van Tull had made one, raising his to eleven.

Not too shabby.

Theda MAB South, 16.59

OPERATIONS HAD HOISTED blue flags and lit guide-path flares. The day was fading in the sky, turning the cloud cover as mauve as a Locust's paint-job. Asche's section was already long home, and Blansher's had landed about fifteen minutes ahead of them. As Jagdea came in, she saw the svelte ivory machines of the Apostles, prepping on their hardstands, their noses bristling with black, antler-like antennae arrays for night-fighting. All the other Navy wings were in the air somewhere.

Busy day.

'Be advised, Operations,' she said as she came in. 'Contrary to briefings, the Archenemy has air-reach beyond the Makanites.' She'd sent this message four times already, with barely an acknowledgement. The bats were over the mountains now. They had much less time than Ornoff had figured.

'Operations. Please recognise my signal.'

'Recognised, Umbra Leader. It has been sent to Tactical.'

In the fading light, she cleared the bright flare path and settled her Bolt onto its stand, gusting down on swivelled nozzles with barely a bump.

The crews ran out.

Marquall landed, shaking with something between fear and delight. He'd survived, but God-Emperor, how he had screwed up. He was for it, he knew.

Van Tull's bird went overhead, slowing to a perfect vertical decline on its smoking nozzles.

Espere had put down.

Ignoring Racklae and the fitters, Marquall jumped off his Bolt and ran over to Espere's machine.

He slowed down as he approached it. The flank was raked to hell, the armour buckled and burst. Huge holes, scorched black, peppered the rudder and the wing edge.

A fitter was running towards the bird, but Marquall pushed him aside and jumped up on the wing, hauling back the shattered canopy frame himself.

'Espere? Espere, are you all right?'

Pers Espere looked up at him. The cockpit armour was splintered. Every dial in the display was cracked. Espere's left arm was a tattered shred, his right a fused lump, glued by the heat of the las-shots to the stick. The left side of his face was a pin-cushion of canopy fragments.

'I'm fine,' said Espere.

DAY 254

Theda MAB South, 04.10

KAMINSKY WASN'T DUE on until six, but the birds were disturbing his slumber. He'd learned to sleep through regular jet sounds, the ruckus that had been going on every night for the last nine months. What bothered his sleep now were the new noises the Navy machines had brought with them: the shrill wails and spitting roars of vector-thrust craft coming and going. He wasn't used to those sounds, and his sleeping self hadn't yet learned to screen them out.

And, Throne, weren't they busy? Kaminsky had counted at least three sortie launches since nightfall, and there'd also been a hell of a noise around midnight, which he was sure was a new wing arriving for deployment.

Things were hotting up. Kaminsky had heard rumours – a friend of a friend in the motor pool, who knew a guy, who'd got talking to a Navy fitter – rumours

that there had already been a few air-brawls this side of
the mountains. Some business had gone down over the
Lida Valley the day before. Someone else said they'd
seen bats over the Peninsula. That was probably crap.
Kaminsky hoped so, because if it was true, that meant
they really were near the end. But the Lida Valley, that
was possible. And bad enough. The bats had got reach.
Maybe even the vaunted Imperial Navy wings couldn't
stop them now.

They were trying, though. Kaminsky left his bunk in
the Munitorum dorm and walked down the dimly-lit
and blast-hardened hallway to section post. The five
guys who were meant to be on standby were asleep in
chairs. The jet roar hadn't woken them. They were all
Munitorum drivers, born and bred. They were oblivious
to the subtle changes in the noise over the field.

Kaminsky helped himself to some caffeine from the
pot on the stove, and went out into the motor pool
yard. The air was cold and the night still very black. Several tech-priests were working on some cargo-8s,
lighting the corner of the yard with the tremulous glow
of their welding wands and incense burners.

Sipping his drink, Kaminsky strolled up the ramp
until he was overlooking the main field. Guide path
flares had just been lit, filling the night with a lambent
green light. Thanks to this, he could see a row of Thunderbolts hunched under mesh-tents to the west. His
guess had been right. They hadn't been there the day
before. A newly arrived wing. More reinforcements.

A shuddering rush swept over him out of the south,
and he turned to watch another wing come in, returning from a sortie. Thunderbolts too. He liked the look
of those big brutes and wondered how they felt to fly.
The twelve machines came in low, following the guide
path, and began to slow, turning their forward rate
into a gentle hover as they adjusted their vector jets

and settled down onto their designated pads. The monstrous, combined howl of their engines made his diaphragm shake.

'Good day, guys?' he called to them, out loud. 'Many kills?' He toasted the distant planes with his cup. He could remember the buzz so clearly: riding home, guns empty, flying on fumes, the rush of a combat survived still twitching in his gut.

As the throb of the mighty turbofans began to fade, Kaminsky turned, hearing voices suddenly audible back in the yard. He wandered back that way, and saw Senior Pincheon standing in conversation with a Navy flier.

Pincheon looked flustered, which was never good for anyone else. The senior noticed Kaminsky approaching and called out to him.

'I need a driver!'

'Ready and willing, senior,' Kaminsky replied. Though he wasn't due on yet, he knew he wouldn't be doing any more sleeping now. He fancied a little distraction. Besides, he didn't want Pincheon blithering into the section post and finding all the standbys asleep. The poor bastards would be on penalty shifts until dooms-day. Which, of course, might be just a few days away…

'I'll take it,' he said.

'Good. Transportation run. Conveyance needed to the Old Town and back. Fill this in.'

Kaminsky took the proffered data-slate and entered his work number and details. He wrote as quickly and neatly as his hand would allow.

'I need to go to a bar called the Hydra,' the Navy flier said. 'Do you know it?'

Kaminsky looked up at the sound of the voice, and saw to his surprise that the tall flier was female. It was the woman whose mob he'd transported in two days earlier.

'Yes, mamzel… forgive me, commander. I know it.'

'Good,' she said. She nodded thanks to Pincheon and fell into step beside Kaminsky as they headed for his transport.

'You'll ride in the cab?' he asked.

'Thanks. Yes.'

He opened the cab door for her and she climbed up. Then he went round to the driver's side, boarded, and turned the engine over.

Lamps blazing, they rumbled out of the compound and left the airfield, joining the empty highway strip into the city. She said nothing, just gazed out at the hooded lights of the field as they went by and receded.

It felt funny having company in the cab. He usually shipped teams of personnel around, loaded in the back. The cab was his private space. He felt embarrassed suddenly by the litter of disposable cups in the footwell, the fact that someone could see the way he had to lock his prosthetic hand around the wheel spoke.

But it would have been rude to expect her to ride in the rear.

At length, uncomfortable, he cleared his throat and said, 'The Hydra, you said?'

'Yes. On Voldney.'

'Yeah.'

Did she recognise him? Half of him presumed not. Just another Munitorum drone. The other half was outraged. *With a face like his?*

The thought made him smile. *Suddenly, August, vain about your looks!*

'Something the matter, driver?' she asked.

'No, commander,' he said. 'I'm to wait for you at the Hydra, is that right?'

'Yes. I shouldn't be more than five minutes.'

'Not going out for a celebratory drink, then?'

'No. Why?'

'Oh, you know. A flier, back from a mission, wanting to wind down. The Hydra is popular with pilots.'

'So I've heard.'

So what's this about, then, he wanted to ask? But he stopped himself. It wasn't his place. He wasn't one of them any more, and he couldn't get away with insolence. He was a Munitorum drone.

As if she sensed his curiosity, she suddenly said, 'I'm looking for an FTR.'

'Ah,' he said. Understanding, he smiled again. He was flattered that she should bother to make even that much conversation. She said nothing else until they were pulling up outside the Hydra.

'Wait here,' she instructed, and jumped down out of the cab.

Five minutes passed. Ten. A trio of drunken Commonwealth troopers staggered out of the bar like a six-legged beast and blundered off down the pavement, singing. It was dark. Just the lights of his truck, the neon bar sign, a few still-lit windows overlooking the narrow street.

He saw her re-emerge, alone. She looked up and down the street, annoyed. She crossed back to the driver's side and he wound down his window.

'Not there?'

'No. Is there anywhere else you know?'

'A few places. Get in.'

He drove down through the Gillehal Plaza, and, as there was no one around, took a shortcut up a one-way ramp onto the shelving streets of the Zagerhanz. The truck's gears wallowed as he downshifted on the steep slope.

'Where are we going?' she asked.

'There are a couple of places up here. The Lullabye and the Midwinter. They're often open after hours.'

She nodded.

'How long's he been gone?'

'Since 22.00 yesterday.'

'And you don't want to make this official?'

'No, I– No.'

'What's your name?' he asked.

'Jagdea,' she said, reluctantly.

He waited for her at the Lullabye and the Midwinter, but she came back from both on her own.

'One last idea. There's a place on the Grand Canal.'

He drove the truck expertly along the narrow Old Town streets. There was just the tiniest hint of dawn in the air now. When they got to the place, he turned off the engine and climbed down with her.

'You can stay with the transport, driver.'

Kaminsky shook his head. 'Actually no, Commander Jagdea. You'll need me to get in.'

'Why?'

'Zara's is an old drinking den. Not a bar. Women are only allowed in if they are the companions of male clientele.'

She stared at him.

'It's true,' he said. 'Maybe… maybe that's why your FTR came here.'

Together, they walked to an iron-hinged door, set down from the street by three little steps. Kaminsky knocked, and the door opened.

The door-guard was a massive Ingeburgan with fat-hooded eyes. He looked them up and down, then waved them through.

The den was almost empty. Some chairs were already up on tables. Half a dozen Commonwealth fliers, all male, were playing cards around a corner table. A yawning waitress was serving them another bottle of joiliq. Two Navy fliers shared another booth, talking in low, fierce voices about something. A few other patrons sat alone, or played the chancer machines with their last pieces of change.

'Is he here?' whispered Kaminsky.

'That's him. At the bar.'

There was a boy sitting at the bar side. A handsome sort, Kaminsky realised. He put the thought aside. Any one of the bastards in the room was handsome compared to him.

But still, this boy was especially handsome. Dark-haired, fair-skinned, tall… clearly from the same gene-pool that had produced the striking Commander Jagdea.

The boy was very drunk. A weary barman was cleaning a glass and watching in horrid fascination as the boy tried to find his mouth with a shot-cup. He missed, emptied the dregs of the liquor down his front, and then settled the glass on the marble bartop again.

He tapped it with an index finger.

'Whu'more.'

The barman shook his head.

'Oh fershizake. Whu'more, s'all I ask.'

'No,' said the barman.

'Time to go home, Vander,' Jagdea said.

The boy looked at her, blinked, and shook his head.

'Yes, Vander. Come home now, and we can forget this.'

'No. No. No-no. I'm woshup.'

'You're in your cups, but you're not washed up. Come on. I've got transport.'

The boy – Vander – fixed her with suddenly probing eyes. 'Espere!' he spat.

'He's in the infirmary. They're patching him up.'

'Espere. He won' fly 'gain.'

'No, he won't. But that's not down to you.'

'I got him hurt.'

'No, you didn't.'

'Yesss! Yes, I got him hurt. I got him hurt. I got him. Hurt. I did. Me. I screwed up.'

'Maybe you did, Vander. Maybe you didn't. No one's blaming you for what happened to Pers.'

'Killacyclone too.'

'What?'

The boy made a shrugging movement with his hands. 'Killacyclone. Killed. Killed a Cyclone. Shot the frigging thing to pieces, like–'

'No, Vander. We went over the gun-cam footage. The Cyclone was stung by a bat. Not you.'

'Yeah?'

'Yes. Not you.'

'Hnh. Thassomething.'

'Yes, it is. Now come on, pilot. Get up. We're going now.'

Vander shook his head. 'Espere...' he muttered.

Jagdea took a step towards him and put her hand on his arm. 'That's it, Marquall. Enough with the self-pity. Get your arse upright and follow me.'

'G'way!'

'Marquall, I've stuck my neck out for you. My whole neck. I came looking for you rather than report you were overdue. So far, it's off the record.' She looked round at Kaminsky. 'It is off the record, isn't it?'

Kaminsky shrugged. 'Sure.'

She shook Marquall. 'See what I do for you? It's off the record. I didn't report you to the Commissariat. I could lose command for letting you run off like this. FTR. Failed To Return. You're four hours late back at billet. The commissars would shoot you for this. Shoot me, too. Don't mess me up, Marquall. Don't you dare earn the Phantine a rep for screw-ups and disobedience. We're running with the frigging Navy now! Get up, Marquall! Don't you disgrace me! I need you!'

He looked at her, blinking to focus. 'Y'don' need me...'

'I lost a pilot yesterday. I'll be damned if I lose two!'

She pulled his arm, and he struggled back. Kaminsky winced as the boy fell off his seat. He spilled Commander Jagdea over with him as he went, and a glass broke.

'That's enough!' the barman cried. The Ingeburgan thug was closing in.

'It's okay,' Kaminsky said, holding up his hand. He helped Jagdea up and pushed her aside. Then he stood over the boy.

'Call yourself a flier?' he said.

'What?' Marquall gurgled.

'What are you doing?' Jagdea began.

'Don't worry,' Kaminsky told her. 'Let me speak to the lad. I don't want any trouble.'

He looked down at the boy again.

'You're a pilot? You get to fly? I tell you what... you're a piece of crap.'

'What?'

'A. Piece. Of. Crap. You disgust me. Your mamzel there has gone out on a line to pull your arse in, and this is what you do? Can you fly? *Can you fly?*'

'Y-yes...'

'Can you fly?'

'Yes!'

'Why don't you then?'

'I... I don't know...'

Kaminsky reached under his coat and pulled out his service auto. He dropped it onto the boy's belly. The falling weight winded him.

'Just use it.'

'What?'

'Use it. Use it now.'

'What?'

'Use the frigging gun, you waste of space. Put a shot through your stupid brain. It'd be quicker than drinking yourself to death. Do us all a favour.'

Marquall stared at the gun on his belly as if it was a venomous arachnid.

'What are you waiting for? Eh? You get to fly, you bastard! You get to fly! Why would you run away from that? I used to fly too! But I got crisped! See this? My face? My hand? They say I can never fly again! I'm not airworthy! I'd give anything to be you! Anything! So pick up that frigging gun and stop me envying your stupid little life!'

'Shit…' said Marquall. 'You can't say that to me…'

'No, he can't,' said Jagdea, kneeling beside him. 'But it seems he just did. Now are we going home or am I going to leave you with him?'

'Home,' agreed Marquall, closing his eyes.

Jagdea tossed the service pistol back to Kaminsky. He caught it. 'Yours, I believe.' Then she hauled Marquall up on her shoulder and carried him out of the bar.

She was sitting with him in the back space of the truck when Kaminsky came out. He looked at her.

'Drive, please,' she said firmly.

Kaminsky got up into the cab. Alone again, he started the engine.

South of the Makanites, 08.30

THIRTY THOUSAND METRES, not a cloud in the sky, just twenty-four silver giants leaving white lines of vapour across the blue.

Viltry felt much more at ease on this early run, Halo Flight's second sortie of the tour. He wondered if it was strength of numbers: Halo was running in formation with Marauders of 2212th Navy, and they had a wing of Thunderbolts five thousand metres above them, flying top cover. Formation safety.

Or maybe it was the soothing effects of a long afternoon spent gazing at the sea.

Whatever, he was more relaxed. *Greta* felt good and responsive. Sunlight filled the cabin with a golden glaze, and the world seemed almost silent. At this altitude, the engines were a muffled throb. The loudest sounds were the hiss of the air-mix and the pump of his mask. He imagined this serenity was what it was like to be deep under the sea.

Lacombe passed a sheaf of plastek-sheathed charts over to him. He took another look at the recon data. As of 17.00 hours the day before, it had been confirmed (thanks, he was proud to note, to the action of a Phantine wing – Jagdea's mob, bless them) that the enemy had secured air-range beyond the mountain limits. That meant almost certainly they had established forward air bases in the Interior Desert, maybe even mobile land-carriers, far further north than had been previously estimated by Operations. Aerial recon had spotted a few probable heat-sources overnight, and now their formation – call sign Hightail – and nine other formations like them were aloft on interdiction missions. If the enemy had air bases in the northern desert, they had to be hit now and taken out, or the show would be over before it began.

Hightail had already spotted half a dozen possibles during their flying time, but all had turned out to be masses of Imperial ground forces labouring north.

From this great height, Viltry enjoyed an awesome panorama of the desert, intractable and vast. It was ragged terrain, resembling worn sandpaper. Over to the west, hundreds of kilometres away, he could make out the margins of the Cicatrice, a huge rift of scarred land that ancient geology had gouged out across the continent, probably around the same time it had lifted the Makanites to overlook it. Flying in that region was said to be tough, especially at lower levels. The scar-valleys caused savage and unpredictable wind shears and crosscurrents.

According to the recon brief, they were now just fifty kilometres short of one of the most likely target areas, a high-density heat and magnetics return from a dune sea region called the Dish of Sand.

There was a Navy Marauder – Hightail One – flying about twenty kilometres ahead of them. Carrying zero payload to remain svelte and fleet, its auspex boosted and amped, Hightail One was their pathfinder.

Viltry waited patiently for the go or no. He had a good feeling about this one.

Then he saw the bats.

It was the strangest thing. It was like no one else had seen them. No alarm had come up, no squawk. There were nine of them, crimson blades, knifing in out of the east across the formation's port flank.

'Enemy! Enemy! Nine o'clock and inbound!' Viltry yelled. He heard the main turret above and behind him whirring as the servos spun it. The vox was suddenly bursting with voices. *Greta* shook gently as, up in the turret, Gaize began firing the twin heavy bolters. Viltry saw tracer fire stitch out and fall to his left. The bats – Hell Razors – smashed in through the belly of the formation, weapon mounts flashing as they came. Where the hell was top cover?

'Vox discipline! Vox discipline!' Viltry yelled, trying to still the agitated shouting of his crew. 'Visual scanning. Conserve fire. We're in a formation, so no wild firing. Pick targets. Track them.'

Hightail was flying in overlapping diamond formations. Effectively, that meant each machine had the protection of its neighbours, and each diamond the protection of the diamond or diamonds adjoining it, plus top cover to fill in as needed. So deployed, and carrying such heavy turret weapons, the Marauders effectively formed a flying fortification that should, technically, be impossible to breach.

But the Hell Razors had gone under them once, and two of the Navy machines were reporting hits taken. The lead Navy Marauder, called *Holy Terra*, had formation command. Viltry could hear the *Terra's*

commander, a man called Egsor, barking orders to the
flight to maintain pattern.

Viltry was checking to his starboard. The bats had
gone that way, and logic said that was where they'd
come back in from. He jumped in his harness as two
Thunderbolts power dived past his starboard wingtip,
burning around west. *Greta* rocked in their slip wake.

'Where the hell were you, top cover?' he voxed.

'No chatter!' he heard Egsor snarl back.

'Six! Six! Six o'clock!' It was Orsone in the tail, and his
yells were echoed by the tail gunners of all the other
machines. The bats had swept out wide and come in
from the rear for their second pass.

'Tail gunner engaging!' Orsone screamed over the vox,
and Viltry felt the shudder of the tail-mount unloading.
A moment later and the top turret, now screwed over to
face the rear, joined in. The twin heavy discharge did
slight but strange things to *Greta's* ride, and Viltry compensated expertly. Then the bats rushed by them. The
tail guns ceased fire, the targets having crossed beyond
their traverse limit, but the top turret continued blazing
as it rotated, following the pass. As the rear ends of the
Hell Razors, bright with full burn, swept ahead and
away from them, the nose turret joined in too.

'Cease! Cease fire!' Viltry cried out. The bats were at
three kilometres now and extending, pulling out of reasonable range. He could still just see their engine flares
as they broke, scattering into a fan.

Damn, Viltry thought. Now they'll be making individual passes.

There was a screech over the vox. Viltry looked
around desperately, and saw one of the Navy Marauders in the adjacent diamond begin to fall out of
formation. It seemed as if its engines could no longer
hold its weight in the air. A gout of black smoke
coughed from one engine, then flames took fierce hold

of the entire leading edge of the port wing. The bats had scored on their second pass.

Trailing flame, the Marauder began to steepen in its descent.

'Eject! Eject!' he heard Egsor yelling to the distant crew.

The dipping Marauder suddenly shuddered and blew up. Its bomb load made a vast fire cloud in the clear sky, jetting debris out in a whirl of scrap. The main part of the nose, burning like a comet, arced away down towards the desert.

'Here they come!' Naxol cried. At least the nose gunner had shown the good sense to keep scanning, instead of watching the Marauder die.

Three Hell Razors were coming in on a frontal attack. Their weapons crackled and flashed brilliantly. Naxol and Gaize opened up on the nearest as it came in across them. Naxol's meaty lasfire chopped the air behind it, but Gaize had held a fine deflection. The bat as good as flew into his bolter stream. It came apart in a drizzle of metal shards and flame, its fore-wings separating and spinning out like broken plate-glass. Whipping over and under as it tumbled away, the starboard wing nearly hit *Greta's* tail.

Viltry sucked in his breath at the near miss. 'Good one, Gaize,' he voxed.

Get Them All Back and one of the Navy machines had also scored good hits. A Hell Razor went into an uncontrolled spin and fell out of the sky, and another pulled a wobbly turn out and began to limp away west, making smoke.

But it wasn't over yet. Another Navy Marauder had been hit and had fallen out of formation, unable to keep up. And *K For Killshot* had taken vector duct damage. The bats were coming in again, and the auspex showed that another wave had now joined them. Over in the western sky, Viltry saw a starburst flash as a Thunderbolt detonated.

His hands were shaking again. Fate's wheel. Fate's wheel.

Turning closer every moment.

Theda MAB North, 12.01

NOISY, CHATTERING, THE streams of Commonwealth personnel flooded out of the station towards the waiting transports. All of them carried kitbags, or hefted crates in teams. They joked in the sunny air, throwing wisecracks and jibes around.

It was a mask, a front. Bravado. Darrow knew that. In a few hours, these men would be on their way to rearline postings down the coast, possibly across the sea. Friendships would be broken, comrades parted from one another. Out on the concourse, hundreds of silent Navy men waited around the transports that had just brought them in, ready to move in and take over as soon as the Commonwealth bodies were gone. Darrow glanced at them. Some smoked, others basked in the sun, stretched out on the rockcrete. Many stared, flat, unfriendly stares. *If you'd done this properly, you know... really fought for your world properly, we wouldn't have to be here.*

That's why Darrow's fellow staffers and crew were laughing and joking. They didn't want to have to look at the Imperials, hovering like vultures over a corpse.

Darrow felt like dropping his own kitbag and returning the stares. *Supercilious bastards! You think we wanted this? You think we're grateful you show up now? Go screw yourselves. We fought for Enothis, we bled, we died. Thanks to us, it's still here to fight for. We did the hard work, now you sweep in to get the glory. And so help me, you had better get the glory. You had better win, or... or...*

'Darrow! Darrow!'

He turned. Major Heckel had appeared on the station steps, waving at him. He made his way back through the mass of personnel to reach him.

'Congratulations, sir,' he said.

'What?'

'I saw you'd been posted to Quarry Flight.'

A muscle under Heckel's left eye ticked slightly. 'Yes. Ah, yes. Lucky me. They've got to keep us old hands going, I suppose.'

Heckel made a high-pitched little laugh, a false sound. His eye ticked again.

'You wanted me, sir?'

'Oh, yes,' said Heckel. He reached into the pocket of his flight coat and produced a docket wafer. It was sealed. Darrow's name was printed on the flap. Darrow noticed how badly Heckel's hand was quaking as he passed it to him. 'This is for you.'

Darrow tore open the wafer.

'Eads had it sent down. I think he was feeling sorry for you. It's not active as such, but he says he hopes it will do.'

'He's... he's posting me to Operations. Effective immediate.' Darrow grinned. Heckel was right, it wasn't active, but it would mean he'd stay at Theda, and be part of the real thing.

'Thanks,' he said.

'Just the messenger,' shrugged Heckel.

'You put in a good word, I'm sure.'

Heckel shrugged again, but he was grinning this time. Then his expression grew serious. 'Just between you and me, Darrow. The enemy got airspace reach into the Lida Valley yesterday. The schedule's really moved up. The Navy's decided it needs local experts who are familiar with the topography to guide them, so they asked Eads to consult at Operations. He told me he wanted a few good bodies to assist him. I suggested you, and a couple of others who'd been moved to reserve.'

'Thank you, sir. I really appreciate it.'

Heckel nodded. 'Just do a good job, Darrow.'

Darrow put down his pack and saluted his former leader.

'Darrow,' Heckel said. His face had a strange, wistful look. 'Darrow, do you think they know I'm sorry?'

'Who, sir?'

'The cadets. Hunt Flight. Emperor save us, so many of them died.'

'You did everything you could, sir.'

Heckel breathed deeply. 'You know, Darrow? That's just what I'm afraid of.'

Heckel picked up his pack, patted Darrow on the arm, and hurried away towards the transports.

Theda MAB South, 15.34

'SHE'S JINXED, ISN'T she?' Milan Blansher said.

'Who's that, sir?' asked Hemmen, the chief fitter. In the shadow of the great hangar, his team was working on the refit of Espere's Thunderbolt. The air was popping with the rattle of power ratchets.

'Her,' Jagdea said, pointing at the wounded machine.

'Serial Nine-Nine?' Hemmen shook his head. 'I couldn't possibly comment, mamzel commander.'

Jagdea shook her head and led Blansher out of the barn. The field was clear apart from Umbra Flight's birds, and a thundering pack of Commonwealth Interceptors taxiing for take-off.

'Espere?' Blansher asked.

'Forget it. He'll be out for months. And even with augmetics, he's a wreck.'

'So we're a man down?'

'Yes. I asked Navy reserve, but they said every able pilot was committed. Unless there's suddenly a bird down and a pilot recovered, or a bird malfunctioned. God-Emperor, Mil, this warfront's stretched really thin. Every man, every plane, thrown in. I think this could be the big one.'

'What do you mean?'

'The decider. The Archenemy's got the Crusade trapped, over-extended. They're attacking here and at Herodor. That's the latest news. Either planet falls, and the Crusade line gets beheaded. Snip, good night. Goodnight Warmaster Macaroth. Goodnight us, and goodnight Crusade. If our line breaks here, they'll be all over us like a bodybag.'

'We'd better fly our balls off then,' Blansher said.

She smiled. 'Speak for yourself.'

'How's Marquall?'

She shrugged. 'Still trying to heave the soles of his feet out through his mouth in the shower block. I thought about slipping him some de-tox tabs, but then I had a bad attack of what the hell. A crippling hangover is the Emperor's way of making us remember our mistakes.'

'He blames himself for Espere?'

'Yes, he does.'

'Should he?' Blansher asked.

Jagdea shrugged. Her reply was totally drowned out by the squadron of prop planes taking to the air.

'Say again?' said Blansher.

'Marquall screwed up. He flew like a virgin and made just about every mistake going. Espere was covering him. So, yes... he should. But he's also a decent pilot. I know that. We need him, and we need him back, confident, learning from his mistakes.'

'I still don't know how you trawled him in,' Blansher said.

'Doesn't matter. I had help. Not the sort of help I wanted, but... Well, it worked.'

Blansher shrugged.

'I'll tell you one day,' Jagdea smiled.

'I'm up at 18.30, I believe,' Blansher said.

'And Larice is taking a unit four out at 21.40. I'll stand down until Marquall is compos mentis.'

'Good flying,' he said, and jogged away to check on his machine.

I wish people would stop saying that, Jagdea thought.

Palace Pier, 15.50

NIGHT HAD ARRIVED early and a wan darkness had settled over the sea. It looked as if a storm was brewing. Afternoon trade had been bad all week, and now with a gloomy pall spreading in the west, it had dried up altogether. Beqa sent Latrice home, and closed up early. It would make a change. A few extra hours' sleep.

She was locking the cafe door when the man appeared. There was a brisk wind coming off the foreshore, tugging at her coat and buffeting her, so she hadn't heard him walk up.

'Oh!' she exclaimed, jumping. It was the sad-faced pilot who'd never tasted shellfish. He was huddled in a heavy leather coat.

'Are you closed?' he asked.

'Ah, yes,' she said, brushing wind-tugged hair out of her eyes. 'Sorry. There was no one around this afternoon. Didn't like the look of the weather, I suppose.'

He glanced up at the sky, as if he hadn't really noticed. The first few spats of rain were falling.

'I understand,' he said. 'I got a decent walk at least. Good afternoon, mamzel.'

'Wait,' she called after him. Beqa shook her head at herself. She was too soft for her own good. 'You're hungry, aren't you?'

'A little,' he admitted.

She unlocked the door. 'Come on. I'll make you something.'

'But you're closed.'

'I can open again.'

She had him sit at the table he'd chosen the day before while she went behind the counter, turned on the water heater and started looking through the pantry bins. Viltry noticed she didn't change the card in the window. The cafe was still shut to others.

'This is very kind of you,' he called.

'It's no problem. You don't like fish, do you?'

'I don't really know.'

'You're in luck. We have some salt-ham today.'

The storm closed in, turning the sky as dark as twilight. Beqa turned on the cafe's oil-lamps. Rain began to patter and drum against the windows and the skylights, running down them in torrents so they seemed to be melting. The whole pier creaked gently as the sea stirred around it.

She'd never been out at the pier-end during a storm before. It felt unnerving, and half of her wished she'd simply been firm with him and gone home. The whole place felt exposed and vulnerable, alone amid the turbulent elements. It was like riding aboard some fragile craft though a maelstrom.

He didn't seem the slightest bit bothered.

When she brought his food and drink, she sat down with him.

'You're an aviator, sir?'

'Yes.' He took a bite. 'This is really very good. I don't think I'd realised how hungry I was.'

'Imperial Navy?' she asked.

He shook his head and wiped his lips with a napkin. 'Sort of, I suppose. Imperial Phantine Air Corps. My name's Viltry. Oskar Viltry.'

'Beqa Mayer.' He held out his hand and shook hers courteously.

'Thank you for your hospitality, mamzel. And act of kindness towards a stranger to your world.'

'Seeing as you've come here to risk your life fighting for my world, I think a plate of ham and bread is the least I can do.'

He stopped eating suddenly and frowned. 'I... I know you from somewhere, don't I?'

'I was here yesterday.'

'No, somewhere else.'

'The templum, early the other day. You held the door for me.'

'Yes, that's it.' An especially fierce gust of wind rattled the windows and threw the rain against the glass with renewed vigour.

'I suppose this place will stand up to a storm?' Viltry asked.

'I think it'd take a lot to bring the palace down,' she replied.

IT WAS ANOTHER hour before the storm abated enough for them to want to risk a dash back towards the town. Refilling his cup, she chatted idly, to no real point, as if simply letting go of conversation that loneliness had dammed up inside her. Viltry was content just to listen. His day had been terrible: the savage air-brawl, the panic and fear. The bats had locked them up so long, they'd finally been forced to ditch their payloads and turn back on the long, exposed slog for home. No target destroyed. No target even seen. Just a portion of the Dish of Sand heat-fused into glass. Halo had lost no one, but five of its machines had been damaged, and several crewmen hurt. *K for Killshot* had been unable to do more than crawl home. Part of its payload had been hung, and Viltry feared that even if it got back, it might stumble on landing and be annihilated by its own munitions. But they'd made it. Three of Egsor's wing, and two Thunderbolt escorts, how-ever, had not.

Some aviators dealt with the pressure of a combat tour by drinking, or hedonistic escapes, others by sounding off about what had happened to anybody in the crew room who'd listen. That had never been Vil-try's way. These days, he was afraid that if he started talking, he wouldn't be able to stop.

But listening to the woman talk eased him. It was like an antidote to the tension of combat. It gave him a touch of perspective, reminded him the universe was not simply him, harnessed into a G-chair, waiting for Fate's wheel to turn. Her life was evidently hard. She was forced to work two shifts: here during the day, and overnight at the munitions manufactory. She was wor-ried about the tide of the war. Fresh food was getting harder to come by. What if the cafe was forced to close? She had a brother called Eido, who was serving in the land army. She'd not heard from him for over three months, since the fighting at the gates of the Trinity Hives. He'd be home soon, she was convinced. She lit a candle for him every day.

'I light three: one for Gart, one for Eido and one for whoever else needs it.'

Viltry smiled. 'I'll remember that. Pardon me, but who's Gart?'

'My husband, Commander Viltry. He was a pilot offi-cer in the Commonwealth PDF. He was lost over the desert the winter before last.'

'I'm sorry, mamzel. Is he listed missing?'

She shook her head. 'I can assure myself my brother is alive, because I've not had proof otherwise. But Gart is dead.'

The Commonwealth had given her a widow's pen-sion, but that had dried up when the war-effort took its latest bad turn. Hence the two jobs. The lack of sleep.

Viltry noticed that the rain had eased. There was a lightness back in the sky. She would be late for her shift if they didn't take advantage of the break.

She locked the cafe doors, and they hurried down the wet boardwalk towards the town, where the evening lamps were coming on.

DAY 255

Theda MAB South, 08.00

'I'M REPORTING AS ordered,' Darrow told the Navy guardsman under the adamantite portico. The guardsman looked at Darrow's docket wafer and nodded him through.

From the outside, Operations could have been mistaken for a Ministorum chapel built in the muscular Early Ornate style. But the many soaring spires and finials were copper and electrophyte-sleeved detector columns, the braced flying buttresses housed pneumatic blast dampers, and where stained glass windows might have glowed, there were deep shutters of loricated steel. Operations dominated the north end of the field area, surrounded on three sides by metal forests of vox masts, auspex towers and modar arrays, where the ground was baked dry and the air smelled cancerously of ozone and electromagnetics.

Inside, a vaulted and soaring atrium lit by caged lumin strips led to the various control areas. Men and women in the dark uniforms of Navy and the Departmento Tacticus bustled to and fro. Vox announcements called for detail rotations. Darrow followed the enamel wall signs, and made his way to a busy staircase that led underground. The main part of Operations was buried in deep, rockcrete bunkers below the ground.

Down below it was cool, and the air was damp and recirculated. He shivered and wished he'd worn his flight coat, despite the hasty patching he'd made to the sleeve.

There was a series of blast doors and another checkpoint, where he had to wait in line under the eyes of three burly guardsmen while a Munitorum servitor checked his papers, conducted biometric tests and issued him with a duty pass.

To Darrow's surprise, Eads was waiting for him at the main hatch.

'Reporting for duty, sir,' Darrow said, saluting.

'Call that a salute?' Eads said. 'Welcome to Operations, Darrow. Stick close by me today as you learn the ropes. Don't be afraid to ask questions; there's a lot to know. If I need you to shut up, I'll tell you.'

'Yes, sir.'

Eads turned and used his sensor cane to trace a path into the chamber. Darrow walked with him.

'Expect to be referred to as "junior", Darrow. Even by me. You're not a pilot cadet down here. You're a junior assistant flight controller.'

Darrow was about to ask a question, but Eads reached out and squeezed his wrist. They had just entered the chamber, and a hush had fallen.

Darrow gazed around him. Central Operations was a vast rotunda, three floors deep. There were two tiers of consoles around the walls, the upper one accessible by an iron walkway. These console stations were manned by Navy operators, some of whom were servitors plugged directly into the interface sockets of the displays. Above them was an observation deck where senior officers gathered to look down on proceedings. In the centre of the chamber was the principal hololithic display, which projected a flickering tactical animation six metres into the air from a wide, brass-edged base unit. Around that stood a ring of semi-opaque glass screens onto which the modar returns were projected. A stern-looking placement operator stood ready at each screen, with a stylus in one hand and an eraser in the other.

Around them lay a further ring of primary control consoles, massive codifier stations that sprouted from the floor like standing stones. Each one, panelled with wood, its instruments turned in brass, had its own valve-screen pict display and hololithic repeater.

All the personnel present currently stood or sat silently, heads slightly bowed.

A rector from the Navy chaplaincy, imposing in his selpic blue robes and sable ruff, was intoning a rite of blessing upon the station. As he spoke, one hand on his breast, the other tucked behind his back, tech-priests moved around the room, anointing the stations and offering holy water from gold ampullas to those personnel in need of personal benediction. Darrow noticed most received it, even the higher ranking staffers.

'Let this day be profitable and successful,' the rector said. 'Let the strength of will and the clarity of sight that is the province of the most high and glorious Imperator, he that is the God-Emperor of all Mankind, inform your work this day. May his glory be everlasting, and his beacon of enlightenment shine to us all in the darkness. For the Golden Throne, everlasting, and in his name's sake, let his will be done.'

The rector made the sign of the aquila across his breast, and everybody did the same.

The deck officer stood, nodded to the rector, and announced, 'Day shift begins, 255, 773.M41.'

At once, activity resumed. A sudden wash of voices, of un-muted vox channels. Deft hands chattered over metal keys. Eads nodded at Darrow to follow him.

As a flight controller, Eads's station was one of the primary control consoles. Darrow helped him into the high-backed seat and stowed the sensor cane where Eads could find it.

'Principal cortical plug and tech-reader link, please,' Eads said as he settled himself. Darrow glanced around, and unhooked the two leads from a bracket on the console's side. He handed them to Eads. Eads read the raised identifier stamps on the plugs with the tips of his fingers, then inserted the cortical plug into the dermal socket behind his left ear. The other lead, from which withered parchment labels dangled, went into a second dermal socket under his hairline at the base of his skull. Eads winced slightly as it went in.

The console came to immediate life. The hololith display lit up and began to rotate. The pict screen shimmered into life, showing a scrolling menu of tight-beamed data. Darrow knew that Eads was now seeing all this for himself, in his mind. Eads began to review the details.

Darrow looked around again. Each of the flight controllers was attended by at least one junior aide. All of the other controllers were sighted, although one had bulky augmetic optics, but many had enhanced their overview with cortical links.

'Vox mic, please,' Eads said.

Darrow unhooked that too, played out the flex, and helped Eads to fit it around his ear so the bead was in place and the wire stalk set by his lips.

'This is Eads, 7513,' Eads said softly. 'I am now on station.' He was answered by a murmur of vox responses.

His fingers began to glide over the mechanical key-board. The data on the screen altered. The cortical plug was simulating a version of the console in Eads's head so he could operate it.

'Climate plot, please,' Eads said to the link. A swollen 3D image bloomed across the hololith. 'Tactical... and quadrant operations.' More changes, more overlays. Hard yellow lines showing aircraft tracks, dotted red lines of mission sequences, winking green runes positioning the machines themselves.

'There's a spare headset if you want to listen,' Eads remarked.

Darrow took the opportunity. What he heard as he wired up was a nonsense of human and machine voices, digital transmissions, and binary codes and atmospherics, which sucked and roared behind the voices.

'Use the dial there to select,' Eads pointed. 'It'll seem overwhelming at first, but you'll learn to differentiate and fine tune. For the next two hours, we're assigned flight control for two fighter units: Umbra Flights Four-One and Four-Two. There are the mission parameters, on screen.'

Suddenly nervous, Darrow read the details, trying not to miss anything. Two intercept units, four machines in each. Routing down across the Peninsula to the head-waters of the Lida, hunting intruders. Time of launch, 08.15.

He looked at the brass chronometer mounted above the console top.

It read 08.14.

Theda MAB South, 08.15

'STRAPS TIGHT?' RACKLAE shouted, barely audible over the rising howl of the fanjets.

Marquall nodded. Racklae gave him a finger-and-thumb 'O', then ordered the ground crew clear. They jumped off, the last of the hoses disconnected and stowed, rolling the primer cart back. One fitter carried the yellow boarding ladder away.

Perched beside the cockpit, Racklae tapped his ears and mouth.

Marquall nodded again. He keyed the vox.

'Test, test,' he said. 'Umbra Eight, Umbra Eight, am I loud?'

'Umbra Eight, this is Lead. You're loud and live. Okay there, Marquall?'

'Yes, ma'am. Lights are green, I repeat green. Ready to lift.'.

'Stand by, Eight.'

Marquall made the sign of the aquila, then looked up at Racklae. He showed him a thumb. The chief fitter grinned, saluted him, and closed the canopy. Immediately, the sound changed. The wail of the jets was dulled, but Marquall was suddenly contained in a resonating box of ultrasonic vibrations.

Marquall checked the canopy lock, then made a gesture almost like a genuflection to his chief. Racklae saw it, nodded, then jumped down and hurried over into cover behind the revetment wall of the pad enclosure.

'Umbra Eight. Locked and ready.'

'Got you, Eight.'

'Umbra Ten, ready.'

'Umbra Seven. Fit.'

'Stand by,' Jagdea said again. 'Four-Two are lifting out ahead of us.'

There was a warble of voices across the vox-channel, then a wailing rush that was loud even with the canopy down and helmet on. From hardstands nearby, four Thunderbolts hoisted themselves up vertically into the air. The space beneath each one was a heat-distorted wash of vectored thrust. Blansher, Asche, Cordiale and Ranfre; Umbra Two: Four, Eleven and Twelve respectively.

On Blansher's expert lead, they began to climb and move forward as their vector ducts gently swung around. In neat formation, they rose, gaining speed. As they crossed away down the length of the field, their primary exhausts lit up hot and yellow as full thrust switched through them. Already, they were receding, climbing higher, accelerating.

'Operations, this is Four-One Leader,' Marquall heard Jagdea say. 'Permission to rise.'

'Four-One Leader, this is Operations. You are cleared for immediate launch. Good hunting.'

'Four-One, this is Lead. Let's go.'

Marquall opened the throttle and felt his machine quiver, as if it had become enraged. Maximum thrust. He felt the gentle wobble as *The Smear* left the stand. Even though it expended masses of fuel reserve, Marquall preferred vector take-offs. He hated ramp launches, and the bludgeoning smack of the rocket boost. He was thankful that no ramps had yet been erected at Theda.

He glanced around, compensating for the wallow of his rising Bolt. To his left, Umbra Ten was coming up. Marquall could almost hear Zemmic fiddling with his rosary of lucky charms as his bird rose. To his right, Jagdea lifted to vertical, and Clovin, two stands down from her. Forty metres up, perfect station keeping.

'Wait for it,' Jagdea's voice cautioned. Blansher favoured the slow, gentlemanly climb from vertical to full forward, but Jagdea preferred the hammer start. The fitter crews knew it. They'd already hit the bunkers.

'Wait…'

Fifty metres.

'On me, extend, full thrust,' Jagdea ordered.

Her machine roared forward, crossing the field at fifty metres, ducts violently thrown to level flight. Clovin gunned after her, then Zemmic. Marquall nursed his throttle and then bulleted after them.

The ground shot away underneath them like speeded-up pict images. The punch kicked Marquall back into his seat. At full burn, they'd cleared the deadlands beyond the field and had already reached close to six hundred kph before they formed up and began to rise.

'Four-One Leader, we have cleared the field. Climbing now to five thousand. Heading south-west, ten-eight-four.'

'Ten-eight-four, copy Leader,' Operations replied. 'Nice launch. Maybe you can apologise to our eardrums later.'

'Copy that, Operations. Fast up, fast away. That's the way we do things where I come from.'

'Understood. What else do you do where you come from?'

'We kill bats.'

'Copy that, Leader. Good to know. Make your level nine thousand and turn south-west eleven-eight-five.'

'Eleven-eight-five. Understood. Four-One, check in.'

'Four-One, Seven. On your lead.'

'Four-One, Ten. At your heels, to port. Nice day for it.'

'Clear as a bell, Zemmic. Count your lucky charms.'

Marquall adjusted his mask. 'Four-One, Eight. Right with you.'

'Stay close, Marquall. This is going to be a breeze.'

It was. He knew it was. He was going to make sure it was.

He'd screwed up on his virgin outing. He could still see Pers Espere, sitting in his cockpit, blood on everything. The image was in his dreams and his waking thoughts.

But Jagdea hadn't given up on him. He could do this. He was Phantine.

He wasn't going to screw up a second time.

* * *

Natrab Echelon Aerie, Interior Desert, 08.16

BARBED LIMBS GLINTING in the fierce light, the slave servitors carried him out onto the foredeck of the aerie in his burnished litter. His pearl-white machine sat in its launch cradle below him, the desert light winking off its stark lines.

The servitors were moaning a litany of providence and blood-hunger. Flight Warrior Khrel Kas Obarkon smiled. The litter came to a stop. Obarkon disconnected the heavy golden pipes that linked his body to the carriage's life-support and slid his helmet down into place so that it locked.

He pulled back the silk drape and stepped out onto the sunburned deck. Tall, lean, encased from throat to foot in glinting black grav-armour, he raised his spidery arms, and the slaves fell to their knees.

The sun was still low in the sky, and the platform beneath his feet rocked slightly as the massive land carrier trundled on over the dunes.

Obarkon waved a skeletal hand and one of the servitors ran up with his speaking cone. Engraved and ornate, it was a bell fashioned from solid gold, mounted on a bronze stand. Obarkon took hold of the dangling lead and plugged it into his larynx socket.

'Fifth echelon!' His digitally corrupted voice boomed out over the upper and lower launch decks. 'You who are of the Anarch, so sworn to he that is Sek! Heed me!'

All along the burnished decks of the carrier, the flight warriors of the fifth echelon stood to attention beside their cradled machines. Their litter bearers were retreating into the blast cavities.

'The Anarch wills us, so we obey! Who shall find blood in the air?'

'We will!' the flight warriors howled back.

'Who will make the kill?'

'We will!' The decks shook.

'Who will stain the earth with the enemy's life?'
'We will!'
'To your machines, your chieftain commands!'

Raising a bloody cheer, the flight warriors clumped to their waiting bats. Obarkon plucked out the speaker cord and walked over to his Hell Razor unsupported. He insisted on doing this, even though he could last less than ten minutes without full life-support. It was a show of personal strength that the crew admired.

Servitors lifted him into his cockpit and automated systems linked him in. He breathed more easily again once the Hell Razor's augmetics took over the mainte-nance of his life.

The spinal plugs engaged. The systems came to life, feeding their data of fuel tolerance, payload and energy into his cortex. His eyes saw through the guns now.

The canopy closed, shutting him in darkness.

Displays lit in his head.

'Clear!' he ordered.

A whining began, rose, exploded.

'Launch!' he commanded.

The ion catapults rose to power and discharged. The pearl-white Hell Razor fired off the carrier deck into the sky. Only his grav-armour prevented Obarkon from being crushed into his seat. Behind him, like darts from a bow, twenty more machines launched into the desert air, some crimson, some mauve, some silver, some black.

They formed up around him as he turned west, towards the mountains. Obarkon switched to his rear pict relays and watched Natrab aerie fall away behind him. The scale of it always delighted him. A leviathan, fully a kilometre long, bristling with weapon ports, rid-ing across the dune sea on a hundred bogeys of five-metre diameter wheels.

Such was the might of the Anarch, sworn unto him that is the High Archon, blessed Gaur.

'Echelon,' he said, adjusting his link. 'Let us kill.'

Palace Pier, 09.12

'YOU'RE EARLY,' BEQA said.

Viltry shrugged. 'The sortie was called off. Repairs, you see. Maybe this afternoon.'

'Breakfast?'

'Please.'

'I have eggs, You eat eggs, right?'

'Not fish eggs?'

'No, not fish eggs.'

'Then, yes.'

'Have a seat,' she said.

Viltry wandered over to his favoured table. The cafe was quite busy. Old folk out for breakfast, and groups of manufactory workers chasing a hot meal after their night shift.

Outside, the sky was spare and pale, a strong wind chasing the clouds out of the air. The sea was dark and moody, rolling with white horses.

A good flying day.

'You know him?' asked Letrice, dubiously.

'Who?

'The mental case. The flier.'

'Yes,' said Beqa, turning the skillet. 'He's okay.'

Over the Lida, 10.01

THEY GOT THE call from Operations about twenty minutes before Jagdea was going to throw it in for the day. *Relief flight under attack, urgent support requested.* According to the grid plot, the fuss was less than fifteen kilometres south of them. Jagdea immediately instructed them to crank to max and burn away down the valley. She called in Blansher's four as support. His unit was coming round in a patrol sweep forty kilometres north.

Marquall swallowed, trying to stay sharp. They were at about four thousand now, and pushing it to twenty-one, twenty-two hundred kilometres. The world was a passing rush. They went over a straggled collection of agricultural stations, then a small town, then a long series of derelict chemical plants. The river basin was stained florid pink and maroon from years of manufacture. Ahead of them, a vast plume of black smoke rose into the sky.

His mouth was dry.

'Gunsights,' Jagdea voxed.

Marquall deftly activated and aligned his targeter.

'Select primary weapons.'

No mistakes this time. Guns live, toggled over to the 'las' setting.

The relief flight had been composed of six super-heavy Navy transports, Onero-pattern, with an escort of six Lightnings, shipping desperately needed fuel out to the retreating ground forces in the desert. Full of promethium jelly and motor oils, the lumbering six-engined transports were ponderous. Easy targets.

Four-One came in on what looked like a feeding frenzy. One transport was already down, having engulfed a square kilometre-plus of the arable valley in its firestorm. The bloom of smoke, fat and black, was what they'd seen on the approach. Another had an engine fire and was dropping badly. At least three of the Lightnings had been stung out of the air.

No less than fifteen black and crimson bats swirled in and out of the convoy formation, evading the tracer streams from the transporters' turrets. Hell Razors. Before they even had range, Marquall witnessed a jet-black

Razor roll in and punch lasfire into the silver flanks of the tail-end Onero. It went up in mid-air. Bright, like a suddenly-lit sun, a massive torus of white flame so hot and fierce no shred of debris survived vaporisation. He winced at the glare, blinded for a moment.

The vox bleeped. Jagdea's voice was hard and curt. Four words: 'Split up. Kill them.'

Zemmic rolled away left, Clovin right. Marquall stayed at Jagdea's seven until they were right into the brawl, then broke left as she split off. The air was full of dancing machines and streamers of contrails, exhaust and smoke. Too many objects to track. He had to stay focused. Concentrate on the bats. Not even all the bats he could see. Just the ones his speed and angle had a chance of intersecting.

Two to port, going the other way. No point even thinking about it. Another, bright red, climbing hard. He wouldn't catch it. There at his ten… no. A Lightning, sun glinting off its aluminoid skin as it turned. Keep jinking, keep moving, keep twisting, keep dancing. Fly straight for more than five seconds and you might as well paint a target on your arse cheeks.

Hexan, his aged instructor back at the scholam. His mantra, his words. Marquall could hear the old bastard saying them.

A bat there. He rolled over on it. No good. It was breaking and turning the other way. Damn it. Another… but Clovin was on it, the nose of Umbra Seven lighting up with las discharge. A hit? Too late to see. Marquall had gone over, past, round again. That put him low under one of the transports. The damn thing's turrets opened up at him, chasing his tail with yellow tracer.

'Friendly! Friendly! Friendly!' he yelled into the vox, knowing they probably didn't care. Terrified beyond measure by now, the gunners were blazing away at anything in the sky.

He banked around again and a crimson bat went across his nose. Without even thinking, he clenched his thumb and felt *The Smear* shudder as its guns lit off. Had he hit it? Chances were low. He didn't care. There was another. He was in the game now.

JAGDEA COULDN'T SEE Marquall. She couldn't worry about that now. This wasn't the place for nurse-maiding. They were desperately outnumbered, by machines every bit as fast and heavyweight as the Thunderbolts. Her initial stooping dive and turn-out had brought her clean in on a bat, but it had the edge on power because she was turning, and zipped out of her target field before she could fire.

She kicked the rudder round and rolled to port, and saw a scarlet Razor streak by underneath her. It was gunning for one of the Lightnings, stuck to its six. The Navy plane was doing everything it could, but it wouldn't shake off.

Jagdea almost had to loop to line up. The angle of deflection was poor, so she saved her shots, and banked around again until she came up right on the Razor's tail.

It must have seen her there, because it broke off furiously. But her instinct was as keen as ever. Jagdea had a natural talent for anticipation. A simple matter of logic, that's how she saw it. She regularly guessed what a hostile was going to do by imagining what she'd do in its place. Blansher once remarked that if it was such a simple trick, why could no one else in the wing do it quite so well? As the Razor pulled off, she was pulling off too, at exactly the same angle. Two bursts. Four las-rounds. All four went straight up the Razor's intakes and it blew apart in a sizzling cloud of debris.

Small parts of the wreckage clattered off her upper hull as she came through the flame-cone. Immediately, she had a lock tone. Something on top of her. Tracers sailed by, pink and bright. She rolled, with a touch of viff from the vectors, and let the bat go wide.

Another one. No, two. One red, one mauve, sweeping in towards the transport with the engine fire. The massive Onero had been holed badly, weeping torrents of fuel mix out into the air.

'No you don't…' she hissed. She cut round, crunched by negative G, grunting out of her defensive 'grip' posture. The angle was bad, but she let go anyway. A long, pumping stream of lascannon. The red Razor lost part of its starboard wing and went into a savage spin, falling away. The mauve one broke off, turning down and out at the limit of pilot tolerance.

Then it exploded. One large blast that skewed it around in the sky, then two smaller ones that shredded what was left of it into metal dust.

Milan Blansher's Bolt ripped past under her.

Four-Two had joined the fight.

Theda MAB South, 10.07

A CURIOUS HUSH had fallen across the Operations rotunda. Eads was the only flight controller who had birds in a fight. Maintaining their own watches, the other controllers were looking his way. Darrow felt like they were in the spotlight. The deck officer had come over to stand at Eads's side.

'Status?'

'Four-One and Four-Two have engaged. Sixteen confirmed hostiles. Four hostiles now show as killed.'

There was a murmur around the room.

'Relief flight situation?' asked the deck officer. His name was Banzie, a short, jocund man in a high-collared uniform of Imperial purple.

'Two tankers lost. One damaged. Three escorts downed.' Eads's voice was frail and distant. He was looking ahead of him into open space, the data swirling in his mind. His hands crept over the console displays, correcting, rewriting. The placement officer at the modar screen in front of Eads's station was making constant adjustments to the glass with her stylus.

Darrow realised why the air in Operations was kept so cold. There was no chance of getting dozy or slack. No chance of drowsiness clouding judgement.

'Assessment?' Banzie asked Eads.

'Tight. Anything in range?' Eads replied.

'Requesting assist!' Banzie cried out to the room. 'Quickly, now!'

'I have the 44th Wing, six machines, fourteen minutes away,' a controller called out from a nearby console.

'No, Deck. Too far,' Eads muttered.

'The 101. Four machines, returning over the Northern Makanites. Three minutes,' called another from across the chamber.

'Tolerance?' asked Banzie.

'They've been up for two hundred minutes, and have engaged once already. If we instruct, they'll have about five minutes of fight in them.'

'Anyone else?' Banzie urged.

Nothing closer than fourteen minutes.

'Controller?' Banzie asked.

'Another Lightning just bought it, sir,' said Eads. 'And... can't confirm, but we may also have lost one of Umbra. Requesting commit.'

Banzie nodded and looked up, his voice rising to drill instructor volume. 'Instruct commit! Bring them in, please.'

Darrow looked over at the flight controller on the other side of the chamber as he began feverish activity. '101, 101, this is Operations. You have an instruction to commit. Please confirm plot.'

There was an answering swirl of vox noise. The placement officer in front of the controller began scribing quickly and expertly on the reactive glass display.

Then Darrow heard the controller say, 'Copy that, Apostles. I'm sure that they'll be happy to see you.'

The Apostles! Holy Throne! Darrow's heart began to race. He looked back at Eads. Beads of sweat were trickling off Eads's brow.

'Confirmation,' he said. 'We've lost one of Umbra.'

Over the Lida, 10.08

'WHERE'S CLOVIN? WHERE'S Clovin?' Jagdea yelled into the vox. She'd just seen a plane go in and make a fireball in the hydro-ponds below. It had looked like a Thunderbolt.

'No visual,' Asche replied.

'Nothing,' called Ranfre.

'Throne, what kind of party have you brought us to?' Cordiale screeched. Jagdea saw him, below and left, turning wildly with a bat on his tail. The air was full of tracer and las. Her own lasers were spent. She toggled to hard cannons and stooped.

Something forked and white bent across her bows and raced after Zemmic's machine.

'See him?' That was Blansher.

'Say again,' Jagdea voxed.

'The pearl-white bat. That's the bastard who stung Clovin.'

Blansher's Bolt slewed in behind her and then rolled away loose. Asche went under her, followed by Marquall.

'Umbra Four-One, this is Operations. We have assist committed to you. Three minutes and closing.'

'Understood,' Jagdea gasped, the G she was pulling compressing her lungs.

She saw Zemmic flick out to dodge his attacker. Smoke was pumping from his port fan.

'Umbra Ten, Umbra Ten, this is Flight Lead. Break off and quit.'

'I can hold it...'

'I don't care, Ten. Break off and quit for home now.'

'Copy you, Lead.'

There was the white bat now, banking over through the tails of a cloud bar. Blansher was on it, Asche too. As good as dead, Jagdea decided.

She was needed elsewhere, anyway.

The burning Onero had finally given up. Its fire-damaged wing tore away and it went down into the valley basement like a meteor. Another bright flash-burst. Another vast section of farmland torched. Jagdea saw the shockwave mash trees, demolish silos, and send segments of plastek hydroponic rafts slewing into the air.

A black Razor swept over her gunsight, rolling hard, firing on Ranfre's machine. She hit the speed brakes, her body arrested by the harness, and fell nose-down onto it, pumping her cannons.

It twisted and turned out as Ranfre pulled clear. Jagdea swung around onto it again. Resighting, she got a decent lock.

'Bang,' she said.

The arcing bat vanished and left a drizzle of fire in its place.

BLANSHER BLINKED IN amazement. He'd had Clovin's pearl-white killer square in his reticule, with a firm tone.

And then it had just vanished.

He banked hard, expecting a trick. But there was no sign of it.

'Umbra Four, Umbra Four... Did you do that?'

'Negative, Umbra Two,' Larice Asche replied. 'Frig it, Mil, he's dummied you. He's right under you!'

Blansher inverted, then curled into a dive. Asche was right with him, popping shots at the merciless white Hell Razor. It stuck and turned, and matched every move Umbra Flight's number two made.

This wasn't right. This was insane. Blansher and Asche were Jagdea's two best pilots, aces both. How could this hostile out-dance them together?

Asche rotated steeply and got a lock, but then pulled her thumb back as Blansher's Bolt got in the way. The bastard was playing with them. Playing them off.

The Razor screwed off left, then punctured Blansher's wing with a flurry of hard rounds. Asche scored a shot that left a dark scorch on the bat's right wing. Then it rolled and fired again. Blansher's port engine exploded.

Trailing smoke, he fell out of the fight. The Razor seemed to consider going after him, but pulled away. Asche turned with him, smiling under her breather mask.

And... he was gone. She switched her head around, looking for it. A las-shot tore through her wing.

It was on her. Lock tone.

Four cream-skinned Thunderbolts came out of the south, nose guns blasting.

One rolled perfectly, came in under her, and fired bursts at the pearl-white Razor.

It side-stepped, and extended at a furious rate.

The white Thunderbolt swung past her.

One of the Apostles. He dipped his wings to her.

'Many thanks,' Asche voxed.

So CERTAIN. So assured. The four Apostles ripped into the air-fight and broke it up, like bouncers in a tavern brawl. Seekan secured one kill, his wingman Suhr another. It was the legendary Quint, ace of aces, who had saved Larice's skin.

The hostiles began to snap off and break away from the tumble.

Then Asche saw the pearl-white razor lining up on Marquall. He was chasing one of the fleeing hostiles, firing wildly.

'Umbra Eight! Break! Break!' she yelled.

She started to turn. Jagdea's machine swept by her, gunning.

The hostile was right on Marquall's six.

Tone ping. Hard lock. He couldn't shake it. Marquall shouted in frustration.

And in desperation, Vander Marquall did the only thing he could think of. He fired his Thunderbolt's rocket drive. It was there only for launch assist. No one ever used it in open flight. It was against text book directives. Fire your rocket and you lose control.

He fired it anyway.

The sky and land became a blur. He greyed out for a moment.

Somehow, he held on.

The pearl-white Razor turned, bemused, as its target banged away.

'Yours, Harlsson,' Seekan's voice sounded calm and controlled over the vox.

'On it, Leader,' Harlsson responded.

Major Velmed Harlsson. Ninety-seven kills. Jagdea watched his consummate skill with humble appreciation. A perfect bank. Not too much throttle. Totally composed. He arched over onto the target expertly, guns blazing.

But somehow, the bat managed to viff out under him, and then swung onto his rear.

She heard Harlsson's voice. Just a hint of confusion in the calm tone. 'I'm locked. I–' Harlsson began. 'Seekan, where are y–'

The bat's guns blew his tail assembly away. Harlsson tried to control his flailing machine. The huge silver bulk of one of the transports suddenly filled his forward view.

The mangled Thunderbolt impacted into the side of the Onero at five hundred kph.

The fire wash lit up the valley.

Theda MAB South, 10.18

'APOSTLE DOWN!' THE flight controller on the far side of the chamber yelled out. There was a brisk gasp from the personnel around them.

Darrow looked at Eads. Eads sighed. 'Enemy has broken off. Bats retreating.'

Banzie nodded. There was some sporadic clapping.

Eads glanced round at Darrow. 'A white bat. Pearl-white. Ring any bells?'

'Sounds like the one, sir,' Darrow nodded.

'He's a devil of a pilot. A real devil. Summarise everything you remember from your encounter and I'll get the report copied out. The wings need to be aware of him. Everything you remember, please, junior.'

'Yes, sir.'

DAY 256

Theda Old Town, 00.10

THE ADDRESS SHE'D been given was a merchantman's house on the Gehnstal, one of a row of elderly mansions on a broad pavement. Many were boarded up now, thanks to the war, but adjacent blocks of cheap habs showed that the area's fortunes had been in decline for some time.

Jagdea brought the staff car she'd borrowed to a halt, switched off the engine and got out. Lights burned brightly around the shutter edges of the house she was looking for.

Nervously adjusting her uniform, she hurried up the front steps. Was that singing she could hear? She found an iron bell-pull and yanked on it. Service bells tinkled faraway in the house.

After a moment, the door opened. The hallway inside was dimly lit. She found herself facing a high-function domestic servitor, its silver form engraved with intricate chasework.

139

'Oh,' she said, surprised. 'I was looking for… is this 133 Gehnstal?'

'Yes, commander,' it replied, digitising the gentle, mannered voice of an elderly male through his voxponder. The servitor had recognised her rank.

'I'm looking for the billet used by the Apostles. The 101.'

'Please come in,' the servitor said.

It was definitely singing she could hear in the background. A recording of Frans Talfer's *Gaudete Terra*, with male voices booming along.

'Follow me,' the servitor said. 'May I ask your name, commander?'

'Jagdea,' she replied.

The servitor's exquisite silver hands reached out and smoothly opened a double set of panelled doors, letting through a bright glow light and the full force of the music.

'Commander Jagdea,' it announced.

The singing stopped, but the music languished on, fizzing slightly through the speaker horn of the recording player on a side table. Seekan rose out of an armchair to greet her. 'Good evening, commander.'

Around the room were the other six Apostles. All of them, Seekan included, were wearing full dress uniforms, heavy with medals. They had glasses in their hands and had obviously been drinking for a while. Faces were flushed, and jackets undone.

Seekan looked as fresh as night frost.

'I'm sorry,' Jagdea said. 'I'm interrupting.'

'Not at all,' said Seekan. 'Domo, a drink for the commander.' The servitor crossed immediately to a lacquered drink stand.

'Is this the Phantine leader?' one of the Apostles asked. He was a big man, his eyes red and hooded from too many amasecs.

'It is indeed, Ludo. Commander Jagdea, may I present Major Ludo Ramia.'

'Mamzel,' the big man nodded.

'Major Ziner Krone, Major Jeric Suhr.'

Suhr was a sharp-faced, skinny man. He nodded curtly. Krone was of noble build, a Glavian perhaps, by the look of his gleaming black skin. His face was badly scarred on the left cheek. He too nodded, then busied himself changing the recorder disk.

'Captain Guis Gettering.' Gettering was pugnacious and jowly, with short, sand-white hair. He was standing by the hearth, a crystal balloon in his hand. 'Mamzel commander,' he grunted.

'And Major Dario Quint.'

Quint. Ace of aces. Reclined in a battered tub chair in the far corner, he seemed more like an observer than a participant. He was a surprisingly small man, well-proportioned, compact, his oval face boyish, though his hair was zinc-grey. His hands were folded across the breast of his uniform jacket. He stared directly at her and held her gaze, though he made no sound.

The servitor handed Jagdea a flute of joiliq, and she took it even though she didn't want it.

'I–' she began, and cleared her throat. 'I thought it was appropriate for me to come here in person and express my wing's appreciation for your assistance. Especially given the cost.'

'You lost a machine too, didn't you?' Ramia asked.

'Yes, I did. But the loss of an Apostle–'

Ramia snorted. 'Harlsson was an odious shit. He couldn't fly worth a fart.'

Jagdea was startled. 'I... what?'

'Detestable man,' Suhr agreed. 'Don't look so bloody shocked, mamzel. Harlsson was all luck and flair. Not a gram of skill in his whole body. It's a miracle he lasted as long as he did.'

Jagdea frowned. She put her drink down, untouched, and said, 'I wanted to express my appreciation and my sympathies. I've done that now, so I think I'll go.'

'Saving the neck of that upstart boy, wasn't he?' Gettering asked suddenly. Jagdea paused and turned back.

'What?'

'Harlsson. Got stung getting a Razor off that boy of yours, mamzel. Isn't that right? The boy who thought naming his machine *Double Eagle* was a bright idea.'

'That matter is over and done, captain, though I believe Pilot Officer Marquall is still waiting on your letter of apology. And no, you're not right. Marquall had already shaken the Razor.'

'Had he now?' said Gettering.

'He used his rocket assist,' said Suhr.

'Did he?' Gettering laughed. Ramia chuckled too. 'So the boy was your casualty?'

'No,' said Jagdea. 'Marquall recovered control of his machine.'

There was a look on Gettering's face that suggested he was about to accuse her of lying. Instead, he just shook his head and looked away. The recorder started blaring again. Krone had put on Nuncius's *Salve Beatus*, loud and strident. Jagdea walked out of the room.

'COMMANDER!' SEEKAN CAUGHT up with her in the hall. Behind him, the drunken singing had resumed.

'You'll have to forgive my men, Commander Jagdea. They're dealing with their loss in their own way.'

'By throwing a boorish party and defaming the dead man?'

'Pretty much,' said Seekan. 'Sentiment does not figure largely in the souls of those men, Jagdea. They're steeped in death. Immune to its touch.'

'Clearly not immortal,' she snapped.

'No. That's not what I meant. Your unit, now. I imagine there's sadness. Low spirits. Mourning the loss of a friend.'

Jagdea nodded. That was exactly the mood in the billet when she'd left. A few were raising a glass to Clovin's shade, but there was a general, numbing gloom.

'I remember that myself,' Seekan said. 'In the early days. But we Apostles are war-weary. When I said we are immune to the touch of death, I meant we just don't feel its bite any more. No sense of grief, no loss, no regret, no sadness. Just an inevitability. When an Apostle dies, we put on our dress white and our ridiculous numbers of medals, and we get filthy drunk. We rage, we sing, we drink some more. We do it to show fate, or fortune, or whatever else lurks out there in the dark, that we don't care.'

She had no reply. His voice dropped slightly. 'We're freaks, Jagdea. Do you know why we're Apostles? Not because we're especially fine pilots. Not at all. We're Apostles because we've had unnatural luck. We should have died long ago, but there's been some oversight and our souls have not been claimed. So we go on flying, and killing. And eventually, the oversight is corrected. Today, it was Harlsson's turn.'

'That's a very bleak view,' said Jagdea. 'Was Harlsson really that disliked?'

'Who knows? Probably not. He was a reasonable pilot. But none of us are friends, you see. There's no point. By the time you become an Apostle, friends are a vulnerability none of us chooses to afford.'

'I pity you,' Jagdea said.

Seekan shrugged his shoulders. 'We don't need pity, either.' He paused. 'Do you know what I have to do tomorrow morning?'

'No.'

'My driver's taking me down the coast to Madenta MAB. There's a pilot stationed there with the 567th. His name's Saul Cirksen. Seventy-two kills, superb service record. I will be inviting him to fill Harlsson's spot.'

'Will he accept?' she asked.

'If you are invited to become an Apostle, Jagdea, you're not allowed to decline.'

She opened the front door. The night air was cold and smelled of rain. From the drawing room behind them, the raucous singing swelled to a lusty chorus.

'Thank you for your pains, commander,' Seekan said. 'They're not as unappreciated as you might think.'

Jagdea made a quick, clipped salute. 'Good flying,' she said.

Coast Highway, 05.50

AT FIRST HE thought it was a summer storm, glimmering the edges of the pre-dawn sky with sheet lightning.

It took him a few moments to realise it wasn't.

He brought his heavy transport to a full stop, and jumped out onto the rockcrete surface of the hardtop, his scope in his hand. The other seven trucks in the convoy grumbled to a halt behind him. The convoy was an overnight munitions delivery to Fetona MAB, already overdue. A couple of the drivers sounded their horns, revved their stacks. Finally, they dismounted too.

They found Kaminsky on the far side of the highway, near to where the pelmet of the road track shelved away into a dry creek-bed. This area of the Peninsula was barren. Straw grasses, fibreweed, salt bars dotting the broken ground. Even in the cold half-light of dawn, there was nothing to spoil the view all the way to the Lida Valley.

Kaminsky was winding his scope.

'What the hell's going on?' asked Velligan.

'Kaminsky, what's the problem?' said Anderchek from behind him.

'See that?' Kaminsky asked. 'That glow? Fire patterns. Towns along the Lida are being bombed.'

Theda MAB South, 06.17

THERE WAS SOMETHING big going on. Darrow had slept badly, aware of a huge launch activity during the small hours. He'd been working late on the report Eads had asked him to write up, and with an hour and a half to go before his next shift at Operations, he went out to find Heckel, to get the major's comments on the tangle they'd had with the white bat.

A pall of exhaust fumes hung in the still air over the field. The majority of the base's machines were gone, on sorties. Darrow spoke to a Commonwealth fitter he knew, and the man told him bombing raids had begun, north of the mountains. River towns had been hit, agro-centres, mills. Someone reckoned the raiders had got as far as Ezraville.

Everyone he passed looked pinched and worried. Everyone was thinking the same thing. This was the start of the end.

Even Commonwealth reserve units like Quarry Flight were on standby. Morose, in full flight armour, they lurked in the dispersal areas, waiting for the call. Wolfcubs were being fitted to their ramps. Cyclones were being wheeled out of the housing barns, attended by fuelling trucks and munition trains.

'Heckel?' No one had seen him, and no one was in the mood to chat for long. According to the posts, Heckel should have been amongst the standby pilots.

Darrow got a room number, and headed down to the blast-proof hab block at the west end of the dispersal yards. By the light of the dingy corridor lamps, he found the right door and knocked.

'Major? Major Heckel? Are you there, sir?'

He knocked again. 'Major Heckel? It's Darrow. Have you got a minute, sir?'

He was about to turn away, but an ominous feeling made him try the door. It was unlocked.

In the narrow room, the cot was unmade. There was a clutter of papers and possessions on the small desk, clothes laid out on top of the officer's trunk. A camp chair lay on its side in the middle of the room.

Major Heckel had hanged himself by a harness strap from the ceiling bracket.

'Oh God-Emperor!' Darrow cried. He rushed forward, seizing the major's legs, struggling to lift him down and ease the constriction. 'Help me! Someone help me!' he shouted out. He couldn't unhook the body. Heckel was a lead weight. Darrow cried out in frustration. He let go, found Heckel's kit knife in the pile on the trunk, then righted the chair and climbed up, sawing at the harness cord. It was aviation issue, tough, designed not to break. Darrow yelled out again, and cut his fingers on the knife as he wrenched it back and forth against the thick fabric.

'Don't you die! Don't you die!' he bawled. 'How dare you do this, Heckel! How bloody dare you!'

Darrow was vaguely aware of two aviators coming in, drawn by his yells. He heard their appalled cries. They grabbed Heckel's legs and raised him.

'Cut it! Cut it!' one shouted.

'I'm trying… I…'

The harness parted. Heckel fell heavily into the arms of the other men, knocking Darrow off the chair and onto the cot.

They wrestled the noose off his neck and started emergency resuscitation. Darrow got up, and dropped the knife. He knew they were wasting their time. The lividity around the neck, the pallor of the cheeks, the cyanotic blue of the lips.

'You poor bastard,' Darrow sighed. 'You poor, stupid bastard.'

In his efforts to perform chest compressions, one of the men had dislodged an envelope from Heckel's flight jacket. Darrow picked it up. The envelope was blank, as if Heckel had been unable to think of anyone to address it to. Inside was a single sheet of paper, inscribed with a single handwritten sentence.

May the God-Emperor forgive me, I cannot do this any more.

DAY 257

Theda Old Town, 07.31

THE SERVICE WAS over. There had been many more in attendance that morning, three times the usual number for the daybreak blessing. Beqa had had to wait in line to light her candles. Everyone was scared. You could almost smell it in the streets. Everyone had been scared for months now, of course, but they'd got used to it, and got on with living through it. But over the last two nights, the fear had intensified.

From the west of the city, it was possible to see the fires in Ezraville. Thousands had died in the Lida bombings, and the raids were ongoing. How long before the bombs started falling on Theda as well? How long before the entire coast was on fire? How long? How long? How long did Enothis have left?

The one shred of good news had come in the hierarch's homily. It had been officially confirmed that the first elements of the retreating land armada had cleared

the mountains and were returning to the coast. There
were soldiers coming home. She lit her three votive candles. One for Gart, one for Eido. One for whoever–

No. One for Viltry.

Over the Interior Desert, 09.07

'IF I'D JUST retreated from the Trinity Hives, marched all
the way back across the desert, not to mention those
mountains, I reckon I wouldn't feel much like fighting
any more after that.'

'You have a point, Judd,' Viltry said to his bombardier
over the internal comm. Halo Flight had just passed
over a shelf of desert upland across which a ten kilome-
tre-long convoy of Imperial armour and
weapons-carriers was slowly toiling.

'I mean,' Judd went on. 'We're meant to be holding
the Archenemy off until the ground forces get home
and regroup. Regroup? That's a laugh. They'll be fit for
nothing.'

'Maybe,' Viltry said lightly. 'Let's just get on with our
job and hope appearances are deceiving.'

Greta was leading a flight of six Marauders. They were
travelling low, skimming the dust seas, striving to
remain under the modar and auspex cones of any land
carriers hidden in the wastes. Meanwhile, recon Lightnings were flying somewhere above at their maximum
operational ceiling, scoping for the elusive carriers. At
any moment, Halo could be called in.

The desert formed an eerie, almost grey landscape
below them. The shadows of the low-flying machines
flickered and danced over the hard-lipped dunes, and
the breaks of rock and scree.

Viltry felt remarkably composed. He wondered to
himself if Beqa Mayer might have anything to do with
his improved demeanour.

'Contact!' Lacombe suddenly said. Viltry stiffened slightly.

'Eight marks at seven thousand, bearing zero-seven-five.'

Viltry looked at the scope. Enemy machines, definitely, heading south-west, twelve or more kilometres away. Not a patrol sweep. Their course was too true, too determined.

'Lacombe – get on the vox and see if Operations can give us a back-plot for them.'

Over the engine roar, Viltry could hear his navigator talking on the main vox. The internal cut back in again.

'They had them on modar about fifteen minutes ago, turning south over the Makanite Ridge.'

'They're going home,' Viltry said. 'They're going home, and they're in a hurry because they're right at the limit of their fuel. Halo Flight, Halo Flight, this is Lead. Maintain level, but come about on my mark, bearing zero-seven-five.'

The six laden machines banked around, still hugging the sand. *Greta* first, then *Hello Hellstorm*, *Widowmaker*, *Throne of Terra*, *Consider Yourself Dead* and *Miss Adventure*. Viltry ordered all birds to go weapons-live, arm payloads, and keep scanning.

Even if they couldn't keep the bats in visual, they had to keep them on the scopes.

Because they were going to lead them straight to a carrier.

Over Ezraville, 09.18

'ATTACKING!' JAGDEA SANG out, and rolled serial Zero-Two into a scream dive, with Ranfre, Waldon and Del Ruth at her heels. Four thousand metres below them, partly obscured by wispy thread-clouds, the air was full of planes, darting and swooping like shoals of reef fish

in a tropical sea. Another nine thousand metres below
the huge air battle lay the vast, dark sprawl of Ezraville,
a collage of blacks and greys beside the mirror-white
expanse of the estuary mouth.

Behind Jagdea's pack, Larice Asche led the second half
of Umbra in: Cordiale, Van Tull and Marquall. Only
two-thirds of the squadron were airworthy. Clovin was
gone, Espere out, probably forever, and both Blansher
and Zemmic were grounded while their machines
underwent repairs.

The power dive was ferocious. Negative G glued them
to their seats, and pulled their faces into rictus masks.
Jagdea's vision was spotty, but she tried to stay fixed,
tried to make sense of the brawl they were coming in on.

They'd been called up to meet a huge wave of enemy
bombers heading for the coast. Nearly two hundred
machines, mainly Hell Talons and Tormentors, with
fighter cover. Poor weather had delayed the auspex plot,
so the raiders were already closing on Ezraville before
the warning had gone up. By now, they were shedding
their payloads on the city.

Other wings had already intercepted. Thunderbolts
2665 and 44, 138 Lightning, and a squadron of late-
model Commonwealth Cyclones. With Umbra, that made
about sixty Imperial machines committed. Others were
inbound. More still, the majority, were engaged against
two other equally massive raid forces over the Lida.

The enemy bombers, hooked, brightly coloured and
menacing, were ranged out in long, straggling Vs, like
migrating waterfowl, holding pattern while they let
their payloads go. The Imperials were milling around
those ranks, trying to pick them off – whilst fending off
the fierce scatter of Locusts that were flying escort.

As soon as their bombs were gone, the big Tormentors
tended to pull out and head for home, but the Hell Talons,
vastly powerful fighter-bombers, stayed on station. Freed

from the weight of their primary loads, they began peeling down to execute rocket or cannon attacks on the city, or even pulled up to provide additional top cover for the rest of the raid.

The air was full of swarming machines, flickering fire and puffs of smoke. Sections of the city below were ablaze.

Jagdea felt the hate fan in her heart. Her dive was bringing her right down on a Talon. She tracked the nose, keeping in her sights, right at the centre of her reticule, and squeezed her thumb.

The Talon detonated in mid-air with huge force. Jagdea had already swept down past it at mach one, banking round under the raid formation and coming up on a Tormentor from below. Her twin-las pumped, and the machine trembled as its belly opened like a gutted fish, spilling out tatters of debris, machine parts and lubricants in fine sprays. Trailing white smoke, it began to tilt and founder. It was dead, but she stayed on it, switching to the quad cannons and raking it end to end. The Tormentor combusted and vaporised. Burning debris showered down towards the benighted city, but better for it to blow up in the air than come down on a hab block with a full payload.

Tight on her heels in the dive, Ranfre and Waldon both destroyed Tormentors with fine intercepts and wheeled off, hunting. In less than thirty seconds, Waldon had lined up on a Talon that was in the process of unloading its bombs, and shredded its cockpit section with quad-fire. As the crimson machine spiralled away, coming apart, Waldon whooped. He'd just made his fourth and fifth confirmed career kills. He was now an ace.

Del Ruth, rearmost of the four, overshot her chosen target, which saw her coming down on it at the last moment and rolled a desperate evade. But she levelled out, and immediately picked up a Locust chasing one of the Commonwealth planes. Tone locked, she stung it hard, and as it began to judder, stung it again and blew it to fragments.

Asche's four came in moments later moving, if anything, at an even higher rate. Asche got a Talon squarely and cleanly. Van Tull took a shot at a Tormentor, damaged it, looped around and finished the kill.

Cordiale, his timing just out, mis-hit a Talon, and then found he had a Talon and a Locust on him. He tried to jink out, but nearly collided with a Lightning coming head on. He screwed over to evade, almost stalling. The Lightning banked hard and its port-wing tip clipped the Talon behind Cordiale. The Lightning lost stability and began to spin, corrected, and then was blown apart by two other Locusts. Trailing debris, the Talon it had clipped came wide, right into Asche's gun cone. She showed it little mercy.

Cordiale swung about and started to chase down a Tormentor. It had shed its load, and was turning for the home run. But it was still a viable target. If it died here, it couldn't come back with another clutch of bombs.

Marquall, the last in, was sure he had a kill. He fired two bursts, but the Hell Talon was still intact as he rocketed down past it.

He tucked in and began to climb again, bleeding off some power so his controls weren't quite so stiff with speed. In a flash, he realised he'd gone up between two Tormentors, both spilling out bombs like egg cases. He cursed his own luck. His haste to correct had made him miss a chance on two easy targets.

Marquall was almost insensible with rage. He was seething with desire to make a kill, to open his account. Bad enough he was the youngest, the most inexperienced, bad enough that Pers Espere had been maimed wet-nursing him. Marquall had no score. No kills to his name. Now his confidence had returned after that disastrous virgin sortie, he was determined to prove his worth in combat.

Hell, the sky was crawling with enemy machines! Surely he could hit one of them?

'Umbra Eight! Umbra Eight! Break left now!'

That was Van Tull's voice. Marquall didn't question it. He stomped the rudder bar and leaned on the stick, inverting as he pulled out to port. A flame yellow Hell Talon rushed over and by him.

'Thanks, Three,' he voxed, coming true and climbing again.

'You okay, Eight?' Van Tull voxed.

'Four-A,' replied Marquall. They were still babysitting him. That rankled. Then again, but for Van Tull's warning, he'd like as not be dead now.

He turned in. Almost immediately, he picked up a Cyclone, running for its life from a Talon. The Commonwealth prop-plane was weeping smoke. Marquall wondered why Operations kept the Cyclones and Wolfcubs in the air. It was suicide, flying machines like that against the enemy's vector-thrust predators.

He cranked the throttle, banked wide, clipped off a wasted but satisfying burst at a Tormentor as he went long over its back, and lined up on the Talon.

This time...

THE PORT ENGINE was dead, and so was Artone. Frans Scalter fought with the Cyclone's leaden stick and called plaintively to his co-pilot and long-time friend. Hard rounds had torn through the machine's cockpit, shattering the glass nose and ripping Artone's torso in half. Wind screamed in through the shattered bubble. There was blood everywhere, and the instruments were plastered with sticky flecks of human tissue.

'I'll get you home! I'll get you home!' Scalter wailed, denying the scene around him, and imagining some

miraculous future where he brought the ruptured
Cyclone down, and the crews rushed in, and Artone was
patched up and made alive again.

Scalter knew he had to keep evading. The Hell Talon
was right on his tail now.

'Seeker One! Seeker One! Someone! Please–'

The Talon's guns lit up.

LIKE A FELINE playing with a mouse, the bastard wasn't
going to let the Cyclone go. It swung from side to side
with muscular power, correcting for every frantic jink
and twist the Commonwealth pilot tried to make.

It had got the blood scent. It wanted the kill. It was
greedy. It was staying on the target.

The first and oldest mistake.

Marquall came around on its five, calculating the
deflection angle with almost leisurely brio.

Then he opened up with his quad cannons, feeling
the heavy slap of them retard his motion, hearing the
breech blocks bang and the autoloaders rattle to feed
ammo from the whirring drums.

Somehow, Marquall had expected the enemy
machine to explode, or catch fire, or do something
equally spectacular.

It simply quivered. Part of one blade-wing deformed,
like foil, and a gulp of brown smoke belched out of its
engines.

Then it fell out of the air. All lift lost in one shocking
instant, it dropped away, turning end over end, like a
toy that had been thrown aside by a petulant child.

It spun away below him, smaller, smaller.

Throne, he'd got it. He'd killed it stone dead.

'S-seeker One, Seeker One,' he stammered, rousing
from a brief fugue. 'This is Umbra Eight. You're clear,
friend. Clear. Get your machine home and down.'

'Umbra Eight, this is Seeker One. Understood.'

Not even a thank you? Marquall didn't care. He had a fire in his belly, a coal of excitement and satisfaction. He was no longer the kid who needed babysitting.

Something threw him into his seat like a kick in the face. *The Smear* inverted, every alarm screaming. In terror, mystified, Marquall dragged on the stick, but it was slack and dead. He saw flame on his port side, sections of metal plating slipping off like fish scales.

Fire licked into the cockpit.

'No!' he yelled. 'Oh no, no, no!'

He fumbled with his harness, trying to reach the eject handle. Half-heard voices blasted out of the vox.

Huge negative G. He was already greying out. He couldn't lift his hand, let alone reach the lever.

In front of him, like a rapidly-spinning kaleidoscope image, the city was rushing up.

Over the Interior Desert, 09.22

THEY KISSED OVER the top of a dune headland and there it was. The size of it took their breath away. Judd voiced a particularly florid oath.

A mass carrier. It was almost a kilometre long, a huge slab of burnished decking and raised ramps, bronze in the desert light. Vast wheel assemblies rolled it across the dust. Viltry had been told the enemy called these behemoths *aeries*, as if they were home roosts for the murderous bats. It was a feat of mechanical genius, a juggernaut, a giant amongst machines.

Nothing could kill something that big. Nothing could–

He caught himself. They would have to try. That was the job the God-Emperor had decreed for them.

'No hesitation, Halo,' he cried. 'We're committed. Line up and shed, then come around with wing-loads for the second pass. The Emperor protects.'

He could see the Talons they had been following sweeping in to the fluted arrestor runs on the carrier's top side. They looked tiny by comparison, little gaudy specks.

The carrier had seen the inbound Marauders, coming down onto it at zero height. Hundreds of anti aircraft batteries tracked round, alert, like the alarmed tails of scorpions, and the air was filled with bursting flak and zipping tracers. A hailstorm of fire.

'Stay on it, stay on it…' Viltry ordered.

A siren screeched. Amongst the blizzard of flak bursts, Viltry glimpsed the trail smoke of missiles banging off from the carrier.

Wordlessly, he hit the chaff switch, and clouds of glittering, distorting material puffed out of *Greta's* launchers. Then heat-flares too. Near-miss explosions shook the airframe. The space between the onrushing planes and the vast carrier was muddy with flash flowers and blooms of black and white smoke.

A rocket struck *Miss Adventure* and killed her dead. The torn wreckage and hull sections, moving at close to mach one, cartwheeled over the desert floor, raking the sand, spitting flame like a firework.

'Nose and top. Anytime you like,' Viltry said.

The turrets opened up, playing fire along the carrier's starboard hull. Viltry, concentrating as hard as he could, saw bats trying to launch from the lower chutes. Naxol had seen them too. A Locust came off its ion catapult and burst like a flare.

Ten seconds. Five. Flak damage to the port wing. Ignore it, hold her true. Two seconds. One.

Release.

Halo pulled off over the giant carrier. Every single bombardier had placed his drop perfectly. Vast eruptions lit up the deck, puncturing the armoured ramps, blasting flak mounts out of their sockets, toppling lifter assemblies and crane gantries. Someone – Viltry's guess was *Widowmaker* – dropped their clutch into the command spire that rose over the top deck section. A massive fireball spread out, felling the spire in ragged chunks.

Four Marauders pulled clear of the blazing carrier. *Throne of Terra*, bombs gone, had been hit by flak. In his rear-picter, Viltry saw it flip onto its back and crash into the sands.

The four remaining planes arced round in formation, turning high, and began their second pass. Monumental palls of smoke rose from the stricken carrier.

They came in with rockets now, turrets blasting again. The wing-loads loosed, and snaked off on spiralling trails of smoke. There was nothing like the same weight of flak on them now.

The rockets splashed, sheeting fire and hull fragments into the desert sky as the Marauders went over.

They began to pull away, climbing.

Something primal and catastrophic happened to the carrier. Most likely, one of the rockets had penetrated the magazine or the drive section. The carrier spasmed, shook, and then incinerated in one stupendously bright flash.

The shockwave almost knocked Halo out of the air.

They soared out, stabilising. A giant cloud of smoke, shaped like a forest mushroom, filled the sky behind them.

Theda MAB South, 09.30

THE OPERATIONS ROTUNDA was frantic with activity and chatter. Between them, the flight controllers were overseeing four major air-fights and nine intercept sorties.

'Darrow?'

Darrow was staring up at the roof dome, where sunlight was spilling in through the collar of stained glass.

'Darrow? Junior?' Eads sounded tetchy.

Darrow started. 'Sir, I'm sorry. My mind was drifting. No excuses. What were you saying, Flight?'

Eads turned his face towards the young man. There was sympathy in its sightless look. Eads held out a scrap of printout wafer. 'I thought you might like to announce this, son,' he said. 'Proof that not just bad things happen in this life.'

'Flight?'

'They told me about Heckel, son. I'm sorry that it had to be you who found him. Think about something else now. Announce that.'

Darrow looked down at the flimsy printout, then smiled. He looked up and cleared his throat. He'd heard junior flight controllers and assistants make proud announcements like this. Now it was his turn. And it beat them all.

'Attention, attention. Halo Flight confirms it has destroyed a mass carrier in the north desert. That is confirmed. Enemy carrier destroyed.'

Darrow's smile widened as the rotunda broke out in cheers and applause. The first carrier found and killed. Even Banzie was clapping and grinning.

Eads said something. Darrow leaned forward to hear him over the tide of applause.

'Say again, Flight?'

'I said,' Eads whispered, 'we might just do this. We might just win this against the odds.'

Palace Pier, 14.02

IT WAS A GREY, flat afternoon, and no one was in. Hardly a surprise, as the smoke wash from Ezraville had been fuming down the straits since daybreak.

The cafe door opened. Beqa looked up from the slates she was reading at the counter and saw Viltry in the doorway. Thirty empty tables stood between them. A Thracian waltz idled in the background.

He smiled, and took off his cap.

'Hello. You look pleased with yourself,' she said, rising. He walked between the vacant tables to reach her and slid a haversack off his shoulder.

'A big success today. A really big one. My crews are away celebrating, madly. They will be draining the vats of Theda dry tonight. And woe betide any ladies of easy virtue…'

'Have you been drinking?' Beqa asked.

'Um, a little, maybe. In dispersal. I do apologise.'

'Why are you here, Viltry? It sounds to me like you're missing parties and celebrations and–'

Viltry opened his haversack. He pulled out two paper-wrapped haunches of vere, a bag of sweet tubers, bunches of fresh greens, dessert biscuits and a bottle of sjira red.

Beqa's eyes widened. Her mouth watered. She'd never seen the like, not even before rationing.

'I was given these. Sort of a tribute. Ornoff sent a hamper down to reward the unit. The men had away with most of the drink, obviously. But I kept the rest. I thought you might know what to do with it. I mean, food-wise. As a cook.'

He looked at her. His eyes were wide and honest.

He added, 'And I couldn't think of anyone else I'd rather share it with.'

'Really?'

'Yeah. Is that all right?'

'Yes,' she said. 'I think it is.'

DAY 258

'THANKS!' JAGDEA SHOUTED, and jumped down off the transport. She strode across the mud to the hut and ducked as she went in through the door. Behind her, Imperial machines thundered up off their hardstands into the smoke-stained sky.

He was sitting on a fuel drum, gazing at his boots.

'You all right?' she asked. He looked, saw it was her, and rose with a quick salute.

'I guess,' said Marquall.

'Tough break, there. Good kill, I hear.'

'Then I got stung. A Talon, I think. Right on my tail. I didn't see it. I'm sorry, ma'am.'

'Don't be. You ejected. You came down alive. That's all that matters to me.'

'Can I fly again?' he asked.

'Yes,' she said. 'Uhm… if you want to.'

'What does that mean?'

163

'The only available bird is Nine-Nine. She's been repaired. You may not want her.'

'Nine-Nine?' Marquall asked.

'Yes.'

Marquall laughed dryly. He couldn't decide which was worse – the fact it was Espere's old bird, or the fact it was rumoured to be badly jinxed.

Then, after a moment's consideration, he realised that the worse thing of all was the prospect of not flying again.

'I'll take Nine-Nine,' he said. 'Maybe my jinx and hers will cancel each other's out.'

Theda MAB South, 16.10

THEY'D SEEN THEM from the coastal highway, and the sight had filled both of them with hope. Wings of Navy machines, in line formations, moving down over the sea towards the Thedan fields. Reinforcements, flying in from mass landing centres in the Northern Affiliation.

Jagdea and Marquall had both got to their feet in the back of the rocking transport, pointing to the sights and talking. Thunderbolt wings turning gently towards Theda North. Two packs of Vulture gunships slimming south into the Peninsula. The afternoon was clear and blue and, despite the sooty sky behind them over Ezraville, and the distant moan of raid warning sirens, they almost felt like cheering.

The mood was buzzing in the base when the transport dropped them off. Eager pre-flight activity around Umbra's hardstands, and dozens of carriers and freight-tractors hurtling to and fro.

With Marquall at her side, Jagdea jogged across the rockcrete, dodging through a slow-striding queue of Sentinel power lifters carrying cargo pods to waiting transport lifters. Blansher and Asche were standing with some of the chief fitters.

'Welcome back, killer,' Asche said to Marquall playfully. He blushed slightly.

'Good to see you in one piece, lad,' said Blansher.

'What's the commotion, Mil?' Jagdea asked.

'Deployment orders,' Blansher replied, pulling a dataslate out of his coat. She skim-read it.

'As of 18.00 hours tonight, Umbra are shipping out to a forward strip in the south,' Blansher said. 'I think they want to make some room here for the newcomers. We'll be flying short notice intercepts from a place called Lake Gocel.'

Jagdea looked at the location on the slate map. It was a vulnerable spot, well inside the enemy's air range. But it would allow them to mount rapid challenges to anything coming north or east out of the Interior Desert, tagging them long before they reached the Peninsula or cities like Theda.

'Operations says that several large sections of our ground forces are now clearing the east of the Makanites on the home run,' Blansher said. 'I think the idea is we'll be protecting them, too.'

'Not just us, surely?' said Marquall.

'No,' said Jagdea, reviewing the slate. 'The 409 are going with us, and there's a Lightning wing already down there.'

'Transports are already starting to ship our crews out,' added Asche. 'We'll be travelling light and fast.'

'We'd better get started,' said Jagdea.

MARQUALL WALKED ACROSS to the hardstand and looked Nine-Nine in the eye. The fitters had done a fine job of patching her up. A slight blemish to the plating and the paintwork. Nothing really to show the pounding she'd taken.

'You're mine now,' he said softly. 'I'll treat you right if you treat me the same.'

Dark, fierce, the Thunderbolt made no reply.

DAY 259

Over the Cicatrice, 13.43

THE SEARCH FOR another mass carrier to pound was going to have to wait.

Viltry turned his wing west and brought them lower over the rushing canyons and gorges of the great rift scar. For the first time, he felt the notorious shake and tear of the Cicatrice winds as they tried to pluck *Greta's* lift away.

Two kilometres dead ahead, a huge blizzard of fire and smoke was coming off the desert.

A section of the shattered land armada, a line of men and machines seven or eight kilometres long, had been struggling down one of the rift's wider passes when the ambush had come down on it. Three at a time, Hell Talons were dipping in and tearing down the length of the column, depositing bombs and rockets, or shooting up ground targets. Dozens of tanks and armoured transports were on fire, and in places so were patches of sand where burning debris and fuel had scattered out.

Tiny dots, individual figures, were running for cover in the jumbled stones of the valley sides. The valley air was striped vertically with rising smoke, and horizontally by tracer fire and jet exhaust plumes. The strafing machines made curious vortices and eddies in the smoke palls with their slipstreams.

At the south end of the valley, squadrons of enemy stalk tanks, bright yellow and venomous-looking, were scuttling in, overtaking the hind part of the crawling Imperial mass. Heavy-gauge lasfire flashed and seared from that section of the fight.

Viltry's Marauders weren't built to intercept air attacks like this, but he hoped their presence would at least discourage the enemy from its relentless strikes. Lacombe had called in for fighter assist, and there were apparently Thunderbolts eight minutes away.

'Head on, low level!' Viltry ordered. 'Drive them off and away from the column, deny their attack runs. If you make it to the south end without having to pull off, unload munitions on those enemy stalkers.'

'Understood, Lead.'

'Right with you.'

Viltry led by example, swinging *Greta* round at the front end of the column and bringing her in down the line in the opposite direction to the raiders' approaches. He kept as low as he dared, whipping through dense smoke streams, feeling the damned rift-winds screwing and twisting the airframe.

As soon as he had lined up and begun his run, he saw three Talons coming in ahead of him. Bolter fire from the ground chopped the air in their direction.

'Make them change their minds!' he growled, fighting with the stiff, jerking stick.

Top and nose opened fire, aiming high. The tracking tracer lines chewed ahead of the Marauder, sizzling into the trio of enemy machines that powered towards it.

Damaged perhaps, surprised certainly, the Talons banked out wildly, left and right, aborting their runs and pulling off the column. Gaize tracked the turret and kept shooting at one that was slow skipping away.

Viltry kept on track. They were almost at the south end of the pass now. The gates of the gorge were coming up fast. A flash of sun caught yellow metal: stalk tanks. The arachnoid war machines were pelting laser cannon fire into the rear echelon of the Imperial column.

'Judd!'

'Ready!'

Viltry clung on, anticipating the jerk-lift of a clean release, but what came was far more violent than that. A sudden, bone-rattling, sideways slam caused by the especially fierce crosswinds at the gorge mouth. *Greta* stumbled. Viltry caught her and held her.

The bombs had gone.

He could hear Judd cursing. The crosswinds had ruined his release. *Greta's* huge payload had dropped wide, detonating across the upper valley slopes.

Viltry brought the nose up and climbed wide, coming around again in a large circuit. Behind and below him, four of his five wingmen were flying in series to protect the pass. *Consider Yourself Dead* had broken off its run and was turning out over the valley tops, mobbed and chased by three Talons.

He heard Orsone open up in the tail. There was another bat behind them. Fire streaked past like scattering sparks. Viltry dived away, turning against the sun so a shadow rolled slowly through the cockpit.

'Lost it!' Orsone voxed.

Down onto the valley fight again, into the smoke, and against the savage wind shear that was as much an enemy as the bright-painted bats.

Viltry banked hard as two Talons went past the other way, just blurs of colour. What was keeping those damn fighters?

G for Greta shuddered. Klaxons wailed. They were flying head on into a blitz of ground to air las. The stalk tanks were ready for them this time.

'We're taking hits!' Lacombe screamed. Terrible noises: fracturing metal, shattering plastek, the blasting tone of an engine-out alarm. *Greta* slewed badly, the wind clawing at her, the controls like iron.

Something exploded in the compartment underneath him. Viltry heard Judd shrieking. A grown man, heavy as a bear, shrieking like a child.

'We're losing it!' Lacombe yelled.

Vibrations, shaking them like toys. Viltry's juddering teeth bit his own tongue-tip. He fought to hold on. The engines were making a terrible, ailing note.

He saw the gorge mouth, the yellow machines, the lasfire hosing into the sky towards him. Wing puncture. Tail damage. Naxol was shouting from the nose turret, virtually inaudible over the raging sounds.

Viltry launched his wing-mounts and saw them puff away on streaks of white smoke. Stalk tanks tore apart, flung into the air, severed machine-limbs scattering. The cockpit canopy shattered, and wind slammed into his face, full of glassite chips.

They came out through the gates of the gorge. The engines howled, two of them churning black smoke. Climb now, climb, *climb…*

Battered by the wind in his face, Viltry glanced around. Many cockpit instruments were broken, burned out. Lacombe hung in his harness. One side of his head, and the seat-rest behind it, were missing.

Fate's wheel.

The instruments told him nothing. But Viltry had flown Marauders long enough to know the feel and the sound of a dying bird.

'Eject! Eject!' he ordered, though he knew they were far too low already.

The ragged, beige wasteland came up under them rapidly. Slicks of sand, rocky outcrops, salt-pans. So huge, so fast, there didn't seem to be any sky left any more.

Viltry closed his eyes.

DAY 260

Theda Old Town, 00.05

THE TEMPLUM WAS all but empty. A few glow lamps were lit along the nave. The main light came from the stand of fluttering votive candles.

'Is there anything you need?' the hierarch asked gently.

Beqa was sitting at the end of a pew stall. She looked up at him.

'I'm just waiting,' she said.

'It's late.'

'I know. I know it is. Can I stay here?'

'Of course, daughter,' he said. 'As long as you wish. I will be in the reliquary if you require my offices.'

When he had gone, she sat where she was for a few minutes more.

Late. It was very late. She'd waited for him past the end of her shift, then waited on the seafront for another hour as the daylight faded. She knew she should have

173

sent a note to the factory chief. Her pay would be docked for missing a scheduled shift.

She had thought about going to the airfield, but realised that she didn't know which one. Besides, the trams didn't run out that far any more, and she had no money for hire-transport. And they'd never let a civilian in through the gates.

She rose and walked to the votive stand. Three small coins in the cup, three fresh candles from the box. She fixed them in place beside the dozens of others already burning, and took up a taper.

One for Gart, one for Eido.

One for–

A main door opened somewhere and slammed. There was a blast of cold air.

All the little candle flames blew out.

THE LAST OASIS
LAKE GOCEL
Imperial year 773.M41, day 261 – day 264

DAY 261

Lake Gocel FSB, 05.32

'GET UP! WAKE the hell up,' the urgent whisper said.

Vander Marquall blinked and rolled over. Van Tull was leaning over him in the violet gloom of the tent, shaking him by the shoulder.

'What? What?'

'Cover drill!' the older pilot hissed. He tapped the aluminoid bracelet around his wrist. 'Didn't your alarm wake you?'

Marquall yawned and shook his head. He glanced down at his own metal strap, which was dormant. Van Tull's had a red rune illuminated on its cover.

'I think mine's broken,' Marquall decided.

Van Tull scowled at Marquall, then took him firmly by the wrist and unclasped the bracelet. He studied it for a moment, then tossed it back to the boy.

'You'll have to get a new one from stores. Not now, later. Come on.'

Van Tull opened the flap-seal of the habitent and let light and warm air in. He was already dressed. Marquall pulled on his breeches and looked around for his boots.

'Come on!' Van Tull called. Marquall yanked on his boots, but there was no time to fasten them. He hurried outside after Van Tull.

The habitent they shared was one of almost a hundred and fifty camo-skinned shelter domes that clogged the ground under the stands of dripping kinderwood trees. Even though it was early still, the air was humid. Bright sunlight filtered down through the lacy leaf canopy and the blast nets strung between the tree trunks, like a roof over the shelters.

The pair of them ran through the mottled shadows, keeping carefully to the flakboard planking where the path crossed the frequent marshy pits and swamp pools. Scops hissed around them like vox static.

As they ran, Marquall saw dark shapes loom out of the twilight groves around them, dark shapes deliberately concealed. More shelters, camouflaged supply dumps, Hydra AA batteries where the crews waited silent and alert, the veiled shapes of warplanes under shimmer netting.

They reached the shelter and scrambled inside. The pilots of Umbra and a gang of fitters were huddled within.

'Overslept?' asked Jagdea.

'My fault, commander,' said Van Tull.

'Really?'

'Marquall's tag was defective and I was slow waking him.'

'I think that rather makes it Marquall's fault, doesn't it?' Jagdea said, looking sourly at the half-dressed boy with his unlaced boots.

'Sorry, mamzel.'

'Shut it,' Jagdea said.

Human silence draped them. Outside the blast shelter, the forest trembled with birdsong and odd animal cries.

Marquall had already decided he didn't like this place. Hot, wet, stinking of rotten fruit. His skin itched. He'd seen bugs the size of fingers crawling on the walls of his habitent and, during the night, swarms of silk-winged beetles flitting around the down-lights of the camp's stealth lamps.

The birds fell silent. Marquall heard the low whir of a nearby Hydra platform as it traversed slowly. Then the sound of jet wash, low, passing overhead. The distinctive warbling note of enemy vector-thrusters. In a moment, it was gone.

A muffled vox signal. 'Understood,' Blansher said, removing his headset. 'All clear,' he reported. Relieved conversations started up, activity resumed. The occupants of the shelter began to file out. The runes on all their bracelets had turned green.

'Begin day duties, please,' Jagdea announced. 'Briefing at 06.30, but get fed and washed quickly. Snap calls can come in at any time. Marquall?'

'Yes, commander.'

'Go to the stores right now, and get a new tag. Before you leave stores, press the test switch and make sure it works. If it doesn't, get another one. Do you understand?'

'I do, commander.'

'Funny, I thought you'd understood last night when I told you the first time.'

'I was slack, commander. It won't happen again.'

'Carry on,' she said. He turned. 'Wait!'

He sighed, and turned back. She was frowning. 'Closer. Right here. Turn round.'

She examined the skin of his shoulders where the vest exposed it, then pulled up the hem and looked at his back.

'You have a dermal condition I should know about?' she asked.

'No, mamzel.'

'Then it's scop bites. They say some people get them worse than others. The sweet-tasting ones. Are you sweet-tasting, Marquall?'

'Don't know, mamzel.'

'The scops seem to think so. See the base medicae while you're about it.'

'Yes, mamzel.'

Marquall laced up his boots properly and then trudged through the base. Now the risk of discovery had passed, the place felt more like a functioning air-base. Personnel hurried about on the boardwalks, and teams of fitters unwrapped hidden machines and resumed work on them. The smell of promethium almost overwhelmed the scent of the swamp.

The forward strike base, a makeshift encampment, lurked secretly in the kinderwood forests on the southern shore of Lake Gocel. The lake itself, immense and nearly a thousand kilometres east to west, was fed by headwaters coming down from the Makanites, and in turn emptied into the Saroja River to drain into the sea on the far-away western coast. This great system of rivers and lakes, around which flourished a gigantic swathe of rainforest, formed a margin between the Interior Desert to the south and the scrubby, temperate peninsula to the north. An enveloping green belt in which they could hide and then strike at anything that passed over.

The vast lake itself, so wide the far shore was all but a smudge, was visible between the thinning shore trees, a broad expanse of sunlit green. The entire territory was swampy and bug-thick: miasmal black ooze and pools of stagnant water interlacing the jumbled kinder groves. Beyond the lake, to the east, Marquall glimpsed the lazy flanks of the Makanites, dust-yellow in the rising sun.

Navy pioneer units and Munitorum workcrews had built a surprising amount at Gocel. Prefab hab modules,

defence batteries, bunkers and covered hangars nestled
under the trees and the ubiquitous shimmer nets. Modar
stacks and vox masts poked discreetly above the leaf
cover, or had been raised as cable-form aerials, cleated to
the trees themselves. Clearings had been cut, dozens of
them, each one levelled and decked with heavyweight
vulcanised matting: thick grey material rolled out to form
temporary hardstands. On each stand sat a warplane: the
ten Thunderbolts of Umbra Flight, the twelve of the Navy
409th 'Raptors', and the eight Lightnings from the 786th
'Spyglass' recon. Unless unshrouded for launch or landing, each matt-decked clearing was all but invisible from
the air thanks to the camo-awnings.

Bulk landers, for support crew transfers, base supply,
and fuel and munitions deliveries, used the wide, muddy
beach of the lake shore, not needing to stay on station for
more than a few minutes. There was no way a permanent
large-scale matt-deck could be concealed from the air.
Sentinel power lifters, striding through the mire, did all
the base's heavy lifting and carrying.

The FSB had a decent ring of Tarantula sentry guns
watching the forest around it, as well as two dozen Man-
ticore and Hydra anti-aircraft batteries. With the PDF
troopers needed to man all these, the thirty pilots, the fitter teams and forward operations personnel, Lake Gocel
FSB had a population of over two hundred.

'Hey, killer. Where you going?'

Marquall looked round and saw Larice Asche jogging
up behind him along the flak boarding.

'Stores,' he said.

Privately, he was in awe of Flight Lieutenant Larice
Asche. She seemed so damn tough. Jagdea was a multi-kill
vet too, but he mainly respected her because she was in
charge. Asche, an ace before the liberation of Phantine
had even finished, was the real thing, respected by all for
her sheer talent. And young, too. Blansher had a huge

tally, but he was an old guy. Larice seemed not much older than Marquall himself.

She was lean and gamine, with bony cheeks and a vicious, toothy grin. The previous afternoon, before they'd shipped out to Gocel, she'd had her famous blonde hair shaved down to a finger width. 'Jungle lice,' she'd announced, adding, 'do not want them.'

'The med-station's near stores, isn't it?' she asked him.

'I think so.'

'I'll tag along. So much for precautions.'

'What?'

She ran a hand through her brutally cropped hair. 'For this.'

'How so?'

She pulled off her jacket and showed him the multiple bites on her bare forearms.

'Scops,' he said.

'So they say.'

'Me too,' he said, dropping his flight coat off one arm and showing her his shoulder.

'Bitching,' she said.

The Munitorum station was a ring of hardened prefabs standing in the blue shadows of a massive frond-tree. They went inside, into the air-scrubbed cool. The duty attendant, his face full of ancient augmetics, looked up from his cogitator.

'I need a new tag,' Marquall said.

'I believe, pilot officer, you mean you need a new tag *please*, senior.'

'Ah... what?'

'I am Senior Lirek. You will address me civilly.'

Marquall glanced at his chronometer. 'There's a war on,' he said.

Asche sniggered.

'Indeed there is. And has civility run out? Where would the Navy be without the constant efforts of the Munitorum?'

'I have no idea,' said Marquall.

'Ah! Indeed!' Lirek said, rising to his feet and adjusting his heavy optics manually. 'You expect us to be at your beck and call, and want this and want that but–'

'Do you know who that is?' Larice hissed at the old man.

'Uh... no.'

'Larice–' Marquall began nervously.

'That's only Marquall,' Asche continued, her eyes fake-wide. 'Killer Marquall. The one who... you know...'

'No,' mumbled Lirek. 'I'm not sure I do–'

'The one who made the kill!' said Asche.

'The kill?'

'The kill. *The kill*. For Throne's sake, and you talk about respect...'

'No, well, yes,' stammered the Munitorum senior suddenly. 'I forget myself. Your device, sir?'

'It doesn't work,' said Marquall, handing his bracelet over.

'So it doesn't. A terrible oversight. Wait one moment, if you will.'

Lirek came back with a fresh tag unit. 'Here, sir. I have tested it. In the event of a cover warning, it will illuminate, and, as required, silently alert or wake you by a gentle, non-harmful electric pulse.'

Marquall signed for it. 'Thank you,' he said.

'I live to serve, sir,' Lirek said, his tortoise-head bowing.

Outside, Asche started sniggering.

'What did you do that for?'

'It got you your tag, didn't it?' she asked.

'Yeah. But you lied.'

'Have you made a kill or not?'

'Yes...'

'Then I didn't lie. What does he know?'

'You're bad, Larice Asche.'

'So they say.'

Next door to the stores, a long prefab huddled under the shimmer hoods. A tall man in early middle age, well-made and masculine, sat on the entrance steps. His arms were folded on his knees, and his head rested on his arms. His hair was matted with what looked like dry clay, forming dreadlocks. He wore the blue silk robes of an ayatani, one of the Beati's priesthood.

'Father,' said Marquall. 'Is the medicae in?'

'He's out,' answered the priest.

'Maybe we can leave him a note?' Marquall suggested to Asche.

'No, I gotta find something. These bites are killing me.'

They went into the med-block. All the surfaces were polished steel and swabbed plastek. The circulating air smelled of mint. Asche began to rifle through the drug cabinets.

'What are you doing?'

The ayatani stood behind them in the doorway.

'Helping myself,' said Asche.

'I told you the medicae was out.'

'Yeah, you did.'

'Now he's in again.'

They both looked at the tall priest. He raised a hand and shook back his sleeve to reveal a Navy-issue ident cuff. Divisio Medicae.

'I'm Ayatani Kautas… I also happen to be serving medicae at this FSB. Take your filthy hands out of my drug store.'

Asche jumped back, causing boxed packets to scatter on the grille floor.

'What's the problem?' the priest snapped.

'Uh, scop bites,' said Marquall, starting to turn to show the practitioner his blisters.

Kautas strode past, ignoring him. He picked up two tubes of salve and threw them at Marquall. The boy caught them, just.

'Twice a day!' he snarled. 'Don't come back unless you get crotch-rot.'

'Thank you, father...' Marquall began.

'Piss off, looters.'

'WHAT WAS ALL that about?' Asche said as they walked away.

'I'm not sure,' Marquall said.

'Oh, who cares?' Asche smiled at him. 'So, killer, what are you–'

They both jumped as their tags went off, zapping their wrists and flashing the red rune.

'Shit!' cried Marquall. 'Who's on? Are you on?'

'No,' said Asche, and pulled him towards the nearest shelter.

JAGDEA WAS ALREADY in her Bolt when the thrill hit her arm. On matt-decks east and west of her, Blansher and Cordiale stood by in their own machines.

Her chief fitter closed her hood and gave her the sign of the aquila.

She sat in her machine, angled seventy-five degrees towards the sky on a hydraulic fast-launch ramp. The base had three, all of them ready to answer a snap call at any time. Above, all she could see was sunlight playing through shimmer net.

Her thumb rolled over the red toggle-cover and rested on the 'rocket fire' stud.

She waited, sweat trickling down her face onto her mask.

Silence. Heat. The distant stir of the forest.

'Umbra Leader...' the vox began.

Above her bird's elevated nose cone, the shimmer nets were suddenly drawing back and daylight spilling in. She knew the order before it was given.

'...you are go for launch.'

Her thumb stabbed down.

With a terrible punch and a roar, she left the world behind.

The Cicatrice, 06.50

'YOU'RE OKAY. You're okay. Trust me.'

'What's the use, sir?' asked Matredes. 'I think he's gonna die.'

'No,' said LeGuin. 'I reckon he's just thirsty. Give him some water.'

Matredes and Emdeen looked at him, unhappy.

'We're down to the last recyc,' Emdeen said.

'I know,' said LeGuin.

'I think we should've just left him where we found him,' Matredes said.

'We're not leaving anyone,' said LeGuin.

'Damn it,' sighed Emdeen, and moved forward to dribble water from his flask into the prone man's cracked mouth.

'Greta,' he moaned. 'Greta...'

'Who's Greta?' Matredes wondered.

'His girl?' suggested Emdeen.

'What's his name?' asked LeGuin.

Emdeen reached into the man's scorched flight coat and pulled out a set of clinking Imperial tags.

'Viltry,' he said.

Over the forests, 07.00

THE FOREST CANOPY was like a vast green rug that had been rolled out over the top of boxes and furniture to form a soft, undulating mass. The three Thunderbolts skimmed as low as possible, following the contours of the tree mass, trying to keep below any ranged sensor cones. Their aftershock rocked and roiled the canopy like

an angry sea, and flocks of disturbed avians and other flying creatures regularly mobbed out into the air like bursts
of gaudy shrapnel.

Blansher and Cordiale kept their birds tucked close to
Jagdea's lead.

'Umbra,' Jagdea voxed. 'Turn zero-six-two west. Contacts presenting at nineteen kilometres and six thousand.
Wait for my order to rise.'

'Read you, Lead.'

Jagdea had a feeling something was not quite right,
and it wasn't just the markedly different terrain. They
were a good few minutes into the flight when she realised
it was her own Bolt, the parts of the nose and wings she
could see from the cockpit. She wasn't yet used to the fact
they were green. The crews at the FSB had sprayed them
with a lime-green wash to aid concealment. She was so
used to a grey shape encasing her.

Up in the cloudless blue, she caught a flash, a glint of
sunlight on metal. A second later, she resolved tiny dots
against the glare, and traces of white contrail.

'Umbra Two, Lead. I see vapour trails at three.'

'Got it, Two. The bastards are coming across above us.
Weapons live, flight. Get ready to climb like hell.'

Five specks. No, six. Small. Razors, perhaps.

'On my mark… three, two, mark!'

The three pilots opened their throttles and heaved on
their sticks, swinging the heavy Thunderbolts up and
away from the forest hood into the clear sky. Jagdea
could see the hostiles plainly now. Six Locusts in cruise
formation.

Umbra was climbing as hard as their turbofans would
allow, pressed firmly back in their seats. The bats
appeared not to have seen them yet, but that would
change very soon. Jagdea settled her hand around the
stick grip, placing her thumb carefully on the fire stud.

Intercept in ten seconds, nine, eight…

Suddenly, startled like the birds that their jets had scared out of the treetops, the bats broke, their formation exploded.

But Umbra was already committed.

'Divide and conquer,' Jagdea instructed.

She went straight up into the heart of the splitting pack, choosing a Locust that was vivid amber and striped with gold. It was already turning out, but she had fine lead time. She banked slightly and let it fly into her sights.

Squeeze.

Electric blue, the las-bursts zapped away from her nose cone. She let off three pairs of shots, and it was the second that caught the Locust squarely. Pieces of its hull flew off in a puff of smoke, and it flopped over on its back. Fire began to rush out of its underbelly, and it described a long, laboured dive down into the rainforest. Jagdea saw a flash deep beneath the thick canopy, and smoke and steam broiled up out of the trees.

Blansher's chosen target, a bright blue machine with vile yellow insignia, evaded his first blasts, and managed a fine power dive under Blansher's trajectory that Umbra Two couldn't hope to follow. Blansher swung around and started to chase a copper-coloured Locust that was fleeing south. He came up, but the Locust was extending fast. The small enemy machines had a terrific turn of speed and climb rate. Blansher cursed, broke off and rolled back into the brawl.

Cordiale was locked onto a crimson bat that was trying to shake him by diving towards the forest. Accepting the invitation, Cordiale stooped, chasing the red speck into the green bosom of the forest. Levelling out at the tree-tops, the bat began to jink and switch, and Cordiale had to stand his plane on one wingtip and then the other to stick fast. He punched off a shot, missed, corrected and fired again.

Another miss.

'Tricksy little bastard…' Cordiale muttered, wrenched back and forth by the centrifugal force of the constant turns.

Above him, Jagdea was hunting down her second scalp. She had her eyes on a yellow bat that was breaking west, but abruptly rolled out as she heard a shrill lock warning. The blue Locust Blansher had lost on his first pass was on her back. It fired twice, gleaming streamers of bolter fire, but she dodged out of line each time and finally managed to throw it by hitting her speed brakes and viffing almost to a standstill. The blue hostile ripped by under her starboard wing, realised he'd been dummied, and broke right and high. Jagdea screwed over to follow its climb.

The yellow bat had decided not to run after all, and had executed a vector turn high above, dropping in like an arrow to find a target. It had missed its chance with Jagdea, so it went for Cordiale, who was still locked in the chase at the leaf-line with the crimson Locust.

It hadn't even seen Blansher.

Umbra Two fell on it from above and behind, quad cannons alight. The Locust shuddered painfully, its hull deformed by the stresses of the multiple impacts, and then blossomed like a flower into bright, radial petals of burning, expanding gas.

At about the same moment, a thousand metres higher up, Jagdea managed to pull off the most perfect Ziegner turn, witnessed by no one, and came in true on the blue bat as it attempted one final slice-roll to port.

Her grouped shots ripped out its nose, then wrenched off a wing-section. As it began to wobble, she fired a third burst that hit the Locust directly under the cockpit mount on the port side. The entire cockpit assembly exploded. An ejector system must have fired, because she clearly saw a burning object fly straight up out of the stricken bat and then fall away like a meteor. Empty, ruined, its pilot already incinerated, the Locust folded up and rained down onto the forest as a hundred thousand burning scraps.

Two of the remaining bats had now fled south on full burn. The last live target was the crimson one that Cordiale was pursuing over the trees.

'Need assist?' Blansher voxed, rolling down.

'Negative, Two. Negative. I've got him. Tricksy little bastard.'

Flying at zero over the canopy at close on four hundred kph, Cordiale whooped as he finally got a fleeting lock tone. He opened up.

At precisely the same moment, his target's shock-wash scared a flock of pink birds out of the trees. Cordiale flew smack into them. They hit his plane like cannon shells. Plating fractured. The canopy smashed. One engine shrieked as feathered missiles clogged the intakes and buckled the whirring fans. There was a mist of blood.

'Shit!' they heard Cordiale yell.

Jagdea and Blansher were already sweeping down after him. They both witnessed the odd, pink flare of organic debris as his machine mowed into the flock. Cordiale had hit the crimson Locust, and it had promptly crashed at high speed into the trees.

But none of them cared about that now.

'Cordiale!' Jagdea screamed.

Umbra Eleven, hammered, one engine totalled, tried to correct, faltered and hit the trees.

'Cordiale! Cordiale!' Blansher could hear Jagdea yelling over the vox.

Suddenly, almost impossibly, Umbra Eleven reappeared, splashing out of the torn and thrashing greenery like a flying fish out of an ocean swell. Cordiale had managed, against the odds, to keep the nose up, and had ripped through the upper foliage of the canopy mass without striking a primary trunk.

He began to climb, pouring a trail of brown smoke out of his port engine that soon turned white.

'Umbra Eleven?'

'Still here, Lead. Bastard bloody birds.'

NINETEEN MINUTES LATER, they settled back at the FSB. Blansher and Jagdea had nurse-maided Cordiale's buckled, limping Bolt all the way home.

The camo-shrouds drew back, exposing the matt-deck hardstands like sockets in the green wilderness.

The three Thunderbolts switched to vertical vector and sank gently onto their stands. As their fans powered down, the shimmer netting folded back over them.

As soon as her stand controller gave her the hand signal for okay, Jagdea yanked out her vox and air plugs, climbed out of her cockpit and jumped down onto the vulcanised mat. She tossed her helmet to the nearest fitter and ran out of the launch area along the decking under the trees.

She reached Cordiale's pad around the same time as Blansher. Umbra Eleven, venting steam and coiling plumes of vapour, was a mess. The canopy was wrecked and the nose armour pummelled. A team of fitters was spraying retardant foam into the clogged, burning engine. The fore-part of the Thunderbolt was a mass of sticky black blood and tattered feathers.

Cordiale was climbing down. He was shaking. One bird carcass had punched through his canopy so hard it had smashed his visor and given him a black eye.

He took off his helmet, dropped it, and wiped the treacly blood from his face. Then he squinted round at Jagdea and Blansher as they came up to him.

'Mental note,' he said, wagging a finger at Jagdea. 'Avoid birds wherever possible.'

'Will do,' she smiled.

Cordiale reached around to the nose of his aircraft and peeled a pink feather out of the sticky mass plastered across it.

He held it up.

'Lucky feather, anyone?'

Lake Gocel FSB, 16.42

THE SCOPS WERE killing him. He'd signed up to fight the Archenemy of mankind, not microscopic flies. Everywhere he went, they surrounded him, unseen, filling his ears with a hiss like a tuned-out vox.

His back was sore. He'd tried not to scratch, but…

Marquall wandered down to the lake shore, wondering if the filthy things would leave him alone out in the open. It didn't seem to help.

The lake's beach was muddy and dimpled. Behind him, the dense rainforest rose like a rotting curtain. The sun was beginning to sink, turning the sky as rose-pink as Cordiale's lucky bloody feathers.

The lake was immense. It occurred to Marquall that he'd never seen a lake before. Standing water, that was a novelty. It was kind of like looking out across the Scald from the ports of a Phantine hive, except that it was so flat. So sheer. The vast green mirror had not changed colour as the sun set, but it had altered tonally. It was murky now, heavy, still.

Slip-snakes danced across its surface tension.

Marquall wondered if he should go check on his bird, but the last time he'd seen Nine-Nine, two Navy Sentinels, fitted out with paint tanks and wash guns in place of the regular lifting claws, had been half-way through spraying it green.

Marquall knelt at the shore line, and dipped his arms into the water. It was warm. He cupped his hands to wash his face.

'Don't do that, you cretin.'

Marquall looked over his shoulder. The ayatani was sitting on a promontory of rock behind him, his blue robes gathered about him.

What was his name again? Kautas, was it?

'Why shouldn't I?' Marquall asked.

'No reason. Go right ahead.'

Marquall let the water fall out of his fingers and rose, wiping his hands dry on the legs of his trousers.

'Come on. Tell me.'

'Baroxyin Biroxas,' said the priest.

'Which is?'

'A microscopic water wyrm. The lake is lousy with them. If they enter the bloodstream, say through the mouth or nose or tear ducts, they infest the brainstem, multiplying at a prodigious rate, bursting blood vessels, severing neural pathways and eventually causing such related symptoms as an inability to remember your own name, an inability to speak, an inability to regulate your own bowel movements and an inability to live.'

'Okay,' Marquall said.

'Just so you know.'

'I was trying to wash off the... the scops.'

'Lake mud.'

'Pardon me?'

Kautas ran his fingers back through his own matted locks. 'Use lake mud. In your hair. That soon sends the scops off.'

'Okay.'

Marquall paused.

'Look, I want to say... I'm really sorry.'

'About what?' the ayatani asked.

'Going into your infirmary like that. Assuming.'

Kautas shrugged.

'Well, I'm sorry.'

'Like I could actually, possibly give a shit,' the priest said, and walked away up the empty beach.

Lake Gocel FSB, 17.20

BREE JAGDEA WAS compiling reports in her habitent when the runner came to her.

'Message wafer, mamzel,' he said, holding it out.

'Commander,' she corrected, taking it from him.

She unfolded the wafer and read it. 'Anything interesting?' Blansher asked, wandering over from his own tent.

The wafer read:

To Jagdea, Commander, Phantine XX

I thought I should inform you that, at around 13.00 hours this day, Captain Guis Gettering of the Apostles was lost in action. I think it appropriate that your boy might now be allowed to name his bird just as he likes.

Sincerely,

Seekan, Wing Co.

'God-Emperor,' Jagdea sighed. 'Another one gone.'

Lake Gocel FSB, 21.12

'How DOES THAT look?' Racklae asked. He pulled off the last of the masking strips and tipped the nearest work lamp so that Marquall could see. Wisp-moths furiously circled the blue light of the lamp.

'That's nice. That's great,' Marquall said.

Along serial Nine-Nine's green flank he could now see the Phantine eagle crest, and the stencil, 'Double Eagle'.

'All right?'

'Really, God-Emperor bless you. That's just right.'

'Not going to get a smack in the mouth for it?' Racklae grinned, wiping his hands on a rag.

'As I understand it, no,' said Marquall. He patted the side of his machine. 'First flight tomorrow,' he said. He'd flown Nine-Nine already, of course, bringing it down to Gocel FSB. What Marquall meant was first combat sortie.

'We're going to get her ramp-ready, soon as we've done the last check over.'

Marquall nodded to the fitter. 'Thanks,' he said and walked off the pad, backing so he could enjoy a last look at his bird. It was framed in a little cocoon of light under the heavy shrouds. All around, night had settled on the forest: a full, deep darkness punctured only slightly by faint lights from the camp.

'Looking good, killer.'

Marquall glanced around. Larice Asche stood in the trees at the edge of the matt-pad.

'It does, doesn't it?' Marquall smiled.

She walked over to him, and produced a bottle of amasec from the map pocket of her flight baggies.

'Better baptise it, for luck.' She took a deep swig and then passed the bottle to him. Marquall drank too.

'Here's to *Double Eagle*,' Asche said. Her eyes were bright in the darkness, and there was relish in her voice. 'Things are coming pretty good for you, huh, killer? An infamous rocket-assist evasion, your first confirmed, a personalised bird… You're really getting in the game. You got the shine, Marquall. The aura that says you're gonna go far.'

'I guess,' he smiled, a little nervous. He took another swig and handed the bottle back to her. 'Maybe my luck is changing at last.'

'Oh, I know it is,' she said, and stepped up to him, her mouth against his. Her enthusiasm took him by surprise.

RACKLAE JUMPED DOWN from Nine-Nine's wing and began searching in the tool trunks for a number three rotator.

'Hey chief,' said one of his men.

Racklae looked up, nodding, and followed the man's gaze, locating the two entwined figures in the shadows of the path. He snorted a laugh.

'And the kid was so sure he wasn't going to get a smack in the mouth...'

DAY 262

The Makanites, 06.47

THE UPPER FACES of the cliffs above them lit up russet in the dawn, and long shadows streaked the dust. It was cold and the air was eerily quiet.

'What day is it?' Viltry asked.

'Two-sixty-two,' LeGuin replied.

'I've lost… three days.'

'I think you must've hit your head pretty hard. We patched you up as best we could.'

'You found me?'

LeGuin leaned back against *Line of Death's* tracks, and took a sip from his water bottle. 'Found your bird. My convoy elements had seen a bunch of trouble ahead. A gorge area. An ambush. Time we got there, it was all done. Lot of mess. We came on your plane belly down in the desert south of the gorge. You were lying in the sand about fifty metres from it.'

'I don't remember ejecting.'

'Thrown clear, maybe?'

'The rest of my crew…?'

LeGuin shrugged. 'Sorry. I'm guessing they didn't make it. Your machine was burned out. We took a look, saw a couple of bodies. I don't think we missed anything still alive.'

Viltry nodded.

'Sorry.'

'Not your fault.'

'Not yours either, I should imagine.'

You have no idea, Viltry thought to himself.

'What's your name?' he asked.

'LeGuin, Captain Robart, 8th Pardus Armoured.'

'Oskar Viltry, 21st Wing, Phantine Air.'

'Don't get many of your sort down this way,' LeGuin joked.

'You're on the home haul?'

'Oh, yes. Part of Humel's great land armada. We've been to the gates of the Trinity Hives, and now we're marching home.'

'What was it like?'

'Trinity? A mess. A bloody mess. We thought we'd roll in and take the place in a week. They had other ideas. And serious reinforcements from offworld. They slaughtered the first waves. Along the farm terraces, the commercial highway, the vapour mills. The sky was black. Fire everywhere. You've never seen anything like it.'

LeGuin wiped a sand midge off his cheek. 'So we fell back, and that turned into a retreat. Right back up through the desert, hunted all the way. I tell you this. Whatever kind of hell we found at the Trinity Gates, it was nothing compared to the hell we've been grinding through out here ever since. Heat. Low water, low fuel, low ammo, low food. Breakdowns. Sickness. Men dying of untreated wounds. Murderous terrain. Constant attacks. There were times I thought we'd never make it.'

'There's still a way to go,' Viltry said.

'I know, but we're in the mountains now. Two days, Emperor willing, and we'll be breaking flat ground on the north side.'

'Some elements have already,' Viltry said. 'Before I… before I left last time, there was news. Convoys entering the Lida Valley, and up into the Peninsula. I think some may have cut through to the west too.'

'That's good,' said LeGuin. 'That's good to hear. Throne of Earth, we're not done yet.'

'Will you go back?' Viltry asked.

'What do you mean?'

'The air operation I was part of. Serious amounts of air power, mostly Navy, brought in to keep the enemy busy and slow him down. To buy you men time to get home. But we can't hold them off indefinitely. I mean, that's the point. We're just flying a desperate holding action. There's still a war to win here.'

'Then we'll just have to win it, won't we?' said LeGuin. He got to his feet. 'Come on. Day's breaking. We should get started. Get a good lead before the real heat settles in.'

He woke his crew, who were sound asleep in the shadows of the tank. Only in the cool of the night was it possible to get some rest. He sent them off to rouse the other crews. All down the narrow pass, armour and transporters were parked and silent.

Engines began to turn over. Voices lifted into the air.

Another day in the great retreat had begun.

Lake Gocel FSB, 08.43

IN FULL FLIGHT armour, Van Tull, Del Ruth and Marquall arrived for the preliminary briefing, which Jagdea held around the camp table outside her habitent. It was a fresh, bright day, with a breeze coming in off the lake, and strong shafts of sunlight beaming down through the shimmer nets, making everything a checkerboard of light and dark. Blansher came along, and brought a pitcher of caffeine from the commissary. For some reason, Larice Asche turned up too, dressed in flight baggies and a vest top. She had a smile about her, but Jagdea didn't really give her presence much thought.

She waited to begin until 08.45 had ticked by. Right on cue, they heard the simultaneous thump of three ramp launches. The Raptors had first slot that morning, punching up into the blue.

'Order of the day is combat air patrols running on staggered overlap,' Jagdea said. 'Three Raptors, three of us, and so on, through the day, six machines aloft at any time. That means you'll probably be up again before sunset. It's going to be tiring, so keep it steady. Overnight picture is this: the enemy is still hitting the coast hard. The word from the Peninsula is bad. They hit Theda for the first time yesterday. But unless a bombing formation comes into our catchment, that's not our concern right now. Large sections of the land retreat are starting to come clear of the mountains. In the next few days, a major evac is going to gear up, getting them across to the northern coast. Recons show several of those columns coming this way, intending to cross the Saroja west of Gocel. They are being hunted.'

'Land or air?' asked Van Tull.

'Both. Mission profile is threefold. If you locate a friendly column, make it the epicentre of your patrol. Stay with it, give it what protection it needs while fuel lasts. If you sight hostiles, engage and prosecute. If you identify enemy land forces, you may also engage. You'll be carrying rockets for that purpose. Targets of opportunity, Umbra. Get out there and see what needs doing.'

'What if we find an enemy carrier?' asked Del Ruth.

'Use your head. Get a fix and get out. We'll call in Marauders. Likewise, if you find a bombing formation up there, or you're outnumbered more than two to one, get on the vox and yell for support. I expect heroism, not stupidity.'

She paused. 'Questions? No? Good, let's go.'

Jagdea and Blansher followed the three pilots to their birds. Jagdea saw how Larice Asche hung around Marquall, laughing with him. At the edge of Nine-Nine's pad, Asche kissed Marquall hard.

'Looks like Larice has made another kill,' said Blansher.

'Marquall? That's a surprise.'

'Not really. His first confirmed, some heroics. He's hot stuff right now. She always goes for that.'

'She ever go for you?' Jagdea asked.

'A gentleman is always discreet,' Blansher replied.

'Oh, what's the matter, Mil? A little miffed you never caught her eye? What is it, an age thing?'

He smiled at her tolerantly. 'If you must know, she hit on me about eighteen months ago. The Urdesh tour. That afternoon I splashed those three Talons.'

'What happened?'

'She had me in her sights, tone lock. But I broke, rolled out and got home safely.'

'She not your type?'

'She's perfectly lovely. It's her motivation that doesn't appeal.'

A hooter sounded. Marquall was ready to go. They moved in behind the blast shields.

Racklae closed the canopy and shot Marquall a grin. Clamped into his mask and helmet, Marquall nodded back. He adjusted his air-mix and settled back. Throne, how he hated ramp launches. He felt sweat trickle inside his suit. He watched the diode counter marking down. Systems on. Hypergolic intermix valves open. Operations chatter on the vox. Rocket was primed.

Buzzer. Five seconds. The shimmer nets began to crank open, revealing the soaring blue sky.

Three seconds. Thumb on the fire stud.

Two.

With a crackling, gut-shaking roar, Del Ruth fired into the air, then Van Tull. Then…

Marquall looked around in dismay. He'd pressed the stud. He was sure he had. He pressed it again. Nothing. He swore.

'Umbra Eight, status?'

'Malfunction!' he called back. 'Restart…'

Again, nothing. Red runes suddenly lit up across his instrumentation. A warning tone sounded.

'Crap!' Marquall snarled.

'Say again? Status?'

'Rocket malfunction!'

'Understood, Umbra Eight. Observe emergency procedures. Stabilise your intermix and activate suppression jets.'

'Yes, Operations.'

He hit several switches, disarming his weapons and payload, sealing his tanks and injecting a neutralising chemical flow into the rocket tanks so that the primed and volatile chemical propellants couldn't accidentally light or trigger late. It would take hours to wash the tanks out and recharge them.

'Umbra Eight made safe,' he voxed.

Only then did the fitters emerge and hurry to the plane. Inspection hatches were opened, cables hitched in to drain off fuel via the tank cocks. A power lifter and a squad of armourers moved in to unload the wing-mounts and stow them in hardened caissons.

A ladder went up at the machine's side.

Marquall popped the canopy. 'Thanks for frigging nothing, Nine-Nine,' he hissed, and hauled himself out.

When Marquall hit the matting, Racklae was beside himself.

'I'm so sorry, sir, I'm so sorry. We thought she was four-A. Not a sign of anything wrong.'

'Jinxes don't show up on your diagnostics, do they?' Marquall said bitterly. He could see Racklae was mortified.

His fitters, however, were not. Many were trying to hide their laughter. Nearby, fitters from the 409th, and other base personnel, were not even bothering to conceal their amusement. His face burning, Marquall heard mocking laughter. There was nothing more amusing, apparently, than a cocksure young pilot, on his first combat sortie, in a newly and boldly decorated bird, getting his pride punctured.

He was a laughing stock.

He strode off the pad.

'Bad luck, Marquall,' Jagdea said. 'We'll get you up again this afternoon.'

'Yes, mamzel,' he snapped, walking past her.

He went towards Asche, who was watching the farce. There was laughter in the air still. Marquall spread his hands in a wide shrug.

'What can I say? How crap is this? Maybe we can catch that breakfast together after all.'

Larice Asche stared at him contemptuously. 'Another time, killer,' she said, and marched away towards the camp.

Over the forests, 09.02

KITTING UP FAST, as if it was a snap call, Jagdea lifted her waiting Bolt off its matt on a standard vector launch, and climbed to join Del Ruth and Van Tull, who were in a holding pattern as per Operations' advice.

'Three, Six? Umbra Lead. Sorry for the delay. Marquall suffered a misfire and he's out. So you'll have to make do with me.'

'No problem, Lead,' Van Tull voxed.

'Always a pleasure, mamzel,' Del Ruth came back.

'Let's get on with the game,' Jagdea said. Serial Zero-Two felt fine, loose and finessed despite the unexpected scramble. 'Let's make our level four thousand, cruise speed, turning one-one-nine.'

'Got that, Lead.'

'Understood.'

'Umbra Three, take the point.'

'Four-A, Lead,' Van Tull voxed back.

They formed a flat V as they climbed hard, with Van Tull at the apex, Jagdea at his port eight. The air was clear and visibility generous, but it was still cold enough for them to be making vapour from wingtips and exhausts. Auspex showed nothing in the sky, except the three Raptors sixty kilometres east.

Jagdea felt uncomfortable. She hadn't expected to be flying so soon, not before midday, given the original schedule. She'd eaten a full breakfast and was still digesting. Pressure was doing nauseous things to her guts. She tweaked the air-mix and felt a little better.

They cruised for an hour, snagging a wide arc eastwards, until the thickness of the forest cover petered away and they were out across the scrublands of the sierra that marked the hinterland between rainforest and desert. The view was huge. Sundogs from the bright daylight hovered in the canopy lense. Open, coarse land slipped by underneath them, scabbed with rocks, thistle, cactus trees.

'I have a hard metal return, point two west, four kilometres,' Van Tull voxed. 'It's cold.'

'Let's check it,' Jagdea replied. They turned tight, pulling a quarter G, but it was enough for Jagdea to feel a twinge of cramp in her stomach.

'You okay, One?' Del Ruth called.

'Four-A,' Jagdea replied.

'Little late on the turn there, s'all I was wondering.'

'Too much breakfast,' Jagdea said.

They came up on the contact, and made a low pass. Straggled out over the ragged crest of a dune sea basin, two Imperial tanks and four troop carriers, silent and still. No sign of damage. Some hatches were open. Auspex showed no heat sources. No engines, no life.

'They're dead,' Van Tull voxed.

'Let's come around again,' Jagdea said.

They banked west, and came in a second time, lower now, throttles idling so they were almost gliding in. A lingering look. Jagdea saw how the wind-blown sands had begun to cover the machines. She saw what could have been a body, a lump in the dust beside one of the carriers.

The enemy hadn't done this, or rather, it hadn't done this directly. This was not the aftermath of an air strike or an ambush. This was extinction brought on by the unforgiving desert. What had they run out of? Fuel? Water? Either one would have killed them. Jagdea supposed it had been fuel first. Grinding to a halt, dry and gritty, power gone. Then heat and thirst. Had any of them tried to walk? The bodies would never be found now.

How miserable. How pointless. Had they known how close they'd come? Another sixty kilometres, and they'd have reached the forest line. She hoped they hadn't. Death was one thing. Death tormented by the knowledge that salvation was just out of reach…

The vox burbled, snapping her alert.

'Umbra, Umbra. Assist request from Raptor Flight, urgent!'

'Coordinates, please,' Jagdea replied. The squirted data flashed up on her main display. 'Received, Operations. We are inbound, nine minutes.'

They banked away and started to climb, opening their throttles.

'Punch it,' Jagdea said.

* * *

Lake Gocel FSB, 09.31

'BITES STILL BOTHERING you?'

Marquall, sitting by the lake shore, glanced up. It was the priest, Kautas. The brisk inshore wind tugged at his blue vestments.

'I was under the impression you scarcely cared,' Marquall replied.

The ayatani shrugged. 'I never asked for this. Actually, I'm not sure what it was I asked for. Not this, anyway. But it is my lot. I am reminded by the regular dispatches from my church that I have a job to do. A calling. So try me.'

'You seem very jolly this morning.'

Kautas sat down beside Marquall. 'An illusion, I assure you. I'm the very same noxious bastard as I was yesterday.'

Kautas slid a metal flask from his robe pocket and swigged. Marquall smelled liquor. The priest didn't offer any to him.

'Ah,' said Marquall.

'Ah what?'

'Nothing.'

'Sounded to me like you'd had some great epiphany, fly-boy.'

'My name is Vander Marquall. And no, it wasn't a... whatever you just said. I just realised why you were in a better mood.'

'Really?'

'Really.'

'Enlighten me, Vander Marken.'

'Marquall. If you start drinking at breakfast, father, no wonder you're happy by nine o'clock.'

Kautas chuckled and took another swig. 'Who said I started drinking at breakfast? That's the behaviour of a hopeless drunkard. Young man, I started drinking many years ago.'

Marquall shook his head. 'With respect, what are you doing here?'

'I saw you here, alone on the beach, looking pissed off, so I thought I'd come and share your gloom. I have an appetite for melancholy.'

'I meant here. Enothis. Lake Gocel.'

Kautas prised a pebble from the shoreline mud and tossed it out into the lake. He had a good arm. It went a long way, and sent a ripple out across the oily green water.

'Why did that stone land there?' Kautas asked.

'You threw it.'

'Yes but...' his voice trailed off. 'No, you're right. I threw it. It's too bloody early for clever philosophical analogies. Or too late. Whatever. I'm here because this is where I stopped. It's a matter I intend to bring up with the God-Emperor, when at last I am granted celestial audience before the Golden Throne as part of the Beati's magnificent host.'

'Good luck.'

'Luck has nothing to do with it. It's all about faith.'

'You don't seem to have much, father. You seem very... bitter.'

'Do I? How crap is that? I meant to supply spiritual reinforcement to this station. And medical assistance. Actually, I think the latter is why they sent me here. I was a medicae first, before I became an ayatani.'

Marquall looked at him. 'Take it from me, you're not excelling at either.'

'Yeah, well...' sighed Kautas. 'Stuff you too.'

They sat in silence for a long moment. Scops hissed around them. At length, Kautas cleared his throat and said, 'Go on, then. Test my worth. What's this mood about?'

Marquall smiled sourly. 'A plane. A woman.'

'Planes I don't do,' said Kautas. 'Noisy great buggers. Can't help you there. Women, more my field. Spurned? Unrequited? Inadequate?'

'Whoah, whoah... the first. Spurned. Last night she was all over me like a body bag. This morning–'

'Well, you must learn to get over it…'

'I hadn't finished.'

'Well. Uhm. Even given that, just get over it.'

'Get over it?'

Kautas nodded sagely.

'Father, you're really bad at this.'

'Am I? Shit.'

There was another long pause. Kautas helped himself to another swig.

'Okay then,' Marquall said. 'You go. Why are *you* so screwed up?'

Kautas scratched his head, then sighed. At length, he said, 'Because I wanted to be there. Right there. When she came back. And I can't, because I'm stuck here.'

'Who?' Marquall asked.

'The Beati, Vander Marquall. The Beati.'

Over the desert, 09.32

THEY CAME IN low and hard, engines really cooking. Jagdea was pleased to see that they'd shaved nearly a minute off the projected intercept time.

Raptor Flight had found a retreat convoy in the open desert, and had been watching over it when an attack had thundered in. Stalk tanks and heavier tread armour, fully powered and fuelled, coming up hard on the limping Imperial group.

The Raptors had already loosed their rocket complement, securing some decent kills. Burning armour wreckage littered the dunes.

'Good to see you, Umbra,' voxed Raptor One. 'We could do with a little more Hellstrike over here.'

'Roger that leader. Coming around,' Jagdea replied.

The Raptors, which had been doing their damnedest with cannon runs, pulled off high, leaving the air open for Umbra. The Raptors were stark, black machines. They had refused a respray on arrival at Gocel. It was a pride thing, apparently.

Below, the enemy tank squadrons were pluming across the desert, lurching over dunes, firing shot after shot from their main weapons at the scurrying Imperials.

Jagdea saw a Chimera go up, and a Hydra platform shred into flames. Blast vapour sheened the air: white smoke trails, puffs of chalky flare from barrel discharges, rising scuds of black flame-smoke from wrecks.

Sporadic tracer fire rose from the enemy AA carriers.

'Let's get lucky,' Jagdea said.

Van Tull went in first, whipping through the mosaic of smoke and vapour. Tracer shot laddered over at him, falling short. He loosed his missile load and pulled out hard at the same moment.

A blitz of flame lit up the desert floor. Two enemy tanks atomised, their warloads kicking off.

Del Ruth was right on his tail, snaking in. She flew edgy, nicking around the flares of flak. Her rockets seared out, and crippled a tank, shredding off its tracks. Instead of pulling out, she stayed low and opened up with her quad-cannons, raking a troop carrier to bits. Then she pulled out wide, whooping over the vox.

Jagdea barrel-rolled onto the approach, setting her wing-load live. She felt like heaving, but suppressed her stomach.

A tank... too close. Another, lined up. She let it slide through her scope and fired. On twists of white smoke, her rockets lit off.

She was already rising off the targets when the tank detonated.

She came up long. Right into the bats.

Lake Gocel FSB, 09.33

KAUTAS SNIFFED THOUGHTFULLY. 'Do you know what's happening on Herodor right now?' he asked.

'Herodor? Where's that?'

'Down in the Khan Group, about nine weeks from here.'

Marquall shrugged. 'No idea. More fighting?'

Kautas sighed. 'It's a trait I've often observed in the – excuse me saying this – common fighting man. He seems to have precious little idea of the big picture. Of the great scheme of things. He seems content to leave that to tacticians and nobility, and the priesthood.'

'The common fighting man tends to have a lot of things to occupy his immediate attention,' said Marquall.

Kautas smiled. 'Fair point.'

'Isn't the true calling of the Imperial warrior to serve and fight? Not to question?' asked Marquall.

'Yes. But a little curiosity never went astray. Why are you fighting?'

'To wrest Enothis back from the clutches of the Archenemy.'

'Of course. And beyond that?'

'To… to prosecute the great Crusade and liberate the Sabbat Worlds?'

'So your greater purpose is…?'

'To win.'

Kautas took a drink from his flask. This time, he offered it to Marquall. The Phantine shook his head.

'Why are the Sabbat Worlds important?' the ayatani asked.

'Well, strategically–'

'No, Marquall. What is their significance?'

'Thousands of years ago, Saint Sabbat purged these worlds of Chaos in the name of the God-Emperor. We are reclaiming what she once established for us.'

'Exactly. These worlds are Saint Sabbat's. They are blessed with her touch. My first duty, as an ayatani, is to the God-Emperor, but I am specifically a priest of Sabbat, the Beati. We ayatani come in two kinds. Those that dwell in the great templums and shrineholds, and those, like me, who are "imhava"… roving priests, sworn to follow her path through the stars and spread her teachings.'

'Okay,' said Marquall.

'This Crusade's been going on for almost twenty years. Warmaster Macaroth, if my information is correct, has pressed ahead, taking a huge gamble in directing an attack into the heart of the Archenemy's core systems. But his flanks are exposed, and the enemy has driven his forces into those weaknesses, hoping to behead the thrusting Crusade force, and leave Macaroth alone and vulnerable. We are those flanks, Marquall: Enothis, the Khan Group. It is the fighting here that will determine the overall success or failure of the Crusade. If we fail here, it doesn't matter if Macaroth achieves victory at the front line. All will be for naught. The enemy knows this. But now, according to rumours, the enemy has an even greater incentive. On Herodor, it is said, the Beati has been reborn.'

Marquall blinked. 'Is that… possible?'

Kautas pursed his lips. 'It tests even the faith of an imhava ayatani, but it seems to be the truth. Right now, Herodor, like Enothis, is under desperate assault by the hosts of Chaos. If either world falls, then the flank is ripped open and the Crusade is doomed. If Herodor falls, and the Beati dies with it, then the Imperium suffers an even greater loss.'

'And you wish you were there?' asked Marquall.

'Oh, indeed. How I wish. In his heart, every ayatani longs to be on Herodor, at Sabbat's side. But it is my luck, my lot in life, to be stuck here, pinned fast by duty and the turmoil of another combat, unable to make the final pilgrimage to her person.'

A breeze picked up, and played across the lake. The frond-trees along the shore swayed and hissed.

'That makes my own problems seem meagre,' said Marquall. 'Maybe you're better at this priestly advice-giving thing than I thought.'

Kautas shook his head. 'I'm good for two things, Vander Marquall. Drinking and being bitter. I waste every miserable day waiting for the end.'

'What end?'

'The end of this war. The end of this world. My own end. Whatever comes first to free me so that I can be with the Beati.'

Marquall got to his feet. 'Don't think that way. It smells too much of pessimism. We can still win, tell yourself that. Here, and on Herodor. The Crusade can still triumph. The Beati can still live. Even one man's sour thoughts can lend the enemy strength.'

'Besides,' he added. 'Did it not occur to you that the Beati must have wanted you to be here?'

Kautas made no reply. Marquall shrugged and headed back up the shore to the base.

'Marquall?'

He turned and looked back. The priest had risen, looking after him.

'What, father?'

'That suggests she must have wanted you to be here too.'

Over the desert, 09.35

THE SKY WAS dark with bats. Literally, terrifyingly dark. A mass bombing wave, perhaps five hundred machines, was passing over like a slow, heavy storm cloud at about ten thousand metres. Two more great swarms, equally large, were following it, ten kilometres back.

Most of it was simply moving past towards intended target zones in the Littoral, unconcerned by the minor brawl down in the desert verges. But a pack of bombers, twenty or more, had peeled off to attack the retreat column, and several dozen escort fighters had committed with them.

Jagdea heard Del Ruth and one of the Raptor pilots frantically calling in warnings.

'Mass raids! Five hundred-plus, coming in out of the desert, turning north-east, ten thousand.'

Jagdea herself was too busy pulling negative Gs to evade the fighters streaking in. Hell Razors, for the most part, but also machines of another pattern with long, dihedral wings cabaned towards the rear of the hulls, so they looked like long-necked birds. The Gs hung on her hard, and made her gut squirm.

Jagdea levelled out in time to hear Operations ordering the Imperial fliers out.

'This is Umbra Lead,' she voxed. 'Negative. I say again negative on that. Get everything up in support or that column is dead.'

As things stood, she and the other Umbra birds had less than twenty minutes left on site before fuel needs would force them to extend for home. The Raptors probably had less than ten.

The enemy fighter-bombers, all of them Hell Talons with lurid paint-schemes, were already screaming down on the beleaguered Imperial ground forces, spilling out munitions pods that lit up the desert with blankets of fuel-air explosive. Tanks, weapons carriers, trucks and men all burned. Frantic Hydra fire stitched up into the air.

She saw a black cruciform shape – one of the Raptors – hammer in under her, gunning for one of the stooping Talons. It missed, then carried on low, strafing the enemy tanks. There was no sign of Del Ruth or Van Tull, but she could hear their urgent calls – both brawling now. They were still in the game.

Jagdea did a high speed barrel-roll, and came in on a Talon that was just commencing its run. Her first las-bursts went wide, but they were enough to scare it and force it to pull out steeply, struggling with the weight of its unreleased payload. She rolled back, corrected her speed, and fired again, ripping las-shots through its aft section. The whole machine disintegrated, a dry, fire-less burst of metal parts and fuselage sections erupting with a cough of smoke. Large pieces of debris whickered backwards across her path, too fast for her to avoid collision. She heard impacts across her armour. Something spinning and black cracked off her canopy and left a star-shaped craze in the armoured glass. Something else smacked across her wing and damaged an elevator, forcing her to compensate hard with trim and rudder. Yet another something – a large piece of drive unit, she guessed – wallowed into her and bounced hard off serial Zero-Two's snout. That nearly knocked her out of the sky.

Jagdea held on and brought the Thunderbolt true. Sitting up in her harness, she could see the buckled plating of her bird's nose cone. She had several damage warning tones.

She checked her display. Lascannons off-line. Either the impact had buckled the cannon barrels themselves, or they'd severed the feeds to the ammunition battery.

She cancelled the alerts, then flipped the toggle over to quad. Hard guns it was then, the only ordnance she had left.

A Raptor went over her in the confusion, climbing hard. Right in its wake came three Razors, unloading on it relentlessly, then Van Tull, chasing the chasers.

Jagdea peeled over and hit the burners, rising fast and acute at Van Tull's four. She closed in time to see him score. Umbra Three's lascannons sparked brightly and the lead Razor blew out furiously like a dirty, smoky promethium fire. Van Tull had to make a violent bank out to avoid the falling, burning lump as it toppled back into gravity's embrace.

Jagdea stayed on, sick in her mouth from the terrible stresses. She barked off a hail of fire, but she couldn't save the Raptor. Struck from behind, it wiggled, then shook. Pieces of it fluttered off and it started to kick out black smoke. It peeled away, straight down, flames encasing it. She saw an eject. A chute in the air.

The remaining Razors had broken as soon as they'd got their kill, mainly, she supposed, to shake her off. They dropped below her, wide, turning out. She pulled a neat vertical reverse, and came back down after one of them.

It was red. She glimpsed some sort of nose art that depicted evisceration. It banked wildly, trying to evade as it plunged towards the blazing desert floor. She let it slide through her sights, left to right, then bellied round so it came back again, rolling through right to left. Tone lock.

Her thumb depressed. She felt the shudder and stammer of the autocannons, saw the streaking shells. The Razor, apparently unharmed, levelled out, then folded up, bleeding smoke, and fell out of the air.

Jagdea rolled off. She saw the chute now, the Raptor pilot, swaying down through the coiling smoke.

He burst.

He spurted apart, like vapour, like shredded meat. His chute ripped into tatters and collapsed.

One of the unknown pattern enemy machines whipped past, flank guns still firing.

Rage engulfed her. She hammered around after the long-necked killer, but the G was too much. She only just got her mask off before her breakfast ejected itself, squeezed out of her body by the turning force.

'God-Emperor… God-Emperor…' she gasped, hoarse. She started to grey out, even though she was now steady and level again. She was light-headed.

She vomited again, then pulled the mask back on, sucking in the air-mix. Her mouth tasted foul, acid. She knew she'd been flying level for too long, even before the lock alarm sounded.

There was something on her. She tried to twist out, but her arms were weak, her body feverish. She felt several solid hits.

Taking a deep breath, forcing herself together, she banked to port, and stormed through a quintet of Hell Talons that had been coming in on the column. She didn't even have time to fire.

Her attacker was evidently good. He stayed with her, maintaining an intermittent lock.

Snaking furiously, she scanned the sky and her rear picters. Where was he? Where was he?

There. Right at her six, textbook. Another of the long-necked raiders. She got a glimpse of it. Enough to see that, whatever these new machines were, they weren't vector-thrust. No nozzles. Fast, slick, but conventional.

Jagdea rose, viffed, and leap-frogged backwards, forcing the bat to slice in under her.

Then she dropped down on its tail and demonstrated how a gun-kill really worked.

The bat went up like a flare.

Jagdea pulled away, avoiding flak. Over the vox, the two remaining Raptors signalled they were done, fuel limit reached. They were pulling out.

'Three? Six? You still with me?' Jagdea called.

'Affirmative, Lead,' Van Tull replied.

A pause.

'Confirm that, Lead,' voxed Del Ruth. Her voice was brittle. 'Little busy…'

Wheeling around, Jagdea saw Del Ruth about a kilometre west and a thousand metres higher. She was dogging it out with two Razors that kept high-turning her and spoiling her attempts to break. Del Ruth's Thunderbolt was making white smoke.

Jagdea hit the throttle and chopped in right across the bats, forcing them to break instead. She reversed, inverting, seeing the killing ground swing up above her.

'I've got them,' she voxed. 'Break off and run, Aggie.'

'Yes, mamzel,' Agguila Del Ruth replied over the vox. 'Sorry.'

'Get home alive,' Jagdea ordered.

She rolled back. With Del Ruth and the Raptors gone, there was only herself and Van Tull left in the air.

Apart from the blizzard of bats.

Three minutes fuel left before critical.

Jagdea saw a Razor and swung onto it, but managed to pick up two or three more behind. She rolled and turned, managing to get a seventy degree deflection on one of them. But when she pulled the trigger, nothing came.

The violent turn was putting nine and a half Gs on her machine, so much that the electric autoloaders couldn't raise ammunition to the cannons.

In hindsight, Jagdea was glad she'd already lost her breakfast. At nine and a half, so weighty the actual guns had slowed down, she'd have choked and died a messy, stupid death.

She came out of the mashing turn, lined up on a Razor, and wounded it with gunfire.

'Time you were gone,' a voice said over the vox. It was Blansher. He torched in, with Asche, Waldon, Zemmic and Ranfre in his wake.

'Good to see you,' she called.

'You might not think so when we get home,' Blansher advised, shooting his way through a loose formation of Hell Talons. 'This is simply extrication. You and Van Tull and Del Ruth... get out now.'

'Del Ruth has already gone. We have to cover the column.'

'Get serious, Bree. Have you seen how many bats are in the air? Besides, there's not much left of it.'

Peeling out, Jagdea looked down. On the desert floor below, there was an awful lot of fire and wreckage, but only a few Imperial vehicles still moving. Despite the fighters' best efforts, the Hell Talons had bombed most of the column into the hereafter.

'Can we go?' Blansher called.

'Yeah. Yes. Umbra, disengage and quit.'

The seven Phantine Thunderbolts broke out of the sky-fight and lit up eastwards. Behind them, the crust of the desert blazed.

Lake Gocel FSB, 12.02

NOW BREE JAGDEA understood the full meaning of Milan Bansher's remark. Showered and cleaned up, she stood in the dispersal chamber of the FSB's main prefab, listening to the air coolers hum. Facing her was the base commander, Marcinon, and Wing Leader Ortho Blaguer, the Raptors' chief. Blaguer, a tight-faced, high cheek-boned man in his fifties, had air command over Jagdea in the base. His flight armour was as black as his wing's planes.

'You were ordered to pull out,' said Marcinon.

She hadn't liked him from the start. Reedy voice, gangly frame, an adam's apple that appeared larger than his nose. Augmetics down his left side. 'I was, sir. However, I appreciated the situation differently, as is the purview of a flight commander. There were lives to be saved.'

'And to be lost,' said Blaguer. Jagdea didn't like him either. Oily, groomed, aloof, the worst stereotype of Navy aviators.

'Indeed, sir,' said Jagdea.

'Gocel Operations decided that was a fight not worth the winning and called you off,' said Marcinon. 'However, five of your pilots... let me see now... Milan Blansher, Larice Asche, Katry Waldon, Orlonz Zemmic and Goran Ranfre... disobeyed Operations. They launched, committed, and fought.'

'To get me and Van Tull free,' said Jagdea.

'Because you had suggested they should. This is not good enough, Jagdea. I intend to discipline all of you, particularly you, commander. Throne, if we didn't need pilots so badly, I'd have you all off active.'

Marcinon's face had become flushed. A vein bulged in his forehead.

'Actually, I don't think you can,' a voice said.

Jagdea looked round. An ayatani priest had stepped into the room, followed by Blansher and Marquall.

'Kautas?' Blaguer sneered. 'Go away father, there's no booze here.'

Ayatani Kautas grinned at the Raptor chief. 'Don't worry, boss. I've had plenty to get me going. I've been chatting with Mister Blansher here. Fine fellow. Second-in-command of Umbra, so Mister Marquall tells me. This is Marquall. Stout fellow. He introduced me to Mister Blansher.'

Marcinon shuffled his papers and slates. 'You're drunk, father. Go away.'

'Drunk? Yes. Right… well, who'd have thought it?' Kautas smirked. 'You can't discipline Umbra Flight. In fact you can't order them around at all. Know why?'

'Oh, please, illuminate me,' said Marcinon wearily.

'You're Navy. Imperial Navy. Every last one of you. You've zero authority over the Phantine.'

'This is ridiculous,' Blaguer began, rising.

'Shut it, hair-oil,' snapped Kautas. Jagdea had to cover a snigger. 'Sit the hell down. You're Imperial Navy.'

'Yes, father,' Marcinon said, evidently ill at ease.

'Right. Navy. No authority over the Imperial Guard whatsoever.'

'None,' said Marcinon, his teeth gritted, suddenly aware of where this was going.

'Then shut up,' said Kautas. 'The Phantine fliers are Imperial Guard. An exception. An oddity. Their world is – how can I put it – just sky. So when they raise Guard fundings, most of them are airborne. They're not Navy. Not now, never will be. You have no jurisdiction.'

'Thank you for enlightening us, father,' Marcinon said. 'Commander Jagdea?'

'I think it's all been said, sir,' she replied. 'The Phantine XX are Imperial Guard. We stand here, on this world, willing and eager to fly alongside the fine aviators of the Navy, in a cooperative venture for the good of mankind. In the spirit of that cooperation, I accept your censure and offer my apologies. But please do not presume to lecture me again. It would open a can of worms, sirs, and likely involve the offices of the Lord Militant and the Commissariat. Our lives are too full and too urgent for such wasteful complications.'

She saluted and turned on her heels.

DAY 263

The Makanites, 13.33

THE PREVIOUS DAY, fate – or the beneficence of the God-Emperor of Man – had decreed them clear passage up through the cold winding passes through the mountains. Not a hint of war had touched them, not an auspex contact, not even the distant murmur of a warplane overhead. Their flasks and cans replenished with cool, brackish water from mountain rills, they had raced ahead, buoyed with a sense of sudden expectation and hope. At nightfall, where previously LeGuin had ordered a rest stop to take advantage of the lower temperatures, they had pressed on, edging on through the dark, grinding along the bottoms of gorges and rock cuts, thundering up across pebble-strewn slopes.

At some hour after midnight, the column passed over the spine of the mountains at a place called Ragnar's Cut, and began its descent into the broad foothills of the north.

Viltry rode with the *Line of Death*. He had been offered the place of a gunner killed on the road some days before. He wasn't expected to perform any tasks. He was simply a passenger.

LeGuin took a turn driving in the mid-period, to relieve the weary Emdeen. Emdeen climbed into the commander's turret seat and immediately fell asleep. In the bare-metal rocker-seat of the sponson below, Viltry found slumber harder to achieve. The noise of the Pardus tank was ferocious, and its motion far more violent than any plane, even under bad turbulence. It was a vibration, a shaking, not at all like the fluid variances of flight. Loose rocks thrown up by the treads clattered against the heavy hull and the track guards. It was hot, despite the night-chill outside, and the moist air reeked of smoke and oil and unwashed flesh. There was also nothing to see. The night was moonless, the dark enclosing. The convoy elements moved with hooded lamps. Within the tank, there was merely the red cabin light and the glow of the thick-glassed displays.

When LeGuin called out that they had at last passed over the top of the Makanite Ridge, Viltry simply had to take the tanker's word for it.

Dawn came in, grey and heavy. Emdeen resumed his driving, and LeGuin and Viltry sat in the turret with the hatches open. The air, cold and damp and filled with exhaust from the long line of trundling machines, was at least refreshing after the stuffy interior.

There was still very little to see.

The trail curled down through bare, grey foothills, snaking through a boulder-strewn landscape that seemed devoid of natural growth. Mist choked the valley beyond, stealing away any distant view. Behind them, the Makanites were towers of shadow against a bleached, starved sky.

The sun rose, but the mist refused to clear, and they bore on down into a layer of haze and poor visibility.

They passed by three Imperial troop trucks, abandoned by the side of the track, evidence of a previous column fleeing this way, and then, at about ten, overhauled the tail end of it. It was twice the size of LeGuin's contingent, and moving much more slowly.

They fell in pace with it. LeGuin moved his machine right to the head of his section of the formation, and made vox contact with the second column's leaders. From the exchanges Viltry could overhear, their new companions were travelling under the same sort of ad hoc command as LeGuin's segment. Proper lines of command through the tank and infantry forces had long since been lost. It appeared the tankers like LeGuin – due to the fact that they were now the defending escort of thousands of truck-bound troops – were calling the shots by necessity.

LeGuin seemed particularly pleased to hear that several tank crews from his own regiment were riding with the other column. He exchanged tart, joking vox conversations with a captain called Woll.

'Good to hear his voice,' LeGuin said to Viltry as he settled the vox-horn back onto its cradle. 'I'd heard rumours that *Old Strontium* had been destroyed at the Trinity Gates. The old rascal.'

Viltry understood LeGuin's delight. He too would have been happy to hear from old friends presumed dead.

Not that it was going to happen.

The mist began to thin, but the day did not lighten. They had reached sparse forest, and the limits of what seemed to be a metalled roadway. The valley of the Lida, heading down all the way to the coast.

Others had come this way before them. There were more abandoned vehicles on or by the road, many stripped of equipment. They passed a number of farm stations and agro-complexes that had been deserted by their inhabitants, possibly weeks before. The places had been comprehensively looted of all stock. Store-barns and silos were empty, habs ransacked or burned out. Livestock pens and the huge tin rotundas of poultry hatcheries were broken down and empty.

In some fields, they sighted rows of fresh graves.

The road approached the river, following its course. More ruined farms stood along its banks, homesteads and land-parcel stations, then a whole village, empty and gutted.

At noon, they came up on a line of burned-out, exploded vehicle wrecks, jumbled along kilometres of road that had been badly holed and cratered. The action was at least three days old. Tanks with dozer blades, and the few remaining Atlas tractors, had to clear some of the wrecks aside to permit progress. It had been an air-strike; Viltry could see all the signs.

After that, damage became more commonplace. The remains of other convoy elements littered further shot-up sections of highway. Unburied, blackened corpses lay in the roadside ditches. More bodies, swollen, floated face-down in the pools of a ruined roadside hydroponics system. All of the next three townships had been bombed to extinction by heavy raids rather than just looted and forsaken.

This was now an eerie, miserable landscape to drive through. Thousands of hectares of field-systems had been burned black by uncontrolled firebomb damage. Farms, villages, entire townships had been levelled. There were stretches of forest where nothing remained but blast-splintered trunks protruding from cindered earth. Craters, many filled with rainwater, punctured the landscape for kilometres. Smashed hydroponic systems leaked rivers of algae-rich soup down across the roadway from ruptured dykes. The column moved on, hissing water up into the air.

It was no longer mist that stained the sky, it was smoke residue from the days of raiding and firedust kicked up by their wheels and tracks. Down the wide, wounded valley, their scopes identified other communities shelled to death, wreathed with the grey vapour of firestorms that had blazed, unchecked, for days.

At 13.33, an alert was given. Ten kilometres north, bright flashes underlit the clouds, and they heard the crump of munitions. A few minutes later, a formation of enemy warplanes was sighted heading south at medium altitude. The machines, their payloads already dropped, ignored the straggling column, but there was no doubt they had been sighted. The contact would be called in.

The Imperial column had begun crossing a miraculously unscathed bridge over a Lidan tributary, just after 14.00, when a second alert came through.

It had started to rain, and the auspex refused to give a clean track. An air of confusion and panic rose in the convoy around them. LeGuin cleared his weapon batteries, and then got on the vox.

'Say again. Track reading. Confirm track reading for hostiles.'

Just frantic chatter.

'Come on!' LeGuin snarled into the vox. 'This is *Line of Death*! Give me a track reading! Get it together!'

Viltry opened the top hatch and craned up at the overcast sky, smelling the cold, wet air, listening. The sound of agitated voices came from all around, throbbing engines, the noise of turret motors as weapons traversed, the timpani of rain pattering off the armour.

And there, concealed behind it all, the warble of vector-thrust engines. Viltry glanced anxiously down at LeGuin.

'What?' LeGuin asked, standing up.

'Hear it?'

'Where? Wait… yes. It's ahead of us.'

'No,' said Viltry. 'That's an acoustic bounce off the valley. It's behind us.'

LeGuin instantly began spinning the Executioner's turret to face rear.

'Get us off the bridge!' he yelled at Emdeen.

'Get moving!' Viltry shouted from the hatch to the trucks all around. 'Come on! Clear the way! Get these vehicles rolling!'

Over two-thirds of the column had still to cross the bridge's ancient pilings.

Viltry heard a change in the vector note.

'Here they come!' he yelled.

Someone back down the convoy had at last got a decent track too. From the end of the long line of vehicles forward, weapon mounts began to fire at the sky. Pintle-weapons, elevated cannons, the few Hydra platforms still carrying munitions. Small-arms opened up as well, men standing up in the back of trucks to unload lasrifles into the sky. Hundreds of other Guardsmen, unarmed or too scared to make such a bold defiance, scrambled out of their transports and ran for cover in the trees and amongst the reed beds of the tributary.

The firing was intense. The convoy's elevated shooting filled the rainy sky with a blizzard of white hot or illuminated rounds. There was still no sign of the hostiles.

'They're wasting most of it...' Viltry said, noticing that LeGuin at least had not started firing.

LeGuin was about to speak.

Something went over, northwards, low and very fast. The jet wash shook them and their ears popped. A brief hint of something mauve or dark red.

Less than a second later, there was a dull, hollow thump. Rippling around itself, a large ball of flame boiled up into the sky on a neck of smoke and sparks some three hundred metres behind them.

Viltry saw the second bat, a Hell Talon. It had just sat its bomb load on the very tail end of the column, and had clearly hit something significant... a tank, an ammocarrier, maybe. A curtain of bright, almost neon-white flame rushed into the air way behind them. Small black specks, which Viltry realised were very probably large pieces of detonating vehicle, flew sideways out of the flash-wake.

The Talon kept low, switching to cannon to rake the convoy. The noise of its jets was terrifying. Crouched in what seemed like a very fragile drum of metal, Viltry experienced the psychological impact of an air attack for the first time. He virtually froze, his body refusing to respond. His teeth chattered.

No, his teeth were chattering because LeGuin had opened fire with the main weapons, the twin-linked autocannons, adding his force to the AA storm. The whole turret shook, and started to turn as it tracked. Gripping the edges of the hatch, Viltry stared at the incoming Talon. A stream of green tracer-shot from a Hydra nearly struck it. It banked slightly, almost daintily, refusing to be deterred from its long, hammering run.

Its cannons were firing. Fast blinks of light-flash flickered around the recessed weapon mounts. Whipping, concussive impacts stripped up the line of the road. A cargo-8 shuddered violently, as if men with rock-drills were working in its flatbed. Its canvas cargo hood shredded, its windows blew out and its tyres burst. Bodywork seams split and exhaled dust and smoke. A second cargo-8, just ahead of it, lurched and immediately caught fire. Viltry saw men burning like brush torches staggering out of the cab. Still running, the truck left the road, bounced down the embankment, and rolled on its side in the reed beds, hissing up a thick cloud of steam as river water hit fire.

The Talon rushed overhead. Viltry flinched as one of its shells glanced off the *Line's* fore-armour. LeGuin's shots streamed after it, but missed.

'Not enough deflection!' Viltry shouted.

'What?'

'Deflection! You're not anticipating him right!'

'Can you do better?' LeGuin asked.

'I can try,' Viltry replied.

LeGuin ordered Matredes down into the lower compartment to free an autoloader that was sticking. He himself switched seats to the commander's position and allowed Viltry to drop into the gunner's seat.

'Bear in mind this isn't a dedicated AA vehicle,' LeGuin cautioned.

'I know,' said Viltry.

'I mean, we don't have a Hydra's elevation, or targeters. I'm just trying to throw up some fire.'

'I know,' Viltry repeated. He was looking around the turret fixtures, familiarising himself with them. 'Traverse?'

'There,' said LeGuin, pointing to a two-way clutch lever. 'You know what you're doing?'

'Well, there are some differences, but it's not that different from a Marauder turret.' Viltry sat back, getting used to the prismatic sight, and test-swung the turret about. 'You were doing pretty well, by the way,' Viltry said. 'But it's a predictive thing. You're not used to airborne targets. You're thinking they're going to move like an arrow or a dart, but vector-thrust don't do that. They'll come up or to the side in a weird way.'

Emdeen had them off the bridge now. Parts of the rearward column was burning fiercely.

'More coming,' LeGuin called, one hand up to his earphones. The Hydra batteries on the road started up again. Viltry strained to see out of the limited scope.

'They're coming for the bridge. They want this column stopped right here.'

Viltry started the turret turning, and then began firing. God-Emperor, it was slow and lumbering, and almost like firing blind. The Talon went over, unharmed. Viltry began to realise why LeGuin had been struggling. The *Line of Death* had been built for savage anti-personnel action, not air cover.

He swung the turret back fast, immediately picking up a second Talon on its inward path. Viltry used the smoke plumes from burning wrecks along the road as a scale, then began firing again at the air above the bridge, the point at which he was sure the hostile would start to lift out.

Elevated as high as they would go, the *Line of Death's* twin cannons punched heavy fire at the clouds, and that stream began to swish in a horse-tail as Viltry dragged the turret around, aiming not for the Talon, but for where the Talon would be when the rounds had covered the distance. Nearly, nearly...

The Hell Talon, blue striped with bone-white, tried to viff hard at the last second, but its forward rate was too high for any kind of instant adjustment. It flew right through the *Line's* fusillade. Riddled, the airframe tore open, fragments flying off. The tank rocked as it went over. The Talon sliced across the main river on one wing-tip, then pancaked and hit the far shore. A throaty explosion followed.

Matredes, Emdeen and the other crewmen started whooping and cheering. LeGuin punched Viltry on the shoulder.

'That was mainly luck,' said Viltry.

'Another one!' the loader shouted, looking at an auspex repeater.

Viltry swung around again. It was coming in much lower. He wasn't going to get anything like as good a lead on this shot. He fired anyway, washing the turret back and forth to extend the cone, an old tail-gunner's trick.

All of it missed, but the raking fire restricted the Talon's line of attack, and it flew straight into sustained fire from a Hydra. The moment the four long-barrelled autocannons of the Hydra found the enemy machine, the targeter system took over and held the guns right on it. On powered traverse, the Hydra managed to maintain heavy hits for over one hundred and five degrees of turn. The Talon began to climb and then blew up in a ragged yellow flash, raining debris down over the river and road.

After that, no more raiders came down the valley for a while. LeGuin shook Viltry by the hand.

Viltry was breathing hard, pulse racing. For the first time since *G for Greta* had been brought down, he felt as if he had a purpose. A worth. He'd helped keep the bridge clear.

The feeling tasted a little like the confidence he'd been slowly winning back on Enothis. The reassurance of a point to life that Beqa Mayer's company had begun to coax back into him.

The crash had torn that confidence away, of course. But now he felt oddly centred. War claimed men. They died. Machines crashed. Leaders, like Viltry, felt guilt and remorse. It would ever be the way, for in the galaxy of man, there is only war.

For one tiny but valuable moment, sitting there in the Executioner's turret, surrounded by the cheering and bellowing of men he hardly knew, Viltry realised that guilt and remorse would truly be his to bear if he didn't make the effort to live. To live, to fight the foes of man, and to make his way back to find the woman who had shown kindness to a stranger.

The column began to move again. The rain grew heavier, and they pulled the hatches shut. The valley ahead was an ashen, dispirited place, and there was a great distance to go before they reached the cities, far away, where the skies were already banded with black fire-smoke.

Lake Gocel FSB, 19.12

IN THE SPACE of about thirty hours, their alarm bracelets had fired eighteen times. With jarring regularity, they were stirred from exercise, prep, sleep, meals and standby in order to rush to the shelters as enemy formations passed through their airspace. Each period of waiting in the gloom of the dug-outs did nothing to soothe already stretched nerves. There was a fight between two Navy fitters and some PDF troopers, and a face-to-face row between Ranfre and one of the Raptor pilots, which was only defused by the calm intervention of Milan Blansher.

The worst argument occurred between Jagdea and Blaguer. The FSB had lofted only three snap calls in the period, and for the rest of the time it had hidden under its camo at the first sign of an alert.

'What possible good are we doing?' she was heard shouting.

Blaguer's argument, supported by Marcinon and the leader of the Lightning wing, was that Gocel FSB was under-strength as an intercept force and should therefore pick its targets. Seven of the alerts had been triggered by mass-raid formations of bombers, three or four hundred machines strong, passing north towards the coast. Gocel's three wings would barely make a dent in such formidable numbers, and launches would betray the base's carefully concealed location. There was no doubt that a mass-raid force would spare a bomber pack to annihilate the source of the ambushers if it was discovered.

'Better to stay low, observe concealment discipline, and only respond to targets we can deal with safely,' Blaguer told her.

'But in another day or two, there'll be so many bats up there we won't be flying at all. We're supposed to be intercept, so let's damn well intercept something.'

'You're talking about a wilful and suicidal approach to the prosecution of this conflict.'

'I'm talking,' growled Jagdea, 'about fighting this war instead of sitting it out.'

LATE IN THE afternoon, the fourth sortie of the day was permitted. Coastal Operations had requested urgent data-gathering from its FSBs along the Saroja. There was a pressing need to assess the disposition of inbound retreat elements so the Munitorum could more effectively accomplish the mass land evacuation, an operation already beginning at Ezraville and Theda. Operations also hoped to locate one or more of the enemy land carriers. Given the terrible strength of the raids now being suffered, it was presumed that several mass carriers were currently established in the Northern Desert, and Operations clearly longed to be able to steer in Marauder strikes to ease the ferocity of the bombing campaign.

Word was that not a single town or city along the Littoral and the Peninsula remained untouched. Quite apart from the huge armour and troop evacuation taking place on the seacoast, a vast civilian exodus had also begun. Deprived for the most part of sea transit or Munitorum aid, the citizens of the Littoral were fleeing west towards Ingeburg and the Northern Affiliation in vast, haphazard caravans. Reports of the public panic and mayhem were filtering through. Several civilian convoys had been hit. The losses were so distressing, Jagdea couldn't bring herself to repeat what she'd read to the pilots and crews of Umbra.

Three recon Lightnings were to go up on a wide track, with a trio of Thunderbolts riding shotgun. According to dispersal rotation, this escort was due to be provided by the Raptors. Blaguer himself was slated to fly, but he clearly felt uneasy about what Jagdea might try to pull if he was absent from the FSB. Blaguer suggested that, if she was so keen to get airborne, the Phantine might take the job.

Jagdea saw through his ploy, and knew Umbra would be better served if she stayed. She declined, citing the damage her Thunderbolt had sustained on the last sortie. In truth, it had already been fully repaired by her devoted techs, but they knew what to tell Blaguer if he asked, and deliberately removed serial Zero-Two's cowling to act out a pantomime of repair work. Jagdea sent Asche in her place, with Waldon and Zemmic.

Marquall could barely hide his disappointment. With Nine-Nine fixed and cleared for flight, he was overdue a run, and should have been chosen over either Zemmic or Waldon.

After the six machines had launched, and the shimmer nets wound back into place, Jagdea went to find him. Marquall was in his habitent, playing regicide with Van Tull.

'Got a moment?' she asked.

'I've got things to do, ma'am,' Van Tull said, and made himself scarce.

'Get your flight suit on,' she said to Marquall. 'I'm moving you up to snap call standby.'

Marquall nodded, but his expression was glum. 'I should have gone on the last run. You know that.'

'Depends what you mean by "should", Vander,' she said. 'You and Larice aren't the best of friends right now. Keeping you out of each other's way is probably a good idea.'

Marquall blushed, but it was largely anger. 'She–' he began. 'I don't know what I've done.'

'You haven't known Larice long, Vander. Not like me. I know what she's like. One of the best pilots it's been my honour to fly with. But also... headstrong, proud. Full of ambition, and a compulsion to prove herself all the time. It's her temperament. To fly the best, get the best score... and be seen associating with the hottest of her male comrades. You had something there that she liked the look of. A reputation in the making. But then, that mislaunch.'

'I was a laughing stock.'

'For about ten minutes. I haven't heard it mentioned since. But Larice... Well, that was a blow to her pride. She'd made a show of picking you as the Next Big Thing, and there you were suddenly, the subject of scorn. Now you might wince and shrug it off, but Larice's pride gets in the way. She felt some of that laughter was at her expense, and maybe it was.'

'So she just cuts me? Freezes me out? Drops me as fast as she latched onto me?'

'I'm afraid that's her way,' Jagdea said.

'Great,' Marquall said.

'Larice is strong… as a pilot. As a person, she's unusually fragile. I know it's easy to say, Vander, but just move on. There's a war to wage. Another sortie or two, I'm certain you'll soon be getting back in your stride, building on the promise you've shown. It wouldn't surprise me if she became interested in you all over again.'

Marquall snorted.

'Of course, once bitten…' Jagdea smiled.

BY 19.00 HOURS, as evening began to drape across the lake, the recon flight and its escort went overdue. Last transmission had been routine, forty minutes before. No vox response. Nothing on the auspex or modar.

The pilots of Umbra gathered, pacing and chatting nervously. The mood in the camp, under the claustrophobic spread of the netting, became charged.

'I want to take a flight up. Combat air patrol. Take a look for the missing planes,' Jagdea said to Commander Marcinon.

'Request denied,' said Marcinon. 'For now, at least. Let's not get precious. They've got an hour left in their tanks.'

'Depending on how they've been flying,' said Jagdea. 'One serious air brawl, and you can halve that. I repeat my request.'

They were standing in the Operations room. Circulation fans whirred overhead and, by the light of caged glow-globes, Navy tactical officers sat before flickering, empty displays.

'Anything?' Marcinon called.

'Some activity in quadrants four and nine-two, commander,' reported the chief operator. 'Enemy movements, but way off. Nothing from our flight.'

'They can't all have been stung,' murmured Oberlitz, the chief of the Lightning wing, the 786th, giving voice to the private fear they had all been hiding. Oberlitz was a short, square-set man with thin lips that he licked as a nervous habit. Like Jagdea, he was now anxious about his crews. She had an ally of sorts against Marcinon and the chief of the Raptors.

'I formally repeat my request,' said Jagdea. 'Let me get machines up now before the situation changes and we're forced to lie low with the nets sealed.'

Marcinon looked at Blaguer. Blaguer nodded.

'Request granted,' said Marcinon.

JAGDEA RAN OUT of the Operations block. The pilots had congregated outside. 'Blansher! Marquall! We're up! Let's go!'

Their machines were already on the ramps. By the time the three pilots had suited up and checked their kit, the fitters had finished pre-flight. Jagdea, Blansher and Marquall ran up to the matt-decks and the ground crews locked them tight in their cockpits.

'Check back,' Jagdea voxed.

'Two, here. Four-A.'

'This is Eight. Ready for go.' Marquall felt his heart rate climbing. He reached out and stroked the edge of the main instrument panel. 'This time, you hear me, Nine-Nine?' he whispered. 'This time, no games. No jinx. Just Vander Marquall and *Double Eagle*.'

The last cues were chopping out from Operations over the vox. The nets began to crank back.

Buzzer. Five seconds. The last of the fitter crew ran to the cover of the blast fences. Marquall sat his thumb on the 'rocket fire' stud.

'You are go, Umbra Flight,' the vox announced.

Marquall squeezed the stud and gravity slammed him back into his seat.

Over the forests, 19.30

THEY CLIMBED INTO the dusk, their burners the brightest things in the air. The sky was violet, streaked with three-tenths clouds ten kilometres to the west. Below, the forest sprawled, almost black.

'Make your height nine thousand, cruising,' Jagdea called. 'Track is four-four-two.'

'Understood, Lead,' said Blansher.

'Received,' Marquall answered. For the first thirty seconds of the flight, he'd been watching the board, waiting for a malfunction light to flash on. Nothing. Even the engines sounded sweet.

In the east, against the darkest part of the sky, stars had begun to rise. Visibility was so good that Marquall could make out distant flashes against the undercast in the far north-west, hundreds of kilometres away, a display like sheet lightning that he knew was pattern bombing.

They flew south for fifteen minutes, then tracked gently west. After another slow twenty minutes, Marquall heard Blansher's call.

'Contact. Strong, inbound, twenty kilometres.'

He sent the signal to the other Bolts, and their auspex systems tracked the lock.

'They're under us, four thousand. Two groups,' Jagdea's voice said. 'Stay at this height, turn onto them. Operations, are you seeing this?'

'Copy, Umbra Lead, but with no more detail than you've got.'

'Closing. Weapons live. Flight, stay tight.'

Another pause. Just the mighty throb of the engines and the hiss of the air-mix.

Marquall stared down into the darkness of the forest twilight. The contacts should have been coming into visual, but it was all too black. Wisps of night cloud were forming at five thousand like banners of smoke.

'I have transponder tracks,' Blansher called. 'Clean signals. It's Waldon, and at least one of the Lightnings.'

'Umbra Nine, Umbra Nine, this is Umbra Leader highside and inbound. Do you copy?'

A squeal of static disrupted the channel, then they heard Waldon's voice. Even with the distortion, there was a note of fear in it. Fear, or pain.

'Umbra Leader, Umbra Leader, this is Nine. Say again.'

'Coming in on you, Nine. What is your situation?'

'Assistance, assistance!' another voice cut in, blotting Waldon out.

'Identify, user,' Jagdea called.

'This is Spyglass Four, Umbra. Requesting immediate assistance.'

One of the Lightnings. The pilot sounded petrified.

'Situation please,' Jagdea called again.

Both the Lightning pilot and Waldon attempted to answer at the same time, and the result was a mangle of signals.

Marquall was still peering down. He saw a glint, a faint trace of thruster flame. Then, against the blackness, several tiny little streaks of light, there and gone.

'Lead, this is Eight. Their situation is they're under attack. I see weapons fire, repeat, I see weapons fire.'

'Stoop and sting!' Jagdea called.

The three Thunderbolts banked over and went into a power dive. As they closed, the jumbled, merging auspex returns resolved. There were four machines below them. Waldon, flying close cover behind a Lightning, and two unidentifieds running after them. Waldon was sweeping his machine from side to side.

They came in. The sky lit up with gunfire traces. Marquall saw the Lightning. It had been shot up, and was trailing long streamers of hot smoke that had blurred the auspex track. Waldon was at its six.

About seven hundred and fifty metres behind them, two Locusts were closing in, weapons pumping.

Waldon's bird took several hits. Metal spalled off it in a spray that caught the last of the daylight. Marquall couldn't believe what he was seeing. Waldon was actually trying to use his better-armoured machine to shield the struggling recon plane. He had never seen anything so selfless and–

Espere. Espere had done the same for Marquall.

'Waldon?' Jagdea yelled.

'Ammo gone, Lead. Losing hydraulic pressure.'

Ammo gone. They must've been in a hell of a fight.

Blansher and Jagdea had the lead, and screamed down into the path of the bats, which both broke immediately. Blansher viffed out on a good guess and began to climb after one of the soaring Locusts.

Unusually, Jagdea misjudged, and the other bat went under her. It was tight, but Marquall managed to pull a break-turn and spill into its roll. He fired. The forks of las-shot were incredibly bright in the low light.

The Locust evaded and turned high. Marquall followed it. He was concentrating hard, but not so hard he missed the call from Jagdea.

'More contacts, closing, ultra-fast.'

Marquall tried to look everywhere at once. Where were the new ones? What angle?

The Locust tried to throw him with a chandelle, but Marquall nursed over on vector thrust. He stood Nine-Nine on its end, let the tail slip out, and turned a tumble into a swing-over.

The Locust was going for Waldon and the Lightning again.

A bright flash lit the sky and, for a second, his instrumentation sobbed with electromagnetic interference.

'Bat down,' Blansher called. He'd blown the other one out of the sky.

'Eight?' Jagdea called.

'I'm on it!' Marquall executed a barrel-roll and swept down after the Locust, which, against the dark shroud of the forest, he could see only on the auspex and by the light of its engines. He pulled in, chasing hard, saw its engine flare slide through his gunsight, corrected, and got a lock tone.

He fired. He hit something, because there was suddenly shrapnel in the air. Where was it?

'It's going high! It's going high!' he heard Waldon yell.

Marquall looked up, and saw the Locust powering up into the violet sky on a vertical track, suddenly visible as a sharp silhouette against the pale light.

It was trailing smoke. He'd hit it, at least, and driven it off.

The vox crackled. 'Umbra Lead, Umbra Lead, is that you?'

'Copy that. Larice?'

'Affirmative. We are inbound to your position, converging. Be advised: bats, bats, bats.'

Marquall heard Jagdea curse. He pulled up and round, and saw the sky above and to their south full of specks and sparkles of light.

Larice and Zemmic, running for home, with ten-plus machines on their heels.

'Eight and Two, with me!' Jagdea called. 'Four, we are crossing to intercept. Can you commit?'

'Negative, Lead. Zemmic and I are nil ammo, repeat nil ammo.'

'Understood. Burn for home. We'll deal.'

Marquall saw two hot lights flare up to his port side as Blansher and Jagdea hit the burners and blasted towards the incoming formation. He opened his own throttle and soared in after them. Zemmic and Asche, cooking at full, streaked past under him, rocking Nine-Nine with their jet wash.

The three Thunderbolts scorched into the leading edge of the Locust pack. The air went wild with dazzling streamers of crossfire. As the bats fired, it seemed like a whole constellation of flashing stars had come out.

Marquall felt the shudder of near-misses, and then a flat slap as something kissed across his port wing. He squeezed the gun-stud, then rolled hard, getting into grip position instinctively as he pulled four and a half negative.

There was a vast fire-splash to starboard, and Marquall was dazed long enough for him to almost collide with a Locust coming fast the other way. From the whoop on the vox, Blansher had evidently scored again.

The bats had broken high. Marquall gunned Nine-Nine and began a climbing turn. His auspex display was just a mass of confused green blobs. He couldn't make anything out.

Something went by him, turning higher and wider than him. He reckoned it was Jagdea. A Locust streaked down past him, guns clattering.

He rolled around and spotted Blansher powering low over the forest, chasing two bats with another pair mobbing at his heels. Marquall put his nose down and streaked after the pursuers.

'Eight! Break, break, break!' That was Jagdea.

Marquall had already heard the whining of the lock alarm. He punched over left, then rolled back right, and fluttered his speed brakes. The tone ceased. Something went over him, turning.

More throttle again, climbing now. The bats Blansher had been chasing had split, and he was alone with Locusts firing at his tail, stuck tight.

'Break, Two!' Marquall yelled. 'Break!'

'They're too tight! Riding me!'

Nose up, Blansher's machine shuddered and yawed as las-shots chewed into its tail fin.

In desperation, Blansher executed a vector brake, but up rather than down, so that the two bats whipped under him. By then, Marquall was tight on them, and he went under Blansher too. Blansher had braked too hard, and was now trying to recover airspeed before he stalled.

One bat disappeared, pulling out so suddenly, Marquall couldn't tell if it had gone high or low. He came in on the other, emptying his batteries, and then toggling to quad-cannon for a second lengthy burst.

The Locust suddenly spluttered out a gout of flame, which flared rapidly into a wide, spiralling fireball and ignited propellant. The bat's doom was so savage that Marquall had to break off to avoid the blast.

He had made his second kill.

JAGDEA BANKED OVER, lined up and ripped a Locust out of the air as it attempted to swing under her. It went over, shaking like an autumn leaf, and caught fire.

Another two streaked past her, but Blansher was on them, firing like a maniac. One blew out, becoming a cloud of sparks that sailed on, slowed, and then began to fall. The other broke south.

Something lined up on Jagdea's bird so fast that the lock tone surprised her. She took three hits that kicked the tail of her Thunderbolt high and caused a mass of alarm runes to light her display.

She fought the stick, stiff with diving speed, and kicked the rudder out to port, piling on the G. She grunted with effort, bringing the nose round.

And there was a banking Locust, moving a touch too lazily, like a gift from the God-Emperor himself.

She was set on quad already. She fired, a sustained burst, enjoying the way the shudder impaired Zero-Two's stable flight.

Mortally wounded, the Locust dipped its nose and began to dive. A long, steady curve of fire-trail marked its passage from air to ground. There was a vivid flash amongst the trees below.

'They're breaking!' Blansher voxed.

She banked wide, checking her auspex. 'Confirm that, Two.'

The remaining bats were fleeing south in a loose line.

'Pursuit?' asked Marquall.

The boy's blood was evidently up.

'Negative, Eight. Turn for home.'

THEY CRUISED BACK through what was now night, each pilot isolated in the darkness. Nine kilometres from Gocel FSB, a large area of forest was ablaze.

IN THE DARKNESS, the nets were back and the lumin barrettes were lit. Umbra One, Two and Eight followed the shine down and settled perfectly on their mats.

Lake Gocel FSB, 21.02

RACKLAE HAULED MARQUALL out of his machine. The fitters were running in for after flight. Vapour fumed the pad. Already, the shimmer netting was closing, the barrettes had been killed, and stealth lighting resumed over the base.

Marquall pulled off his helmet. The night air smelled good. Insects were screaming in the thickets and under the dark trees.

'Okay, pilot?' Racklae asked.

'About time I started a tally,' Marquall said. Racklae grinned. It wasn't done for a pilot to stripe up a single kill. But once it was more than one...

'How many should I put, sir?' Racklae asked.

'Keep it modest. I got another one, Racks.'

'Number two!' Racklae yelled, and the ground crew began jumping around and cheering. Several ran up to shake Marquall by the hand.

'There was a fire in the forest,' Marquall said, trying to make himself heard over the jubilation.

'I wouldn't know about that, sir,' Racklae said. 'You'd better go to dispersal.'

Marquall nodded, and patted Nine-Nine's flank.

'Look after her, Racks,' he said.

'Will do, sir,' said the chief.

The fitter crew gave him a series of hearty cheers as he left the matt-deck. Weighed down by his flight armour, Marquall limped down the path through the trees towards Operations.

There was a commotion there. Still wearing their flight gear, Larice Asche and Zemmic were in the process of recounting some furious dogfight to Del Ruth, Cordiale, Ranfre and Van Tull. Base crew, and some Raptor pilots gathered around, listening.

Marquall saw Blansher standing in the shadows of the awning outside Operations, talking to someone.

He went across. The cries and laughter from the gaggle of pilots was loud and vigorous.

It was Kautas standing with Blansher. Both men were smoking lho-sticks. Marquall saw how pale and drawn Blansher was. The older man smiled as he saw Marquall.

'Over here, Vander,' he called.

Blansher shook Marquall's hand. 'Thanks,' he said.

'For what?'

'I think that double stern attack might have stung me if you hadn't been chasing them down.'

'Rubbish. You got yourself out of that one.'

Blansher shrugged. 'Well done, by the way. Two, was it?'

'I wish,' said Marquall. 'One, clean and definite. I hit another, but he stayed up.'

Kautas reached into his robe pocket with his left hand, pulled out a silver stick case, and opened it, offering the contents to Marquall.

'No thanks, father,' said Marquall.

'Such a clean-living boy,' Kautas said to Blansher as he put the lho-stick case away. In his other hand, the priest held a bottle of amasec. 'How about this, then?'

Marquall took the bottle and knocked off a finger that burned in his mouth, then his throat, then his belly. He handed the bottle to Blansher.

'To your three kills, sir. What is it now?'

Blansher took a swig. 'I forget, Vander.' He passed the bottle back to the priest.

'Do we know what happened yet?' Marquall asked.

'Not entirely. What I've been told is the flight got into serious trouble on the edge of the desert. The Lightnings had picked up something important, and then there were hostiles all over them like a swarm. Forty-plus machines. From what Asche has said, it must have been a monster of a fight. One of the Lightnings was stung almost immediately. Then another of them got a kill, and was promptly killed itself. Meanwhile our three went into the brawl. Waldon splashed two and then, ammo zilch, he pulled out and started to nursemaid the remaining Lightning, which had been shot to crap and was running home. Asche and Zemmic stayed on station, and kept going until they were out, trying to buy Waldon and the Lightning some time to get clear. We're waiting for gunpict confirmation, but allegedly Zemmic bagged four, and our dear Larice got nine.'

'Nine?'

'That's what she says,' Blansher nodded.

Blansher had made three, Jagdea two. Amazing scores for one sortie. Zemmic himself put them to shame. But nine. *Nine*. That made Marquall's triumphant one seem so paltry.

'Nine?' Marquall said again.

'Seems so,' said Blansher.

'She's a foxy one,' said Kautas.

'That must be a record,' Marquall murmured.

'I've not heard anything to match it,' agreed Blansher.

The bottle came back to Marquall. He wiped the snout and took another sip.

Nearby, the crews were clapping and cheering Asche as she reached the climax of her turn-by-turn account. Knocking back a drink, she leaned over and mashed her lips into Zemmic's. There was laughter and whoops.

Zemmic. A clean four. The new hot stuff. The new one with the shine.

Marquall turned away. 'Who belonged to the fire I saw?' he asked.

Blansher looked down. 'Waldon,' he said.

WALDON HAD GUARDED the wounded Lightning back home, every step of the way. Just short of the FSB, his damaged Bolt had given up and dropped nose-down into the rainforest. No chute, according to their Lightning pilot, who had landed safely. No chute.

SOMEONE CAME OUT under the awning behind Marquall, and Blansher stiffened. Marquall turned. It was Jagdea. Oil still smeared her face. She looked grim. 'Come in,' she said.

The three of them crossed to her.

'What about the others?' Blansher asked.

'Leave them,' Jagdea said. 'They're having fun. I don't want to spoil it.'

They walked into Operations. Blansher and the priest stubbed out their sticks before entering.

Blaguer was there, leaning over a display intently with Oberlitz. The operators sat at their stations.

Commander Marcinon sat at a desk, reviewing pict slides on a back-lit writing slope.

'Kills confirmed,' Jagdea said. 'Two for me, three for Mil. One for you, Vander. Good work.'

'Thank you, mamzel.'

'Zemmic got his four. Turns out, from the picts, Asche got ten.'

Kautas whistled.

'Unheard of,' said Jagdea. 'Though by the look of the footage, the sky was so full of bats it would have been hard not to hit something.'

'Why so grim?' Blansher asked her.

'We've studied the recon data the Lightning was so desperate to bring home.'

Jagdea went over to the light table and cycled up some images into the projector. Hololithic shapes formed in the air.

'What's that?' said Kautas. 'I can't–'

'That's armour, father,' said Jagdea. 'Seen from above at high altitude. Stalk tanks mostly, but also lines of main battle tanks, troop transporters and some super-heavies.'

'It just looks like specks,' Kautas said.

Marquall stiffened. He was more used to reading aerial picts than the priest.

'Holy Throne…' he sighed.

'Summary count is nine thousand units,' Jagdea said. 'Coming in out of the deserts. These enlargements here modify for dust cover. See this? Identified as the sigil markings of the Blood Pact.'

'They're coming north,' whispered Blansher.

'Undoubtedly,' said Marcinon, coming over to join them. 'The Archenemy clearly believes its air war has been successful in hammering the Littoral. The ground forces of Chaos are now invading. I have sent word to the coast. The evacuation is being stepped up. I… I somehow doubt we will be ready in time.'

'What about us?' asked Marquall.

'Us, boy?' Marcinon asked.

'Sir, we're in the direct path of this. The enemy land forces must already be in the forests.'

'Yes. Auspex returns paint them sixty kilometres south and moving fast. Operations has ordered our immediate withdrawal. Us, and all the other FSBs in the forest region. Transports will arrive tomorrow at 08.00 hours.'

Jagdea looked at Marquall and saw his sadness. 'Time to retreat,' she said. 'It happens.'

DAY 264

Lake Gocel FSB, 06.30

THE EXTRACTION TRANSPORTS were an hour and a half away. Marquall watched the dawn come up. All through that long, humid night, the personnel of the base had moved with a single purpose, crating up equipment and spares, bagging possessions, collapsing habitents and getting them stowed, deactivating secondary detection systems. The prefabs would have to be left, and the mats and the ramps probably. Certainly the ring defences. The pilots would fly the planes out, the transports would extract the rest.

Marquall had spent the small hours of the night lugging packages around and making sure his fitters were clearing out swiftly. Racklae insisted they run a full pre-flight on Nine-Nine before they went, and told Marquall plainly that two fitters would stay on station to see him aloft.

The pathways were full of hurrying bodies under the lamps, and the huffing shapes of laden Sentinels.

251

Everyone was active and alert. No, not everyone. Several of Umbra Flight had drunk too much enjoying Larice Asche's celebration, and had to be whipped into shape by Jagdea and Blansher.

Asche herself, and Zemmic, had disappeared. Their tent-mates, Del Ruth and Cordiale, picked up their gear. Marquall volunteered to gather up Waldon's belongings, but Jagdea said she'd do that herself.

The sun was just rising. There was rain in the air, beating on the leaf canopy and the shimmer nets. It was cold.

Weary, strung out, Marquall sat down by a tree bowl, and wiped the rain off his face. He had to go to dispersal to suit up, and then to his bird in time for the pull out.

Shades hurried past him along the pathway. Fitters carrying crates. A power lifter.

He jumped as he heard a strange, crackling noise. It went on for some seconds, so odd and loud, that he failed to realise at first that his alarm bracelet was sounding.

Panic hit the base.

Marquall realised that the crackling noise was the sound of the automated Tarantula guns along the perimeter firing out into the forest.

They'd been tripped.

'Oh hell!' he yelped and leapt up. His kit was nearby, and he reached into the haversack, yanking out his service pistol and a belt of battery clips.

There was a bright flash in the trees ahead of him as something went off. Marquall could smell fyceline and burning oil. Gunfire chattered.

The enemy had arrived, far earlier than expected.

Lasfire zipped through the air, ripping apart shimmer nets and sections of the arboreal canopy. The chunter of the Tarantulas increased.

'Throne alive!' Marquall said. Klaxons were now wailing. Pistol raised, he ran across to one of the maintenance shelters and ducked inside.

Heavy gauge lasfire crisped the air outside. The flakboard shivered.

Marquall ran across the floor space of the shelter and fell over something.

'What the bloody hell...?' a voice murmured.

Marquall looked down. Asche and Zemmic, both naked, were curled up together, half-covered by a section of blast curtain.

'Marquall?' Larice narrowed her eyes, bleary and annoyed. 'There better be a bloody good reason why–'

A shelter nearby exploded loudly, raining debris out.

'Shit!' Larice Asche said, leaping up and pulling on her flight pants. She kicked Zemmic.

'Get up! Wake up!' she cried at him.

Zemmic sat up, blinking.

Asche had got her vest on now. She turned to Marquall. 'What's the situation?' she said.

'They've found us,' Marquall replied. He was hunkered in the opposite doorway, looking out, gun ready. 'I think they–'

He shut up quickly. Three figures, armoured in red, were running up towards the side of the shelter. Without thinking, Marquall leaned out and shot the first one through the head.

He dropped hard.

Shaking, Marquall realised the warrior had been wearing a snarling mask of black metal.

Blood Pact. *Blood Pact.*

Shots ripped his way, punching holes in the side of the shelter. Her boots still undone, Asche joined him by the doorway, and started shooting her own service pistol into the trees.

'Where's Zemmic?' Marquall asked.

'Running? Who cares?' Asche replied. She fired again.

Bright yellow, a stalk tank ripped into the outer clearing of the concealed base. Its underslung turrets recoiled as they spat out bursts of heavy las.

A section of the maintenance block exploded, sending shingles and pieces of spar into the sky. A kinderwood tree creaked and fell over. Stripped-away shimmer netting revealed pale slices of dawn sky. The clattering stalk tank felled more trees, and their collapse severed a series of power cables that showered white crumbs of light out in a savage flurry.

The Blood Pact warriors rushed them. Marquall and Asche, decently covered, opened fire into the charging figures and killed both of them. It took a surprising number of shots to stop the enemy shock troopers. The necessary blasts exhausted their clips.

Asche threw up noisily.

'Not so easy when it's face-to-face, eh?' Marquall asked, dragging the retching girl upright.

'It's the drink, you idiot,' she coughed, spitting.

Lasfire tore past them. The stalk tank reached one of the matt-decks.

A Commonwealth trooper with a tube launcher killed it dead. The blast tore out a section of the canopy and lifted smoke into the air clear of the forest.

CALM RETURNED FOR a while. The attack had been from an advance force. Marquall prayed no more would arrive until the final minutes of the evacuation had counted off. Just before eight, they heard the sound of Navy mass-lifters powering in across the lake. The huge transporters settled on the shoreline mud and opened their gaping maws to accept the lines of aircrew personnel, fitter teams and Sentinels. Pack after pack of machinery and material was carried on board.

About then, drawn in by the land attack, the enemy air cover reached Gocel. The base's planes were just beginning to lift off.

Razors swept overhead, dropping submunitions. One of the transporters at the lakeshore went up in a haze of flames. Blansher launched clear. So did Van Tull and Del Ruth, then Cordiale. Ortho Blaguer's rising Thunderbolt collided with a Razor on a strafing run. The blast lit the sky. Two of the fleeing Lightnings, one of them Oberlitz's, were stung hard as they attempted to climb. Oberlitz went down in the lake, the other into the trees on the far shore.

Asche pulled away. Then two of the Raptors. A Lightning. Another Raptor launched, and was blown apart. Zemmic got away. Ranfre. Then Jagdea, her Bolt struck twice by heavy passing fire.

Marquall ran to Nine-Nine. The sky was on fire. He found Racklae and the chief fitter's number two waiting for him.

'Go! Leave now!' Marquall yelled.

'Not before we see you safe, sir!' said Racklae.

'Your transport is about to leave, mister!' Marquall shouted.

Las-rounds ripped out of the trees. Racklae's number two dropped, his head fused into a misshapen blob.

'Racklae, go! Now, for Throne's sake!'

Marquall fired his pistol into the tree-line.

'Cables are disconnected, sir. You're clean!' Racklae bellowed.

'Go, Racklae! Go! Go!' yelled Marquall.

'Give that to me, for Throne's sake,' Kautas shouted, appearing from nowhere and snatching the pistol out of Marquall's hand.

'Run now, Mister Racklae,' Kautas said. Racklae turned and began to sprint for the shore. The air was full of hard rounds and las-streaks.

Kautas started to fire the pistol.

'And you, Vander Marquall,' he said.

'Father…'

'Close your bloody lid, boy.'

Marquall slammed his canopy home. He lit the engines, and kicked over the vector thrusters, ripping up through the remains of the shimmer tents into the smoke-filled air.

He managed one last, frantic look down.

Far below, amongst the trees and flames, Marquall saw a figure with its arms spread wide, as if in benediction. Ayatani Kautas, his robes tugged by Nine-Nine's down-draft, turned and ran towards the red-armoured soldiers pouring in along the pathways.

The last time Marquall saw him, Kautas was a distant shape, sinking to his knees. Bright las-shots flickered in all directions. Kautas held Marquall's pistol out before him, firing over and over again.

FATE'S WHEEL

THEDA

Imperial year 773.M41, day 264 – day 266

DAY 264

Theda MAB South, 08.30

EVEN TO SOMEONE unfamiliar with the arcane sigils of
Navy plotting symbols, it would have been obvious that
a huge fight was going on over the Littoral. Nine of the
flight controllers were now involved, Eads included. Darrow stood by and watched with mounting concern.

It had become ceaseless, day and night. They came in
on shift, and took the reins of some ongoing brawl from
a controller almost dead on his feet from fatigue. Weary
and strung out, they handed fights off to replacements at
shift rotation. The enemy attacks – mass bombing operations, lightning raids, opportunistic intercepts – were
happening all the time.

Currently, the rotunda had four points of focus. Two
controllers on the far side of the chamber were negoti-
ating interceptions on a wave of bombers over
Ezraville. Another had a fighter-on-fighter clash in
progress above the Lida Valley. A fourth had control of

a Marauder formation heading south. The nine on Darrow's half of the room were handling the big battle: close on four hundred and fifty enemy bombers, a hundred escorts and fourteen Imperial wings.

The chatter and roll of voices was incessant. Reports, plot statements, corrections, vox transmissions and updates volleyed back and forth. At their screens, the placement officers were inscribing hideously complex tactical maps, constantly adding, deleting, rewriting, reassigning.

The controllers were locked in worlds of their own, fixed on their own tracks while trying to accommodate the overall situation. Most were head-down over their cogitators, but Eads sat like an orchestra conductor, sightless gaze fixed directly ahead as his hands danced over the display. Darrow knew the commander was dog-tired. His face was pale, and he hadn't been eating or sleeping properly.

'Forty-Four, call off. Nine-One, rise to ten, bearing five-eight-five. Rimfire, make your track eleven-two. Say again, Quarry Leader. You're breaking up. Switch to channel four. Understood, contacts west of you at nine kilometres. Brass Flight, correct and descend to two thousand. Bat group under you, turning east, three kilometres. Sixteen contacts, you should have visual. Confirmed, Lancer, I show you as attacking.'

The klaxons started to ring, and the deck officer cancelled them at once. Raid warnings had been going off regularly, but no one in Operations ever quit for the bunkers. There was too much at stake. Twice, Darrow had felt the great chamber shudder as bombs quaked the Thedan ground.

His days with Eads had taught Darrow a lot. Once he'd picked up the basics, he'd been able to do more than merely stand by and run simple tasks. They'd evolved a good working pattern. Eads now expected Darrow to monitor peripheral tracks, and pass them over if they impinged on primary activity.

The displays on Darrow's substation were alive now. But he wouldn't just cut in and interrupt his chief. Darrow had developed a habit of touching Eads on the left shoulder to let him know he wanted his attention.

'Speak,' Eads said.

'Counter track, Flight. South-east, two hundred kilometres, closing. Formation of forty. Modar reads heat-wash patterns as Locusts.'

'Heading?'

'Four-one-six.'

Eads's hands drifted. 'That'll fall into catchment twelve. Run it to Scalter.'

'Yes, Flight.'

Darrow noted the details down carefully on a data-slate, took off his headset, and hurried along the busy companionway behind the controller stations to the third one down from Eads.

Major Frans Scalter had been section leader of Seeker Flight up to the moment it had been decimated in a dog-fight over Ezraville on the morning of the 257th. Scalter had lost his co-pilot and his bird had been crippled beyond hope of repair. It was a miracle Scalter had got home at all. His hands and face were still scabbed with healing cuts.

He was an experienced aviator and, in Eads's opinion, a level-headed pilot officer. With no available machine or unit to transfer to, Scalter had been drafted to Operations, to help out with the increasing pressure. Shifts were back to back, round the clock. Operations needed all the clear-thinking and experienced flight personnel it could rope in to work the stations.

Scalter was good at Operations work. His fine service record stood him in good stead. Like all of the Commonwealth fliers who had been switched to Operations duty – Darrow included – Scalter thought of it as a demotion. But it was vital work, and he took it seriously.

'Make your height five thousand, Ransack,' Scalter was saying tersely as Darrow came up to his station. 'Turn eighteen north. I repeat, north. If you pull west, you'll be over them and dead. Do as you're told.'

'Flight?'

Scalter held up a hand without looking round. 'I don't care what you can see, Ransack. I can see more. Five thousand, eighteen north. There's a block of bats under you, out of your visual, that will mince you if you commit west. Copy? Thank you. Lamplight, as you were. Clear for eight kilometres. Be advised, hostiles west sixteen.'

Scalter looked round at Darrow. 'Junior?'

Darrow held out the slate. 'Coming into your catchment. Eads wants you advised.'

'Express my thanks,' Scalter said. Darrow noticed the man's hands were shaking as he took the slate. He thought of Heckel. Should he say something?

'Anything else, junior?' Scalter asked. Like all of them, Scalter looked monstrously tired. Darrow knew why. It wasn't just the stress. All the Commonwealth pilots pulled from active duty had been spending time in the simulators when they should have been sleeping, keeping their skills honed. Darrow had certainly been doing that, and he'd seen Scalter several times in one of the rigs. The Navy had brought in new training programs, simulation routines for Thunderbolts and Marauders. They'd all been eager to try them. To experience what they were missing.

'Nothing, Flight.'

'Hang on, Darrow,' Scalter said. 'While you're here.' He turned back to his station, snapped off a few commands over the air, then scribed some details on a slate. 'Eads will need this. I was going to get my junior to run it over, but I'm damned if I know where he is.'

Darrow took the slate. 'Thanks, sir.'

That tremble in the hand. The first symptoms of a self-destructive fall? Or just fatigue?

'Off you go,' said Scalter.

Darrow turned. As he moved away, he heard Scalter bark, 'Ransack, that is not, repeat *not*, eighteen north! Correct, you blasted dunce!'

Darrow dodged back through the tide of hurrying deck juniors, aides and Navy staffers. He reached Eads.

'Come about point three-five, Orbis. Rise and climb, for Throne's sake.' A pause. Darrow waited. 'Orbis Flight, Orbis Flight,' Eads said. 'Your plot is merging with Ganymede Seven-Seven. Correct and come about. Yes, I have bats confirmed, extending at eight thousand. Take your fix on my beacon mark and turn out, climbing, point three-five. Be advised, hostiles at eight, breaking.'

Darrow placed his hand on Eads's arm.

'Harp Flight, proceed north by ten. Hostiles now at two and closing. Yes, Darrow?'

'Plot from Scalter, sir.'

'Out loud, junior.'

'Inbound, broken formation, six thousand variable, heading north-east four-two. Units from Gocel FSB. They're thirty minutes out, requesting touchdown instructions.'

'How many?'

'Estimates at twenty fighters, mixed, plus extraction transports, heavy.'

'You'll have to deal with it, Darrow. I've got a major scenario here. Send the transports to us, priority. Discover the operational status of the fighters. If any can still manage combat, we could use them. Get fuel and ammo from them.'

'Yes, Flight.'

Darrow put on his headphones and adjusted his dial. Eads was already back on the line to his formations. Darrow tried to settle his nerves.

'Gocel inbound, Gocel inbound, this is Theda Operations. Do you copy?'

A crackle. 'Operations, this is Umbra Lead, we have you clear.'

'Report your situation, Umbra Leader.'

'We've quit in a hurry, Operations. Enemy overrun. Umbra is nine, repeat nine machines. 409 Raptors are now eight, repeat eight. Spyglass 786, three, repeat three machines. We have five transports, heavy. Flying protective cover on those. Be advised, hostiles behind us, possible pursuit.'

'Time on Theda, Umbra Leader?'

'Twenty-six minutes.'

'Transports are cleared for MAB south, priority. Any of you combat ready?'

'Umbra and Raptors show willingness, Operations. We came up fuelled and loaded. Spyglass were half-tanked, so I'd advise no to them.'

'We could use you, Umbra Lead. Skirmish bearing nine-two west.'

'Copy that.'

Darrow took a deep breath. He was making control decisions now.

'Gocel inbound, let the Lightnings cover the transports home. All other elements break and rise, nine-two west.'

'Received and executing.'

Over the Littoral, 08.34

FOUR-TENTHS CLOUD AND southerly cross-wind. A pale blanket of sky streaked with grey.

Jagdea led the turn west, watching as the massive transport ships sailed away north with their Lightning escort, lost into the cloud.

'Raptor Flight, this is Umbra Lead. Blaguer is gone, Throne rest him. Operations has just called the play, as

I'm sure you heard. I'm leading now, so nuzzle up and make nice. We can argue on the ground later. Any objections?'

'Umbra Leader, this is Raptor Two. Lead us well, and we'll follow you to hell and back.'

Jagdea smiled. She'd met Blaguer's deputy a number of times during their brief stay at Lake Gocel. His name was Rapmund; a decent sort, broad-faced, quietly professional. His confident response pleased her.

'Four diamonds, I'll fly sprint,' she ordered. 'Nice and slow, no clipping. We've got enemies enough out here without killing each other.'

With a burst of throttle, she ran forward then watched her rear pict-screens as the other machines settled into formation. Four diamond shapes, each containing four Bolts. They settled in with extraordinary simplicity, Raptors and Umbra mixed. Cooperation at last. No grandstanding, no pecking order. Just air warriors, uniting without argument for a common good.

'Lead to wing, compliments to all. This is how the Imperium conquers its foes.'

Jagdea's Thunderbolt was flying ahead of the four diamonds, directly in front of the second formation, creating an asymmetrical structure. Diamond Two was at her tail, Diamond One at her four o'clock, Diamond Three at her seven, and Diamond Four seven o'clock of Diamond Three. She was flying what the Navy called *sprint*, and what the Phantine knew as *pointer*, the sharp end of a medium, ranged fighter shoal. She got the Raptor pilots to vox in their numbers and positions, marking the details on the data-slate fixed to her thigh. Then she flicked channel.

'Operations, this is Umbra Leader. Umbra and Raptor elements now under me as one flight. Do you have us?'

'On the modar, Umbra. Good and clear. Adjust heading three points and climb to eight thousand. Skirmish is four kilometres and closing.'

'Copy that.'

They flew on through a cloud bank, billowing like fog, and then came clear. The skirmish was ahead of them.

Skirmish. What an inadequate word. The voice of Operations sounded like a boy, a child.

This was war.

Hundreds of machines whirled and danced in the sky across ninety cubic kilometres of space. There were planes everywhere... some loners, some in formations, some in tight, complex patterns of combat. Most of them were hostiles, as far as Jagdea could see. A lot of bombers, a large number of gaudy Interceptors and fighters. Imperial birds flashed and mobbed amongst them, struggling. The air was full of shot and smoke. She could see at least six machines burning towards the ground.

The ground. Down through the clouds, she could see the broad expanse of the Littoral and the outskirts of Theda City. Hundreds of fire points lit it up. That was the bombers' target.

'Umbra has visual,' she voxed.

'Okay, Umbra.' Operations suddenly had a different, older voice now. 'High to your eleven, hostiles wide. Can you engage?'

Jagdea peered up into the sky, and checked her glance against the auspex track.

'I see them, Operations.' A flight of Razors, twenty-plus, storming in towards the mobbing Navy machines a thousand metres below.

'This is Umbra, we will commit.'

'The Emperor protects,' said the older voice from Operations.

'Track up and round,' Jagdea ordered. 'Full burn. Hit those bastards!'

Umbra's enlarged formation peeled upwards and accelerated, coming in head-on to the Razor flight. Some were already firing.

The Razors, surprised, fired back and started to break.

'And here we go…' Jagdea said to herself.

Light-flash bursts. Streamers of hard rounds. Puffs of smoke. Two of the Razors sawed out of line, issuing trails, dropping. A third exploded in a haze of flame. One of the Raptors, four, lost its port wing and spilled over like a falling weight.

Cordiale was hit.

A large piece of his fin blew off, and then sections of flank plating. Shots had punched through his wing.

His Bolt started to plunge away, but to Jagdea's relief, he leveled, holding the machine steady with what little trim he had left.

Jagdea arced round behind a hard-running Razor and started to dive.

'Umbra Eleven,' she yelled. 'Are you stable?'

'Just a flesh wound, mamzel,' Cordiale replied, as if merely passing the time of day. The damage to his bird was nothing like a flesh wound.

'Pull round and descend,' Jagdea ordered. 'Theda Operations, Theda Operations, we have a crippled bird inbound.'

'Copy that, Lead. Strips are open.'

Jagdea glanced to port. Two Razors had dropped low on vectors to chase Cordiale.

'Cordiale! Break!'

'Break? I can barely stay level!' Cordiale replied.

Jagdea gunned the throttle. 'Blansher? Take over. I'm following Eleven in. Umbra Flight, Two has command as of now.'

'Read that, Jagdea,' Blansher voxed.

Jagdea brought Zero-Two down in a rapid pass. Cordiale's Bolt was now spewing smoke.

She got a tone lock on one of the Razors and just grazed it with her cannon-fire. It broke away. The other bent in, intent on Cordiale's stricken craft.

Jagdea banked hard and adjusted. The Razor was slipping through her gunsight.

She lined up, with about forty degrees of deflection and hammered it. The Razor belched black smoke, rose nose-up as if to flee, and then exploded in a flurry of burning chunks.

Something as hard as a wrecking ball smashed into the left side of Jagdea's cockpit. Part of the canopy shattered, her instruments blew out, and buckled armour plating tore in, slashing across her left arm.

She screamed in pain. The Razor went past her, turning for a second strike.

Shaking, she tried to level.

'Theda Operations,' she gasped. 'Two, repeat *two* cripples coming in.'

The field lay before her.

She saw the spread of the city, the firestorms, the battered air-base.

Wind sucked and whistled through the split cabin. Smoke gushed from under the instrument display. Jagdea could see nothing through the left hand side ports of the canopy because they were painted with blood... her blood. She glanced down. She could see torn flight armour, blood, flesh. A glimpse of white bone.

Her port engine flamed out.

She dropped harder, woozing in and out of shock.

She heard an odd sound, and finally realised it was the target lock warning. She'd been locked up.

The Razor dropped towards her, its guns opening up, then it detonated like a triggered mine, fluttering scrap out in a broad circle.

'Get down safe, Bree,' Blansher called as he ripped over. 'In the name of the God-Emperor, get down safe.'

THE CRATERED STRIP-WAY came up. Jagdea fought with her thrusters, trying to correct. At the last moment, she distantly remembered her cart, and dropped it. Cordiale was already down, the crews around his smoking bird.

Jagdea passed out. Then she snapped awake, smacked by the juddering impact, and heaved on the stick.

Zero-Two slid twenty metres on its claws and came to rest.

Cordiale was first to reach her. He punched off the hood using the emergency release, and reached in to kill the screaming jets before the Bolt lifted off again.

Jagdea looked up at him. Her helmet visor was speckled with drops of blood. She wiped it, but that simply smeared it.

Using her right hand, she pulled off the helmet and threw it out.

'You're going to be okay,' Cordiale said.

It was the last thing she heard.

The Peninsula, 11.21

THE ROADS WERE blocked, as far as the eye could see. LeGuin stood on the top of the *Line's* turret and stared. It was a dismal sight. Thousands of vehicles, most of them military, nose to tail through the town, and out beyond it onto the northbound highways.

Many of the machines had turned off their engines to conserve fuel, but the air was still rich with exhaust fumes. Men milled about, and LeGuin heard more than one angry outburst.

'See anything?' Viltry asked. He was sitting on the edge of one of the top hatches.

'Nothing that's moving.'

The town was called Nivelle, a market burg on the broad flood plains of the Lida some sixty kilometres south of Ezraville. Like so many of the places they had travelled through, it had suffered bombing damage, and seemed empty of civilians.

Once the column had passed down onto the decent
hard roads along the Lida, the going had been good,
despite cratering and the constant threat of air attack.
They'd met with relief units along the route, which
brought them much needed food, medicae supplies
and fuel. It had begun to feel like they were rolling back
into civilisation after the weeks of hardship and struggle.

But the war had somehow overtaken them. The Littoral
and the Peninsula had taken a pasting. From Nivelle, the
skies of Ezraville formed one vast storm-cloud of black
smoke. Aircraft, often too high to identify, went over all
the time. They had grandstand seats for several huge air
battles over the valley: specks moving and circling, spiralling and turning, leaving brief, intricate filigrees of
contrails, darting sparks and flashes. Burning machines,
like meteors on re-entry, had fallen out of the heavens
into distant pastures.

Operating at rooftop height, Munitorum lifters and
Valkyrie carriers passed overhead regularly, zipping back
and forth along the column. Many were extracting the
more seriously wounded for treatment at the coastal
hospitals.

Munitorum directives had ordered the columns to
Ezraville where mass-barges and VTRPs were waiting to
evacuate them to the northern shores. That was the plan,
at least.

In reality, the roads had become increasingly full as the
column caught up with other convoys, or met more elements moving in from other directions. And the mass
exodus wasn't all military. They'd driven past long pro-
cessions of civilian refugees, families with children,
walking by the roadsides, pushing their abbreviated lives
on hand barrows.

Matredes rejoined them. LeGuin had sent him off
looking for any Munitorum seniors working the file.

'There's some good news,' Matredes said as he clambered up. 'We're jammed here because the evacuation is almost overwhelmed.'

'That's good news?' said LeGuin.

'According to the senior I spoke to, yes, sir. About thirty per cent more of us have made it home than they were expecting. They've been scrambling to organise more VTRPs from the northern shores to help with the demand. Lord Militant Humel didn't manage to kill quite as many of us as they'd feared.'

'Not like a lord militant not to do his job properly,' sniped LeGuin.

Viltry smiled, but he knew that it was good news in the long run. If more of the land force was making it home, then a stronger host could be regrouped for the phase of war to come. It made his efforts, and the labours of all the pilots, seem much more worthwhile.

'The other problem appears to be people,' said Matredes. 'Civilians are leaving Ezraville in droves, and refugees are pouring in from the Littoral. Whole highways are shut down with refugee traffic.'

'So we're stuck here?'

'The Munitorum are advising any units with decent fuel and fair running to divert east. Evacuation centres are being established at several of the coast towns along from Ezraville to ease the pressure there. It means cross country, that way–' Matredes pointed. 'Then we should hit some decent roads.' He pulled a scrap of paper out of his pocket. 'I wrote down the names: Fetona, St Chryze, Langersville. I can find them on the chart.'

LeGuin shrugged. 'We've got fuel and traction. What do we think?'

'Better than sitting here,' Matredes ventured.

'What's another few kilometres?' said Emdeen.

'East suits me,' Viltry said.

'Let's do it,' said LeGuin.

It took them another hour to spread the word and recruit about forty machines to come with them. LeGuin made sure they were all in decent repair. He didn't want stragglers. The damaged, the struggling, they could stay with the main tide of traffic.

After that, once he'd voxed numbers and details into Munitorum despatch and got an all-clear, it took another two hours to manoeuvre out of the line. It was hard work, like a stalemated round of regicide, with nowhere to back up or turn. Arguments flared. LeGuin and Viltry had to jump down and break up a brawl between the crew of a Gerzon regiment halftrack and the men from a 44th Light Chimera that had accidentally rammed it.

Finally, the commander of a Pardus Conqueror, *The Stuff of Legend*, managed to find a turning space in the gateway of a canning plant, and lanced the pressure by creating a new exit route with his dozer blade. He leveled a line of stone privies and yards behind a terrace of habs, then churned forward through a blighted orchard and a series of fenced-off market gardens, boisterously cheered on by the onlookers.

Vehicles began to edge out and follow him. Roaring smoke, the *Line of Death* was the sixth vehicle clear. They clattered across the ruin of the market gardens and out onto pastureland, where they rolled up and waited as the others trickled out and joined them. Nine Pardus tanks, eleven from the Gerzon Heavy, six from the 2nd Balchinor Tracked Company, three Hydra platforms, and sixteen assorted troop carriers and half-tracks laden with Guardsmen. By common consent, LeGuin had command. This was due in part to the fact it had been his idea, but also because the *Line* had earned itself a reputation by bringing down the bat on the previous afternoon.

LeGuin gave the command, and they rolled out, kicking up mud as they crossed the pasture onto uncultivated land.

It was a rough ride. Viltry sat in the turret and clung on.

But they were moving at last.

Theda MAB South, 14.02

'HANDING OFF,' SAID EADS.

'Thank you, Flight,' said his shift replacement. 'I have control.'

As the replacement controller took position, Darrow helped Eads remove, clean and stow his augmetic links. Both of them were light-headed, frazzled. The demands of their work had not slackened one bit for the duration of their shift.

'Good luck,' Eads said to the new flight, but the man was already too busy coming to terms with the pandemonium in his catchment to respond.

Darrow waited while Eads spoke quietly to the deck officer, then escorted him up out of the hubbub of the rotunda. Eads had his cane, but he held Darrow's arm and allowed the younger man to lead him. He was exhausted.

They went up into the atrium.

'I can see you all the way back to your quarters, sir,' Darrow said.

'No need, Enric. A little walk, a little solitude, that might do me good. You should get to your own bed. Deck says we're needed again at midnight.'

'Yes, sir.'

'Darrow?'

'Yes, sir?'

'This is off the record, you understand?'

'Yes, Flight.'

'When you get back to your billet, pack your things. Pack them now, so you can travel light and fast.'

Darrow frowned. 'Why, sir?'

'Banzie reckons we're all going to be pulled out. It's not official yet, but he's sure that's the Navy thinking. Another four or five days, and Theda will be unviable as a field.'

'God-Emperor...' Darrow breathed.

'They're winning, son. No matter how hard we fight, this sky pretty much belongs to them. The Navy's going to pull its wings out, general evac. Move them to safer fields.'

'Where, sir?'

'Maybe Zophos, the Midwinters. Possibly St Hagen. Apparently, Tacticus is evaluating.'

Darrow felt hollow. He looked away. The echoing atrium was empty apart from other Operations personnel plodding out from their shift.

'Are we–' he began. 'Are we going to lose this?' he asked.

'No,' said Eads. 'Retreat is a hard thing to deal with, but you'll be a better warrior, Enric, if you realise that sometimes that's the only way to win. Throne, if retreat equalled defeat, then we might as well have run for the hills the moment the land armada was turned back from the gates of Trinity.'

'Sir.'

'I know it hurts, Darrow. It wounds a man's pride. But you have to see it all.' There was no irony in Eads's voice. 'Retreat, regroup, gather our strengths, try again. That's what we're doing. That's why we've fought so hard to get the land forces home. So they can turn and fight again, renewed. Go read some history slates, Darrow. Wars have been won that way. And many others have been lost by men too proud to acknowledge the sense of a tactical withdrawal.'

Darrow nodded.

'Darrow?'

'I nodded, sir. My apologies.'

'Get some sleep. I'll see you at midnight.'

Darrow saluted. Eads moved away across the marble floor, his cane twitching. 'Call that a salute?' he said over his shoulder.

DARROW WANDERED OUTSIDE. The air was murky and stank of fyceline. A few Operations personnel from the last shift loitered around under the portico, smoking and chatting, or just lounging on the damp steps in aching relief.

He saw Scalter nearby, smoking a lho-stick. Even from a distance, Darrow could see how much Scalter's hands were shaking. He had just decided to go and confront the man, when he realised something.

He drew his own hands from his pockets and looked at them. They were shaking too.

'Need something?' asked Scalter, noticing him.

'No, sir. I'm fine.'

'Something wrong with your hands?'

'No.' Darrow joined him. 'Actually, just the shakes.'

'Tell me about it. We all get that. Tension and fatigue.'

'Yes, sir.'

Scalter offered Darrow his pack.

'No thanks, sir.'

'Heading for the simulators?' Scalter asked. 'I've seen you there.'

'I might. You?'

Scalter nodded his head at the airfield before them. 'What do you think?' he asked.

Darow looked out across the MAB. Parts of the field were shredded with craters and bulldozed heaps of debris. Along the east fence, the wrecks of bombed out and crashed planes had been piled up, simply to clear usable space. Smoke twisted up from recent hits. Navy craft were landing in flocks, some pouring vapour. Crews rushed out onto the field. In the hardstands, the Apostles were warming up, munitions trains clattering clear. Darrow heard the brutal, buzzing pulse of primers starting engines.

Beyond the field, the towers of Theda itself rose in crumpled majesty. Columns of smoke writhed from the city, darkening the sky. Fires blazed. There were gaps in the city skyline where familiar buildings had been destroyed. Raid sirens were wailing.

'I think I'll head for the simulators,' Darrow said.

DAY 265

Western District Theda, 10.02

THE INTAKE OF wounded had filled the infirmaries of Theda
to bursting. Jagdea had been transferred right across the
city to a hab clinic in the Western Districts, a four storey
pile of rotting brick that had been, over the years, a sani-
torium, a refuge, and a scholam for wayward youths. The
building was in poor repair. The air reeked of disinfectant
and mildew.

Blansher found her at the end of a long, grim gallery,
gazing out of the windows onto a street where files of civilians were waiting in the rain for travel permits.

She looked pale and thin. Her left arm was bound up in
a heavy sling. Blansher noticed that under her dressing
gown, she still wore the trousers of her flight suit.

'Hey, Mil,' she said.

'Bree. How's the arm?'

'Okay. Another day or two, they reckon.'

'We miss you. The wing all send their best.'

'Keeping them in line, I hope?'

'They wouldn't dare mess with me.'

She grinned. 'Want a seat?' she said, getting up out of her bathchair.

'I'm fine,' he said.

'Sit down, Mil. You look fit to drop. I've been sitting all day.'

Shrugging, he sat down in the old, wheeled invalid chair. He settled back, elbows out.

'So… how are these for speed?' he asked.

She leaned against the wall by the window and gestured down the long, lino-floored hall with her good hand. 'Try it out. Not much reheat, but if you really push it you can achieve lift by the time you reach the dispensary.'

Using his hands, he milled the big handwheels back and forth.

'How's it been?' she asked.

'We've been up once. A nasty tangle over St Chryze. Aggie stung one, and so did I.'

'All safe?'

'A hard round went through Zemmic's side-pane and snapped his chain of lucky charms, so he's really low. But yes. All safe.'

'Cordiale?'

'Fixed up, and fit for the next sortie.'

'How's my baby Zero-Two?'

'A mess, Bree. But she'll live. They're working on her now, but she'll have to be shipped by carrier t–'

Blansher stopped. 'Damn,' he said. 'And there I was going to break it to you gently.'

'Shipped out?' asked Jagdea. 'Since when?'

'Since 06.00 hours this morning. Navy directive. Apparently, Ornoff's decided it's time to quit the coast.'

'Where to?'

'For us, Lucerna MAB in the Midwinters. That's need-to-know, obviously.'

'Of course.'

'The mass land evac is now well underway. Theda's almost empty, the population fleeing. We're giving ground. From the islands we can keep our bases out of strike range of the enemy for a while, and keep them off the evac fleets. Throne alive, Bree, you've never seen so many mass-barges!'

'I like islands,' said Jagdea thoughtfully. 'They remind me of home.'

'We're flying the Bolts out at 09.00 on the 268th, three days from now, situation permitting. Your bird will be packed off this afternoon on one of the freight barges.'

'Don't you bloody leave me here!' Jagdea said.

'Of course not, Bree. I'll arrange a transport to collect you, maybe around 08.30 that morning. The Navy will be scooping off personnel using Valkyries and Oneros. You'll be with us by noon.'

'I'd better be,' Jagdea warned. 'I don't want to die here in this dump.'

'Oh, trust me,' said Blansher. He was still rolling to and fro in the bath chair, playing like a child. 'When have I ever let you down?'

'Never,' she replied.

'You see?'

'What about Espere?' she asked.

'Already gone north, medicae evac. I checked. He's in a care unit in Enothopolis as we speak.'

Blansher got up out of the chair, and rolled it around for her to sit again. 'I should go,' he said. 'We're due up at 11.00 hours and my ride is waiting.'

'Good flying,' she said.

'Take care of yourself.' Blansher paused. 'Well, well, looks like you've got another visitor.'

Jagdea looked around. Wing Leader Seekan, splendid in his white suede coat, was coming down the hallway.

'Friends in high places,' Blansher said.

He walked away, giving Seekan a salute as he passed him. Seekan returned it respectfully, and then walked on to join Jagdea under the stained, aged window. She remained standing.

'Leader.'

'Commander. How are you?'

'Alive. I didn't expect to see you here.'

Seekan shrugged.

'Have a seat,' Jagdea suggested, nodding her head towards the bath chair.

'I'm fine, commander. I… I came for two reasons.'

'Did you now?'

'The first is as a matter of courtesy. From one flight leader to another. Major Ludo Ramia of the Apostles was lost in action last night.'

'I'm sorry to hear that, leader.'

Seekan cleared his throat, awkward. 'I intend to offer his place to Flight Lieutenant Larice Asche. Her record, especially in recent days, has been remarkable. Ten kills in one sortie.'

'Ten indeed.'

'I wanted to ask your permission, commander.'

'My permission?'

'Before I ask her.'

Jagdea limped over to the bath chair and sat down in it. She felt dazed, hurt, as if something precious had been stolen from her.

'Larice is one of my…' She stopped and corrected. 'Larice Asche is my best pilot. I will miss her. But I know the form. The Apostles ask, you don't refuse. I'm flattered you even ran it past me at all. Larice will be overjoyed. It's an honour. Of course she'll accept. The first Phantine aviator to make the Apostle grade.'

'The first female…' Seekan said.

'Not a distinction we ever make on Phantine, sir.'

'The Navy is rather old fashioned, mamzel,' he smiled. 'So, I have your permission?'

Jagdea shook her head and chuckled. 'It's as if you're asking me for her hand in marriage.'

'I am, in a way. Till death parts us.'

Jagdea looked up at him. 'Make her a hero. A legend. That's all she wants, Seekan. That's all I want for her.'

'I will,' he said. 'Thank you.'

'What's the second reason?' she asked.

'Pardon me?'

'You said you'd come here for two reasons. You've robbed away my best wingman. I dread to think what the other cause is.'

'I merely wanted to enquire after your health. I was concerned when I heard the news.'

'I thought you Apostles didn't care about injury or death?'

'We just don't care about each other,' he said. He looked round for a moment. 'I must be getting along. May the Emperor protect you, commander.'

She nodded.

Only when he was out of sight down the length of the long hallway, did she notice the long stemmed bloom, its petals a rich Imperial purple, that he had left on the window's sill.

Langersville, 15.16

FROM THE HILLS above the foreshore, it looked as if parts of the coastline were breaking off and drifting out to sea.

LeGuin's convoy had reached the headland, and was now crawling down into the seaport, just one small part of the teeming forces seeking evacuation.

Threatening skies drifted above them, and a brisk sea breeze washed them. Schools of Valkyries burned off fields on the lower slopes, heading out to sea. Viltry could see Oneros prepping for take-off.

At the docks, VTRPs, pontoons and mass-barges slugged away from the shore. The mass-barges were enormous cargo ships, belching smoke from their stacks, their open bellies laden with armour and carriers. As they plied out into the deeper waters, others, riding light and empty, were piloted in to the dock quays.

The VTRPs – Vertical Thrust Raft Platforms – were colossal. Each one was an armoured rectangle five hectares square, suspended over the water by monumental vector engines at the corners and edges. As they slid up to the quays and dropped their metal ramps, squadrons of armour rolled onto them. The noise of their thrusters filled the bay.

Marshals directed the boarding armour to their stands, lining them up. An entire regiment-strength could be swallowed onto one raft.

Humming like monsters, laden VTRPs gusted out into the open sea.

'There's our ride,' said LeGuin.

Viltry nodded. 'Theda. How far, do you think?'

LeGuin consulted his chart slate.

'About three hundred kilometres east. Why?'

'Time I got going,' Viltry said.

LeGuin frowned. 'We'll miss you, Osk.'

'You too. It's been quite an experience.'

Viltry shook LeGuin by the hand.

As Viltry got down off the tank, Matredes hugged him, and Emdeen slapped his arm.

'Good luck!' Viltry shouted as the *Line of Death* began to roll forward.

'And to you!' yelled back LeGuin.

'The Emperor protects!'

LeGuin said something, but the racing engines blotted it out.

Viltry stood on the hillside for a while as the slow column threaded past him and LeGuin's tank was out of sight.

Then he ran down the grassy bank towards the coastal highway, and began to flag down the Munitorum transports speeding east.

Theda MAB South, 16.10

As SOON AS his skids settled on the hardstand, Marquall killed the fans and let the ground take the fourteen tonnes of serial Nine-Nine 'Double Eagle'. He sat for a moment, canopy still locked, his head resting back against the seat and his eyes closed. They'd just run their third sortie of the day, a snap call up and into a bomber pack. Brief, bitter fighting had followed. Marquall had nearly been stung twice, on both occasions, by fighters he hadn't seen.

Racklae knocked on the window and Marquall opened his eyes. The fitter mimed opening the lid and Marquall nodded, pulling off his breather and goggles.

The canopy lifted and cool, fumy air blew in across Marquall's face. It let in the roar and whine of the field too.

'Everything all right, sir?' Racklae asked.

'Four-A,' Marquall replied as he was helped clear, and had his suit leads unplugged. 'I need her turned around quick. We could go up again before evening.'

'Understood, sir.'

'I think the port lascannon needs cleaning or refitting. I was getting an odd fire-pattern.'

'I'll see to it, sir.'

'Any chance of rockets?'

Racklae shook his head. 'Between you and me, sir, munitions are getting pretty low. We're okay for hard rounds, but all the rack weapons are going to the Marauders.'

Marquall left the fitters to their work and walked out of the revetment shelter. At the mouth of the hardstand next door, Van Tull was stripping off his jacket and gloves.

'Nice one,' Marquall said. 'I saw you sting that Tormentor.'

'Thanks,' said Van Tull. 'I thought the bastard was going
to get past me for a moment. Any luck yourself?'

Marquall shook his head.

'I thought I saw you on a Razor.'

'Yeah, but it slipped out and I lost it.'

'There's always the next time,' said Van Tull.

Zemmic wandered up to join them. His lucky charms
jingled about him on a new chain. 'What's that about?' he
asked, gesturing down the line of hardstands.

A large staff limousine was approaching, pulling to a
halt. The driver, a Navy cadet, got out, went around to the
other side, and opened the rear door, saluting. A figure got
out.

'That's the Apostles' chief, isn't it?' asked Van Tull.

'Seekan,' said Marquall.

'What the hell does he want?' said Zemmic.

They watched as Seekan crossed to number three stand.
Asche was just dismounting from her Bolt. She saluted
Seekan, and was saluted back. Seekan began to speak and
handed her something. A data-slate, it looked like. Even
from a distance, they could see the strange, startled look
on Asche's face.

'What's going on?' Zemmic said.

Seekan and Asche exchanged salutes again, then Seekan
shook her by the hand and returned to his car. As it carried
him away off the field enclosure, Asche remained where
she was, studying the slate.

Marquall, Zemmic and Van Tull jogged down to her.
Blansher had appeared, and Ranfre, Cordiale and Del Ruth
were also approaching.

'Larice?' Zemmic said.

She glanced up. There was such a strange look in her
eyes. 'Hey, Zem.'

'What's going on? What did Seekan want?'

'Me,' she said.

'What?'

She looked at them all for a moment. 'You're not going to believe this…' she began.

DAY 266

Theda seafront, 06.02

VILTRY'S FIRST GLIMPSE of Theda City was from the cab of a Munitorum fleet transport in the small hours of the night. It was the first time he'd set eyes on it since the morning of the 259th when he'd taken *G for Greta* aloft on her final flight. Things had changed.

In the dark, from many kilometres distant, the city itself was invisible because of black-out regulations, but the shape of it was defined against the sky by the ruddy glow of firestorms throbbing in its heart.

'Holy Throne...' he'd breathed.

'Told you it was bad,' the driver had said.

Viltry had made the journey along the coast overnight, begging lifts from a series of transport drivers. There was activity all along the seaboard, part of the frenzy of evacuation. Munitorum transit fleets were pouring out of Theda and the surrounding towns, laden with materiel and personnel for the evacuation ports, and then streaming back to depot empty for another run. The vast night sky was a maelstrom of tracer, flak bursts and burner trails. At Madenta, trying to find a ride to hitch amongst the chaos of traffic in the town centre, Viltry had been about three hundred metres from a bomb strike that had destroyed a templum, nine habs and a machine shop. Everywhere he went, he could hear the drone of the Archenemy's engines in the sky.

THE CARGO-10 DROVE into Theda's outskirts at first light, stopping at several Munitorum or Commissariat checkpoints. The streets were deserted, apart from other military traffic. The slowly rising light, pale and thin, revealed a dusty, smoky world. They passed row after row of bombed-places, fire control teams fought with blazing tenements and hab stacks gripped by swirling infernos. Some streets were closed. Medicae shuttles, bells clattering, rushed by.

Just after five thirty, they reached the Old Town area. Like everywhere else, it had taken a pasting. Viltry had a clawing, sick feeling in his chest.

'I'm due at the assembly yards in Danzerplatz,' the driver said. 'Any good to you?'

'No. Uh, just let me out here.'

The driver pulled the truck up at a street corner.

'Thanks,' Viltry said, climbing down.

'No problem. Good luck rejoining your unit. Shoot some of them bastards down for me.'

'I'll try.'

The driver nodded, and then pulled the truck away.

Viltry began to walk. His tattered flight jacket still had the emergency compass sewn into the cuff, so he followed the needle and went north. It took him about thirty minutes to skirt up through the ruins of the Old Town to the seafront.

The air was cooler here, fresher, despite the cloying smoke that wrapped the whole city. He heard the strange yet familiar sound of rushing breakers, the clatter of pebbles. He smelled the sea. How ironic that a smell, so recently new, so alien to his background, should now be so evocative.

He wandered down the broad seafront road for a while, trying to get his bearings. He was sure he should be able to see the piers. Finally, almost by accident, he realised he was standing by the familiar entrance arch. There was the chalkboard, propped up against the ironwork gate. 'Palace Refreshments. Table service, sea views.'

Beyond the arch, there was nothing, except a tangled mess of black iron and charred wood sprawled out into the surging tide. The piers were gone, destroyed, all three of them.

I think it'd take a lot to bring the palace down, Beqa Mayer had said.

Oskar Viltry felt his legs go numb and weak. He leaned against the cast iron railing and closed his weary eyes.

Theda Old Town, 06.30

THERE'D BEEN A plan. A trip down to the Hydra on Voldney, all of Umbra, and the fitters too, to toast Asche on her way. Blansher had sent a message, ordering cases of joiliq and the private hire of the main bar.

But then the snap call had come in at 20.00, and they'd gone aloft into the night, into the mayhem of darkness and fire. By the time they'd returned, debriefed, showered and been stood down, Larice Asche had already packed her bags and departed to meet her report time. She'd left a note.

Good flying, Umbra. See you up there, somewhere.
Larice.

There was an empty feeling in the billet. A dark mood, somehow worse than if they'd lost a comrade in action.

'We're going anyway,' Blansher said.

THEY'D REACHED THE Hydra at four in the morning, just as the staff were hoping to close, and tried their level best to rouse a party mood. But it was like a wake. Blansher said a few words about Asche, and they were good words too, but they'd have sounded better coming from Jagdea. The crew of Umbra sat around, morose. The fitters, always up for a free drink, got drunk and loud, but kept themselves to themselves. Van Tull and Cordiale left after an hour. Zemmic, who had been discarded by Larice Asche as quickly as Marquall, got brutally intoxicated and then violently ill. Ranfre took pity on him, found a driver with a truck, and took him back to the base.

Which left Marquall, Del Ruth and Blansher.

'Not exactly what I'd planned,' Blansher said. The three of them sat around a table, toying with shot glasses. On the other side of the bar, Racklae and the fitters were playing drinking games, roaring out with laughter and good humour. The red-eyed bar staff sat behind the counter, longing for them all to go home.

'We could join them,' Del Ruth suggested, tipping her head in the direction of the fitters.

'And spoil their fun?' Blansher said. 'Pilots need fitters and fitters need pilots, and there is a bond close to love between them. But socially? No. Different worlds. Different classes. We go over there, try to join in, we'll be as welcome as a turd in a foot bath.'

Agguila Del Ruth had been halfway through a sip, and snorted with laughter, choking so hard Marquall had to slap her on the back.

It was the best laugh they'd had all night.

'Throne save me,' Blansher sighed. 'This is so not what I'd planned.'

'Story of my life,' muttered Marquall, pouring out another measure of joiliq for each of them.

'What's this now?' said Del Ruth. 'Self-directed misery too?'

Marquall shrugged. 'Do you know, I was top of my class at Hessenville.'

'Weren't we all?' said Del Ruth, raising her eyebrows at Blansher.

'No, not me,' said Blansher sadly, reaching for his drink. 'I was… bottom. Pilot-cadet voted most likely to wash out. I failed every exercise. Not just failed, mind. Failed dismally. One day, my instructor took me to one side, led me out to an obs deck overlooking the Scald. He pointed to it. He said, "Milan, this is your birth-world. Plenty of sky, not very much land. If you can't fly, boy, what the frig else do you think you're going to do? Swim for the Emperor?"'

Del Ruth snorted her drink again and started coughing.

'Damn you!' she gagged, wiping her mouth on a napkin. 'That's twice.'

Blansher smiled.

'I was top of my class,' Marquall said. 'Accelerated program, right at the end of the liberation war. I mean, I was good. I longed to fly combat. Kill bats. But now I'm in it, in the combat zone… I screw up. I can't hit a thing. My birds break down on me. I get people hurt.'

'That's one way of looking at it,' Blansher said.

'There's another way?'

'Well, for a start there's the matter of two fine kills. Besides that, you've saved my life in the air, and I can't speak for others. You survived an eject from a slain machine… not many do that. And there's that heroic use of rocket drive to break out of a kill-shot. That last thing alone, Vander, that's one for the archives. I don't know of anyone who's even tried that, let alone come back to talk about it. Seekan should have come to you, not Larice.'

Marquall managed a smile. 'Thanks,' he said.

'I mean it.'

'You're a very good exec, sir. Just what Jagdea expects. You say the right things and boost morale.'

'Maybe,' said Blansher. 'Personally, I think there's an up side to everything. You just have to see it. Say to yourself, is the glass half full or half empty?'

'They're shot glasses,' said Del Ruth flatly, staring at her own. 'They're either full or empty. Anything else, and someone isn't trying.'

'I'll drink to that,' said Blansher, and reached for the bottle.

THE THREE OF them left the Hydra at twenty past six in the morning, dim light filling the sky. The fitters were still carousing. Blansher led them to the nearest Munitorum depot, booked out three transports and drivers from the pool, and then returned to the Hydra to collect the reluctant ground crew.

They drove out along the highway. It seemed otherwise deserted. The strip of road was littered with trash and discarded possessions. Some broken down vehicles sat on the hard shoulder. Marquall was riding in the back of one of the trucks with Racklae and a group of the ground crew.

'You hear that?' he said suddenly.

Racklae turned and cocked his head, trying to hear above the noise of the truck engine. 'Fan drives. Lots of them.'

'Another raid?' asked one of the men.

'Doesn't sound like bombers,' said Racklae. 'Heavier…'

'Oh shit… look!' Marquall cried, pointing to the southern sky.

Massive, multi-vectored drop-ships were sliding in across skies above the eastern suburbs. Thousands of dots were showering out of them, like windblown pollen.

Storm troopers, on jump packs.

From the depths of the war-torn city behind them, sirens began to rise into a howl.

The mass invasion had begun.

Theda MAB South, 06.39

THE FLASHES OF the detonations were coming so fast the early daylight appeared to be strobing. There was a gritty, sizzling noise from the continuous bombardment. How could the sky hold up so many aircraft?

Darrow ran towards the Operations centre. Bombs were falling on the inner city, and several Tormentors had swung over the field wide, loads gone, turning out over the sea. The airfield's defence batteries were hurling everything they had at the sky. Tracers spiked up and danced, flak turned the air into a broiling mass of flame-lit smoke.

Fighters were already lifting off the field, either to fight or flee. Darrow heard mounting engine-roar from several Oneros and other mass lifters. Figures mobbed across the landscape.

'Extraction?' Darrow yelled at a Navy officer.

'Everything, now!' the man yelled back, still running. 'We're pulling out now!'

Darrow looked to his left in time to see the Apostles lift off. They'd been prepped for a first light call, and now they launched, climbing north-east in the turmoil of the air. Their cream paintjobs made them look like blades of ice in the fire-lit sky.

A sonic boom split the air like the muzzle bang of an artillery piece. A Hell Talon streaked long and low over the field, and left a crop of furious blasts in its wake. Two Marauders were blown up on their hardstands. Darrow was one of the many who threw themselves flat as the Talon thundered over.

The wind was full of smoke and scraps of airborne ash. The furious metallic hammering of a nearby Hydra almost drowned out the background roar of explosions and jet engines.

Darrow got up and started running again. Another aircraft went over, and he saw running personnel not twenty metres away from him thrown into the air by cannon fire. Then there was a tremendous, vibrating roar and a prickling wash of heat as a laden Onero took off and crawled past overhead.

There was blood in Darrow's left eye. He'd caught a scratch in the left eyebrow, shrapnel probably, and blood was running down into his vision. He kept running. Another big transport took off, kicking up dust and grit.

Darrow saw bodies on the ground. Two Navy airmen and three ground crew. The force of the strafing fire that had claimed them had punctured the ground in a long, broken gouge, stripped most of their garments clean off, and left them lying in impossible, dislocated poses.

Darrow glanced away. It was a hard thing to look at.

People still ran past in all directions. Some were wounded and being helped by others. Two pilots staggered past carrying a fitter upright between them. The fitter was making an odd, sobbing noise. His face was–

Again, Darrow turned his eyes aside. Over on the hardstands, the latest enemy strafing run hit a bowser, and a huge sheet of yellow flame splashed up into the air.

On the northern-most pads, squadrons of Valkyrie carriers were warming up, their stern hatches open. Personnel streamed towards them from the base buildings.

More planes launched, mainly Thunderbolts. One of them was hit by a seeker-rocket as it tried to lift, caught fire violently, and belly flopped down into a loading bay, killing at least twenty ground crew. Darrow winced at the heat of the blasts.

Then he saw Eads. Feeling with his cane, Eads was approaching the entrance of the Operations building. Navy crew ran past him. A low-flying Locust chewed a line of shots up into the side of Operations ripping out brick dust and pieces of tile and shutter. Protecting his face, Darrow ran towards Eads.

'Sir!'

'Is that you, Darrow?'

'Yes, sir. Come on. I'll get you onto an evacuation flight.'

'I should go to Operations. This attack needs proper–'

'There's no point, sir!' Darrow yelled above the concussive noise of the bombing. 'It's all gone! Everything's gone! The enemy is here, right at the gates! We're pulling out now!'

A clutch of submunitions detonated forty metres away, killing a dozen people. The pressure of the blast-wave knocked Eads and Darrow flat. Scrambling up, Darrow fought to get Eads on his feet.

'Someone help me!' he cried at the figures running past. Most just ignored them. One went by, then stopped and ran back.

It was Scalter.

He helped Darrow lift Eads and they started moving.

Scalter yelled something about the Blood Pact over the din.

'What?' said Darrow.

'They're saying Blood Pact are dropping into the suburbs. Ground forces, certainly.'

'God-Emperor protect us all,' Eads said.

'Pardon me, sir,' said Scalter. 'But right now it feels like he's forgotten all about us.'

Western District Theda, 06.40

THE SIRENS WOKE Jagdea. Her room in the hab clinic was cold and damp. The window was rattling.

She lay still for a moment, listening. Apart from the blare of the sirens outside, there was a murmur of disquiet in the old building. Her window rattled again. No, it was more than a rattle. The glass in the old wooden frame was vibrating.

She got out of bed, and went to look.

Pulsing air pressure was making the glass shake. Jagdea could see the blistering flashes of pattern bombing detonations underlighting the sky behind the immediate cityscape. Hundreds of smoke plumes were curling up into the murky dawn sky.

In the clinic's courtyard below, staff members and patients were fleeing in droves.

Jagdea hurried across the room, got down on her knees beside her bed, and started to pull her clothes and effects out of the bedside locker. She found her boots, her flight coat–

At that moment, a high yield bomb landed on a building across the street, levelling it instantly. The entire clinic recoiled as if its foundations were set on bedsprings. The window of Jagdea's room blew in with the shockwave, ripping a blizzard of glass across the room.

Jagdea cried out involuntarily, hammered by the concussion, but her bed had shielded her from the shredding force of the glass. She crouched on the floorboards for a moment, tense with shock. She could smell smoke, fyceline and heat scorching. She could hear the crash of rubble, the flames and the screaming coming from outside.

Cursing her sling and the pain in her arm, Jagdea pulled on the trousers of her flightsuit, and then her boots. She had a vest top on, so she put the coat on over that, good arm through the sleeve, slung arm under the coat.

Then she went out into the hallway. Smoke was pouring into the clinic through the smashed windows on the courtyard side. She headed the other way. In the hall, she passed several patients and medicae staff lacerated by window glass. Most were alive, calling out, helpless.

There was nothing she could do. The able-bodied staffers that she saw were simply running for the exits.

Jagdea found the stairs, then made her way out through the half of the building away from the blasted courtyard. Outside, she found herself in a back street. A few people hurried past her. Looking up, she could see strings of enemy bombers creeping overhead.

She ran down the side street and halted at the corner where it joined a main road. Several commercial premises were on fire, and there was debris in the street. People rushed by, some crying and wailing in blind panic.

A truck went by, then a car. She tried to wave them down, but they ignored her. In fact, the car almost hit her, so determined was the driver not to stop. Jagdea yelled in frustration. She'd lost her bearings, and didn't even know which way the base was from there.

The only thing she did know for sure was that it was more than walking distance.

But she didn't seem to have much choice.

Theda MAB South, 06.59

DARROW AND SCALTER hurried Eads onto the northern pads. Some of the Valkyries there had already started lifting clear, fully laden, probably overladen. One had been hit before take-off, and was burning furiously on the hardpan. Frantic personnel swarmed around the ramps and side doors of the others. The door gunner teams were trying to organise boarding, but the panic was such that fights were breaking out.

Darrow looked around. He felt a knot of panic in his own gut. 'Throne's sake,' he said, aware of a tremulous quality in his voice that he couldn't help. 'There won't be enough places.'

'We'll try there,' Scalter said, determinedly holding his nerves together. On the far north edge of the pad area, almost by the field's blast fences, three old bulk transport-lifters were warming up. The machines were a good distance away from where they stood. But it seemed most of the evacuees wanted a place on one of the faster, better armoured Valkyries. The trio started across the pads towards the transporters. Other individuals, unable to get aboard a combat carrier, or unwilling to endure the fight that would entail, began to break off from the clamouring groups around the Valkyries and head the same way too.

Still moving, Darrow looked round sharply at the sound of small-arms fire. Someone had snapped and drawn a handgun, trying to shoot his way onto a Valkyrie.

In response, the door crew slammed the hatches shut and the carrier lifted off, scattering the crowd that had been trying to get on it. Denied their chance of escape, the mob turned on the man who'd fired the gun.

The Valkyrie went over them, and then, to Darrow's amazement, came back in to land ahead of them.

The door gunners opened the ramp again and started to wave at them. The machine's crew had clearly not been able to stomach the idea of leaving Theda empty when lives were wasting.

Darrow and Scalter ran Eads bodily towards the ramp, in under the tail booms and into the embrace of the gunners.

'Get in! Inside! Find a space and a handhold!'

The compartment was dark, a hot metal box. As they got Eads into a scissor-seat, the door crew brought aboard several more stragglers. A buzzer sounded. The ramp began to retract again, and the engine noise rose to a scream.

With a lurch, they left the ground, nose down, and began to accelerate and climb.

Theda MAB South, 07.02

BEFORE THE TRUCKS had even come to a halt, the last three pilots of Umbra Flight had jumped clear and started to run towards their hardstand shelters. The fitters followed them.

'I need just five of you!' Racklae bellowed above the raging bombardment. 'The rest… get going. Evac transport over there!'

Racklae turned and kept running with the five men who'd volunteered. The others started sprinting towards the last two Oneros that were loading near the main drome hangar.

The truck drivers ran with them.

The whole airfield seemed to be on fire. There were bodies and shell-holes everywhere, overturned vehicles, buckled munitions carts. Some hardstands were ablaze, and in some burned the wrecks of planes that had never made it up. Two Lightnings launched, and swept away north. Marquall fully expected to find *Double Eagle* in pieces.

But it was intact, and so was Blansher's bird. Del Ruth's, however, had been caught by strafing fire. The engines and cockpit were just mangled ribbons of metal.

All the other Umbra machines were gone. Cordiale, Ranfre, Zemmic and Van Tull must have made it out. Into the air, at least.

Three Razors went over, low, drives shrieking. In the western sector of the airfield, Tormentors were drizzling submunitions on the machine shops.

Racklae sent two of his men to ready Marquall's plane, and two to do the same for Blansher's. 'Basic checks, clear them off, and then head for the transports!' he emphasised.

With Del Ruth and the remaining fitter, Racklae ran across to the adjacent row of hardstand shelters. The Thunderbolt wing that had occupied this area, the 76th Firedrakes, had already quit, but they'd left two of their mustard-yellow Bolts behind. Bodies on the ground nearby left little doubt that both pilots had been mown down, along with members of the ground crew, on the way to their machines.

One of the abandoned Bolts had tail and elevator damage, but the other seemed okay. Racklae started work getting Del Ruth airborne.

Marquall dropped into his own cockpit, and switched primary systems on with one hand as he wrestled to strap up his harness. One of the fitters rolled the primer cart close for connection as the other disengaged the fuel and data-feed lines, and then jumped up on the wing plates to pass Marquall his helmet.

The primer fired and surged, and after a second, Nine-Nine's mighty turbofans began to turn. Marquall leaned out.

'Unhook the primer and get out of here!' he yelled at the fitters over the rising whine. 'Just go!'

They ducked out of view under the cowling. Marquall closed and locked his own lid, fastened his mask, and then did a last preflight overview of vitals. Pressure, coolant, fuel, electronics, air-mix, ammunition. Green all around.

The fitters reappeared, and waved him double thumbs. He signalled back okay, and the two men turned and began to run.

The last Marquall saw of them, they were crossing the asphalt apron towards the heavy lifters.

Ducts angled to vertical, Marquall eased open the throttle and brought *Double Eagle* up and away from the ground.

'Two, this is Eight. I'm going clear.'

'Copy that, Eight. Just get out of here.'

In the present circumstances, no pilot needed to be dawdling about on lift. Still low, he swung the nose, and lit the burners as he wound the ducts round to level.

Marquall's Thunderbolt crossed the blazing airfield at rooftop height, power building. He glimpsed bats crossing behind him, but he ignored them. No tone warnings.

He turned into a wide climb north, and in thirty seconds was crossing the coastal ramparts and the long white seam of the shoreline strand. Sea was under him now.

'Two? This is Eight. Are you clear?'

'Confirm that, Eight. Coming up at your five. Don't wait for me. Turn and punch it.'

A THOUSAND METRES below, Blansher watched Marquall's Bolt blasting eastwards. He waited, then banked firmly, turning back towards the field he had only just left.

'Four? Where are you? Aggie, are you launching?'

From his high vantage point, the true extent of the destruction was finally clear. Blansher could only half-see the ruined airfield through the blanket of black smoke and the sudden blooms of white and yellow flame. Beyond it, Theda City was encased in a vast nimbus of smoke. The air to the south was crawling with formations of enemy planes, dots that caught the sunlight and twinkled against the dark clouds.

'Aggie? Where are you?'

He made another pass over the MAB. Below, Blansher saw two fat Oneros plough up out of the boiling vapour and thunder away in a tight track eastwards. Then a smaller transport plane came up, but it seemed to be in trouble. His blood chilled as he saw a pair of Locusts streak over it diagonally and turn it into a fireball.

'Two? Two, are you receiving? This is Four.'

'Go ahead, I hear you.'

'Coming up now.'

Blansher banked again and saw the tiny, cruciform shape of Del Ruth's yellow Thunderbolt as it emerged from the smoke line. It was rising cleanly. Instinctively, Blansher turned his rudder and rolled down so that he was coming in behind her as she climbed.

A Hell Talon, having just emptied its payload onto the field's main drome, swept out of the smoke and saw the flare of her burners. Opportunistic, it lined up immediately, using its pull-out momentum to propel it into a rear attack.

It was five hundred metres lower than Blansher, and about the same distance ahead. Blansher hit the throttle, punched back into his seat, and dropped low, flicking on his targeters and activating his gunsight. He selected quad. He didn't want to risk hitting Del Ruth with lasfire if he missed.

All Thunderbolts had their own feel, their own temperament. Del Ruth was still getting used to the individual character of her new machine, and as a result was flying slightly erratically.

It saved her life.

The Talon's first bursts, which looked like the sparks of a striking tinderbox from Blansher's position, went wide.

Blansher tore down, levelled out, viffed slightly to adjust, and got the tone ping he'd been praying for.

His thumb pressed hard.

A cone of smoke gouted out around the nose of his bird as the quads chattered.

A sudden, savage spray of fragments burst out of the Hell Talon. Blansher kept firing, smacking his shots into its midsection. Fire guttered out, then the enemy machine split into two large sections, almost divided along its centreline. The shorn segments fluttered away below him.

'You're clear, Four. Get moving,' he voxed.

'You shouldn't have come back for me, Mil,' her reply crackled. 'You should already be gone.'

Not true, he thought. Not true at all. As acting flight commander, it was his duty to make sure all his pilots got clear, even if it meant his own life.

And the real tragedy was Umbra Flight had left one pilot behind, and there was now nothing any of them could do about it.

Western District Theda, 07.26

JAGDEA STRUGGLED ALONG the transitway between hab stacks, yelling at every vehicle that rumbled by. Nothing stopped. There were people in the streets, and a penetrating, sickly air of distress, something which the word 'panic' no longer did justice to. Every few seconds there was a flash or a rumble from the east, and the ground shook several times. One particularly large detonation away to the south was followed by a failure in power supply betrayed only by the sudden cessation of the raid sirens. After that, in the strange quiet, there was just the distant booming, the whistle and crump of munitions, the drone of aviation engines. Once or twice, Jagdea thought she heard distant gunfire, small-arms. She put that down to her imagination.

Her wound throbbed. She'd brought no meds with her, and she had managed to knock her sling half a dozen times during dashes for cover when bombers came over.

Fatigue overcame her, quite suddenly. Fatigue, and a sense of hopelessness. She sat down on a kerb and felt tears running down her cheeks. How weak was that? How bloody weak was that?

A truck went past. She didn't even look up. She heard a screech of brakes.

Jagdea lifted her head. A Munitorum transporter, laden with packing cartons, had pulled to a halt twenty metres away, and the driver was dismounting.

Jagdea rose to her feet. It was the driver, the man with the burn-scarred face. What was his name? She couldn't remember. She wondered if he'd told her. She wondered if she'd ever bothered to ask.

'Commander Jagdea? Is that you?'

She nodded. He hurried over to her. 'I saw the jacket. Recognised an aviator's uniform. God-Emperor, are you all right?'

'No,' she said.

'You need a lift?'

'Of course I bloody do.'

He helped her over to the cab and supported her as she climbed up. Then he ran around to the driver's side and got in.

'What are you doing here?' he asked as he threw the truck into forward gear.

'I was in a hab clinic. Wounded on a sortie. I heard the raid begin and... I started to walk.'

'What? To MAB South?'

She wiped her face. 'I'm not sure I know where I was going. Just... trying to rejoin my unit.'

'Of course. Wouldn't want another FTR,' he said.

She hesitated. 'I never did thank you for your help that night.'

'What help? I was out of line, talking to the boy like that. You had every reason to be angry at me. Apart from that, what did I do? A bit of driving for you. That's all I'm good for these days. The Munitorum gives me instructions, and I do some driving for them.'

'Even now? In the middle of this?'

'Even now. I am a servant of the Throne, commander. I do as I'm bid. My senior sent me to Kozkoh Administorum, with orders to collect a bunch of Munitorum record files that someone somewhere didn't want falling into enemy hands.'

Jagdea shook her head. 'Record files? Not people? You could be carrying a couple of dozen human lives to safety in this truck.'

'That had occurred to me, commander. The Munitorum has curious priorities, especially at times like this.'

She looked round at him. He was concentrating on the road ahead. She realised for the first time that he had probably been a good looking man before half his face had been melted.

'I don't even know your name,' she said.

'Kaminsky,' he replied. 'August Kaminsky. Munitorum Transit Division, vehicle 167.'

'You were aircrew before that.'

'Combat pilot, Commonwealth Airforce. Wolfcubs and the like. Sixteen years. But that's ancient history.'

'Look, Kaminsky,' she began. 'Can you get me to the field? I know you have orders, but I really need to rejoin my command.'

He shrugged. 'I don't know. Really, I don't. From here, it would be a long slog, especially given the circumstances.'

'Then I need to evac at least. Anywhere closer?'

'Well, I've been told to report to an extraction centre at Mandora Point on the north shore. That's where these damn record files are supposed to be delivered. There should be mass-barges there, maybe even lifters. Good enough?'

'Okay, that'll do. I just need to get out. Get out and clear and then back in the game.'

He smiled.

'What?' she asked.

'I've been thinking that for months,' he said.

They rode on for fifteen minutes without talking. Kaminsky drove hard, almost recklessly, through the shattered streets. Several times, Jagdea winced as he ran them into walls of smoke that washed across the roadway, without knowing what might be concealed by them. Twice, Kaminsky had to brake hard to avoid debris and slopes of rubble.

'Theda's done for,' he said at last.

'Yes. I'm afraid it might be.'

'I guess these are the end times.'

'There's still a chance,' she said.

Swinging the wheel, he laughed at her. 'I don't think so. Not now.'

'If a member of my flight spoke like that, I'd have them up on charges. There's always a chance. While we still breathe, by the grace of the Emperor, there's still a chance.'

'Then I count myself fortunate that I'm not a member of your flight, mamzel. Enothis is my homeworld, and I gave everything I had to protect it. There comes a time when a person has to be pragmatic.'

'I fought for my homeworld too. Now I'm here fighting for yours. Don't talk to me about effort. Don't talk to me about contribution. And as for being pragmatic, that's sometimes just another word for defeatist.'

'Well, screw you too, mamzel–'

'Kaminsky! Look out!'

They'd just come through another drift of smoke. In the suddenly-revealed road ahead, a group of figures, dressed in dark red uniforms, turned to face them.

Jagdea saw leering iron masks, bowl helmets, lasrifles.

'Blood Pact!' she blurted out. 'Turn round! Turn us around!'

Kaminsky was already hauling on the wheel. He swore loudly, fighting to avoid a full skid. The truck slewed around madly, stripping tread from its fat tyres. It came side-on to the Archenemy troopers.

And stalled.

'Kaminsky! Kaminsky!' Jagdea yelled.

'Stop shouting at me!' he yelled, gunning the starter. The Blood Pact drop-troops began to fire at them, running forward. Las-rounds smacked into the truck's side and one crazed the door window.

'Kaminsky! For Throne's sake!'

'Will you shut up, woman?' A las-round went clean through the cab in front of their faces, shattering Kaminsky's side pane.

The truck's engines burst back into life.

Jagdea was thrown back against the seat by the violent restart. Her left arm cracked against the door jamb and she howled in pain.

Kaminsky swung them round to the left, standing on the accelerator. The big truck side-swiped the burned-out shell of a car, and slammed it out of the way. Then the Blood Pact squad was behind them and they were barrelling away down a side street at nearly sixty.

'Are you hit?' he said.

'No.'

'You cried out.'

'I'm not hit.'

'I'm sorry I shouted at you.'

'It doesn't matter.'

'Looks like we're not going that way,' Kaminsky said.

Theda Old Town, 07.43

ALL ALONG THE canal side, recent bombing had felled the ancient buildings and tenements, even the old Kazergat Bridge. But the templum was miraculously unscathed. Coughing in the smoke and brick dust, Viltry hurried along the canal's bank and went down to the church door.

He paused there, and glanced up at the effigy of the God-Emperor.

'Remember me?' he asked.

Viltry opened the door.

It was almost disturbingly calm inside. The air was clear, though he could still smell the stink of smoke from the firebombing. The templum was empty. The rows of pews, the alabaster columns, the faint residue of camphor and incense.

He walked down the aisle, his boots clipping on the mosaic flooring. Saints and daemons passed under his heels. The Ministorum priests had long since fled.

He came to a halt in front of the votary shrine.

Three candles burned there. Just three.

'God-Emperor…' he sighed.

'Oskar?'

Oskar Viltry turned slowly.

She had been sitting at the end of a pew row, hidden behind a column. He hadn't seen her. She was shivering in her thin coat.

He took a step towards her, almost laughing out in strange delight.

'What are you doing here?' he whispered.

'Where else could I go?' Beqa Mayer said. 'How else would you know where to find me?'

Northern Theda, 08.12

THEY TORE OUT of the dying city and onto a coastal highland where the habs became infrequent and scattered. Jagdea glimpsed the sea beyond the headland.

'Kaminsky? Where are we going?' she asked.

'Not the field, that's for sure. Or the extraction either. The bastards have the whole place locked down. I'm running on a hunch.'

'What sort of hunch?'

'The sort of hunch that will disappoint you if it doesn't work.'

'Kaminsky?'

'I think there comes a point,' said Kaminsky, 'where the act of being pragmatic and the notion there's always still a chance become the same thing.'

They went under a road-bridge and then down a steep hill between rows of fish processing plants. Kaminsky suddenly turned right, and drove the truck down an access way into a yard behind the manufactories.

Ahead of them stood a line of flakboard sheds facing the edge of the sea cliff. The sheds were painted green. The nearest had a large, shuttered door in the side of it. It was barred and locked.

'Get out, commander,' he said.

She looked at him.

'I mean it. Get out.'

Jagdea climbed down from the cab and slammed the door.

Kaminsky reversed and then drove the truck at the shutter. Jagdea winced at the impact. Trailing a fender, the truck reversed and drove in again.

'Throne's sake, Kaminsky!' Jagdea cried out.

A third battering run, and the shutter tore away at the sills, partially crunched out of its flakboard frame. Kaminsky got down out of his mashed truck.

'Come on,' he said.

Jagdea hurried over to him, and they bent in low to pass under the crumpled metal sheets of the door shutter.

She found herself in a damp, echoing chamber. It smelled of rotting plyboard and salt water.

'What the hell is this?' she asked.

'Shut up and follow me,' he said.

They edged through the gloom, Kaminsky leading. Jagdea saw fitter trolleys, compact bowsers, shelf-racks of tools. There was a scent of promethium jelly in the air.

Kaminsky opened another hatch and daylight spilled through.

'This way,' he said.

She followed him through the hatch and out onto a metal catwalk. They had entered a deep, flakboard-built hangar. The mouth of the bay, facing the sea, was open to the air, the floor cut away right down to the lip of the cliffs. Pale light flooded in through the opening. Jagdea could hear the breakers far away and below.

Directly beneath them, in the shadows, two Commonwealth Cyclones sat on steam catapult launch racks.

'Coastal defence,' said Kaminsky, clattering down the metal staircase ahead of her. 'They haven't been used in months, but I hoped they were still here.'

'My lord,' gasped Jagdea, following him down.

Kaminsky ran to the nearest machine, opened the cockpit door, and leaned in.

'It's got electrics, but we'll need fuel. And a primer cart.'

Jagdea came up behind him. 'And then what? Fly one out of here?'

He looked at her. 'Exactly.'

'We can't…' Jagdea began.

'Of course we can. You'll quickly get the hang of it. Simple, basic, that's all a Cyclone is.' Kaminsky ran back along the machine's length, and opened the tank cocks. He hefted a fuelling line from nearby bowser and connected it, fumbling slightly because of his prosthetic hand.

'I can't fly that,' Jagdea said.

Kaminsky started the bowser's pump motor. The fuel line wriggled and flexed as pressurised liquid surged through it.

'I know you're not used to props, but she's real easy to handle, I promise,' he said, and hurried to the catapult stations at the back of the bay. Kaminsky threw some switches, and got a generator firing. Then he pulled down a handle that started the catapult's steam engines, pumping up the piston track mechanism.

'No, Kaminsky,' Jagdea said. She held up her slung arm. 'Even a machine like this needs both hands. Throttle and stick. Remember that, airman? With the best will in the cosmos, I can't do it.'

Kaminsky came to halt. 'I suppose you can't,' he admitted. He seemed deflated.

'But you could,' she said.

'Me? I'm not rated airworthy.'

'Right now, this deep in the shit, I hardly think that's the point any more. Let's be pragmatic, shall we? I'm a wing leader. I'll clear you as airworthy. I have the authority.'

'I'll need your help,' he said, uncertainly.

'Anything,' she promised.

'Keep an eye on the fuel dial.'

Jagdea peered into the cockpit. The gauge was barely registering.

'Slow,' she called. 'How long?'

'Maybe fifteen minutes to full tolerance. The pumps aren't famously efficient.'

Jagdea did what all pilots have done since the beginning of aviation. She leaned over and flicked the glass dial with the fingers of her good hand. As with all pilots since the beginning of aviation, it made no difference.

The steam pressure was rising. Between them, Jagdea and Kaminsky unhooked the support hawsers and suspension straps holding the Cyclone in place.

'Can you do a cockpit check?' Kaminsky asked. 'You're more familiar with the layout.'

'Yeah, but there's something I need to do.'

'What?'

'The record files. I think I should burn them. Not just leave them here.'

'I'll do it,' Jagdea said. 'You finish the prep.'

'You sure?'

'Yes. How long have we got?'

Kaminsky checked his chronometer, and then looked at the fuel gauge. 'Ten minutes.'

'I'll be five,' she promised, and hurried towards the stairs.

Kaminsky checked the catapult controls. They'd reached full pressure. He locked them off and tripped the lever that switched release control to the plane itself. Then he went to the bowser. Its pump seemed to be ailing.

'Come on!' he hissed. There wasn't time to find another and switch over.

He clambered into the tiny cockpit.

He'd done a few hundred hours on Cyclones. It was oddly familiar. He tested the electrics, the glycol levels, the radiator levers. Then he checked the trim, leaning out of the cockpit to look backwards as he pitched and turned the stick and the rudder bar, watching the ailerons and the fin respond obediently.

'Come on, Jagdea,' he hissed. He looked at the fuel gauge. It was still so very low. 'And come on pump,' he added.

IN THE UPPER part of the shed, Jagdea fumbled around and filled a can with liquid promethium from one of the tank trolleys. It was hard to do, one-handed. The only light came in under the buckled shutter. Hefting the heavy can in her right hand, she ducked out into the open air.

A few papers from the truck's load were fluttering free in the breeze. Jagdea set the sloshing can up on the tail gate and then hauled herself up after it.

She started to spill fuel onto the record boxes. It was a huge effort. She felt stupid and weak, having to set the can down so often to catch her breath.

She heard an odd, clattering noise.

She resumed the work, dousing the entire pile. Then she jumped down, biting back the urge to cry out as her left arm jarred, and poured the last of the can into the truck's cab.

That sound again. Not a clattering so much as hammering. Like steel pistons.

She checked her chronometer. She'd already been five minutes.

Then there was the matter of ignition.

Jagdea cursed herself for not thinking it through.

She hurried back into the shed, and started to search in the gloom. Tool boxes crashed over. Drawers upturned. Something. Anything.

Nothing.

Panting, she stepped back. On the flakboard wall, a distress gun hung on a hook in a glass-fronted box. She picked up a ten mil wrench and smashed the box off the wall.

The distress gun was smooth and old, and it had started to rust. She snapped its barrel open and rummaged for a shell.

That noise, again. *Clatter clatter.* Louder.

She chambered the flare cartridge and closed the gun, then ducked back outside, aimed it at Kaminsky's truck and–

Hesitated.

Jagdea took several long paces backwards and aimed again.

She fired.

The flare barked out, white hot, struck the side of the transport and ricocheted off up into the air, where it spattered out streamers of green fire.

'Shit!' she cried, and ran back into the shed to find another shell.

The clattering noise was getting much louder.

She found another flare and tucked a spare into her belt for good measure. Loading the distress gun, she ran outside again.

The glow of the first flare was beginning to subside. She raised the gun again.

To her right, at the mouth of the yard, a stalk tank strode into view.

It was painted bright red. Its striding metal limbs screwed it around and it galloped in down the access way, hunting for the source of the distress flare.

Clatter clatter clatter went its feet.

Behind it, Blood Pact troopers ran in squads, weapons raised.

Jagdea fired the distress gun. The flare struck the record boxes and in an instant, the entire vehicle was consumed in broiling fire.

The heat-blast knocked her over.

Approaching, the stalk tank started firing. Its heavy laser batteries recoiled and spat as they fired off volleys at the sheds.

Jagdea got up and ran towards the broken shutter. Inside, she kept running, colliding with a munitions cart and bruising her thigh. She yelped and pulled her head down as the ferocious shots of the stalk tank punched through the flakboard wall behind her, splintering holes, letting in daylight. The air was full of swirling fibres and ash.

She darted through the hatch, onto the catwalk and down the stairs.

'We have to go! Now!' she was shouting.

'We're not fully fuelled!' Kaminsky yelled back from the open cockpit.

'Tough!' she replied. She ran to the bowser, deactivated the pump, and then struggled to disconnect the line from the cock.

'Just start her up!' she screamed.

'I've not connected the primer–' Kaminsky yelled back.

'No time! Just do it!'

Kaminsky threw the starter switches. The port engine growled, turned over and then burst into raging life, kicking out blue smoke from its exhausts.

The starboard engine cycled once and then froze.

Jagdea clambered into the cockpit.

'Come on!' she urged. She could heard sustained lasfire above them.

'Trying!' Kaminsky yelled over the single, roaring engine.

He switched off the starboard power plant, fluffed the throttle, and opened the choke.

'We don't have much time,' Jagdea said. She closed her door, and strapped up.

Kaminsky turned the starboard engine over again. Dry fire. Again. Another cough. Again.

This time it took. The prop howled into life. They both felt the airframe shaking.

'Okay, we're good,' Jagdea said.

In the pilot's seat, Kaminsky seemed to freeze.

'You all right?' asked Jagdea.

'It's… been a while. Didn't think I'd ever–'

'Kaminsky, will you shut up? We don't have time for the whole emotional thing now.'

'Right. Of course.'

Jagdea threw some of the switches. 'Launcher at pressure. Current on. Armed.'

'Props at thrust,' he said.

'So… gun it,' she replied with a smile.

The hangar was clogged with dense smoke from the engines.

'Jagdea?'

'What?'

'Help me. Help me fit my hand on the stick.'

'Of course. Sorry.' She leaned over, closing his prosthetic hand around the control stick. His other hand was busy regulating the twin throttles.

'Now I need you to hit the release,' he said.

'Okay. Ready?'

'No. So just do it,' said August Kaminsky.

Jagdea hit the switch. The steam catapult engaged and flicked their Cyclone out of the hangar and into the air with bone-jolting force. For a second, it began to drop, but Kaminsky nursed it, and opened the throttles, lifting the delta wing-up over the coast in a fast ascent.

Jagdea felt the steady purr of the props and smiled.

'How's that feel, mister?' she asked.

He was grinning. 'Like coming home. You torch my truck?'

'As promised.'

They rose, banked around and turned east.

'Smooth,' said Jagdea.

'Old habits,' said Kaminsky. He was grinning.

They were rising to about a thousand metres when the Cyclone's antiquated detector systems emitted a warning beep.

'Someone's got us!' Jagdea cried.

'Where? I can't see him?'

'I don't know! What does the auspex say?'

'This bird isn't equipped with an auspex.'

'Oh frigging great!' Jagdea began craning her head around, turning as far as she could to scan out of the Cyclone's bubble nose.

'Locust! Eleven o'clock!' she yelled.

She got a brief glimpse of a bright red bat stooping in, cannons lit, then Kaminsky turned the Cyclone over in a suicidal bank.

'Kaminsky! Kaminsky!'

'Will you shut up, woman? Will you ever shut up?'

The sea rushed towards them. Kaminsky suddenly leaned on the throttles and rolled the Cyclone.

'Guns,' he stammered.

'Uhh!' Negative G was slamming at her. 'What?'

'Guns, dammit, Jagdea! I can't press the gun stud! I don't have a thumb! You'll have to do it.'

She wrestled over, all her blood in her feet, fighting against the centrifugal force of the turning Cyclone. She clamped her fist over his dead, prosthetic hand.

'Tell me when!'

'Wait!'

He feathered the Cyclone up on a corkscrew and then wafered it down violently as the Locust slipped under them.

'How the hell did you do that?' she yelled. 'You just out-danced a vector-thrust machine!'

'Shut the hell up and shoot,' Kaminsky replied. 'Fire! Just fire! Fire!'

He rolled the Cyclone hard and Jagdea heard the sudden, sweet sound of target lock. She clamped her hands around the grip. Around his plastek hand.

Flame-flash blitzed from the Cyclone's gun ports. The Locust banked out, rising hard.

Then it ignited and blew apart.

'Holy hell!' Jagdea whooped.

'Got him,' hissed Kaminsky.

'Yes you did,' said Jagdea, as Kaminsky banked the Cyclone east. 'Yes, you damn well did.'

OPERATE TO DENY

THE MIDWINTER ISLANDS

Imperial year 773.M41, day 267 – day 269

DAY 267

Lucerna AB, 12.30

MARQUALL WAS DOZING in his flightsuit when the hooters started their strident blaring throughout the base's deep, rock-cut hallways and buried decks. He jumped up out of his seat, grabbed his helmet, and ran out of the dispersal room, down the narrow companionway onto the floor of the hangar bay. Zemmic and Ranfre were close behind him, and Van Tull followed them, though more slowly. Van Tull's airline had taken a hit during the exit from Theda, causing an intermix fault that had allowed carbon dioxide to leak, undetected, into his supply. By the time he'd reached Lucerna, he'd been suffering from border-line hypoxia and had only just made it down.

Marquall paused and let Zemmic and Ranfre go by. 'You okay?' he asked Van Tull.

'Four-A,' said the older pilot. He was over the worst effects, or so he said. But he was now suffering with bleeding gums and sinuses, and kept dabbing at his mouth and nose with a folded handkerchief, like a consumptive.

'Sure?'

'I'll be fine once I'm up,' Van Tull said flatly.

They hurried across the bare stone floor onto the rigid deck plating. The entire air-base had been hollowed out of the island's rock. Hangar three, assigned to Umbra, was a gigantic rectangular cave, its floors and walls smoothed by industrial mason-cutters. Both ends of the cave, north and south, were open to the sky.

The Thunderbolts of Umbra Flight waited, lined up in three ranks facing the south. Fitter teams were disengaging the last of the cables and fuelling lines, and whirring elevator platforms carried the empty munitions trolleys down to lower levels.

Cordiale and Del Ruth were already with their planes. Blansher ran out across the gratings of the deck, reading a wafer of printout paper.

'Air cover, evac protection!' he shouted. 'Immediate launch, track six-nine-two, no higher than two thousand.'

There was a chorus of acknowledgements and the pilots dropped into their cockpits. The chief fitter of each plane crew made sure his pilot was secure, closed the canopy then signalled to the primer technician to start as he jumped off the wing. Each primer cart fired and the Thunderbolt engines began to turn over. Within moments, the engine noise in the enclosed space was so loud that it drowned out the screeching hooters.

Deck crews with goggles and ear protectors took up position in front of the formation, directing with lumin paddles. Signal to go.

In the front rank were Blansher and Ranfre. Behind them, Marquall, Cordiale and Del Ruth. The third rank was Van Tull and Zemmic. The flight rose up in a swaying hover almost simultaneously. The deck chief swung both his lumin paddles together and pointed, then dropped down onto one knee, head down in a braced position as the front rank rushed out over him, swiftly followed by the second and the third.

They came out into the open, exiting the hangar through a rectangular slot in the sheer cliff face. The sea was two hundred metres below them. The seven machines immediately started to turn and come onto their track.

The sky was greenish-blue with two-tenths of long, wispy cloud. The sea was a richer, more intense green. Lucerna Island dropped away behind them, a plateau of craggy pink granite jutting out of the water. Marquall could see the AA defences nested in the cliffs and on the headlands. Two more flights of Thunderbolts were coming up after Umbra from other hangar mouths. Far below, he could see the masses of shipping and barges that had been arriving at the island's jetties for the last twelve hours.

They climbed higher, steady. Marquall adjusted his nitrous mix carefully. He watched the formation around him, and kept his eyes on the auspex returns of the other Thunderbolt wings that were running below and behind them. From this altitude, he could see out across the range of the Midwinter Islands, an archipelago of pink atolls that filled nearly seven hundred thousand square kilometres of ocean at the eastern end of the Zophonian Sea. It was to the larger of these islands, places like Lucerna which had airbases and ports, that the majority of the planes, transports and extraction barges from Theda had fled.

The islet-speckled sea below him was full of shipping, powering east towards safe ports in the island chain. The auspex was also alive with air contacts. A few Imperial machines were still heading in from the mainland retreat, but the rest of the activity was Navy wings, coming back out of their new island bases to guard sea convoys or hunt for Archenemy intruders. Marquall could see the patterns of a large dogfight going on, twelve kilometres south of them, and another, more condensed, nineteen kilometres

to the south-west. To the east, there was a progressive intercept on a bomber formation, and another large air-brawl,
down at low level amongst the islands.

Visually, the southern horizon line was a smudged belt
of black, at odds with the clarity of the clean sky and the
sparkling sea. That was the smoke line, the vapour of death
and destruction that crowned the Thedan coast for hundreds of kilometres. The filthy mark of the Archenemy,
branded across his newly-taken territory.

Blansher called them to focus. They were closing on the
designated target. A convoy of thirty-seven mass-barges
and VTRPs out of St Chryze was moving up one of the
archipelago's clear-water channels, under attack from
enemy raiders.

'Brief said sixty-plus bats,' Blansher voxed.

'I have visual on the convoy,' reported Ranfre.

'Copy that.'

Down through the clouds, the mighty vessels were now
in plain view. Some were staining the air with trails of
exhaust smoke from their turbines, but others were pouring out cones of black and white smoke.

'Auspex contacts,' Del Ruth reported. 'Two groups of hostiles. One high at six thousand, circling, the other low,
crossing the convoy.'

Marquall checked his own auspex screen and got a sim-
ilar report. Multiple contacts were milling around the
surface vessels like flies around a wound. He could even
see them now, little flitting dots against the sea, catching
the sunlight.

'Umbra Leader to other flights. The contacts showing
high could be a second wave of attack planes waiting their
turn to come in, or they could be top cover. Suggest Umbra
and Sabre go in after the raiders; Cobalt stays high to
watch for fighters.'

The split made sense. Sabre Flight, part of the
333rd Navy wing, was short four machines, and so

under-strength like Umbra. Cobalt, also part of the 333rd, was twelve strong.

'Umbra, this is Cobalt Lead. Acknowledged.'

'Umbra Leader, Sabre will comply.'

'Stoop and sting,' Blansher ordered.

The two flights committed down, rolling off from the front of the formation to the rear in a formal cascade. Marquall tried to keep his breathing even as the power dive began. He switched on the targeters and lit his gunsight. Guns on, las selected.

The glittering water was coming up fast.

He saw the great black hulks of the convoy vessels, trailing wakes of white water, and the tall, thin spurts of foam around them where detonations were hitting the sea. And there were the bats, streaking in on horizontal approaches against the sides of the ships, attacking with rockets and cannon.

They were Hell Talons, painted in various red, black and coral-pink shades.

The Thunderbolts tore into the mob of them. For a second, there were aircraft and gunfire tracks going in all directions around Marquall. He pulled the stick back slightly and brought Nine-Nine up level. A Talon swept by, heading across onto one of the barges, and Marquall banked around after it.

It started to fire, churning up a track of impacts across the water towards the barge's hull, and Marquall opened fire too. He missed, but the Talon broke off to starboard, trying to get out of his cone of fire.

Marquall didn't manage to turn as tightly and overshot the barge, passing briefly through the clouds of smoke it was emitting. He turned the plane's nose and saw the Talon climbing furiously, so did likewise.

Two Thunderbolts, wearing the combat blue of the 333rd, shot past him, both chasing Talons. Then a red Talon swept in and Marquall had to roll out stiffly to avoid it. A wash of bright tracers, snaking and rippling like a wind-blown streamer, crossed past his right wing tip. Marquall rolled again and saw a black Talon zip under him. He inverted, falling after it, and dropping low to bob back up on its tail. The Talon tried to turn but he stuck with it, watching its ducts for the tell-tale swivel that announced a sideslip viff. The Talon rolled left, then right, but it couldn't shake him. He got a lock-tone but before he could fire, two machines went past in the opposite direction, so fast he had no time to identify them, so hard their jet wash rocked him out of line.

More throttle. The Talon was extending slightly. It tried a little viff but Marquall held on tight. Lock-tone for the second time. He fired.

He hit it. Buckled pieces of plating flew off. But it wasn't a clean kill. The Talon rose, finding speed in desperation.

'No you don't…' said Marquall.

Suddenly, the air lit up around him. A rain of las-fire.

'Umbra Flight! Break! The bastards are above us!'

It was Blansher's voice. Marquall broke high, somehow coming out of the blizzard of shots unscathed.

'Umbra Flight, Umbra Flight! Bats at eleven. Climb like hell!'

Marquall looked about desperately and saw twenty or more Hell Razors diving in through the dogfight. Either Cobalt Flight had screwed up completely and let them through, or these were newcomers to the brawl.

Marquall came up fast, gripped by the heavy G. He couldn't even see the black Talon any more and cursed his own luck. He'd come so close.

He saw Zemmic diving past, nose cone lit up in a blaze of gunfire. The Talon he was after started to spin and then lost something – probably coolant – in a gush of fluid. It fell into the sea like a stone.

Marquall looped and saw two green Razors turning out wide over another of the barges. He knew if he

pulled away they'd be after his tail, so he went straight
in for a frontal attack. Coming head to head, the closing speed was alarming. Marquall fired and saw shots
burning back his way. The Razors shook past. He had
no idea if he'd hit anything.

To the west of him there was a blue Thunderbolt, one
engine on fire, descending slowly on a long, lazy curve. A
brief puff of white erupted as it hit the water.

A glance right. Del Ruth and Ranfre, locked in a barrelling acrobatic tumble with three Razors. The machines
kept trying to turn in under each other, jockeying to get on
the six. Ranfre was firing and his chosen target viffed out
of the tangle so frantically it rammed its wingman. The
colliding machines exploded in the air. Del Ruth and Ranfre broke and blasted on past. The remaining bat screamed
out the other way.

Marquall was on it immediately. He came round on its
seven, let off a burst, then a second. The bat plunged. For
a moment, Marquall thought he'd stung it, but it was simply viffing out hard to switch onto his tail. Nine-Nine
shuddered and bucked as it was hit. Marquall pulled a violent evasive turn. The bat shot past and away.

'Umbra Eight. Are you okay?'

Marquall checked the instruments. No critical warning
lights had come on.

'This is Eight. I'm okay.'

'Eight, this is Lead. You're trailing fluid. I think it's
hydraulics. Break off and head for home, do you copy?'

Marquall's heart sank. 'Copy that, Lead. I am breaking
off.'

By the time he began his approach to Lucerna, Marquall could feel the damage by the way *Double Eagle*
was handling. He lined up on the transponder signal,
and made a good landing in hangar three via the north
entry.

Racklae got him out. The chief fitter's head was bandaged. The transport that had got him out of Theda had been attacked, and he'd been sliced by shrapnel.

They inspected the damage to Nine-Nine.

'Superficial mostly,' said Racklae, 'but you've taken a hit to the hydraulics.'

'It didn't show on the instruments.'

'Sometimes it doesn't, sir. But I'll check your critical indicator too. Any luck, by the way?'

'No,' said Marquall. He didn't have the heart to admit he'd come so close on two only to lose both. 'Still shaking off the jinx.'

Lucerna Processing, 16.30

'PUT SIMPLY,' SAID the Munitorum senior. 'You're dead.'

'Well, I hate to fly in the face of facts…' Viltry began.

'Don't worry,' said the senior. 'I'll just run it again. Could you check the details as I have them?'

Viltry looked over the data-slate, and handed it back. 'That's correct.'

The senior began to enter the codes in the large, brass-levered cogitator that dominated the chamber. Robed clerks hurried in and out of the room, collecting data-slates or depositing scroll-cases in the alphabetised pigeonholes along one wall. Viltry shrugged apologetically to the man waiting in the doorway. He was at the head of a long, slow-moving queue that stretched right back down the hallway of the Munitorum complex and out down the stairs. Viltry had already spent two hours in it.

The dirt-stained windows of the chamber looked down onto one of Lucerna's giant docks. The scene was artificially lit by frosty blue lumin spheres because it was inside a giant sea cave, protected by the overhang of the island cliffs. There was a hum of industry outside. Hoists clattered, men shouted. The wharfs were lined with extraction barges, disgorging hundreds of men and machines, crates and equipment onto the docks.

'It's coming up the same again,' the senior said. 'Viltry, Oskar. Listed as killed in action on the 260th, along with the rest of his crew. I'm afraid as far as the records are concerned, you don't exist.'

'And yet,' said Viltry.

'Quite,' said the senior. 'We're getting this a lot, I'm sorry to say. War is not conducive to competent record management. And the withdrawal from the Peninsula, well… let's just say whole sections of the data archive are missing or inaccurate. You didn't fly in with a unit, did you?'

Viltry sighed. He'd been through this four times: once to the wharfinger, once to a junior clerk in the downstairs annexe who was running a kind of logistical triage on the influx of refugees, and once already to this man.

'I've been detached from operations for over a week since my flight went down in the desert. I made it back to the coast as part of a retreat column and then reached Theda. I just got on a barge. Whatever was available. Things were pretty wild. I'm travelling with a woman.'

'Your wife?'

'No–'

'Fiancée?'

'No, sir–'

'But there is an attachment?'

Viltry shrugged. 'Yes, we left the city together. She needed to get out too. The Blood Pact was everywhere. I couldn't leave her. I wasn't going to leave her.'

'Where is she now?'

'She went to civilian processing. I had to come here. Military. I hope she's secured a place in a refuge.'

'I'm sure she's fine.'

Viltry cleared his throat. 'Sir, I just want to rejoin my wing. I don't even know where they are.'

'Well, not here at Lucerna, I'm afraid. Actually, I can't tell you where the Phantine XX is. More gaps in the record.'

'Can't you just… correct your data?' Viltry asked.

'Not that simple, I'm sorry to say. Once the records say you're dead, I'm not allowed to argue with it. The best I can do is register you as pending.'

'What does that mean?'

'It means I have many thousands of new arrivals to process, disperse and reassign as quickly as possible, and I can't afford to spend several hours now trying to correct your listing.' The senior took up a stylus and filled in a paper docket which he then stamped a number of times. 'This is a temporary document of registration. It officially recognises your presence here at the base, and clears you to receive accommodation, food and so on.'

Viltry looked at it. 'It doesn't even have my name on it. Or my service number.'

'Of course it doesn't. If I register you by your name or service number, the system will reject you. This is a new number, freshly issued, so the system can accept you. Come back in a few days. Once the pressure's died down, I promise I'll attend to your case with all urgency. That's the best I can do right now.'

'Very well,' said Viltry.

Clutching the docket, he walked out of the chamber.

'Next!' the senior called, and the next in line hurried forward.

Viltry wandered away down the busy, rock-cut hallway. Fate had got him after all.

Oskar Viltry was dead, and he was just an anonymous body with a number.

Lucerna AB, 19.17

BLANSHER WALKED OUT onto the hangar decking. The pilots of Umbra, kitted up, were waiting in a group near the parked machines where the fitters were working hard, repairing the damage to Marquall's machine, and patching hits taken by Del Ruth and Zemmic. It had been a furious brawl, and had continued for another fifteen minutes after Marquall's departure. Zemmic had bagged one, Van Tull another and Blansher two. Despite struggling with her adopted and repainted Firedrake machine, complaining she couldn't get used to the damn thing, Aggie Del Ruth had also scored a good kill. The Thunderbolts had finally driven the bats away from the convoy at around 13.30.

Blansher raised his hand. 'A little quiet, please, Mr Racklae?'

Racklae obliged, and the sound of rivet guns and power drivers stopped.

'What is this, Lead?' Zemmic asked. 'A snap call?'

Blansher smiled. Very quietly, he said, 'Officer on deck.'

Bree Jagdea walked up out of the dispersal tunnel and came across the floor towards them. She'd had a shower, medical check and an issue of clean clothes, but the flight jacket was still her old, battered original.

There was a moment of disbelief. Then the pilots and the fitters began whooping and clapping. Del Ruth ran forward and hugged Jagdea. Van Tull shook her by the hand. The others all grouped around.

'As you were, Umbra,' she said.

The clamouring died down a little.

'Good to see you too, wing,' she smiled.

'We prayed you'd make it to an evac,' Del Ruth said.

'Actually, that's not quite how it happened,' Jagdea replied.

'Then how in Terra's name did you get here, commander?' asked Ranfre.

'You wouldn't believe me if I told you. Okay, okay! Quieten down! I will tell you. Later. For now, I want–'

She paused and glanced at Blansher. 'I apologise, Umbra Leader,' she said. 'I quite forgot myself.'

He grinned. 'For the record, Acting Wing Leader Blansher hands command to Bree Jagdea, 19.18 hours.'

'I accept command,' she said. 'And also for the record, may I commend your leadership in my absence, and also extend my highest compliments to the pilots and crew for their sustained work. You may applaud yourselves loudly.'

And they did.

'Right,' she continued when the ruckus abated. 'I want the flight ready to go in an hour. Combat patrol. Manageable, Mr Racklae?'

'Yes, ma'am!'

'Excellent. We'll go up, two hour sweep, then down. Snap calls permitting, I want everyone rested overnight. No card schools, no drinking. We'll be going again early. I've met with the base commander, Vice Air Marshal Dreyco, and I'm appraised of the situation. This is how it stands, and if I'm blunt, you'll forgive me. The forces of the Archenemy have, as you are well aware, stormed the southern Littoral. According to Tactical, they hold the coast from Theda through to Ezraville. Despite our best efforts to maintain air superiority over that area, they have beaten us back into the sea.'

Jagdea looked around at their faces. All of them looked grim.

'We could not have predicted their air power, nor the efficiency with which they advanced their mass-carriers to extend strike range. Nor could we have countered the manner in which their bombing campaign paved the way for drop deployment of Blood Pact ground forces. They outplayed us, it's as simple as that.'

She took off her flight jacket and hung it from the claws of a power lifter. The cavern air was humid. Her arm was out of its sling now, though it was still packed with dressing pads.

'But understand this,' she continued. 'Our efforts – and the lives of our comrades in this unit and the Navy at large

– were not wasted. We held them. We delayed them. Face it, all we ever hoped to do was delay them. We bought the land forces time to get clear. As I speak, extraction convoys are sailing north across the Zophonian Sea, heading for the main islands there or the northern coast itself. Reports say large elements of armour and infantry are crossing the Festus by land on the way to the Commonwealth fortress hives at Ingeburg. We've made it possible for a considerable portion of the Imperial land army to get clear of the war zone. Now they can regroup and prepare to stage a counter-attack. Reinforcements are en route from the Khan Stars. Due in eight days. The Imperium is on the back foot, but Enothis is far from lost.

'There's always a chance,' she added.

'There's gonna be a "but", isn't there?' said Cordiale.

Jagdea nodded. 'Naturally, pilot. Whoever said the life of an Imperial combat flier would be easy?'

'The aviation recruiter back in scholam,' said Ranfre, and raised a laugh.

'The enemy has driven us into the sea,' said Jagdea. 'But the sea is our secret weapon. We've got the islands. Navy wings are regrouping here at Lucerna, at Onstadt, Viper Atoll, Longstrand, Salthaven, and also on the hive islands of Zophos and Limbus. Long range squadrons have taken station on the northern coastline at three dozen airfields including Tamuda City and Enothopolis itself.'

Jagdea walked across to the nearest Thunderbolt and placed her hand against its flank, like an ancient warrior patting their destrier. 'In order to mount his final offensive, the Archenemy has to get over or around the Zophonian Sea. He will achieve this by way of an air offensive. In the next few days, enemy machines will be flying in force from the southern Littoral with the intention of sinking the retreat convoys and attacking the northern shore. Unchecked, a blanket air assault such as that will crush Enothian hopes. The Northern Affiliation would be wounded and reeling by the time the invasion comes.'

She turned round to look at them straight. 'All viable Navy wings have been charged by Admiral Ornoff to deny that air assault. I repeat, we are commanded that we should operate to deny Archenemy air superiority over the sea. If we can just hold his squadrons back, we will block the sharp end of his invasion, and stall its malign force at the southern coast.'

'And if we can't?' said Zemmic.

'Then we will have failed. And Enothis will fall. Any other bloody silly questions?'

THE BRIEFING BROKE up and everyone resumed work.

Blansher joined Jagdea.

'Tall order. You think we can do it?'

'We can do what we do, Mil,' she replied. 'After that, it's down to the almighty God-Emperor and the currents of fate itself.'

'But realistically?' Blansher had a habit of rubbing the scar tissue that bisected his lips and chin when he was anxious. He was doing it now.

'Realistically? How's this for realistic? It took them two weeks to smash us out of the south. How long do you think the remainder of our broken, under-strength, scattered wings can hold the sea zone?'

'Throne!' he said. 'But–'

Jagdea cut him off. 'Or try this for realistic instead. The sea is a real buffer that will slow the enemy more than the desert or the Peninsula ever did. We are the best pilots in the Imperium… I don't just mean the Phantine, I mean the Navy boys too. We fly to our limits for another week, keep knocking the bastards back, and maybe we have a chance. Once they start hitting the northern coast, it's checkmate, but they've got to get past us first. Regular combat patrols. Snap calls. Up and into them. We could fend them off. Unless…'

'Unless what, Bree?'

'Unless they send everything they have at us at once.'

Blansher sighed. 'That's not a scenario I want to think about.'

An odd look abruptly crossed Jagdea's face. She turned. 'It just occurred to me. What the hell am I going to fly?'

'We'll find you something,' Blansher promised.

He walked her over to one of the freight elevators and dropped them down into the storage chamber under number three hangar. Teams of fitters were at work down here too. In the glow-globe half-light, welding sparks showered up, bright and thick, and panel-guns whirred and thumped. The cradle bays down in the storage chamber were circled around a central elevator platform that lifted planes up onto the main deck.

Serial Zero-Two sat on one of the repair cradles.

'Came in on one of the heavy transports,' said Blansher. 'The techs say she's fit to fly.'

'Great throne of gold!' Jagdea exclaimed. 'I never thought I'd see her again. I expected to make do with a spare from the depot.'

'Praise be the God-Emperor and the diligence of his Munitorum. Despite the urgency, they got a hell of a lot of equipment out of Theda at the end there.'

'Speaking of spares,' Jagdea said, raising her voice to be heard over a blast of riveting, 'what are those?'

Alongside Zero-Two, four other Thunderbolts sat on cradles.

'Oh, they shouldn't be here. The transports brought in a lot of unassigned machines. Spares. Or leftovers from units that don't exist any more. That sort of thing. They gave us four of them because Umbra was listed as a twelve element wing. I explained to the Munitorum clerk we only had eight pilots, and he just got concerned I was upsetting his book keeping.'

Jagdea walked round the machines. One was an ex-Raptor bird, in a scratched black livery. Another was from a unit that favoured pale tan with dazzle patterns. The other two were bare-metal silver, recently delivered replacements that had yet to be assigned.

'Anyway, I've got the depot working on it,' Blansher said. 'I don't want them wasted. And I'm sure we're not the only wing to have been given machines we can't use. They'll get shipped out in the next few days to units that can use them.'

'No,' said Jagdea firmly.

'What?' Blansher asked.

She looked at him. 'Mil, the Imperium needs to get everything it's got aloft now, not in the next few days. We've got planes without pilots. Good for us! I'll bet the evac barges brought in dozens of decent pilots without machines. Let's find them! Let's use them now!'

'Well, I guess…'

'It's called pragmatism,' she said. 'Inform the clerks that these planes are assigned to Umbra. Cancel the transfer.'

'Are you sure?'

'Yes, I'm sure.' She turned and called out. 'Mister Hemmen?'

The fitter ran across to her. 'Mamzel?'

'Make these planes airworthy and dress them in Umbra paint schemes.'

'Yes, mamzel. Directly.'

'Soon as I can,' she said to Blansher, 'I intend to have Umbra up to full strength. I'm going to find us some willing volunteers.'

* * *

Lucerna AB, 23.12

THE FAN ASSEMBLIES were still venting thick exhaust fumes out of the hangar. Jagdea took off her helmet and got down from Zero-Two.

She glanced at the three cannon-shell holes in the tail plating. 'Patch that, please,' she said to her head fitter. 'Rearm and refuel.'

'Yes, commander.'

She walked up the dispersal tunnel and entered the ready room, throwing her helmet, mask and gloves onto the couch. The man who had been sitting in one of the armchairs for some time stood up swiftly.

'At ease,' she said. 'Thanks for coming. You'll have to forgive my temper. A patrol turned into a full-on brawl. But we stung two for no losses, thanks be.'

She went over to the cradenza and poured herself a stiff amasec. 'I told my crews this was a "no drinking" night, so be good and don't let on.'

The man nodded.

'Commander, I was wondering why you sent for me?' said August Kaminsky.

Jagdea slid open a filing cabinet drawer and pulled out a bulging file and some data-slates.

'A bit of driving, Mr Kaminsky. That's what you told me you were good for these days. A bit of driving for the Munitorum.'

'Yes, commander.'

'Well, I'd like you to do a bit of driving for me. There's an I-XXI Thunderbolt downstairs, and I'd like to have your name stencilled under the cockpit.'

Kaminsky gazed at her. His eyes shone with what seemed like anger. The skin of his unblemished cheek flushed almost as pink as the mass of burns on the other side.

'Is that a joke, commander? If it is, I think it's in pretty poor taste. I can't fly Thunderbolts. I can't fly, period.'

'I beg to differ. I was in that Cyclone with you. That was instinct, Kaminsky. Pure instinct. I've never seen finer.'

'But, commander…'

'I'm offering you a place in my wing, Mr Kaminsky. Or should I say "Major"? I called up your log records. Sixteen years, wing leader grade, a career tally of seventeen confirmed kills. This is your chance to get back in the game. To fly and fight for your world. Are you going to refuse me?'

Kaminsky raised his stiff, plastek hand. 'Commander, I was rated not airworthy because of this, not because I was unwilling to fight. The Commonwealth just hasn't got the augmetic resources to fix up pilots like me. With this hand, I can't control throttle, stick and guns. Shit, you know that, Jagdea.'

Jagdea nodded. 'Yes, that's a problem. The Navy could resource you a proper augmetic implant, but we don't have much time. Certainly not enough time for you to undergo implantation surgery. So I talked to my fitters. They're an ingenious lot, fitters. One suggested mounting the trigger assembly on the top of the throttle lever, but we all thought that might get in the way. Then Mr Racklae had a notion. He's going to wire up the weapons systems to a voice activator. It'll take a little getting used to, I realise, but you've got some serious familiarisation to do anyway. Bottom line, Kaminsky, your guns can be voice controlled. Your impairment need not bar your from combat service.'

Kaminsky continued to stare at her. 'I–' he began.

'Think it over, major. If you decide to pass, I have other candidates to consider. But you were my first choice.'

There was a knock on the door.

'Yes?'

Marquall looked in. 'Commander? Do you have a minute?'

'Be right there,' she said. She glanced back at Kaminsky. 'Help yourself to a drink if you like. I'll be back in a while.'

She left Kaminsky in the ready room and went outside. Marquall peered back through the doorway with a frown. 'What's he doing here, commander?' he whispered, dubiously.

'He's having a long, hard think, Marquall. What did you need?'

'A guy's just turned up in the hangar. Says he knows you.'

'HELLO, JAGDEA,' SAID Viltry.

'The Emperor protects! Viltry?'

She hurried to him and shook his hand. He looked like hell. Unshaven, his clothes dirty and torn, and he'd lost a lot of weight.

'Viltry, it was posted that you were dead,' she said.

'So they keep telling me. The Munitorum refuses to believe I exist.'

'But your machine did go down?'

'Yeah.'

'Your crew?'

Viltry shook his head.

'I'm sorry.'

'By the time I got back to Theda, everyone was leaving. I jumped on a barge, wound up here.'

'Where's the rest of Halo Flight?'

Viltry shrugged. 'Don't know. I was talking to a Navy crewman down in the food line, and he said he thought a Phantine outfit was stationed here, so I came to see for myself. I can't pretend I'm not disappointed you're not Halo, but it's good to see a face from home.'

'What are you going to do?' asked Jagdea.

'I don't know, exactly,' he confessed. 'Even if I do find out where in this theatre Halo's been posted, I don't stand much chance of rejoining them. Until the Munitorum acknowledges my existence, I'm not eligible for transit back to my outfit. I'm... stuck.'

'Not necessarily,' said Jagdea. 'Do you want to fly?'

'Well, yes. If I can.'

'You're fit. You've done tours on Thunderbolts too, right?'

'Yes. Bree, what do you have in mind?'

DAY 268

Lucerna AB, 07.30

A CLEAR DAY over the desert. Fine, bright, light conditions.
Slight crosswind. He opened the throttle and the big,
brutal Imperial plane climbed effortlessly.

Ironic, Kaminsky thought. Conditions had been just
like this that day he'd–

The last time he'd flown.

'Make your track four-one-six,' the vox said.

'Copy that, Lead,' Kaminsky replied.

'And keep an eye on your auspex. The dial top right of
the screen-plate adjusts gain if you need better resolution
on a merged return.'

'Got that, thank you.'

Kaminsky pushed the stick over gently, depressing the
rudder bar. Good response. The Thunderbolt was everything he'd imagined it would be.

'Contacts! Ten o'clock!' the vox suddenly chimed.

343

Kaminsky glanced round, saw the flash on the auspex. Nothing in visual... No, there it was. A glint of sunlight off metal, hard and high up.

He started to climb again. The bat came down sharply, screwing out of its dive. He thought he'd paced the intercept well, but the hostile had gone under him.

'Break! Break, or he'll have you!'

'Trying!' Kaminsky responded. He made a violent left-hand roll. It was right on his tail now. How the hell had it managed that?

'Break! Break!'

Tone warning. He was locked hard.

'Holy Throne!' he cursed, and tried one last twist.

The bat began to fire.

Kaminsky's Thunderbolt exploded.

The stick went dead. So did the sky. Blansher slid back the hood.

'Bad luck,' he said.

'I was stupid,' Kaminsky said. 'It was a basic mistake.'

'You're still getting used to the bird. Thinking too much about the controls and how they operate. It's natural. Once the mechanics become so familiar you don't have to think about them, your mind will be freed up.'

Kaminsky nodded.

'Besides,' said Blansher. 'I know you don't have much experience of vector-thrust aircraft. Vectoring gives us all sorts of tricks we can play in the air. The bat got you just then because it viffed out under you. And if you'd done the same, you'd probably have evaded.'

'I know,' said Kaminsky. 'But it's difficult not to think in terms of forward motion. Sidestepping, stopping... that sort of thing doesn't seem natural.'

'It needn't be that dramatic. Just a little touch will put a slight non-ballistic behaviour into your performance.'

Blansher glanced at his chronometer.

'You've been in the simulator rig for two hours. We can take a break if you like. Get some breakfast into you.'

'How many times have I died in those two hours?' Kaminsky asked.

'Six,' Blansher grinned.

'Let's try it again.'

Lucerna AB, 07.43

'COMMANDER? COMMANDER EADS?'

Jagdea ran to catch up with the man. They were crossing a busy gantry walkway deep in the heart of the base. Tannoy announcements kept booming out, and personnel jostled and hurried past.

'Commander Eads?' Jagdea said.

The man turned, his head cocked. 'Who's calling my name?'

She'd been told he was blind. *Look for the blind officer*, several people had said.

'My apologies, sir. I'm Commander Jagdea, Phantine XX.'

'Are you indeed? And why were you after me?'

'I was hoping to talk to you, sir. Get some advice.'

'About what?'

'Pilots. I'm looking for pilots to replace losses in my flight.'

'Then surely you should be talking to Navy reserve,' he said.

'I started there. Navy reserve has no one airworthy. The handful of able pilots who have come in with the evac have already been assigned to Navy flights. So I asked the Munitorum for lists of airworthy Commonwealth pilots here on Lucerna.'

Eads chuckled. 'You can't do that. Navy doesn't take pilots from the PDF.'

'Because the Navy believes it is an elite service and chooses to draw only on its own. I know. That's what the

Munitorum officer told me,' Jagdea said. 'The thing is, the Phantine XX isn't Navy. It's Imperial Guard. An aberration, but one that permits me the scope to recruit from the PDF if I choose.'

Eads shook his head, amused. 'The Navy won't like that.'

'The Navy can lump it. The precedent is already well established, thanks to a priest who– Look, I won't bore you with the story. The point is, I have the list of Commonwealth fliers.' Jagdea patted a fat folder under her arm. 'I was told you were the man to ask about recommendations.'

'Can we walk and talk?' Eads asked. 'I'm due on shift at Operations at eight.'

'Of course.'

They moved away off the gantry and along an equally busy rock-cut corridor. Jagdea noticed how even the most hurried-looking personnel they met respectfully stood aside to let Eads pass.

'You know the men. You had command at Theda North.'

'Before the Navy arrived. I'm afraid I can't read your lists. I left my code-reader behind in the haste to evacuate. I'm lost without it.'

'I could read out the list to you, sir.'

'As I said, my shift starts at eight. Maybe later, commander.'

'With respect, sir, time is very short. Is there no one you can think of?'

The main hatch into Lucerna Operations lay ahead of them.

'Well, there is one. Good pilot. I know he's here because he came in with me. And I know for a fact he's done simulation time orienting on your machines.'

'That's a good start.'

'His name's Scalter. Frans Scalter. I recommend him highly. He works Operations too, but he's not on this shift. Someone can track him down for you.'

'Thank you, sir. Can I come and find you later? Run through the lists?'

'Of course.'

They'd reached the doorway. Jagdea could hear the frantic chatter of the busy Operations floor beyond the hatch. Juniors ran in and out with data-slates and chart reports. A young man was standing by the hatch. He seemed to be waiting for Eads. He looked somehow familiar to Jagdea.

'Good morning, Flight,' he said to Commander Eads.

'Call that a salute?' Eads replied. 'Ready to go, Darrow?'

'Yes, sir.'

'I'll expect you later then, commander,' Eads said to Jagdea, then allowed his junior to lead him away into the hustle of the Operations deck.

Lucerna AB, 08.30

THEY STOOD ON an observation platform high amongst the island cliffs. It was a fine, clear morning, though the wind was strong and tugged at their hair. A hundred metres below them, the sea crashed in against the foot of the pink crags.

'Almost romantic,' said Beqa. 'The sea and the islands. My family took me on holiday to the Midwinters when I was young. Me and Eido. We stayed on Salthaven. There are beaches there. Eido loved it. That was before the war really took hold, obviously. A time when holidays were something that people did.'

'One day, I'll take you on a holiday. I promise.'

She smiled at Viltry. 'Don't make promises you can't keep.'

'No, really. I mean it, all I've got to do is defeat the enemy, and we can have all the holidays we want.'

She shook her head, amused.

'So you say they've found you a job?' he said.

'In munitions prep. The senior who assigned me seemed impressed by my skills. All those long night shifts at the manufactory weren't a waste.'

'That's good.'

'I start this afternoon.'

'You haven't said anything about the way I look,' Viltry said.

'I'm trying not to think about it. It's difficult, because you're very handsome in that new flightsuit, all shaved and groomed. You've found your squadron, haven't you?'

'No,' said Viltry. 'But I found a Phantine unit here that needed a pilot. Fighters, would you believe? That'll take some re-learning. It's called the Phantine XX. Umbra Flight.' He showed her the insignia pins and badges on his new flight coat.

'Very nice,' she said, and looked away at the sea.

'I have to fly, Beq. It's what I do. They need every pilot they can get right now. I would be failing the Throne if I didn't do this.'

'I know.'

'And maybe when the war's done here, I can apply to leave the service and stay here with you.'

Beqa Mayer smiled. 'The war is never done, Oskar. If it finishes here, a fine pilot like you will be needed somewhere else. They won't let you leave. You're a resource. They'll keep you flying until the enemy finally claims you. Remember what I said about promises you couldn't keep?'

'I'm sorry,' he mumbled.

'It's all right. Really. We've had some time. It's been brief, but very sweet. I thought I'd lost you once, and the Emperor allowed you to come back. I couldn't go through that again. You fly. I'll be proud of you. That's all that needs to be said.'

The wind had picked up again. She shivered.

'That blasted old coat of yours,' he snapped. He bent over his kit bag and pulled out his ragged Halo Flight jacket. 'Take this. It's a bit battered and torn, I'm afraid, but it's got a fleece lining.'

He put it over her shoulders, then pulled her close.

'Thanks,' she said, pressing against his side. She rested her head on his chest.

'You're right,' he said, gazing at the view. 'It is almost romantic.

There was a boom like the end of the world, and eight Thunderbolts slammed up into the air from a hangar in the cliff beneath them. The throaty roar of the formation's afterburners shook their diaphragms.

As the planes climbed away, they both laughed.

'Until something like that happens,' Viltry said.

She kissed his cheek. 'To hell with them. We can make our own romance. You go and fly, Oskar. I've told the Emperor to protect you.'

Over the Midwinters, 14.10

UMBRA FLIGHT WAS barely up when they spotted the air battle. To the west, the pale green sky was bright with flashes and tinged with smoke. And it wasn't the only battle. Wings from Onstadt were coming in on a major fight to the east, and everything Viper Atoll had was lofting against a thousand-bomber wave heading out across the Sea of Ezra towards Limbus.

'Umbra, rise to four thousand,' Jagdea ordered. She had four machines with her: Marquall, Van Tull, Cordiale and Viltry. Viltry's first flight. She had sensed his nerves as he'd run to his bird.

Umbra Flight had already been up twice that day. A full flight sortie at 09.00 hours that had lasted two hours and seen them turn back a ninety-plane bomber formation with the help of three Lightning wings out of Tamuda MAB. Three kills – Ranfre, Del Ruth and Jagdea. Then Del Ruth, Ranfre and Zemmic had gone up just before noon with Blansher as lead, and had a short but ferocious duel with the top cover of a Hell Talon formation. Zemmic and Blansher had scored kills, but they'd been grateful to see the 56th coming in to help break the wave up.

All four were now on refit turnaround and Blansher was spending time coaching Kaminsky. Blansher was patient, but he seemed to have doubts about Kaminsky's talent.

'He's getting the basic layout of the Bolt, but he refuses to relax,' Blansher had told her. 'Maybe he's not the best choice.'

'Stick with it,' Jagdea had ordered.

They could see the hostiles now. Sixty Tormentors pounding across the sea towards the Northern Affiliation, laden with bombs. The 51st had already engaged.

'Any sign of escort?' Jagdea voxed.

'Nothing on the scope,' replied Cordiale. 'But you've got to assume.'

'Start assuming,' she said. There was also no sign of the promised support for them from Longstrand. Jagdea keyed the vox. 'Lucerna Operations, this is Umbra Leader. Confirm other units aloft.'

A buzzing crackle. 'Operations, Umbra Lead. Kodiak Flight and Orbis Flight show as launched. East of you, seventy kilometres, closing low. Twenty, repeat, twenty machines.'

'Thank you, Operations. We have visual on the enemy. Closing to intercept.'

Jagdea was reassured to hear that the Phantine wing commanded by her friend Wilhem Hayyes was inbound. She switched on her gunsight and toggled her lascannons to active.

'Guns live, Umbra. Come back.'

'Umbra Eight, copy.' That was Marquall.

'Umbra Three, four-A.' And Van Tull.

'Umbra Eleven, check and ready.' Cordiale.

A pause.

'Umbra Four? Come back,' Jagdea voxed. 'Umbra Four? Do you copy? Viltry? Dammit, Viltry!'

'Copy you, Lead. This is Umbra Four. Sorry, I just tried to switch on my gunsight and appear to have turned on the de-mister and the cockpit light instead.'

'Viltry?'

'Just kidding, Lead. Guns live. On your command.'

Jagdea smiled. 'Operations, Show Umbra as attacking. Umbra Flight… Attack, attack, attack!'

Viltry was nothing like as confident as he sounded. As he nursed the throttle, following Jagdea's shallow dive, he saw the lumbering packs of Tormentors filling the sky ahead. The slow, medium bombers were already firing from their turret mounts, chattering out streaks of heavy fire.

Viltry had flown Bolts before, but this seemed strange after so many tours in Marauders. It wasn't the differences in cockpit layout, or the considerably greater agility. It was the fact that he was alone again. One man, one machine. No trained crew manning other stations.

So focused. So very concentrated. It was all down to him.

Viltry decided he'd better enjoy it. The Thunderbolt certainly felt like a tiny, speeding dart compared to *G for Greta*. They sliced down into the enemy lines.

He was reminded that air tactics were now utterly different too. Ordinarily, he'd have been the one flying the heavy plane in formation, fighting off the interceptors. Not the other way round.

Jagdea and Van Tull went over the formation, blitzing fire. Viltry followed them, seeing Marquall and Cordiale go under.

Immediately, three enemy machines started to drop out of line, making thick smoke. One suddenly pitched down, violently. Umbra came up and around for the second pass.

'Must do better,' Viltry said to himself.

Cordiale had the lead on the turn and prosecuted the attack. His lascannons flashed white. One of the Tormentors wavered for a moment then blew up in a huge cloud of flames as its payload ignited.

Burning debris rained down. The Tormentors in immediate formation wallowed away in the shock burst, two collided and the destroyed plane's sheared apart. Viltry saw scrap metal and bodies falling.

He had a decent line-up. The nearest Tormentor was pumping streams of tracer his way, but the shot-stream was dropping low. He smiled as he got a clean lock *ping* and started firing.

The Thunderbolt tugged hard, its airframe pulsing as it discharged its cannons. Bree had warned him it would do that. He compensated and turned high.

'Umbra Four, this is Lead. Nice kill.'

'I didn't even see it,' he said. 'Did I get it?'

'Yes, Four.'

He rolled back, exhilarated by the light performance of the Thunderbolt, and pounced on another Tormentor.

Its turrets tried to pin him. He knew from bitter experience how a fighter could ride up underneath a straight-flying bomber. It was all a matter of judging the cones of fire.

There was always a sweet spot.

He found it.

Viltry fired, lancing dazzling bars of las energy from his nose cone.

The belly of the Tormentor burst, and then it started to dive, ablaze, leaving a curl of brown smoke in the air behind it.

'Scratch two,' he voxed. 'Think I'm getting the hang of it, Bree.'

MARQUALL BANKED, QUIETLY furious. He'd missed his targets on both passes. And this man, Viltry, had just come along and in the space of two minutes, he'd equalled Marquall's career score. The bastard! It was insufferable. The upstart was even on first name terms with Jagdea.

Who the hell did he think he was?

Nine-Nine shuddered as bolter rounds kissed its flank. Marquall banked out. Part of the formation went by under him, and he dropped back onto the lead pair.

He was too high. The tail guns nailed him hard, cracking his canopy and ripped out part of his cowling.

He dropped out of the line of fire. How the devil did Viltry know where to place himself? He climbed again, hammered at by gunfire from the enemy pack.

He snuggled in, lining up on a bomber, but before he could deploy the trigger, the thing exploded in a giant wash of smoke. Van Tull had nailed it.

'Oh give me a break!' Marquall exclaimed. 'Someone give me a frigging break!'

THE 51ST, TANKS spent, had pulled off. Now Kodiak and Orbis Flights powered in and entered the engagement. Kodiak, a flight from the 789th Navy, were flying dark green Bolts; Orbis were dressed in Phantine grey with blue trim.

'Hello Orbis, hello Orbis,' Jagdea voxed. 'Nice to see you.'

'Umbra Lead, this is Hayyes. Any left?'

'Plenty. Take your pick, Orbis Leader.'

Hayyes turned his Thunderbolt long and peppered a Tormentor that went down in flames at once. Two of his wingmen scored, and Kodiak Flight ripped another three hostiles out of the sky.

'All wings! Break left! Now!' Kodiak leader voxed. 'Fighters coming in!'

Hell Razors stooped out of the high clouds, hammering down at full thrust. They were firing.

'Break wide!' Jagdea ordered.

Viltry felt his machine buck as shots scorched by. He started to climb steeply.

Marquall started to dive.

The enemy fighters slammed through their scatter. One of the Kodiak planes broke apart under fire. Another sank on a wide turn towards the sea.

The Razors were crimson and black, except for their leader, who was pearl-white.

Lucerna AB, 14.30

'Switch.'

'And say it again.'

'Switch.'

'Okay, sir,' called Racklae. 'Now give the command "fire".'

'Fire!' said Kaminsky.

'Again?'

'Fire!'

Racklae stood up, checking his tech-plate, and looked down at Kaminsky in the cockpit.

'Right, the system now knows your voice. The commands are logged.' Racklae leaned in across the cockpit well and pointed to a brass switch on the panel beside the throttle.

'That's your arming toggle. Throw it, guns are live. After that, it's all voice. You say "fire" and the system will fire a burst from whatever's selected. Default is las. You say "switch" and it auto-toggles to the quads or back. Is that clear?'

'Yes, thank you,' Kaminsky nodded. 'And if I want continuous fire?'

'Just keep saying "fire", sir.'

Kaminsky pulled himself up out of the cockpit. 'Thanks, Mr Racklae. You've done a fine job.'

The fitter seemed distracted.

'What's up?' asked Kaminsky.

Racklae jumped down off the wing plate. 'The boys are monitoring the vox, sir. It sounds like Umbra's in trouble.'

Kaminsky followed the fitter across to the clutch of crewmen around the vox set. Blansher was tuning the dial. Ranfre, Zemmic and Del Ruth were crowded round amongst the techs. At least Kaminsky was pretty sure that's who they were. He'd only just been told the other pilots' names.

'What's going on?' he asked Zemmic. The young man was playing with a chain of lucky charms.

'Jag's gone into a Tormentor formation,' Zemmic said. 'And now they got bats. Bad bats. The Killer's there.'

'The Killer?' Kaminsky asked.

'The pearl-white bastard,' said Zemmic.

Over the Midwinters, 14.33

VILTRY SCREAMED HIS Bolt round. The fighter pack was all over them. He tried to twist out. Jagdea and one of the Orbis birds swept in under him crosswise, gunning. He saw a Kodiak explode in mid-air, stung by a red bat.

He got a brief warning *ping* and rolled. A black Razor was trying to tag him. Viltry swept down and, ignoring the turret ordnance whipping up at him, plunged in amongst the Tormentor formation. The Razor slowed, unwilling to risk hitting one of the bombers it was supposed to be protecting.

Pleased with his ruse, Viltry throttled hard and came back up through the formation, this time with his guns alight. Firing impaired his climb rate, but it was worth it. As he came up diagonally under a Tormentor, he hit it two or three times. Its engines began to gush blue vapour.

Rising clear, Viltry could no longer spot the black bat.

But there was the pearl-white Razor, the leader of the enemy pack. It came around about five hundred metres starboard of him, moving a lot faster than Viltry's machine, and dipped low. Another Thunderbolt, Orbis Six, was ascending past it.

'Orbis Six! Watch yourself!' Viltry called.

The pearl-white Razor executed a perfect viff correction, a deft little simultaneous climb-and-slide, and spat fire at Orbis Six.

Hit, the Thunderbolt folded, spraying out burning fuel.

The lead Razor was already climbing out, hunting for another target. Viltry started to go after it, but suddenly found he had his hands full evading hard as the black bat reappeared.

JAGDEA AND CORDIALE banked together, and began chasing a red bat down towards the formation. What had been clean, bright air was now thick with exhaust trails, vapour, bars of smoke and weapons discharge residue. Nevertheless, she could see the white bat.

The red Razor they were after was beginning to outrun them. She gave up on it and banked out, searching for the white bat again in the chaos of the rolling dogfight.

A black Razor chopped across her, head to head, and they traded shots. She checked her fuel. Low. The demands of the brawl had really emptied the tanks.

'Umbra Flight, fuel status?'

Cordiale responded, then Viltry and finally Marquall. All of them were virtually running on empty like her.

'Lead instructs flight, disengage and turn for home.'

'Umbra Four, copy.'

'Umbra Eleven, yes ma'am.'

'Marquall? Umbra Eight? Respond.'

MARQUALL HAD JUST spotted the white hostile too, and recognised it at once. Most definitely the one that had nearly killed him on his second sortie, the bat that had claimed the Apostle.

'Umbra Eight?'

'One moment, Lead.'

He turned towards the bat, but immediately had to crank away because he had inadvertently run into the range of a pair of cruising Tormentors. Marquall pushed Nine-Nine's throttle, dropped the nose and looped in under the bomber string, taking a futile pot-shot at the now-ascending white Razor. Another bat started firing at him as it crossed his two and Marquall banked, barely avoiding a Tormentor that was dropping, engines burning.

'Umbra Eight! Break off now!' Jagdea sounded mad.

Marquall heard a persistent warning chime. Fuel limit reached.

'Copy that, Leader. I'm coming.'

He took one look back, and saw to his dismay that the white bat had lined up on Orbis Leader.

'Orbis Lead! Break! Break wild!' Marquall yelled.

Orbis Leader turned to the right. Cannon fire from the white bat chewed his Bolt into pieces. The debris flew out on a spear of flame for almost half a kilometre.

Marquall climbed out of the dogfight, chasing the other three Umbra birds.

'Did you see?' he voxed. 'Did you see? That damned white Razor! He got Orbis Leader!'

'I saw,' Jagdea replied. She felt nothing except numb and sore from the physical extremes of the engagement. She knew the misery would hit her later. Hayyes had been her friend since flight school.

Right now, only one thing stuck in her mind. In the turmoil of the last part of the clash, she'd finally remembered why she'd recognised Eads's junior.

Lucerna AB, 15.10

THE NOISE OF the jets died away. As Jagdea and her wingmen dismounted, the fitter teams and the other flight pilots applauded. Jagdea knew they were saluting a hell of a fight, a clutch of good kills, and the fact that all four were back alive. They were also showing support for Viltry on his successful debut.

But it felt wrong. Not just because of Hayyes. How many Imperial planes had she seen go down in that one brawl? Men were dying at a hell of a rate.

'Good work,' she said to Cordiale, who had sat down on the deck to unlace his boots and massage circulation back into his feet. Exposure to multiple negative G events often left a pilot with pins and needles, or worse.

'Thanks, commander,' he said.

Viltry was removing his helmet. He looked pale, shaken, but there was a grin on his face.

'Enjoy that?' she asked.

'Of course not.'

'You did well, Viltry. Like you've been on Thunderbolts for years.'

He smoothed his sweat-flattened hair. 'I must admit it was fun cutting loose in something so agile. You forget how heavy Marauders are.'

Marquall was just climbing down from Nine-Nine.

'Nice going, Marquall,' she said. 'You kept your head.' She dropped her voice so only he could hear her. 'Don't *ever* ignore a direct instruction again, pilot. I called you out because it was time to go. That happens, you obey without question. Are we clear on that?'

He looked at the deck. 'Yes, commander.'

She walked away. 'Rearm and refuel, please!' she shouted to the fitter crews, knowing they were already on it.

A tall man in a Commonwealth uniform was waiting for her with Blansher.

'Major Frans Scalter,' Blansher said, by way of introduction. Jagdea shook Scalter's hand and looked him up and down. Scalter had a slightly stunned expression.

'I take it you've explained the basics to Major Scalter, Mil?'

'I took the liberty of spoiling your surprise, commander.'

Jagdea looked at Scalter. 'Well, major? Are you interested in taking a place in my flight? Commander Eads has given you his personal recommendation.'

Scalter opened his mouth, but couldn't find any words immediately. He nodded, and then said, 'I would be honoured, Commander Jagdea. I have been longing to get the chance to fly for my home world again.'

'That's agreed then. Good. Your designation will be Umbra Seven. Mil, if you're busy with Kaminsky, find someone like Del Ruth or Cordiale to get Mr Scalter oriented, kitted up, and checked out on a simulator.'

'Yes, mamzel,' said Blansher. 'You off somewhere?'

'I won't be long,' said Jagdea.

MARQUALL STOOD BY his bird for a while, stripping off his jacket and gloves, not wanting to mix with the others.

'Everything all right, sir?' asked Racklae.

'Fine,' he replied. He was hardly going to tell his fitter that he was still smarting from the dressing down Jagdea had given him. At least she'd had the decency not to do it in front of the others.

He wandered across the hangar space, through the teams of working fitters, skirting a power lifter as it offered up munitions drums, stopping to let an electric bowser trundle past.

Kaminsky was seated on a jerry can beside his Thunderbolt, carefully studying a data-slate of specifications and procedures.

'Hi,' said Marquall.

The shockingly-scarred face tilted up at him. 'Hello. Marquall, right?'

'Yeah. So... you got your wish, then?'

'I beg your pardon?' Kaminsky replied.

'That night in Zara's. You said you'd give anything to be like me. To fly again.'

'Ah, I did, didn't I?'

Marquall nodded. 'I can't quite remember if it was before or after you called me a bastard and a waste of space, and suggested I shot myself to make the sector a better place.'

'Damn,' said Kaminsky. He put the slate down carefully, but still did not get to his feet. 'I was kinda hoping you'd forgotten about that. Yes, I got my wish, Marquall. And what about you? Fallen off any barstools recently?'

Marquall coloured. 'No,' he said.

Kaminsky picked up the slate and started to read it again. 'Then it sounds like things are working out for both of us,' he said.

Lucerna AB, 16.01

EADS HAD QUARTERS in the lower levels of the base. The evacuation influx had put huge pressure on accommodation. The rock cut passages down here smelled damp, and the glow globe lighting was poor. Some of the rooms she saw were storage bays, and she was sure the quarters she passed had also been storage bays until recently.

She found Eads's room and knocked on the metal hatch. After a moment, it opened and Darrow peered out.

'Commander Jagdea?'

'I've come to see Eads.'

'Yes, mamzel. He's expecting you.'

Darrow opened the door and let her in. The room was small and bare. Litter had been swept into one corner. There was a camp table and two chairs, an unmade cot, and a bottle of amasec with a dirty glass.

The one concession to comfort was an old, tatty armchair. Eads was sitting in it, apparently asleep.

'I can come back,' Jagdea whispered.

'I'm awake, Jagdea. Just resting my thoughts. It was a long and demanding shift.'

Darrow collected up a stack of data-slates and paper files from the table.

'I was just finishing the shift reports,' he told Jagdea. 'I'll get out of your way.'

'No, stay,' she said. He paused, and put the paperwork back down.

'Excuse the drabness,' said Eads. 'I'm told it's drab. I can't help it. I came out of Theda with just the clothes I was standing up in. Take a seat and let's get down to business.'

Jagdea sat down, and put the folder she was carrying on the table. 'I saw the white bat today,' she said.

'Did you?' said Eads. 'That devil's still out there, then?'

'It reminded me of the notice of report that had been circulated at the time of the Lida incident. This report,' she said, tapping the folder. 'It contains a written account of a brawl with the bat. Very useful, very cautionary. It's been required reading for the Navy wings. You wrote it, didn't you, Darrow?'

'I did, commander,' the young man replied.

'The report also contained your commanding officer's account. I forget his name.'

'Major Heckel,' Darrow said.

'Major Heckel. Not confined by modesty as you were in your part of the file, he describes the most extraordinary piece of flying.'

'Heckel was not exaggerating,' said Eads quietly. 'He said it was one of the most gifted displays of natural ability he'd ever seen.'

'So it seems,' said Jagdea. 'Out-running an expert killer, probably an echelon commander, a pilot at the height of his powers. What's more, doing it in a totally out-classed machine that lacked the speed, power and vector abilities of the enemy's bat. What puzzles me is this, Commander Eads. When I came to you asking for recommendations, you chose to ignore the young pilot serving with you on a daily basis.'

Eads was silent.

'Commander?' Darrow said softly. 'May I ask… recommendations for what?'

'My wing is short a frontline pilot, Darrow.'

'You… you'd consider me?' he said, astonished.

'I understand you've been clocking simulator time on Thunderbolts,' Jagdea said.

'I have,' said Darrow. 'Sixty hours. Who told you?'

'Major Scalter. So where does this leave us?'

Eads sat forward, his hands on his knees. 'Enric's not the one you're looking for, commander,' he said.

'Why not?' Darrow asked sharply. 'I'm sorry, sir,' he added, adjusting his tone. 'Why not, sir?'

Eads addressed his answer to Jagdea. 'He's barely a cadet, Jagdea! His combat hours are minimal. Oh, he's got talent. But that one dogfight? It was luck. He got very lucky indeed. If you send him into combat now, he will die. He's not ready. My recommendation would be an act of murder.'

Darrow rose to his feet. 'I disagree, sir.'

'It's not up to you, Enric,' Eads said.

'Isn't it?' Jagdea asked.

'How will I ever be ready if I don't get the experience?' Darrow said.

'This is not the time,' said Eads.

'Oh, I think there's no time like it,' said Jagdea. 'Enothis needs all her pilots for this war, Commander Eads. If men like Darrow don't try, then there may not be a future available for other chances.'

'I won't have his blood on my conscience,' said Eads emphatically. 'I will not recommend him.'

Jagdea looked at Darrow. 'I think it's up to an individual wing leader to decide if she needs a man to be recommended before she takes him. Your objection is noted, commander, and your loyalty in trying to protect him is admirable. Cadet Darrow, I'm offering you that place. Will you take it?'

'Yes, commander. Gladly.' Darrow looked over at Eads. 'I'm sorry, sir.'

Jagdea got to her feet and collected her folder. 'You'll have to report immediately, Darrow. You can come with me now.'

They walked to the hatch. In the doorway, Darrow turned and saluted crisply.

'Call that a salute?' Eads said.

'Yes, sir.'

Eads rose to his feet stiffly, and then saluted back.

'That's a salute,' he said, and sat down again. 'Good luck, son. Prove me wrong.'

DARROW FOLLOWED JAGDEA down the passageways to one of the main staircases. They clattered up the stone steps, side by side.

'You alright?' she asked him.

'Yes, mamzel. I'm very fond of the commander. It's sad to see him upset like that.'

'You know he was only trying to protect you, don't you?' Jagdea said.

'Yes, but I think there was something more,' said Darrow. 'These last few weeks, he's lost everything. His command, many of his men and his friends, then the base itself, and all his possessions with it. I think my company was the last thing he had to hold onto.'

'This is war,' said Jagdea. 'War calls for sacrifices.'

DAY 269

Lucerna AB, 06.30

'THIS WAY, GENTLEMEN,' Jagdea called, walking out into the middle of the hangar three deckway. The four aviators followed her, wearing their flight armour, carrying their helmets. Viltry, Kaminsky, Scalter and Darrow. The latter looked especially nervous.

'Relax,' Scalter whispered.

Jagdea stopped beside the ranks of parked planes. 'We have no time for proper induction. Apparently, there's a war on or something.'

The crew laughed.

'This is an orientation flight, a shake-down. It's the best we can do to get you used to the feel of the real thing before we start hitting combat. When I say you, I mean Mr Darrow, Mr Scalter and Mr Kaminsky. Mr Viltry has already been on one sortie. But I figure the more flying time he can get in a Bolt, the better. Zemmic and I will be flying chaperone. Follow my lead. Any questions?'

'Commander?' said Scalter. 'What's with the pink feathers you all wear?'

'Lucky feathers!' Cordiale called out. The rest of the Umbra pilots were waiting by the birds. He came forward, stuffed a hand in the pocket of his flight pants and produced several more which he handed out to the newbies. They put them on their lapels dubiously.

'Right,' said Jagdea. 'Lucky feathers. That's got the important stuff out of the way. Let's mount up.'

'ARE WE SCRAPING the barrel or what?' Marquall whispered to Ranfre. 'Two Commonwealth no-hopers, one of them a kid, that poisonous cripple, and a Marauder pilot who's been through the ringer. I mean, he's got that look in his eyes.'

'Viltry did pretty damn well yesterday,' Ranfre said.

'Even so,' said Marquall. Viltry's score from the previous day still irked him.

Primers began to crackle and fire the engines on the six planes. Scalter settled into his cockpit and ran his hands around the edges of it with a grin on his face. Kaminsky allowed the fitter to fasten his harness, then used his good hand to fix his prosthetic around the stick.

'Okay, sir?' said Racklae.

'The usual nerves.'

Racklae leaned into the cockpit, strapped the speaker phone for the voice system around Kaminsky's neck, then plugged its trailing leads into the instrument panel on his left.

'Comfortable?'

Kaminsky settled his mask and nodded. Racklae closed the canopy.

Darrow's heart was beating fast. He kept licking his lips. Nothing was how he had imagined it. The weight of the kit on his body, the sound of the Lightning engines, the smell of the cockpit as he lowered himself in.

One of the fitters patted his own ears and Darrow noddded, switching on the vox and testing it.

'This is Umbra Leader, let me know you're ready.'

'Lead, this is Ten, ready.'

'Thank you, Zemmic. I assumed you were.'

'Leader, this is Umbra Four. I'm all set,' voxed Viltry.

'Umbra Five, Leader,' called Kaminsky. 'Ready to lift.'

'Umbra Seven, check, Leader,' Scalter said.

'This is Umbra Nine, Umbra Lead,' Darrow said. 'Systems clear. I am ready.'

The deck officers waved them go, and ducked down.

'Flight, go to lift,' Jagdea voxed.

The Thunderbolts' engine pitch increased sharply as they rose into the air.

'Launch to forward flight,' Jagdea instructed.

The flight rushed up and away out of the hangar mouth and into the sky, lifting their landing gear.

JAGDEA TURNED THEM right, across the atolls, and they spent a while practising formation flying and basic manoeuvres.

Then she started to push them a little harder. Fast ascents, rolls and power dives.

'Keep looking around you, flight,' Jagdea voxed. 'Get in the habit of checking both auspex and visual on a regular basis. And get used to what you can't see from your canopy as much as what you can. Learn how to compensate, how to pitch your plane to get a better view.'

After ninety minutes, she chose a small, uninhabited atoll near the edge of the island chain.

'Line up, flight,' she said. 'I want each one of you to test his weapons. To feel how they affect the airframe. Zemmic and Viltry can sit this one out.'

Scalter went in first: a long, low dive, and raked the rock, both las and then quad.

'Good aim,' said Jagdea.

'Throne, it really shakes the plane,' Scalter observed, banking away.

'You next, Umbra Nine.'

'Copy that, Lead,' Darrow responded. He switched on his gunsight and armed his weapons with quick, assured flicks. Then he pushed the stick and swung down into a dive. Water and rocky outcrops flashed by under him. He set the sight reticule on the rock, closed to range, then fired his las. The shots streaked ahead of him and he saw the fluff of impacts. He toggled to cannons and chattered off a burst, then brought his bird up.

'Excellent, Nine. Little high with las, but the cannon was good. You might want to calibrate your gunsight down a few points.'

'Copy that, Leader.'

'Umbra Five? You're up.'

Kaminsky acknowledged and began his run on the target atoll. With his left hand, he threw the arming switch and turned the weapon system on, then returned his grip to the throttle. The sight was in.

'Fire!' he said.

The lascannons blasted.

'Select! Fire! Fire!'

Now the quads blasted, twitching the machine's track.

Kaminsky rolled off the target and started to climb out, disarming his gun system.

'Racklae's little toy seems to work,' he said.

'Very nice,' Jagdea voxed.

She let all three of them do it again a few times, then pulled the whole flight up to five thousand.

'We'll swing wide on three-three-two and then turn for home,' she voxed.

They'd been going for ten minutes, and Jagdea was about to call the turn, when Zemmic called.

'Auspex contact,' he reported.

'I'm watching it,' Jagdea said.

In another ten seconds, they could make out the flash and smoke of a dogfight ten or fifteen kilometres to the north-west, out over the sea.

'Operations, Operations,' Jagdea called. 'This is Umbra training. What are you showing in our vicinity?'

'Umbra Leader, mass intercept underway on a bomber stream. Suspected escort cover. Advise you push it home and clear the area.'

'Acknowledged, Operations,' said Jagdea. 'Umbra Flight, what you can see has nothing to do with us today. We're turning for home. Come about, bearing—'

'Break! Break!' Viltry was shouting.

Jagdea and Zemmic broke at once, Viltry and Kaminsky going the other way. Scalter and Darrow were taken by surprise, but began to turn out the moment they saw the formation scatter.

Jagdea looped up in time to see three Razors run clean through the parted formation. Escort cover no doubt, taking a pop at them.

She engaged. 'Zemmic, stick with me. Guns live. The rest of you, pick up Lucerna beacon and follow it home *now*!'

Jagdea and Zemmic burned after the bats, but they were already breaking. She scanned her auspex frantically, and saw one of the Razors descending through the light cloud. She stooped after it.

It dropped to under a thousand metres, then turned up again sharply. Jagdea saw passing shots slip by her wing and realised she'd picked up another of them.

'On him!' Zemmic voxed.

Umbra Ten rolled in on the second bat's tail and fired three bursts of quad. The Razor caught fire and went into a screaming climb that ended three thousand metres above them in an expanding fireball.

Jagdea was chasing the other bat when she heard Scalter on the vox.

'He just went right over us! Break! Break!'

The third bat must have found the trainees.

THE FOUR THUNDERBOLTS had split, and now Darrow couldn't see the hostile at all. The only aircraft in sight was Viltry's, three hundred metres down to his right.

Darrow's skin crawled. Eads was right. He wasn't ready and now, as soon as he'd got into the air, he was going to be killed.

He saw a flash and looked left. Scalter's bird was climbing and trying to evade. The Razor was on his tail, firing.

'Break! Break!' he heard Viltry shouting.

Kaminsky's Thunderbolt swept in out of the clouds, guns crackling. His shots went wide, but they were enough to check the bat and allow Scalter to break and dive out. The bat went over Kaminsky, then managed to viff round. Within seconds, Kaminsky had got the bat on his six.

Two shots crashed into Kaminsky's wing.

'Dammit!' he cursed, imagining the disappointment on Blansher's face.

Instinctively, feeling it now, he eased the vector thrust, and to his delight, the bat overshot him and started to turn.

Darrow saw it. He'd already turned his gunsight and weapons on.

It was trying to extend, its sport denied by the four pilots. Darrow opened the throttle and gave chase, following its attempts to evade. He let the sights roll through it...

Lock.

He fired.

The bat blew up. Just like that. A vivid backdraft of flame and flying scrap.

JAGDEA SAW AN aerial explosion underlight the clouds ahead and screamed in rage. She let the bat she was chasing pull out and flee, and raced towards the flash.

'Flight? Flight? What was that?' she voxed.

'Hello, Leader,' she heard Viltry respond. 'That was Darrow making his first kill.'

Lucerna AB, 10.20

THEY'D ALL MADE a big fuss, which had made Darrow blush. All of them, that is, except the young pilot called Marquall, who just looked sick or something.

Darrow stood by his Thunderbolt in the hangar for a long while, just staring at it.

He could do this. Starting tomorrow, he was going to be flying and killing for Enothis and the Emperor.

He felt certain that after a day or two, he'd begin to get a real feel for it.

Natrab Echelon Aerie, Theda, 19.10

THE IMPERIAL CITY was burning.

From the deck of the giant carrier which now occupied a headland above the sea, a site that had once been an enemy air-base, Flight Warrior Khrel Kas Obarkon gazed upon what the forces of the Anarch had wrought.

The sky had turned black, and the flames from the burning habs were stark and red. The sea itself glowed amber with their reflection.

Overhead, the echelons of war machines flew past, gleaming in the firelight. He listened to the lusty purr of their engines and smiled. As much as his woven face would allow him to, anyway.

His litter carriage awaited. The slaves abased themselves as he stepped into it, then carried him down into the deck space of the giant aerie.

In their hundreds, the other senior echelon leaders and flight warriors had gathered. The bronze horns were sounding and the kettle drums beating. Obarkon drew back the silk drapes of his litter and greeted the nearest of his fellows. Sacolther, his armour engraved like alabaster. Coruz Shang, clad in chrome, his fingers sheathed in golden claws. Nazarike Komesh, echelon ace, impassive behind his green visor.

The drums and horns fell silent, and there was only the expectant murmur of the company. In the centre of the great chamber, the giant hololith projector rippled into life, projecting a translucent blue image ten metres into the air. The flight warriors howled in adoration, their augmetic voices shaking the hangar's rune-scribed walls.

The image was of a face. Obarkon thought the face quite beautiful, though it also terrified him. He knew it was appearing simultaneously on every other mass carrier and command base in the conquered southlands. Hundreds of thousands of warriors, echelon chieftains, Blood Pact officer-lords and death-priests were all seeing it, and worshipping it.

But as usual, Obarkon felt it was looking directly and only at him.

The face of Anakwaner Sek, Magister Warlord, great and awesome Anarch, sworn lieutenant of the mighty Urlock Gaur himself, began to speak.

'Tomorrow,' it boomed. 'The day of days. Who will find blood in the air?'

'We will!' they howled as one.

'Prepare! And let the enemy fall in flames!'

GOOD FLYING

THE BATTLE OF THE ZOPHONIAN SEA
Imperial year 773.M41, day 270

DAY 270

Lucerna AB, 05.01

'Jagdea? Jagdea?'

She woke, heavy-headed and slow, and for one fleeting moment, forgot where she was. Then she remembered and it was like a lead weight in her stomach.

'Jagdea?' Blansher was standing over her. The ready room was half-lit. Jagdea had been slumbering on the couch, wearing most of her kit. Aggie Del Ruth was asleep in the armchair.

'Give me a second, Mil,' Jagdea said, sitting up and dropping her feet to the floor.

'I don't think I can,' he said.

She followed him into the briefing room. Viltry stood there, arms folded. The big, glass-screened auspex, which relayed tracks from the main systems in Operations, lit the room with its pulsing green light.

There was nothing on the screen, except for a half dozen returns that the system had identified as Imperial patrols.

'It's been quiet for three hours,' said Viltry. 'Totally quiet.'

'You've been watching it for three hours?' Jagdea yawned.

'I couldn't sleep,' said Viltry.

'I think it's a woman,' Blansher smiled.

Viltry laughed, but for some reason Jagdea thought Blansher might have touched a nerve.

'You got me up to see nothing?' she said.

'Since when has it been this quiet?' Viltry asked. 'They've been coming thick and fast since the moment we deployed on this world. Before that even. Ask Kaminsky.'

'So?' she shrugged. 'They wanted a night off. All that murder and destruction can take it out of you.'

'Bree...' Blansher said, a touch of disapproval in his tone.

'I apologise. Extreme fatigue makes me flippant. You think something's coming?'

'Yes,' said Viltry.

'So do I,' said Blansher. 'I've been on to Operations. They're jumpy. They know this is odd. Every base in the Zophonian is on standby.'

'Get the crews up and prepped,' she said.

Viltry nodded and hurried off.

'Something you said,' Blansher remarked.

'What?'

'That we could fend them off, deny them, unless they sent everything they had at us at once.'

'I must stop talking so much,' said Jagdea.

'Why would they all be down, Bree? All of them? Every last machine? Why would they be doing that if they weren't arming and fuelling and fitting their entire air command?'

A buzzer sounded and Jagdea jumped. It was the vox intercom. Blansher lifted the set and answered.

'Hangar three Umbra. Yes, sir. I see. Show us ready.'

He hung up. 'We've just gone to primary standby. Long range auspex has detected a significant background temperature rise in the air above the southern coast.'

'Meaning?'

He shrugged. 'Maybe an awful lot of engines just started up at the same time.'

THE HANGAR LIGHTS came on. Fitters scrambled to perform last minute pre-flight. Only the vaguest hint of dawn fell in through the hangar mouth. Marquall could smell the cold sea, the air. He fought his nerves. Everyone was tense. Some because they seemed to know what might be coming. Others precisely because they did not.

'All right, Vander?' Van Tull said, walking over. He was eating dried rations. How could the man eat under pressure like this, Marquall wondered?

'Four-A,' he replied. Van Tull smiled. There was blood on his gums. He was still suffering from the hypoxia. Throne help me, thought Marquall, of all the ways to die, all the ways I've imagined and had nightmares about, wouldn't that be the worst? Poisoned by the air-mix. Dead without realising it.

Van Tull nodded over at Darrow, who was doing a walk round of his Thunderbolt.

'Lad did well yesterday, didn't he? Fine debut.'

'Yeah,' said Marquall. He was deciding whether or not he needed to dash to the latrine to vomit. 'He'll be fine. They all will.'

'You've changed your bloody tune,' said Ranfre, joining them.

Marquall shrugged. 'Just hoping for the best, I think. I hope they'll be fine– because if they're not, we're all screwed.'

VILTRY BUTTONED UP his flight coat and adjusted his gauntlets.

He saw Jagdea approaching.

'Anything?' he asked.

She shook her head.

'Look, Bree,' he began, 'There's something I–'

'What?'

He smiled. 'No, now's not the time. I'll talk to you later.'

Jagdea nodded. She passed through the waiting pilots. Zemmic was sitting on a camp chair, counting off his chain of charms, one by one, over and over. Cordiale and Del Ruth were playing knuckles to take their mind off the tension.

'All set, you two?' Jagdea asked.

'Yes, ma'am,' said Aggie Del Ruth. She had such an appealing smile. Not what a man might call a pretty woman, Jagdea thought. Too stern in the face, too heavy in the jaw. Del Ruth was what Jagdea's father had liked to call 'comely'.

'Cordiale?'

Cordiale grinned, and patted his lapel. 'Got my lucky feather, commander.'

Scalter was chatting to Blansher, asking him some technical question about fuel pumps. He seemed calm enough. Pretty stable, that man, Jagdea thought.

Kaminsky was standing alone, staring out of the hangar mouth at the slowly lightening sky.

'Are you set?' she asked as she came to stand beside him.

'I think so,' he said.

'Just… do your best,' she said.

'I've been waiting a long time for a chance to do just that, mamzel,' Kaminsky replied. He held out his left hand. 'I never did thank you properly for this opportunity.'

She shook his hand. It seemed odd to do it left-handed, but she knew he didn't want to use his dull prosthetic.

'I never thanked you for getting me out of Theda,' she said. 'Shall we call it even?'

He smiled.

'What do you think?' she asked.

'Everyone's scared,' said Kaminsky. 'That's what I think. It's natural, I suppose. Frankly, I can't wait.'

He didn't have to. The klaxons began to howl.

Over the Midwinters, 05.39

UMBRA FLIGHT CLEARED the dock and began to rise in formation, burners bright. Every other hangar bay in Lucerna spat out its flights. Seventy-two Thunderbolts darted up from the island plateau, which was now glowing pink in the rising daylight.

Operations chatter was constant. All along the archipelago, the airbases were launching en masse. Squadrons were snapping up from Limbus, Zophos and the major islands, and also from the northern coast and the Ingeburg stations.

From carriers on the Littoral and the Peninsula, a broad and solid auspex return had manifested.

Jagdea had indeed tempted fate. It seemed like everything the Archenemy had was coming for them.

'Climb to eight, Umbra. Hold formation. Make your speed two and a half.'

They called in. The sky was four-tenths cloud, and there was a strong northerly that would aid the enemy's approach speed.

'Everyone tight?' she called.

'Leader, this is Eight. I've got an engine warning.'

'Can you sort it, Marquall?'

In his cockpit, Marquall fiddled with the throttle. His port engine kept misfiring, juddering *Double Eagle*.

'Trying now, Lead.'

The engine stuttered and then died altogether. Nine-Nine wobbled back out of the line.

'Umbra Eight, please advise status.'

'Engine out,' Marquall said. He pressed restart once, twice. Nothing.

'Leader, engine is definitely out.'

'Peel off, Eight, Get home and get it fixed. You're no good to me running on one.'

'Copy that,' he said and dived away.

'Snuggle up, flight,' she said. One down already and they hadn't even fired a shot yet.

The auspex started showing a mass of contacts at fifty kilometres. She fiddled with her gain control. It couldn't be that massive.

But it was. Auspex assessed overlapping bomber streams, five hundred units in each.

'Holy Throne of Earth,' she murmured.

'Umbra Flight, this is Lead. Mass targets at fifty kilometre. Climb to ten thousand and let's go in onto them. Targets for all.'

'Copy that, Lead,' voxed Blansher, and the planes began to climb.

Darrow adjusted his air-mix and stuck to Van Tull's eight. He could feel the pulse in his wrists against the tight strapping of his gloves. He toggled his guns on and off to make sure he got a green rune.

The vox channels started going mad. Via Operations, they were getting the first reports of contacts. At St Hagen, the Sea of Ezra, the Festus Delta. Navy flights had encountered vast waves of Archenemy bombers and their fighter support. Monumental air battles were now igniting over the Zophonian Sea.

'Five kilometres and closing,' Jagdea called. 'Hold steady. Keep scanning for fighters.'

High altitude seemed empty, by visual and auspex, but there was a huge mass of returns from the lower level.

Could there be that many machines in the air, wondered Darrow, or was his auspex faulty?

'Umbra Flight, weapons live, sights on, targets below at four thousand. Stoop and sting.'

The Thunderbolts peeled off and went into their attack dives. Nose down, reaching maximum velocity, Darrow saw the clouds stream away. Below them, the bombers. His auspex had not lied. The air was studded with mass bomber formations.

'Attacking!' Jagdea voxed.

The air lit up. Festoons of tracer streams hosed up from the enemy formation, filling the air. Darrow felt the thump and bang of close detonations rattle his bird. The dive was intense. Pick one, he thought, pick one, you bloody fool or you'll just go through them. Explosions blossomed below. Two or three of the bombers in visual range had gone up.

He chose one, a massive thing, bright red, with four wings and eight vector engines. He had no idea what pattern it was. It was the size of an Onero at least. Its multiple bolter turrets ripped up at him and he felt a solid hit against one wing.

Diving vertically onto it, he opened fire. His lascannons lit up. The huge machine's dorsal plating ruptured and burst apart. Darrow realised that he was diving so steeply and so hard he was going to impact into the back of it. He tried to pull out. Velocity had frozen his stick. He fired again and again. *Hit, hit, hit–*

The enormous bomber blew up. A fat, hot, torus of flame out of which little white tendrils of smoke spat and trickled. Darrow shot through the flames and out under the formation. If the bomber hadn't exploded, he would surely have collided with it. He fought to raise the nose. It was a huge effort. He gripped the way Jagdea had taught him, but still nearly blacked out from the G.

His bird climbed, the stick looser. He saw Scalter's machine whirl past, chasing down another of the massive super-bombers. Scalter's sustained shooting dropped it into the sea.

Darrow ascended, nursing the throttle. Perspiration was pouring down his face and making his mask itch. He blinked the sweat-drops out of his eyes. His targeter pinged as another of the super-heavies filled his sights. Bright blue bolter rounds cindered down around him from the belly guns.

He viffed up, adjusted to the right, and gave the thing four bursts of las. It lost a wing. The damage caused the huge craft to wallow and then invert suddenly. It was on fire by the time it hit the water.

JAGDEA KILLED A Tormentor on her way down, and another on her way back up. Las batteries drained, she wound over onto a heavy bomber, and switched to quad. She gave it a few bursts, but its turrets forced her to back off.

To her left, she saw Zemmic make a kill, and Del Ruth zoom over, chasing a Tormentor that had broken from formation, wounded.

Jagdea kicked her rudder bar and rolled down under the heavy. Viltry had been telling her about the sweet spot, the point that no turret could track.

Two rounds went through her tail armour before she was sure she'd found it. She chattered quad fire into the beast's stomach.

It slumped to port, dropping out of its line, making hot smoke, and exploding long before it reached the sea.

WITH BLANSHER TO his port, Kaminsky dropped in on a Tormentor, letting it come wide into his gunsight.

It had been a long time since he'd felt this right.

'Fire!' he said. 'Fire! Fire!'

The lascannons charged and unloaded. The Tormentor broke like an eggshell and fell into a tumble.

'One to you, Kaminsky,' Blansher voxed.

Yeah, he thought. *One to me.*

* * *

VILTRY FOLLOWED RANFRE and Cordiale down through the chaos of shots and wafting smoke. He rolled right and got a lock on a Talon that was attempting to climb.

Before he could commit to shoot, he saw stripes of fire coming up from below. He rolled and looked down.

The air below was full of bats, ascending, shooting. The bomber waves had escort all right. But low, not top cover.

'Bats! Bats! Bats!' he yelled. 'Six o'clock and coming up vertical!'

Lucerna AB, 06.01

FLOUNDERING ON ONE engine, Marquall came into hangar three and set down. He did it badly, denting the deck plating and slewing hard, leaving deep gouges from his landing claws.

The fitters ran to Nine-Nine. Marquall clambered out, throwing off his helmet in disgust.

'Sir?' asked Racklae. 'Damage?'

'No! No, it's the bloody port engine! She's cut out on me!' Furious, Marquall kicked his helmet across the deckway.

'We're on it, sir,' Racklae said, running to open the cover.

'Just fix it! Fix it! Bloody fix it!' Marquall yelled at them.

Racklae stopped, and turned, dignified. 'We're trying, sir,' he said.

Marquall saw the look on his chief fitter's face. He raised his hands for calm. 'I'm sorry,' he said. 'I'm really sorry, Racklae. It's just that I should be out there. I should be engaged. It's this bloody jinx. The jinx of Nine-Nine! It's frigging with me and–'

'There's no jinx,' said Racklae sharply. 'Why don't you shut up, boy? Always blaming your failures on something. Your fellow fliers… the pilots who score better than you… your jinxed plane. Anything, just so long as it isn't you. Wake up. Look closer to home. and start doing something about it, or by the Throne, I'll lamp you with a wrench myself.'

Marquall stuttered and took a step back.

Racklae turned away. 'Crews!' he yelled. 'Get this bloody bird airworthy now!'

Over the Midwinters, 06.15

THE RAZORS AND LOCUSTS swept up amongst them, trying to force them away from the monstrous bomber formation. Kaminsky decided he wasn't having that.

He banked over and went to meet the fighters head on.

'Umbra Five, where the hell are you going?' Blansher yelled over the channel.

Kaminsky didn't say anything except, 'Fire. Fire. Fire. Fire.'

Blansher followed him down through the fire-streaked air. He saw a Razor vibrating as it fell away, bleeding smoke. He saw a Locust blow out as it climbed. Kaminsky was ploughing into them with deliberate, single-minded fury.

Blansher pulled in beside Kaminsky's port, took a shot at a rising Locust, then banked out as he saw a crimson Razor turning close. The Razor was looping to line up on Kaminsky. Blansher took him with the last three bursts of his las.

Switching to quad, he barrelled down. Kaminsky had lined up on a Locust and was peppering it with las-fire. Cordiale and Del Ruth rushed past, gunning at three Locusts that had turned away in a harsh dive.

He saw a Razor going across him, viffed his Bolt to get deflection, and ripped the hostile down its length with quad rounds.

Kaminsky came up out of his long stoop, and locked a Locust.

'Fire.'

Nothing. His las batteries were exhausted.

'Switch. Fire. Fire.'

The quads burst off at empty sky. Kaminsky soared around, and found a bomber right ahead of him.

'Fire. Fire. Fire.'

The bomber tilted and began to come around. Several engines out, it was turning back for home.

'Fire. Fire,' Kaminsky said.

The stricken bomber went down, suddenly encased in a shroud of its own burning fuel.

Bats blazed up past Kaminsky. He rolled over to greet them.

TWO THUNDERBOLT WINGS and a formation of Lightnings had now converged on their air-brawl. Jagdea had taken a hit to her rudder and Zero-One wasn't steering very well, but she tanked out of the fusillade three Locusts were laying on her, bent right and hammered another Tormentor to fragments.

Her fuel load was getting low. The rest of Umbra would be the same, unless they hadn't been doing their jobs right.

'Umbra Flight, prepare to turn for home. Refuel run. Re-arm. Come back.'

Del Ruth, Cordiale and Zemmic quickly acknowledged. Then Darrow, Scalter and Van Tull.

Viltry's affirmative came in a moment later.

'Umbra Two?' she called.

'Heard you, coming out,' Blansher replied.

'Umbra Five? Kaminsky?'

'Understood, Leader. Fuel is low. Breaking off.'

'Umbra Twelve? Umbra Twelve? Ranfre? Copy me!'

She looked around, scanning the packed sky for some sign of Ranfre.

Far below, unseen by Jagdea, a Thunderbolt descended.

Ranfre's bird had sailed through the shot-storm of the bomber pack. Every bolt round blasted out by the turrets had missed it, except the one that had shattered its canopy and burst Ranfre's skull.

His Thunderbolt, uncontrolled, slowly dropped away and hit the sea.

Lucerna AB, 08.13

THE FLIGHT CAME in through the south entry of the hangar. Del Ruth's machine was making smoke and Jagdea's rudder was flapping like a weather vane.

'Refit, rearm and refuel!' Jagdea yelled to the fitter crews.

Power loaders and tank trucks were already spurring torward the vapour-swathed machines.

'Where's Marquall?' Jagdea yelled to Racklae over the noise.

'He was here, ma'am! We fixed him up! He's gone up again!'

Promethium jetted out of a hose poorly fitted to Cordiale's machine. Racklae ran towards the problem, cursing his crew.

Jagdea looked up out of the hangar mouth at the sky.

Marquall was alone out there.

Over the Midwinters, 08.45

THE SKY WAS lit up by the fight. Marquall took a deep breath. It was amazing. He'd never seen so many air machines in combat before.

He put Nine-Nine into a dive and came in on a pack of Locusts, thirty strong. He didn't care. Effortlessly, he rolled into them and fired the moment he had a tone lock.

One of the small Archenemy fighters bucked, then flew apart in a dazzle of heat.

'Three!' Marquall whooped to himself. 'Three! Frigging three!'

The Locust pack broke and looped. Suddenly, they were all over him.

He took three holes in the port wing, two in the starboard and four through the tail.

Gasping, Marquall turned out high, trying to evade. The Locusts swarmed after him.

He saw a flash. A passing glint.

Eight Thunderbolts, painted cream, streaked down past him into the Locust swarm.

The Apostles.

Throne of Earth, *the Apostles!*

'Larice?' he whispered.

Holy Terra, those Apostles were punishing the Locusts hard. Perfect timing, perfect formation. They blitzed into the pack and killed most of them in one pass.

So fast. Marquall felt almost stationary, even though the speed gauge said he was topping eight hundred.

'Larice? Larice Asche?' he called.

'Who's that?' snapped a hard voice.

'Umbra Eight,' he said.

'Marquall? Emperor's teeth! This is no time for reunions. Get your arse out of here!'

'Copy that, Larice. I'm going.'

'Get the hell gone. And don't call me that. I am Apostle Five.'

Over the Midwinters, 09.18

BLANSHER LED UP the first four Bolts that were ready: Van Tull, Cordiale, Scalter and Zemmic. The others would follow under Jagdea the moment her rudder was fixed.

Blansher turned them south-west, in the direction of Theda. Another wing of eight Thunderbolts that had just turned round at Lucerna launched and fell into step with them.

Ahead, it seemed like a great storm had slid down across the horizon. There was a wide, brown cliff of smoke along the sea, extending as far as Blansher could see, filled with sparks and flashes like lightning.

As they closed, the cliff began to resolve. What he'd been seeing was the glare distortion of thousands of exhaust plumes and engine fires, ribboned into a lattice across the sky, so dense that from a distance it seemed solid.

They passed several Imperial machines limping for home. Blansher kept calling for Marquall. The vox was still burbling with hundreds of intersecting transmissions. According to Operations, the massive clash they were prosecuting here was matched by a vast battle over the Sea of Ezra, and another near the east coast approaching Ingeburg. Other reports said that bomber streams had got past the Midwinter line, and were beginning to hit Zophos and even the northern shore. Every available Imperial machine was now aloft on at least its second sortie of the day.

Contacts were closing. A large pack of Hell Talons cruising north.

'Umbra Flight,' he ordered. 'Engage!'

Over the Midwinters, 09.50

IT HAD TAKEN an age for the fitters to fix Jagdea's rudder. Even now, Hemmen had warned, it wasn't a solid repair. She ascended at maximum speed, tailed by Del Ruth, Kaminsky, Viltry and Darrow. It was no longer a matter of getting track instruction from Operations. The sky above the archipelago was loaded with machines everywhere she looked.

They picked up a quartet of Marauders, all damaged, that were being harried by a formation of nine blue Locusts. The bats seemed to move as one, skilled and disciplined, as if they were somehow controlled by one fierce mind.

Jagdea rolled the wing into them.

One of the Marauders was finally overwhelmed, and went down towards the atolls. It was hard to keep a focus on the brawl at hand. Parts of other dogfight clashes kept impinging, as the edges of one skirmish overlapped another. Umbra was rolling with the blue Locusts when seven Lightnings blundered into their fight-zone, tumbling around three pairs of Razors. Jagdea found herself having to deal with one of the Razor pairs which switched from the Lightnings they'd been chasing onto her. Any semblance of strategic formation in Umbra vanished.

Darrow turned tightly over one of the ailing Marauders and locked onto a yellow Hell Razor that seemed to be either confused or suffering from vector damage. He led his shot, expecting it to break left, but it didn't, or it couldn't. As a result, Darrow's first burst missed. He banked to the right, floating the machine into his reticule and fired again, killing it instantly.

Kaminsky and Viltry had been forced to the eastern part of the skirmish, separated from the others by the Razors going through their midst. They found themselves mugged by all nine of the blue Locusts. Both of them began turning and firing, and the blue bats danced away like a shoal of fish, triggered by a single impulse. They switched, and came around again, almost in line. Kaminsky broke hard, and Viltry executed a savage vector-assisted turn, representing so the Locusts were almost head on to him.

He got a good but momentary lock on the lead plane and fired his quads, leaving his thumb on the stud so that the salvo would rake. The first Locust blew out and because they were running tight, in line, Viltry's target lock carried his bombardment onto the second one, which also disintegrated.

Then Viltry had to bank abruptly to avoid the others. Something blinked past over his canopy and he saw

Kaminsky coming in on a barrel roll into the thick of them, forcing the Locusts to lose cohesion for the first time.

Kaminsky hit one, then damaged a second, and hunted a third round, at its six. The blue bat was so eager to avoid the Thunderbolt on its tail that it ran blindly across Viltry's field of fire and he stung it with his lascannons.

Kaminsky and Viltry scissored past each other. Their pack cut in half, the Locusts pulled out.

Over the Midwinters, 10.10

BLANSHER'S ELEMENT FLEW out of their tangle and enjoyed a brief respite of quiet air before a vast swirl of fighting planes engulfed them from above. They were forced low, then lower still. Burning engine parts, wing fragments and pieces of elevator rained past them from craft destroyed in the upper levels of the brawl. One large fragment bounced off Scalter's nose, destroying his las battery and stripping the cover plating off his starboard turbofan. He cried out in alarm and fought with the controls to steady the plane. Peering forward, he could see energy from the split las-cables crackling and sparking on the dented nose. He deactivated the power magazine and switched to quad.

'Umbra Seven! Pay attention!' Blansher yelled.

Scalter had been so intent on his damage that he'd been flying straight for too long. A mauve Hell Talon came sweeping down out of the frothing smoke wash above and started to fire.

Scalter sat down in his armour plating, flinching as the shots went by. He seemed to have frozen. Blansher was too committed to a pair of Razors to help him.

Cordiale came out of the north, firing heavily. The Talon took a hit or two in its rear armour and forgot all about Scalter. It dropped low, towards the sea, running to escape. Cordiale stormed after it.

They went across the water at less than ten metres, kicking up wash and spray with their thrusters. The Talon slipped back and forth, around atolls and cliffs, determined not to climb and thus make itself a target. Cordiale stuck to it, banking as it banked, slicing around islets and surface rocks. They came around a tall, sheer cliff in a hard turn, the noise of their engines reflecting oddly off the cliff face, and immediately had to leap-frog two mass-barges lying at anchor in the cove. Cordiale missed the vox masts of the big tubs by centimetres. The Talon rushed low across the basin, chased by Hydra batteries along the beach, and bent right around the shoreline of the atoll.

Cordiale steered after it, standing his plane on its starboard wing. He laughed as he saw that their passing rush had caused seabirds to take off in panic out of the rocks.

The Talon twisted to port, skimming over a pattern of low, semi-submerged islets. Following, Cordiale heard the lock tone and fired.

The Talon lurched and plunged nose-down into the rocks, detonating with huge force. Cordiale shot past it, glancing back at the fireball gleefully.

Travelling at seven hundred kilometres an hour, his plane tore into another flock of startled seabirds erupting from the low rocks. Each one weighed a kilo or more, and they shredded his nose cone and front plating like jack-hammers. Two annihilated his right engine, and one punched through his canopy, shattered the gunsight and hit him square in the face, driving his goggles into his skull and snapping his neck instantly.

Umbra Eleven hit the outer line of the rocks and disintegrated in a blizzard of hull plates, cables and machine parts.

* * *

Over the Midwinters, 10.45

SWINGING WIDE FOR home, Jagdea's flight had come up on a Tormentor wing that had broken from the thicker fighting and was heading towards the Sea of Ezra. They harried it until their tanks were too low.

Gaining altitude for Lucerna, they sighted Marquall.

'Umbra Eight,' Jagdea voxed. 'Where the hell have you been?'

'Not really sure, Lead,' Marquall responded. 'But wherever it was, there was an awful lot of planes there.'

Lucerna AB, 11.30

'TURN THEM AROUND as quickly as you can!' Jagdea said as she jumped down. Her four had brought Marquall back with them. According to Operations chatter, Blansher's element was five minutes away.

'Yes, ma'am!' Racklae replied. Smoke was coming out from under Kaminsky's machine, and Racklae yelled at a deck crewman to get it doused. Turning back to Jagdea, he indicated the trolleys of ammunition at the hangar side waiting to be loaded.

'We've not got the whole of our last order, commander,' he said. 'I've called down to the base arsenal, and they told me we're draining the magazines. This morning so far they've fetched up as much as they would usually in eight days.'

'They'll have to work harder,' Jagdea said.

'It's not that, mamzel. The magazines are actually emptying. They're having to pull munitions supplies that came in on the barges and haven't been unloaded yet. It's slowing things down.'

'I'll go and put in a good word,' Jagdea said, heading for the briefing room. As she walked, she turned round and shouted, 'Pilots! Make sure you all, I repeat *all*, get some fluid inside yourselves! Maybe a little food too, if you can stomach it, but not too much. Fluid is a necessity.'

Marquall dismounted and took a water bottle that one of his fitters offered him. He spat out the first mouthful, trying get rid of the thick taste of rubber his mask had left in his mouth.

'Running better?' Racklae asked.

Marquall nodded. 'Look, I want to apologise f–'

Racklae shook his head. 'Least said, soonest mended, sir.'

'I got my third,' Marquall said.

The chief fitter grinned, and clapped him on the shoulder. 'There, you see? What jinx?'

IN THE BRIEFING room, Jagdea got on the vox to the armourers and had to listen while someone told her the same story she'd heard from Racklae.

'Just take a look up at the sky and see if that helps you any,' she said and hung up.

While she'd been making the call, Jagdea had been gazing across at the main auspex. It looked more like the climate plot of a tropical storm than aircraft tracking.

Viltry came in, put down his helmet and came to look at the screen too.

'Operations say they're breaking off,' Viltry said.

'Operations can kiss my arse, they're not up there.'

'No,' Viltry pointed to the southern sections of the display. 'I can sort of see what they mean. Overall. That was a huge wave pattern they threw at us at dawn. The sky may be full of machines and plenty of fighting, but a lot of that's involving hostiles that are turning back for home, fuel out, or coming back from target if they made it. This whole area here, see?'

He tapped a section east of Zophos. 'That's all medium bombers, all going south. The actual wave has broken.'

'The first wave,' Jagdea said. 'A mass onslaught like this is all or nothing. They'll be coming again as soon as they've rearmed and refuelled.'

Viltry nodded. 'Of course. I have a feeling they're going to keep this up until they've crushed us. The Archenemy is many things. Subtle is not on the list.'

'Very true,' said Jagdea. 'We go up as soon as we can. Hunt stragglers, and steal some altitude before the second mass comes in.'

'I'll see if Racklae can scare up some rockets,' Viltry said.

'You'll be lucky,' Jagdea laughed.

'But with rockets, we could seek out a mass-carrier and have a go. I don't care how many bats they've got, they can't refit and refuel without a carrier.'

'Yes,' said Jagdea. She looked up at the log board that the fitters were keeping. Times of launch, times home, damage, work done. Ranfre's log line was ominously blank.

'Ranfre?' Viltry asked, guessing what she was thinking.

She nodded. 'Hasn't been seen since about six-thirty. Even flying to conserve fuel, there's no way he's still in the air.'

'Maybe he put down at another base?' said Viltry. 'Or… ejected… or…'

She appreciated Viltry was trying. She picked up a stylus and wrote 'Missing' next to Ranfre's name.

'It's something I've been thinking about a lot in the last few days,' Viltry said quietly. 'You know… death, I mean.'

'You and everyone else,' said Jagdea.

He shook his head. 'No, in particular. As far as the Imperium is concerned, Oskar Viltry is dead. I'm just a… a scrap of paper, a pending number to be assigned.'

'So?'

'Will you promise me something, Bree?'

'Yes,' she said immediately.

'You haven't heard what it is yet. I'm here, at your side, proud to be a member of Umbra. And that's how it'll be until the end.'

'I know,' she said. Few men were as loyal and committed as Oskar Viltry.

'But when this is done. When we win this fight. I don't mean today, I mean however long it takes… will you forget you ever saw me?'

'What are you talking about?' she laughed. Then she saw in his eyes he was entirely serious. Viltry took the paper registration docket the Munitorum had given him out of his pocket and smoothed it flat.

'Forget you ever knew that Oskar Viltry came back from the desert and flew with you. List this pending number as missing in action. Let me disappear here, on Enothis, when the fighting's done.'

She blinked. 'Is that what you want, Viltry?'

'Yes. Not just me. There's someone…' he paused. 'There will be lives to rebuild here, after the war.'

She thought about it for a moment, then picked up the paper.

'I promise,' she said.

OUT IN THE hangar, as the fitters worked feverishly, Darrow sat in silence, his back against the wall. His hands were no longer shaking. They were completely steady. What was shaking now was inside him, some deep core part that had been rocked and rattled and squeezed and slammed and wrenched. In one morning. No clear image remained to him of the day's fighting. Just a blur. A smell of fuel and fyceline. A sound of thunder.

Nearby, he heard some of the ground crew cheering as they added a third stripe to Marquall's plane. Marquall looked triumphant. Even in the short time he'd known him, Darrow had been able to tell that Marquall was desperate for glory.

Darrow thought for a moment, and realised, to his shame, that he couldn't precisely remember how many kills he'd got himself. He tried to picture them all. The fluke the day before, then the bombers...

He realised that his tally was now five. He was an ace.

Darrow decided not to tell Marquall.

Buzzers sounded. Blansher's element came in at last, shrieking down through the north entry. Darrow leapt up. He saw immediately how damaged the snout of Scalter's plane was.

Scalter himself seemed all right, but dazed. Jagdea ran out to inspect the damage.

'Las systems completely shot,' said the lead fitter. 'It will take hours to mount in a new system. We can replace the plating quick enough, but if you want him up again, he'll have to make do with quads.'

'Then he'll have to make do,' Jagdea said. She glanced round as Blansher, Van Tull and Zemmic plodded across from their machines.

She froze. In her concern for Scalter and his bird she'd missed the obvious.

'Where's Cordiale?' she asked.

Milan Blansher shook his head.

Over the Sea of Ezra, 13.16

THE SECOND WAVE rolled in an hour after noon. Though the day was bright, the pollution of the morning's combat had now stained the sky with a strange, yellowish opacity. Volcanic columns of smoke rose from Theda, Ezraville and Limbus, visible for hundreds of kilometres.

Umbra was already up. So were all the other wings from Lucerna, Viper Atoll and the other Midwinter bases. The techmages had blessed their craft and sent them on their way.

Umbra climbed high, to about fifteen thousand, and formed two packs. Jagdea, with Viltry, Darrow, Del Ruth and Marquall, and Blansher leading Scalter, Kaminsky, Zemmic and Van Tull. Once again, the ominous track on the auspex showed the tide of Archenemy airpower rolling north. Jagdea had heard a flight controller estimate that at the peak of the morning's activity, the Imperial planes had been outnumbered eleven to one. She wondered how the kill rates had compared.

Reserves had been added. Commonwealth units were mobilised now after the morning's surprise, and had their machines – mostly pulse-jets and reciprocating-engine birds – standing ready in fields along the northern coast, a last ditch defence. Those old craft wouldn't stand a chance against the Archenemy's vector planes, Jagdea knew. The point was, if the enemy wave reached the north coast in any numbers, nothing mattered any more anyway.

That morning, despite terrible losses, the Navy wings had denied the bulk of the enemy wave. The north coast had been hit, but not with the full fury the onslaught had threatened.

Now it was round two.

Tactics had changed. Now spearhead groups of fighters were storming ahead of the bomber strings to disrupt the Navy interceptors and prevent them from flushing the bombers.

Jagdea saw condensation trails crawling out. The bats were clocking in at maximum thrust, lashing forward to meet the Imperial line.

Air flashes lit up to east and west. The first contacts had been made. Operations traffic suddenly became frenetic.

Umbra's scopes showed a fighter group, nearly thirty strong, coming in at twelve thousand.

'They're moving bloody fast,' muttered Zemmic.

'Let's slow them down,' said Jagdea.

In the paired packs, Umbra stooped, and began to fire as soon as the racing bats were in range. They were a squadron of Locusts, some maroon, some yellow, some gold, and they broke upwards into Umbra's attack.

Viltry killed a bat head on, but Jagdea picked up two that refused to let her go. Darrow and Del Ruth almost converged, and managed to smack las shots into the same hostile, chopping it into fragments. Marquall avoided getting his tail shot off in the first pass, then climbed hard again to help Jagdea.

The two maroon Locusts had locked down on her despite her violent slips and turns. Any tighter and she risked a high-speed stall.

'Can't shake them!' Jagdea snarled, gripped tight against the lousy G.

'Umbra Leader! Speed brakes and drop out!' Marquall yelled as he came howling in.

Vision closing into a grey tunnel, Jagdea deployed the speed brakes into the slipstream and slammed violently back out under the still-turning Locusts. Immediately, she started to recover with vector thrust. Marquall came in over her guns firing and the Locusts swung out of his way with some haste. One darted up out of sight, but the other went into a dive and Marquall committed after it.

The pilots in Blansher's half of the flight all made kills within twenty seconds, though Van Tull was himself hit and took wing damage.

'You okay, Three?' Blansher called.

'Four-A,' came the expected response.

Blansher could hear Kaminsky distinctly over the link. 'Fire. Fire. Fire. Switch. Fire.'

As he came up, mushing off speed, Blansher looked up and saw Kaminsky's plane flick-roll, quads firing, and make his second kill of the sortie.

The remaining bats retreated. Marquall came back up from his chase empty-handed. Umbra reformed, and immediately sighted the front edge of the bomber wave, low and south of them. They scoped more fighter escorts.

They began their attack run anyway.

Over the Sea of Ezra, 14.02

THE BATTERIES OF the mass formation opened up as the fighters stooped in amongst them. In the flat, yellow light, the bombers looked like a mezzotint image. Four Thunderbolt wings were now attacking this gigantic string, and two more were duelling with its Razor escorts.

Viltry's anti-bomber expertise earned him two stings straight off and Jagdea followed his example, damaging a heavy raider that Del Ruth polished off in her wake. Darrow found a Tormentor and blew away part of its engine assembly. It hung in the air for a second, then pitched away as if it had fainted.

Del Ruth did a split-S then swooped onto a super-heavy that was dark red, like carrion. Chains fluttered out behind the huge machine and Del Ruth realised they were strung with human skulls. She banked in, not even waiting for the sights to lock. It would have been difficult to miss. She put eight pulses of lasfire into the swollen flank and, as she pulled away, saw the aluminoid skin shred and burst as fuel-air explosions blew it apart from within.

Even as the giant craft died and burned, its turrets kept firing. Del Ruth felt her bird shudder as something hit the underside of her nose with huge force, tearing the stick out of her hands for a moment and knocking the plane's attitude through twenty degrees.

She recovered control.

'Six, are you okay?'

'Yes, Leader,' Del Ruth responded. She checked her instruments and saw two warning lights lit, indicating damage to the starboard autoloaders. 'Hit, but not critical.'

Kaminsky and Zemmic had both taken out bombers on the first pass, but Blansher, Scalter and Van Tull were intercepted by the Razor escort before they could do any harm. Van Tull had to fly an almost complete figure of eight before he shook a purple Razor, then almost immediately got the drop on another, chequered black and white, that had lined up on Scalter. As the chequered hostile vaporised, Scalter peeled away towards a heavy bomber, firing on it from its seven.

The purple Razor that Van Tull had shaken reappeared, swooping steeply and opening fire on Scalter's machine. Bolt rounds sliced down into the starboard engine, the midsection, and the tail, shredding part of the rudder. The impacts destroyed Scalter's auspex, ruptured his coolant system and crazed the side screens of his canopy white.

'Umbra Seven! Umbra Seven!' Van Tull yelled.

Dazed, Scalter heard the voice and looked around. The air of his cockpit was full of blue smoke. He stared at the shattered instruments. The few panels still functioning were a mass of warning lights. _Overheat, leak, pressure loss, power failure…_

'Scalter, can you hear me?'

Scalter looked down and let out a sob. At least one of the rounds had gone clean through his lower torso. He couldn't believe the bloody mess was anything to do with him. He couldn't feel his legs. He couldn't feel anything much at all.

'Scalter!'

'Four-A…' he whispered. 'Taken a little damage.'

'Seven, if you're not flyable, eject for Throne's sake!'

With effort, Scalter touched the stick. It was dead, slack, all control gone. His ruined machine was just flying straight. He looked down again. There was no way he could eject. No point, either.

He looked up. The heavy bomber he'd been targeting was still ahead, cruising on.

Scalter put his hand on the throttle. 'For Enothis and the Emperor,' he murmured and pushed the throttle open.

Umbra Seven accelerated in a straight, unswerving line and hit the heavy bomber in the port ribs. A huge halo of flames engulfed them both.

'SEVEN'S GONE! SCALTER'S GONE!' Marquall could hear Van Tull yelling. Negative G was preventing him from replying. He was cranking round in a murderous loop with a mauve Razor on his back. He felt hits skinning off his armour. He banked hard – a bone-shaking shudder – and managed to force the Razor to fly past under him. Now he was behind it. It would break at any second, Marquall knew. But which way?

Which way would you go? Jagdea had always told them.

Marquall went right, and the Razor did just that in the same instant.

Target lock.

Marquall was screaming as he fired. He knew it was a kill before *Double Eagle* had even started firing. The mauve Hell Razor started to spin, then spiralled away like a leaf.

Marquall hoped someone had seen that. He dearly hoped that someone–

'Umbra Six! Umbra Six! Status?' Jagdea started shouting over the vox.

There was no obvious hostile on her, but Del Ruth's Thunderbolt looked like it was taking hits to the nose. Explosive crackles rocked her airframe and plating blew out.

'I don't know–' she began. It was the hit she'd taken in the autoloaders just minutes before. Overheated damage or a late detonating round wedged into the mechanism had explosively cooked off the drums of ammunition. The rippling blasts were her own shells exploding in the caissons. In horror, Jagdea saw several detonate up through the main hull, blowing out both sets of engine pipes, and another flurry wrecked her radiator.

Mortally wounded, the Thunderbolt began to dive.

'Aggie! Pull out! Pull out!' Jagdea yelled.

'I can't! Negative! Dead stick!' Del Ruth screamed back.

'Eject, Aggie! For Throne's sake, eject!'

The machine plunged away. Jagdea saw a flash of glitter and a shape in the air. Far below her, a chute opened, a tiny dot against the tungsten sea.

Lucerna AB, 15.20

AS THEY REFUELLED and reloaded, no one spoke much. Fatigue and nerves had almost wrung them out, but the losses made it much worse. Their hearts ached as much as their joints. For most of the pilots, circulation and balance were seriously impaired. Just walking around the hangar was difficult.

Just before 16.00, as they were preparing to launch, Operations reported that the second wave had broken short of Zophos. Fought to a near-standstill after four hours, the Archenemy formations had turned back.

If a third wave was intended, they'd see it within the next five hours.

'Third time lucky,' said Zemmic.

'Who for?' asked Kaminsky.

Over the Midwinters, 18.23

THEY CAME BACK early. As if hungry, somehow sensing that they had their enemy on the ropes. Or desperate. That's what Jagdea told herself.

The third wave came out over the coast in the early and unnatural dusk, seemingly just as immense as before. How could they have shot down so many of the bastards and there be so little sign of a thinning in their ranks?

The remaining eight machines of Umbra Flight climbed
with four other Thunderbolt squadrons to nine thousand,
and circled in over the archipelago as the enemy formations approached. The other bases had put up their wings.

The line was drawn.

Combat began at 18.45. Another new tactic was immediately revealed. Frustrated by the Navy's staunch
resistance, the Archenemy had committed the front elements of its bomber waves low, to pattern bomb the
islands in the hope of annihilating the hidden bases there.
From its overall heading, this arm of the wave was intending to cross the Straits of Jabez and target Tamuda once the
islands were done. The radiant ripples of furious detonations began to light up the southern part of the island
chain.

The Imperial planes went in amongst the bombers, cutting them out of the air even as they dropped their
warloads.

'I don't see fighters,' Marquall called.

'There'll be fighters,' Blansher said.

Darrow made his eighth kill of the day, then throttled up
to join Viltry in an attack on a super-heavy. The tracer patterns were torrential and bright in the stale air.

Jagdea turned in tight. She couldn't see Zemmic or Van
Tull in the mayhem, but she could hear them over the link.
Blansher and Kaminsky were attacking a trio of Tormentors. She was about to start a run onto a Hell Talon when
she saw the escort bats coming in across them.

'Bats! Twenty-plus! Two o'clock!' Jagdea yelled.

They were Razors. Black and red, a few bright crimson.
One pearl-white.

The Killer and his circus came on. Two of his wingmen
attacked and destroyed a pair of Navy Thunderbolts from
the 96th who didn't react anything like fast enough.

'Umbra! Split! Split!' Jagdea ordered and opened her
throttle, going for the pearl leader. His evasive roll left her

wrong-footed, but she turned hard and tried to get on his tail. He refused to sit, vectoring to port and coming up underneath her. Desperately, she flick-rolled and dropped down around him to his right, but he turned off sharply to port.

For a moment she wondered if she had actually scared him into a break, but then saw in dismay that he'd simply been lining her up for his two crimson wingmen. Serial Zero-Two shuddered as laser bolts went through its wings. Jagdea slammed the stick over and tried to barrel under the Razors, but they were as agile as their master, and stuck tight to her tail.

'Throne of Earth!' Jagdea cursed, fighting to break out. Moving far too fast for such close quarters, she almost rammed a Hell Talon, and bled speed miserably as she was forced to duck under it. Another shot clipped her tailfin. Two more ripped through the sensor clusters and her auspex screen flickered and died. She vectored, came round stubbornly and started to climb between a pair of Tormentors that lashed at her with their weapon mounts.

Viltry saw her plight. He pulled away from the superheavy he had just crippled and lit his burners, spearing down through the bomber formation into the denser smoke

'Jagdea! Come left!' he called. She turned, but the crimson bats would not let her go. Viltry fired on them and tucked in. He couldn't get a lock. He wasn't going to get them in time.

BLANSHER AND KAMINSKY left the bombers alone and stooped after Jagdea too. Kaminsky saw the pearl-white bat first. It seemed to come out of the vapour of fyceline smoke like a spectre, gun-pods flickering. Umbra Two wrenched violently as gaping wounds punched into its tail plane.

'Blansher!' Kaminsky yelled.

Blansher tried to viff, tried to shake it just the way he had taught Kaminsky. But his vector ports were damaged. The white bat fired again, a stream of illuminated shells, and a spray of flames sheathed Blansher's entire tail. The shots had penetrated the tanks of the Thunderbolt's rocket motor, and the hypergolic propellants had ignited. The huge thread of flame was greenish-white with intense heat. Blansher started to dive.

Ignoring the white killer, Kaminsky scream-dived after Umbra Two. Blansher's plane was now on fire from nose to tail.

'Get out! Get out, Milan, eject!'

'...can't! I... can't... canopy's jammed!'

'Blansher!'

The Thunderbolt no longer resembled a plane. It fell like a comet. A meteor. An attenuated ball of fire, almost too bright to look at. But diving with it, Kaminsky could not look away. He knew fire. He knew the terror of a burning plane all too well.

Blansher started screaming. The fire was inside the cockpit now. The voice on the vox no longer seemed human.

Kaminsky was strangely relieved when the inferno hit the sea.

OBARKON WATCHED WITH curiosity as the Imperial's wing-man made the strange choice to follow his burning leader down. How odd. As if there was anything he could do.

It rendered the wingman an extraordinarily easy target. Obarkon turned into a dive, feeling the grav armour clench around his body and the cardio-centrifuges throb. He blinked to settle the gunsight focus and put the orange pipper on the wingman's tail.

Attention...

Target found.

Just a little more.

A warning sounded. Obarkon glanced up and instinctively raised his nose, losing the target immediately. Shots stripped past him.

'Someone's eager to die,' he muttered.

DARROW CAME IN hard and tight, firing as soon as he dared, but leaving it late enough to be in positive range. The white bat pulled out of his line and banked away.

Darrow turned and chased it. This wasn't going to be like the last time. He wasn't going to run, frantic, in an outclassed machine. He was a Thunderbolt pilot now. The bastard white bat that had slaughtered all of Hunt Flight – and Heckel too, in a way – was going to be the one doing the running.

A vector-aided roll and a burst of speed put Darrow closer and closer still, despite the enemy's excellent outrolls. Darrow got two brief locks, but lost them both. He waited for the third.

INTERESTING, OBARKON THOUGHT, his pulse not even drifting in its rhythm. This one has some merit. He flies by the claws. If this had been a quieter hour, he would have enjoyed sport with this child. But this was the day of days, and there was still great work to be done. This duel was over.

THE WHITE BAT dropped down to an altitude of no more than fifty metres and proceeded to whip in and out of the inlets and bays at speeds that Darrow thought he'd never be able to follow. Every turn threatened to smash them into a sheer cliff or clip a rocky outcrop.

He stayed on the bat as long as he could and then was forced to climb by a jutting atoll that he knew he would not otherwise avoid. The white bat let him go over, then sliced up after him, firing. Darrow twisted out, but the bat locked him cold.

Then shots sprayed in from a second Thunderbolt.

It was Marquall.

VILTRY PUT ALL his power into a last turn and fired again. Now at last he disturbed the crimson bats enough to break them from Jagdea's tail. One looped back to engage him.

'Switch out!' Jagdea ordered.

Viltry obeyed. Ignoring the looping attacker, he kept on after the other one, lining up. Jagdea broke wide and turned up to face the threat to Viltry.

Viltry opened fire and the crimson bat erupted and came apart.

A moment later, Jagdea caught the other one in a head-on attack and ripped it out of the sky.

MARQUALL'S FLUNKED ATTACK gave Darrow time to break. The white bat turned out to meet Umbra Eight.

'I've got him!' Marquall cried. 'I've got a score to settle!'

So have I, thought Darrow. And I wouldn't be so sure that you've got him either.

Marquall fired again, but the Razor rolled on its axis and slid under his fire cone. Marquall banked, exactly the right way, but the white bat had already viffed as it looped, and it fell on him. Its gunpods roared.

Darrow watched in horror as shots tore into the midsection of Marquall's plane.

Marquall wrenched the stick. He saw an engine tube explode off, and felt the airframe shake as rounds went into the hull around him. Two shots buckled his airmix canisters and punctured the radiator. Two more ripped through his ejector mount and packed chute, shredding the chute and bursting shrapnel from the seat frame. A chunk of metal chopped Marquall's left calf and another whickered up from under the seat itself and punched clean through the meat of his left thigh.

He screamed in pain and his bird fell into a sharp dive, but he hauled back on the stick and came up again. There was a track of blood spots glued to the inside of his canopy.

Darrow banked. Wounded, Marquall was dead meat. Darrow hit the throttle and shot across the pearl-white bat, deliberately turning out, drawing his aim. The Razor followed him.

THE WOUNDED ONE wasn't going anywhere. Obarkon knew he should take care of the one with the real merit first. Especially as the child had now made a very basic mistake and lined himself up, vulnerable for the Echelon chieftain's guns.

The auto-sight reconfigured. The orange pipper drifted in.

DARROW WENT LOW through the atolls. He'd made himself a target for Marquall's sake. Running for his life did not seem like the best way to fight the enemy.

But he remember what Eads had said. *Retreat is a hard thing to deal with, but you'll be a better warrior, Enric, if you realise that sometimes that's the only way to win.*

'Come on! That's right! Come on!' Darrow yelled. 'You couldn't catch me before, you won't catch me now!'

Darrow raced between the islets and the jagging rocks, lifting spray in his wake, flying on pure nerve and instinct. He had no idea how he avoided some obstacles. There was no time to think. The pearl-white bat was right at his heels. It fired twice, three times, missing Umbra Nine and spraying chunks of rock from the island stacks.

* * *

By the claws indeed. Such skill. It reminded Obarkon of a chase he'd once enjoyed in the Makanites. Another young pup with promethium in his veins.

But the game had to end.

Attention...

Target found.

'Goodnight,' said Obarkon, as his hardwired thumbs dug at the trigger paddle.

Darrow heard the target lock shrilling.

'Umbra Eight, for Throne's sake! How long have I got to keep him occupied?'

The pearl-white bat fired.

Two shots tore into Darrow's tail fin.

Vander Marquall, travelling at over nine hundred kph, came up over an atoll's flat top, head on. He went right across Darrow's plane and blazed his quads on sustain at the white bat dead ahead.

The furious fire needed no angle of deflection. Obarkon's machine flew straight into it, without any time to evade.

For a millisecond, the pearl-white Razor deformed. Its multi-punctured hull shredded. Stress fractures peeled away armour like dead skin. The blitzing cannon shell vaporised the pilot. Then the engine and weapons batteries detonated in a cataclysmic flash.

Marquall rode out of the sheet of fire and came clear on the other side. Fluttering hunks of pearl-white armour scattered wide and rained down across the lagoon.

'I think,' said Vander Marquall, 'that makes me an ace.'

Over the Midwinters, 19.30

Darrow climbed back into the raging air brawl.

'I thought we'd lost you, Nine,' Jagdea voxed.

'Copy Leader, I'm okay. Marquall's been hit. I told him to turn for home.'

'Copy that.'

'Umbra Lead, he got the bat. He stung the white bat. Definite kill.'

Jagdea rolled Zero-Two through the streaming tracer. That news was the only thing worth smiling about she'd heard all day.

The sky was full of aircraft and fire, like some great scene of damnation on a templum frieze. With Viltry turning high to her left, she stooped into the pandemonium and started to avenge Blansher.

Lucerna AB, 21.00

IT WAS NOW almost dark, and strangely quiet. The third wave had faltered and broken half an hour before, and some gut instinct told Bree Jagdea that there would be no fourth wave. Not that day.

The fitters had to almost carry her out of her battered Thunderbolt. Zemmic and Van Tull had just landed. Van Tull, sneezing blood, had lost a third of one wing. Viltry and Kaminsky sat with their backs to the hangar wall, drained of all strength.

She crouched down with them. She wanted to speak, but there was nothing to say and no effort left to say it with anyway.

Darrow was last back. He had taken fifteen of the enemy. A triple ace.

He climbed out of his aircraft, dropped his helmet from his trembling fingers, and made the sign of the blessed aquila. The sacred double eagle.

'Commander?' he called out. 'Commander Jagdea?'

She rose. 'What's the matter, Darrow?'

'Where's Marquall?' he asked.

* * *

Over the Straits, 21.01

STILL FLYING LEVEL and true, Thunderbolt serial Nine-Nine *Double Eagle* crossed the Straits of Jabez at six thousand metres, cruising, with the fuel dwindling in its tanks. The ocean lay before it.

Vander Marquall sat in his seat, his head hung forward slightly.

The vox crackled. 'Umbra Eight? Umbra Eight? This is Lucerna Operations? Do you copy?'

Marquall did not answer. The damaged air-mix system had filled his cockpit with carbon dioxide over half an hour earlier.

The plane flew on, true to its nature at the very last, out across the ocean and into the folds of the night.

EPILOGUE

No FOURTH WAVE came. Not that day or any day. Though the air war on Enothis continued for three further weeks, the losses suffered by the Archenemy air force on the 270th were so severe that a willingness to try such a venture again seemed to leave them.

THE BATTLE OF the Zophonian Sea, as the history texts now call it, was not the final fight of the Enothian War, but it was the most decisive. In the weeks that followed, Lord Militant Humel's counter-offensive began and, with reinforcements from the Khan Group, the Imperial Guard began to strike back into the south, into a demoralised enemy. The Trinity Hives finally fell, after months of savage fighting, on the 62nd day of 774.M41. By that time, the Archenemy Magister Sek had fled the planet. Records show that the first unit to breach the Trinity Gates was an armoured regiment commanded by a Captain Robart LeGuin.

DURING THE BATTLE of the Zophonian Sea, Imperial air losses were nine hundred and forty-eight compared to seven thousand eight hundred and forty confirmed Archenemy machines. Of the Navy wings involved, the highest kill tally per individual pilot was achieved by the 101st Apostles, but three other fighter wings, including the Phantine XX, exceeded the Apostles' combined score of kills.

THE RECORDS SHOW that Captain Oskar Viltry, a Marauder pilot, was killed in action in the interior desert on the 260th day of the Imperial year 773.M41.

ABOUT THE AUTHOR

Dan Abnett lives and works in Maidstone, Kent, in England. Well known for his comic work, he has written everything from the *Mr Men* to the *X-Men* in the last decade, and received particular acclaim for his five year run on *The Legion* for DC Comics. He is currently writing *Majestic* for Wildstorm, and *Sinister Dexter* and *The VCs* for 2000 AD.

His work for the Black Library includes the popular strips *Lone Wolves*, *Titan* and *Darkblade*, the best-selling Gaunt's Ghosts novels, and the acclaimed Inquisitor Eisenhorn trilogy.